S0-BNY-614

Girls of Summer

Girls of Summer

Barbara Bretton

BERKLEY BOOKS, NEW YORK

This is a work of fiction. Names, characters, places, and incidents either are the product of the author's imagination or are used fictitiously, and any resemblance to actual persons, living or dead, business establishments, events, or locales is entirely coincidental.

GIRLS OF SUMMER

A Berkley Book / published by arrangement with
the author

Copyright © 2003 by Barbara Bretton.
Cover illustration by Wendy Popp.
Cover design by George Long.
Interior text design by Kristin del Rosario.

All rights reserved.
This book, or parts thereof, may not be reproduced
in any form without permission.
The scanning, uploading, and distribution of this book via the Internet or via any other means without the permission of the publisher is illegal and punishable by law. Please purchase only authorized electronic editions, and do not participate in or encourage electronic piracy of copyrighted materials. Your support of the author's rights is appreciated.
For information address: The Berkley Publishing Group,
a division of Penguin Group (USA) Inc.,
375 Hudson Street, New York, New York 10014.

ISBN: 0-7394-3909-X

BERKLEY®
Berkley Books are published by The Berkley Publishing Group,
a division of Penguin Group (USA) Inc.,
375 Hudson Street, New York, New York 10014.
BERKLEY and the "B" design
are trademarks belonging to Penguin Group (USA) Inc.

PRINTED IN THE UNITED STATES OF AMERICA

For my husband, Roy,
because sometimes a woman gets it right the first time.
I love you, BDH. Always have, always will.

Sincere thanks to the charming and gifted T. C. Loehr, and to her sister, the equally charming and gifted Sharron Dupree, for sharing their passion for music. My undying gratitude goes to talented author Elizabeth Doyle, whose eye for detail helped bring the Celtic harp to life for me. And a special thanks to Jo Beverley and the amazing members of the NINC loop.

Also a big loud rowdy thanks to the usual cast of characters whose eclectic knowledge and willingness to share never fail to amaze me: Dwayne Webb, Kit Wells, Tracey Robinson, Susan Lacy, Joanne Garland, Annette Nunez, Michael Elizabeth Chastain, Tim Bowden (and Scoob), Lorin Hart, Jeannie Perrin, Kay Butler and her son Wendell Rote, and Michael Poszlusny who should one day rule the world.

Girls of Summer

One

The last time Ellen O'Brien Markowitz woke up in a man's bed it was three weeks before her wedding and the man on the next pillow was her fiancé.

A very temporary situation, as it turned out. She could still see Bryan propped up against the headboard, Palm Pilot in hand, as he patiently read her the list of reasons why it would be better for both of them if they called off the wedding. She was dressed and out the door by the time he reached number eight, his cry of "But there's more!" ringing in her ears.

It wasn't as if she hadn't seen it coming, because she had. In fact, she often wondered if she hadn't chosen him for those very qualities that doomed the marriage before they ever took the vows.

That was over four years ago. One thousand six hundred and eighty-five mornings of waking up alone. Not that she was counting, mind you, but numbers like those were hard for a woman to ignore. Would one more solitary morning have tipped the heavenly balance and brought civilization crashing down around her shoulders? Would worlds collide if the Goddess of the Morning After rewound the tape back to last night, to the second before Ellen made her fatal mistake?

There had been a moment there in Hall Talbot's shadowy bedroom when it could have gone either way. He was a gentleman through and through. Despite the bubbly haze of champagne, he would have stopped if she had shown the slightest reluctance—but she hadn't. Instead she had opened her arms to him and tried very hard to close her heart to hope.

She was very good at closing her heart to hope. She had learned early that nothing was quite the way it seemed, not family and certainly not love. The drawbridge was up and the door bolted, but last night, in an unguarded moment, hope slipped in through the window just the same.

She opened one eye and peered across the wide expanse of bed. "Oh, God," she whispered. The sight of him, so warm and so close, made her light-headed with remembered pleasure and more than a hint of remorse.

She hadn't imagined him, hadn't conjured him up from a lethal combination of too much champagne and three years' worth of dreams. Hall Talbot, Shelter Rock Cove's most beloved OB-GYN, her good friend and colleague, her boss, was snoring softly not two feet away from her.

Even in postcoital repose he managed to look like your average middle-aged Adonis. His silvery-blond hair shimmered against the pale blue sheets. His muscular torso loomed gorgeous in the gathering light. She remembered how he had looked last night when she slid his fine white shirt off his fine tanned shoulders and—

Stifling a groan, she buried her face in her pillow.

In the grand scheme of things, it really wasn't such a terrible mistake. People slept with the wrong people every day of the week and somehow the world managed to keep on turning. She and Hall had been good friends before last night, and there was no reason to think their friendship couldn't survive a night of passion.

Even if he had called her by another woman's name at a very inopportune moment.

And this came as a big surprise, Markowitz? The first two things she had learned when she moved to Maine were her new phone number and the fact that Annie Galloway Butler was the love of his life.

Hall blamed it on the champagne, and he had tried to make

it up to her in some amazing ways, but the damage had been done. There were three of them in that bed, and Ellen already had too much experience being second-best. Everyone in Shelter Rock Cove knew that Hall Talbot had carried a torch for the former widow Galloway for more years—and through more of his own failed marriages—than even the most blunt Yankee would acknowledge. Not even Annie's marriage to Sam Butler had seemed to dim Hall's devotion. It had taken the birth of the Butlers' second perfect baby girl to force him to acknowledge the fact that he had lost Annie before she ever had a chance to find him.

Hall and Ellen had attended Kerry Amanda Butler's christening yesterday as honorary members of the family, and the sight of that beautiful baby, that miracle of love and fate, had turned Ellen's heart inside out. She could only imagine what it had done to Hall. The Galloway and Butler clans descended on Shelter Rock en masse, filling Sam and Annie's little house with food and music and laughter and enough love to make you believe happy families not only existed but flourished. They were a big, handsome, fertile lot, and Ellen would have sold her soul to be one of them, but, as always, she was on the outside looking in.

The only time Ellen had ever felt more like an outsider was at one of her father Cy's infrequent family gatherings where she needed a name tag in order to be recognized as part of the clan. Family always did that to her, like a private club, the kind that didn't want her as a member. When Hall suggested they split early, she had been almost pathetically grateful.

"Hungry?" he asked as they walked down the Butlers' driveway toward her car.

"Starving."

She avoided Cappy's, where they were bound to run into someone who would ask them about the christening, and, at Hall's suggestion, drove over to the Spruce Goose, a small inn on one of the back roads between Shelter Rock Cove and Bar Harbor. Good food, better lighting, the kind of place where you could pretend to be someone you're not and maybe get away with it for a little while.

She should have known it was dangerous. Scratched wooden tables and paper place mats were more her speed.

Linen tablecloths and soup spoons meant trouble. Colleagues grabbed a lobster roll at Cappy's or a pizza at Frankie's near the Yankee Shopper. Friends didn't dine by candlelight with soft music wafting past them and the scent of possibility in the air. Not if they wanted to stay colleagues and friends.

But loneliness had a way of playing tricks on even the smartest women. Hall had needed someone last night and she had needed to be needed by him. It was that simple.

And it should have been enough. God knew, it was more than she had ever expected. She had enjoyed nurturing a low-grade lust for him. It had been delightful to enjoy the way his shoulders filled out his lab coat or how he somehow managed to look *GQ* in scrubs. If you had told her last week that she would wake up this morning in Hall Talbot's bed, with Hall Talbot's pricey sheets wrapped around her naked body, she would have laughed out loud and suggested therapy.

And then she would have made an appointment for a pedicure and a bikini wax.

As it turned out, she went to him smelling of soap, with fingernails filed short and smooth, and a hairstyle that could best be described by the more charitable observer as casual. He had invited her in for a glass of champagne to celebrate Kerry Amanda's christening and one glass led to another and he said she couldn't drive home after that much champagne and she said she would sleep on his sofa and suddenly they were in each other's arms and for the first time in her life it seemed that reality was going to win out over fantasy, hands down.

He made her feel beautiful. Nobody had ever made her feel beautiful before, not even in her dreams. When he traced the curve of her bare hip with his long, elegant fingers, she knew, at least for an instant, how it felt to be adored.

Of course, then he had to go and ruin everything by calling her "Annie" at the moment when she wanted desperately to believe she was the only one on his mind, if not in his heart. She had tried to push past the embarrassment and sink deeper into the fantasy, but the ragged sound of his voice as he said Annie's name was in her head and it wouldn't go away.

Maybe she should thank him for the mistake because only something that hideous could have brought her back to earth before she made an even bigger fool of herself.

At least she hadn't said anything ridiculous. Nothing that would come back to haunt her for the rest of her life and somehow end up on the front page of *The Shelter Rock Cove Gazette.* She had somehow managed to gather up all of her unruly emotions and hold them tightly to her. Lust was easy to explain away; emotion was almost impossible. The world looked very different when you were naked and horizontal with your body throbbing pleasantly in some unfamiliar places.

Like your heart?

Now, there was a thought to push as far away as possible.

She inched the covers down and slid toward the edge of the bed, wincing at the sound of her naked limbs moving across his crisp cotton sheets. Even her heartbeat sounded too loud. How he could sleep through the racket she was making was beyond her, but his breathing remained regular and his eyes didn't flicker open and she was old enough to know her luck wouldn't hold forever. She swung her legs over the side of the bed and stood up. He didn't move a muscle. Moving quickly, she gathered her clothes from the floor and the wing chair in the corner of the room, fished her heels from under the armoire, then darted for the bathroom.

Hall Talbot opened his eyes as soon as he heard the bathroom door swing shut. The room was dim, bathed in shadow. The nest of robins outside his window was silent. He peered at the clock on his nightstand: 4:52, it read, in screaming green flashes of light that made his eyeballs ache. You were in bad shape when your clock made you feel like you were strapped to the nose cone of an Atlas rocket that was about to lift off inside your skull.

He hadn't felt like this since he was an intern pulling seventy-two-hour shifts. What the hell was going on? It wasn't flu season. He hadn't sustained a head injury. There was no reason for feeling like roadkill.

Or was there?

His skin smelled faintly of carnations and woman. He had dreamed about a woman last night, about long legs and soft skin, about losing himself in her warmth and wanting to stay lost. Was it possible he hadn't been dreaming? His sheets were rumpled and the other side of the bed was warm beneath the flat of his hand. Bits and pieces from the night before began to swim to the surface: Kerry Amanda Butler's christening; single-malt Scotch at the Spruce Goose; a bottle of champagne on his back porch; Ellen's long elegant legs wrapped around his waist; the sweet taste of her mouth; the way he called out Annie Butler's name when—

Shit. He'd been hoping that part was nothing but one of those caught-naked-walking-down-Main-Street dreams, but the echo rang loud and clear. The funny thing was—if anything about the situation was funny—that he hadn't been thinking about Annie at all. For the first time in years, he had been completely there with a woman, completely into the moment, and wouldn't you know his damn champagne-fueled subconscious had to rear its head and hit Ellen right between the eyes.

What the hell had he been thinking when he asked her in for a drink? He was old enough to know where those things usually led. He could take the easy way out and blame the single-malt, but Scotch usually made him more circumspect. She deserved better. There was no doubt about that. He had been on the wrong side of a triangle for most of his adult life, and he wouldn't wish it on anyone. But something had been different yesterday, from the moment she swung by the hospital to pick him up for the christening. Maybe it was the way she looked in her party dress, like a summer flower, or maybe it was the soft sound of her laughter as she held Kerry Amanda in her arms.

He had seen her face minutes after Kerry came into the world. He had seen the look of wonder, of joy, the kind of look you saw in Renaissance paintings but not in the post-modern, post-everything world.

The rest of the crowd in Annie Butler's garden faded away and he saw only Ellen, heard only her voice.

He didn't know what impulse on her part had brought her into his bed, but he had been deeply grateful for it, grateful for her warmth, and her kindness, and the way she moved beneath him. Grateful for everything that made her who she was.

He never mixed work and pleasure, never lost sight of the

importance of his vocation, or of what he owed the women who entrusted their lives and the lives of their unborn babies into his care. That was what had prompted his decision three years ago to find a partner. Young couples had been moving into Shelter Rock Cove faster than new housing could keep pace, and with them came a rapid rise in the birthrate that had tripled his workload before he knew what hit him. If he wanted to continue to give his patients the care and attention they deserved, he realized he would have to bring in a partner.

He had interviewed candidates from every part of the state, and while they all came with impeccable qualifications, none seemed the right fit. He had seriously considered a woman from Boston, but her reluctance to commit to life in a small shore town forced him to rule her out. Just when he was about to put aside the search for a few months, Ellen showed up and his problems were solved. Nobody was more surprised than Hall when the perfect partner turned out to be a tall, reed-slim New Yorker with curly red hair and the uncanny ability to charm even his most straitlaced Yankee patients with her dry humor and gentle hands. He had worried about the old guard's reaction, but for the most part even the dowagers of Shelter Rock had accepted Ellen. Maybe not as one of their own but definitely as a welcome addition. Even Claudia Galloway finally broke down and stopped canceling appointments if it meant seeing his partner rather than him.

Progress came slowly to small New England towns, but when it came in the guise of someone like Ellen, it couldn't be denied, not even by those who could trace their lineage back three hundred years just by walking past the cemetery behind the church.

She was part of the community. Part of the clubs and fund-raisers, welcome at church barbecues even though she didn't attend the church in question, a familiar face at parties and parades, christenings and funerals. She had earned their friendship, their trust, and their respect. No small thing in a town like Shelter Rock Cove.

And now, with one act of supreme selfishness, he had put all of that into jeopardy.

He had to do something or say something, but the question was *what*? As well as he knew her, there was much about

Ellen that remained a mystery. This wasn't your standard morning-after where you shared one of Dee Dee's doughnuts and French roast on the back porch while the day unfolded itself before you. The moment he had uttered Annie's name, he had seen to that.

Would she be casual about it, as if they had shared nothing more than dinner and conversation? He doubted it. They knew each other too well to play games. Maybe they should go for a walk on the beach and he could somehow find a way to apologize to her. Apologies of that sort were tricky beasts. He'd seen too many heartfelt apologies backfire, heaping embarrassment upon the one who least deserved it. Or he could lie there pretending to be asleep while she let herself out of his house and delay the moment of accountability, but that was the coward's way out and she deserved better.

She had deserved better last night, but it was too late for him to undo the damage. The only thing he could do now was to follow her lead and hope for the best.

Maybe somewhere in the world there were women who waltzed into affairs armed with a change of clothes, toothbrush, and blow-dryer, but Ellen wasn't one of them. Standing there in Hall's bathroom, wrapped in a dark green towel that barely covered the essentials, she found herself looking at the reflection of a woman in trouble.

She looked too needy. The expression in her eyes was too open, too vulnerable, too everything. She looked the way she had looked the summer she was fourteen when her entire world turned upside down.

There wasn't a soul in town who wouldn't know what she had been up to when they saw her driving down Harbor Road toward home wearing the same clothes she had worn to the Butlers' christening party. And, to make matters worse, her car had spent the night in Hall's driveway. She might as well have hung a flag from his bedroom window with the words "Dr. Markowitz Slept Here" embroidered across it in big scarlet letters.

Back home this wouldn't have registered on the radar screen. A private life was possible in Manhattan, something she hadn't given much thought to before moving up to Maine. You could order in Chinese every night for a month or send a lover home each dawn and the only one who could tell the tale was your doorman, and if you tipped him well enough each Christmas, he would take your secret to the grave. Her friends loved the anonymity that provided them, but Ellen had always yearned for something more. She wanted to feel as if she was part of a community, a neighborhood. What she lacked in family ties, she longed to make up for in friendship. When one of the doctors she worked with in the big impersonal clinic they euphemistically called the Family Care Center told her about a position that was opening up in Maine, she was ready. Jack and his family summered each year at Shelter Rock Cove, and he had spent some time fishing with Hall and had come to both like and respect the older doctor.

"It's pretty rural," he had warned Ellen the day she left for her interview. "Big change for a city girl."

But that city girl had been ready for the change, and when she first saw Hall Talbot, her fate had been sealed. He was tall and golden, one of those lucky few who were blessed with good looks and a good heart to match. They talked through the afternoon on topics ranging from prenatal care to geriatric gynecology and they found themselves to be in perfect harmony. Later, as the sun began to set over the harbor, the talk veered toward the personal, and she found herself telling him about the life she had planned with Bryan and how it had all fallen away without warning.

He listened the way a woman wanted a man to listen to her. His eyes, so warm and so blue, never left hers. He leaned across the glass-topped table as if every word she uttered was of vital importance. And yet there was nothing false about it, nothing calculated. He listened because he cared about what she was saying and that caring had been a revelation to her.

The last of her doubts vanished as the moon rose high above the harbor.

They must have sat out on Cappy's patio and talked until ten or eleven o'clock. He ordered a bowl of chowder for each of them and some lobster rolls, and she found herself devouring the simple food with a lumberjack's appetite. He told her that he had a checkered past when it came to love and marriage. "You might as well hear it from me," he had said as he signaled for another iced tea, "because you'll certainly hear it from someone else before long." After all, there were no secrets in small towns.

Four daughters. Three failed marriages. She tried not to show her shock, but he must have seen something in her face because he'd smiled and leaned back in his chair. "It's okay," he said. "I can't believe it, either." He never told her about Annie Galloway Butler, but then he wouldn't. He wasn't that kind of man. By the time she had been a resident of Shelter Rock Cove for six months, she had heard at least twelve different variations on the story. The details might have differed but the plot was always the same: Hall loved Annie and Annie loved someone else.

A smarter woman might have learned something from that revelation. She would have ignored the way her heart leaped into overdrive every time he walked into the room. She would have learned to stop noticing the way his skin always smelled faintly of lime and sunshine, even in the dead of a New England winter. And a smarter woman would definitely have stayed out of his bed, no matter how much champagne had passed her lips.

But Ellen had never claimed to be a genius when it came to romance, and the fact that it was Monday morning and she was standing almost naked in Hall Talbot's bathroom wondering how she would get home without alerting the whole town to the fact that she'd spent the night with the town's most eligible—and most married—bachelor was proof of that fact.

Hall tugged on a pair of faded jeans and his favorite cotton sweater and went down to the kitchen to start a pot of coffee. He had a few jelly doughnuts in a bag on the counter. They were probably pretty stale by now, but maybe he could freshen them up in the microwave. He could always go out to Dee Dee's for a fresh batch, but that would be like waving a red flag in the face of the town bull. The news would be all over town before he walked back through his front door.

He settled for nuking the doughnuts he had and pulling

some bagels from the freezer. He was pretty sure he'd seen a tub of cream cheese hiding behind a quart of milk. The thing was to keep it simple. Don't ratchet things up to the point where they were both any more uncomfortable than they had to be.

He paced the kitchen while the sound of running water filtered down from the second-floor bathroom. How could one woman take so long to get ready? It wasn't as if she was trying to decide what to wear. He was beginning to wonder if she'd slipped out the bathroom window and headed for home, but her car was still in the driveway.

He drank some juice, popped a handful of vitamins, poured himself a cup of coffee. The sun was rising over the ocean, bathing his yard in the pastel lemons and pinks of early morning, burning away the wispy fog that carpeted the grass. He considered going back upstairs and knocking on the bathroom door, but that seemed poor form. She couldn't stay up there forever, no matter how much she wanted to. She was closing on her first house that afternoon and had a walk-through scheduled for eleven.

Of course that meant, if the mood struck her, she could stay holed up in his bathroom until after he had left for the hospital and still have plenty of time to make her appointment.

Was that her plan? To outwait him and avoid confrontation? He had to admit he could see the appeal, but there was nothing to be gained by postponing the inevitable. They needed to see each other face-to-face. They needed to talk. And they needed to do both of those things without any prying eyes or ears.

That did it. He would pour her a glass of juice and take it upstairs to her. Maybe she needed some more towels or soap or a hair dryer and was quietly trying to make do without bothering him. Whatever was going on, they had to talk and they needed to do it before any more time passed.

He was reaching for a glass when he heard footsteps on the stairs and then the sound of his front door opening.

"Ellen." He put the glass down on the counter and made for the hall. "Wait!"

She was halfway out the door, looking fresh-scrubbed and

extremely uncomfortable in yesterday's clothes and sky-high heels.

"Ellen!"

She stopped on the top step and turned around, and he saw in her face all the things he had prayed wouldn't be there. Hurt. Confusion. Embarrassment. And something else, something he hadn't expected: a yearning so sweet and clear it almost brought him to his knees.

"I didn't mean to wake you," she said, her voice little more than a whisper. They both knew how easily sound carried on the early morning breeze.

"I made coffee," he said, gesturing toward the kitchen. "At least let me give you some caffeine before you go."

"I shouldn't. I have to get home and—" She glanced down at her clothes. "I don't think Claudia Galloway would appreciate seeing me in this outfit again, do you?"

He didn't respond. They both knew Annie's former mother-in-law would figure it out in a nanosecond.

"You have time for coffee."

"I'll pick some up at the drive-through."

"They're not open yet."

"You're making this harder than it needs to be, Hall."

"That's not my intention."

"You should be getting ready," she said. "You have Mc-Intyre at eight, don't you?"

"You're changing the subject."

She met his eyes. "There is no subject. I'm going home. That's all."

"Ellen, I—"

"Let it go," she said, fumbling in her bag for her car keys. Her damp curls danced around her face and tumbled over her shoulders. He wondered if she still smelled of carnations, that sweetly spicy scent that suited her so well.

"I want you to know—"

"Don't." There was no mistaking her tone of voice. "If you really want to make things better, you won't say another word about it."

"If that's what you want."

"It's very much what I want."

She turned again and he stopped her. "Your dress," he said. "You didn't finish buttoning the back."

Her huge blue eyes suddenly filled with tears, and it took all the restraint he possessed to keep from pulling her into his arms and holding her close while she cried. She would hate it if he did that, and, even worse, she would hate him for seeing her in a weak moment. You didn't work with a woman every day for over three years and not learn a little something about what made her tick.

She reached back and fumbled around, too distracted to be able to handle the simple task. It was clear she couldn't wait to be out of there.

"Let me," he said.

He stepped behind her, and, lifting her heavy, damp hair off her neck with one hand, he quickly fastened the buttons with the other.

"You're good at that," she said. He tried not to read anything into her tone.

"Practice," he said. "I have daughters."

She made to leave, but he placed his hand on her bare shoulder. "Believe it or not, you were the only woman in that bed last night, Ellen."

"Nice try," she said and left without a backward glance.

Two

It seemed to Ellen that everyone in town watched her make the two-mile drive from Hall's house to her condo. She felt like a float in last week's Memorial Day parade, rolling slowly down the main street clad in nothing but one of Hall's dark green bath towels. Since when did the entire town hit the street by six-thirty in the morning anyway? Ceil, the checker at Yankee Shopper, looked up from the ATM at the corner of Harbor Road and Shore Drive. Fred Custis from the hardware store nodded as he popped out of Dee Dee's Donuts with a sack and a cup of coffee. The Fontaines and their Bernese mountain dog named Lola actually stopped dead in their tracks and watched while she waited for the town's one traffic light to turn green.

Sweeney, head of the Artists' Co-op, waved at her from the back of her motorcycle, then roared by en route to her daily swim at the beach near the lighthouse, and Ellen was sure she saw her fishing buddy flash a thumbs-up as she disappeared around the curve.

It wasn't as if she had broken a local ordinance or violated any zoning rules. All she had done was sleep with her boss, then leave her car (the only fire-engine red PT Cruiser in Shelter Rock Cove) in his driveway overnight. Fortunately, stupidity wasn't punishable by law, even if it should be.

She wasn't sure what had happened between the bathroom and the hallway, but the moment she saw him standing there with that glass of orange juice in his hand, she had wanted to deck him. Before that she had been hurt but calm about the whole thing, embarrassed but not even the slightest bit angry. And then she saw his face and a wild surge of anger almost knocked her off her feet.

A few moments before she had been worried only about her dignity. Standing there in his foyer while he buttoned her dress, she had been worried about getting out of there without causing him bodily harm.

Up until last night his unavailability had been one of his most attractive assets. What could be better? A warm, witty, accomplished man with more baggage than LAX the day before Thanksgiving. The kind of man you could watch, observe, commiserate with, and lust over and never have to worry about it going anywhere at all.

In other words, her perfect man.

Nothing like a night spent in the arms of harsh, cold reality to show a woman the error of her ways. It was easy to fool yourself when you were home alone with a bag of Oreos and *When Harry Met Sally* in the DVD player, but let's see how good you were when the man you'd been dreaming about was dreaming about someone else.

It was time to say so long to those elaborate fantasies of showing up at the hospital one day to find her office awash in red roses or waking up to the sound of Hall serenading her from the parking lot of her condo. Oh, she was an expert at conjuring up scenarios worthy of Hollywood in its heyday, where the women were witty and the men were wonderful and everyone knew exactly when to say goodbye. No awkward slips of the tongue. No red-faced embarrassment. No explanations a woman could go to her grave without hearing. Worthless fantasies that she could pack away with yesterday's newspapers and chipped dinner plates and toss into the trash.

She wasn't quite sure when she had stopped looking at him simply as her colleague and started looking at him as a man, but it had been fairly early in their association. He was warm, funny, charming, and gorgeous. A woman would have to be made of stone to resist him, as his track record would attest. She had heard chapter and verse about his way with the ladies, but up until last night she had seen little evidence of a social life. It seemed as if he spent most of his time at the hospital, at the office, or with his two younger kids. If he had been seeing anyone the last few years, she was the best kept secret in town, and they all knew how tough it was to keep a secret in Shelter Rock.

"There you are." Mary from next door popped out onto her porch just as Ellen fit her key into the lock. "Somebody's been looking for you all night, hon. She said you wouldn't mind if I let her in, but since you didn't mention anyone, I wasn't about to give her the spare key."

"Did she give a name?"

Mary frowned. "Dorothy? Doris? Dee Dee! That's it. I think she said her name was Dee Dee like the doughnut shop."

Ellen rested her forehead against her front door. She didn't know whether to laugh or cry. "A small blue-eyed woman with curly red hair like mine?"

"Yes," said Mary, "and the loveliest hands I've ever seen."

"That's my sister Deirdre." Deirdre who floated from job to job and town to town like a soap bubble on the breeze. Deirdre who never answered her e-mail, her snail mail, or her phone calls until she needed something.

"Well, I'll be a monkey's uncle. And here I thought you were an only child!"

"Nope," said Ellen, trying to stand in the shadows so Mary wouldn't notice she was still wearing the same garden party dress that the elderly woman had admired the previous afternoon. "Actually I have two sisters. Mary Pat and Deirdre." Half sisters, but Mary could do without the full version of the story. She looked surprised enough as it was. Ellen knew exactly how she felt. She had been every bit as surprised to learn about them herself.

"I don't think I ever saw your sisters around here before, did I?"

Ellen took a deep breath. Most families were dysfunctional to one degree or another. Why should hers be any different?

Funny how after all these years, the embarrassment still ran deep.

"We're not the closest family," she said. "Mary Pat has her hands full with her five kids and Deirdre—" She shrugged her shoulders in a gesture she hoped conveyed benign bewilderment.

"She had a harp in the back of her car."

"A harp!" The last time she'd seen Deirdre, her sister had been carting around a tenor sax and a pair of bongos.

"And a dog."

"What kind of dog?"

"A big one," Mary said, spreading her arms wide. "The kind that slobbers. Let me tell you, that windshield was a sight. I don't know how she could see the road."

A minor sex scandal, a harp, and Cujo, and it wasn't even eight o'clock yet. The day was off to a great start.

She glanced around the quiet parking lot, then back at Mary. "Do you have any idea where she went?" Deirdre's plans often did a 180 while she waited for the traffic light to change.

"Sorry, honey, but I didn't ask. I heard her ring your bell again around midnight. She stayed a few minutes on your front step, then drove off. Maybe—" Mary's thick gray brows knotted in a frown. "Hope you don't mind me asking, but isn't that the same dress you were wearing yesterday?"

Hall's cell rang as he was pulling into his parking space at the hospital. He angled his Rover into position and grabbed for the phone.

"Dr. Talbot speaking."

"What the hell were you thinking?" Susan Galloway Aldrin's melodious tones launched themselves straight into his cranium. A cold shower and black coffee had restored his equilibrium, but nothing short of full-body anesthesia could have protected him from Susan on a rampage.

"Care to ratchet it down a few decibels, Suze? I'm in a hospital zone."

She tried. He had to admit she gave it her best shot, but she could still be heard in three counties.

"You slept with Ellen!"

He neither affirmed her statement nor disavowed it. "I take it you saw her car in my driveway."

"Everybody in town saw her car in your driveway. I saw it there last night when we were driving home from Annie's, and Ma saw it there this morning on her way to six o'clock mass."

"She had car trouble."

Susan was his oldest friend and confidante, but she didn't suffer fools gladly, if at all. "Save that crap for the rest of the world, Talbot. This is me you're talking to, the woman who held your hand through both of Annie's weddings."

That was the trouble with living in one town all of your life. Your secrets were public knowledge and you were never allowed to forget them. "I don't have time to get into this with you right now. I have to prep for a C-section."

"Right," said Susan. "Every time I try to say something you don't want to hear, you conveniently have a C-section planned."

"Don't push it, Galloway."

"What? You mean there's no population explosion in Shelter Rock?"

"You know damn well Jamie McIntyre was scheduled for her C-section. I saw you talking to her at the party yesterday."

"Apparently it slipped my mind."

"Good thing it didn't slip mine. That baby's ready to see what he's been missing. Looks like Jamie's going to pop an eight-pounder."

Hall wasn't a fool. Mention a newborn to Susan and she turned to mush. "I'll let you go deliver Jamie's son," she said with obvious reluctance, "but don't think this is the last you'll hear about this. You screwed up big time, friend, and you'd better be prepared to take the heat for Ellen. The least you could've done is park her car in your garage."

He disconnected without saying goodbye. He was Shelter Rock Cove born and bred. The rhythm of the small town was in his bones, a part of who he was and how he saw the world, but there were times, like today, when he wished he lived in Boston, where nobody knew his name.

"Hey, Doc, how's it going?" Marie at the reception desk

waggled her fingers at him as he crossed the small lobby. He had delivered her twin daughters nearly three years ago.

"Not bad for a Monday, Marie." He smiled at her desk mate, Leandra, who was manning the phones. Leandra was one of Ellen's patients, a high-risk prima gravida who required careful observation and a gentle hand, two of Ellen's specialties.

Was he imagining things or did Leandra lean over to Marie as he was passing by and whisper something that sent Marie's finely plucked brows arching skyward? He felt the heat of embarrassment rising up his neck. He hadn't reddened since he was fourteen and his voice changed halfway through his recitation of the Gettysburg Address in Assembly.

Get used to it, he thought darkly. If Susan was right, and to his dismay she usually was, he was going to be fielding arched brows and quizzical looks all day. *If you think this is bad, try walking in Ellen's shoes this afternoon.* She was closing on her purchase of Claudia Galloway's house on the hill and would have to face everyone from Claudia to Susan to a battery of attorneys over a conference table. He had the sinking feeling she was going to be fielding a whole lot more than a few raised eyebrows.

Damn that bottle of champagne. Damn the loneliness that filled his nights. Damn the way Ellen had looked with her auburn curls tumbling over her shoulders and those big eyes watching him across the table at the Spruce Goose, the way her own loneliness mirrored his, the way he had wanted her so badly that nothing else seemed to matter.

And damn him for taking advantage of that fact.

On the other side of town Susan Galloway Aldrin was taking out her aggressions on an innocent pan of scrambled eggs.

"Lighten up, Susie," Jack said as he poured two mugs of coffee, then set them down on the kitchen table. "Those eggs didn't do anything to you."

She turned around, spatula aimed like a semiautomatic. "What was I thinking, Jack? Can you tell me what in holy hell possessed me to tell my mother Ellen spent the night with Hall? I might as well have handed her a loaded gun."

"At least you called to warn him."

She leaned against the side of the counter and aimed the spatula right between her eyes. "I swear to you the words popped out before I knew what hit me. I never meant to tell her I saw the car there last night."

"You're your mother's daughter, all right."

He was trying to be funny and she knew it, but she wasn't in the mood for levity. "Meaning what? That I'm controlling or nosy or gossipy—feel free to stop me any time, Jack."

The poor man looked as if he would rather be anywhere else, but, trouper that he was, he didn't try to escape. "You knew something she didn't and you couldn't resist passing it on."

"After I told her, she asked me if I knew what Ellen was doing there! Can you believe that? The woman's seventy-six years old. I think she knows what it means when a woman spends the night with a man."

He poured at least a half cup of sugar into his coffee cup, tasted it, then added a half cup more. "Did you ever think she was trying to protect Hall and Ellen?"

"Oh, please. She was the first one to tell all of her friends that Eileen was pregnant when she got married, and that was her own daughter."

"You asked my opinion, I gave it to you. I don't know what else you want from me, Susie."

"I don't know how that man made it through med school," she fumed, moving the terrified eggs around with the business end of the spatula. "Everyone knows you don't sleep with an employee."

"She's not an employee."

"Oh, yes she is. He owns the practice. She's just a junior partner."

"I thought she was a full partner."

"Nope," said Susan. "Not yet. At least, I don't think so."

"Tell him it's like getting married. He doesn't seem to have a whole lot of trouble with that."

"Not funny," Susan said. "Maybe I should call him back and—"

"It's not your business," Jack warned. "Stay out of it."

"Then I'll call Ellen," she said, lowering the flame beneath the pan. "Maybe we—"

"—can screw things up even more? Great idea."

She gave him one of the withering looks that had worked much better in the earlier years of their marriage. Over twenty years of cohabitation had dulled the impact considerably. "I want to remind her about the walk-through at Mom's house this afternoon before the closing."

"You reminded her three times yesterday at the party."

"Only once," she corrected him. "Ellen's a doctor. She has a busy life. It's my job to make this easy for her."

"If you really want to make it easy for her, stay out of whatever's going on between her and Hall. They're both adults. Believe it or not, your old high school buddy doesn't have to run his girlfriends by you for approval."

Now, that hurt. She and Hall had been best friends since grade school. When it came to his private life, it was all public knowledge as far as Susan was concerned. If she didn't know about it, it hadn't happened yet.

"Damn," she muttered, scraping at the pan with the tip of the spatula. "Stupid eggs." She hadn't been paying attention and the moist yellow morsels were turning dry and brown. She pulled cream cheese from the fridge and dropped a good-sized blob of it into the pan, swirling it into a regular cholesterol festival. Welcome to the cardiac care unit.

"You've got to quit this matchmaking," Jack was saying as he slathered blueberry jam on a slice of toast. "The guy's forty-five years old. He's been married three times. I don't even want to speculate about how many women—" He shrugged. "Maybe the white picket fence isn't in the cards for him."

She opened her mouth, expecting a clever retort to fly out, but nothing happened. He was right. She didn't want him to be right. It hurt her to think her dearest friend might never find the happiness he deserved, the happiness she had spent the last twenty-five years of her life trying to manufacture for him, but she couldn't deny the truth.

She thought about Hall, about his ex-wives, his former lovers, his kids. He was a wonderful father, and the best ex any woman could possibly ask for. He went into each new relationship determined to make it work, confident that this time he could be everything his partner deserved, but somehow it never turned out that way. Sooner or later the woman involved began to realize there were three people in the marriage and that she would never be number one.

When Hall realized what she had done, he was going to be furious. She should have kept her big mouth shut when Claudia called and let her mother think Ellen was making an early morning visit to think of a way to back out of the house closing that afternoon. Claudia's leaps of logic had always gotten under Susan's skin, and this morning, with too little sleep and too much on her schedule, she had been eager to point out the error of Claudia's ways.

If only it hadn't been at Hall and Ellen's expense.

How was she going to face the woman during the walk-through later that morning, knowing that she had helped spread the news far and wide like some kind of town crier on commission?

Not that the gossip would be fatal. Oh, tongues would wag furiously for a while and they just might lose a few patients to other doctors, but when the smoke didn't turn into a fire, the furor would subside. Unfortunately most of the damage would be to Ellen's reputation, because this was a small town and she was still, in many ways, an outsider, but it was nothing she couldn't repair with time.

Give it a month or two and some other hapless couple would be caught slinking out of the Cozy Cottage Motor Court outside of town, and Hall and Ellen would be relegated to the back burner.

It couldn't happen fast enough for Susan.

Simon Andrew McIntyre was born at 8:32 A.M. and weighed in at over nine pounds. Hall congratulated both parents, then quickly set about closing up the mother so the McIntyres could embark upon the important business of becoming a family.

"Good job," he said to his surgical intern as they elbowed out of the delivery room. "You're catching on quickly."

She was a wide-eyed brunette with a smile that managed to glow from behind a face mask. "It's so unbelievable," she said, stumbling over her words. "I mean, to be there when a new life begins—" She shook her head and he caught the glitter of tears in her eyes. "Tell me it never becomes routine, Dr. Talbot."

"If it ever does," he said, "then it's time for a new specialty."

He thought about that a little later in his office. That was one of the many things that had made him choose Ellen as his partner. He had seen her dead tired at the end of an exhausting day, so wiped out that she could barely drag herself from the office to her car, and then her pager would go off and she'd find out one of her patients was in labor and the exhaustion and everything that went with it all fell away right before his eyes. All it took was the thought of being present for one more miracle, being there for that moment when the newborn sees the world and lets out with that first glorious cry—it was all there each time in Ellen's eyes.

Sometimes the fates weren't so kind. If he had the power, he would make sure no woman ever endured a stillbirth; that no husband had to hear the words, "I'm sorry but we couldn't save her." Every baby would be as perfect as the babies in magazines and on television, plump and rosy with ten of this and ten of that, all in the proper places. But life was inherently unfair and sometimes terrible things happened to the finest people, and it was often his job to carry the news. It took its toll over the years. He whispered a quick prayer before each delivery, for the ease of the mother and the health of the child, for the wisdom to make the right choices. Still the sharp claws of dread clutched his heart every time.

They had fallen into the habit of touching base after every delivery. A quick acknowledgment of the everyday miracle of life. Sometimes a silent moment that marked the passing of hope. It had become a ritual he looked forward to, even counted on to mark the importance of it all.

On any other day, after any other delivery, he would have been on the phone to her with the news. Nine pounds, two ounces, he would say. Twenty-four inches long with lungs to match.

Another day, another miracle, she would say, and they would both laugh softly, then sink back into their daily routines.

All he had to do was pick up the phone and dial her number, same as he had done hundreds of times over the last three years. A few words exchanged between them and everything would be back the way it had been this time yesterday before he made the biggest mistake of his life.

But he didn't pick up the phone because he couldn't say the words. The words he needed to say were the ones she didn't want to hear, the ones that would only make things worse between them than they already were.

"Damn it, Elly," he said out loud to his empty office. "What the hell have I done?"

Three

There was little doubt in Ellen's mind that the day was deteriorating fast. She was afraid to think about what the rest of the morning might have in store for her. The way her luck was going Claudia Galloway was probably sitting at her breakfast table, rethinking the sale of her house. Any minute now she would pick up the phone to tell Susan the deal was off. Or maybe Claudia wouldn't back out of the deal and instead a giant sinkhole would swallow the entire property thirty seconds after Ellen signed the papers and she would be left paying off a thirty-year mortgage on a hungry hole in the ground.

Mary from next door had accepted her mumbling, bumbling excuse for still being in yesterday's party dress, but Ellen doubted if the old woman believed a single word of it. And who could blame her? Yes, obstetricians were called into the hospital at all hours of the day and night (it was part of the job description, after all), but you couldn't fabricate an emergency in a town like Shelter Rock Cove without finding yourself tangled up in your own lie before you reached the end of the sentence. Everyone knew everyone else. They knew who was pregnant, who was trying to become pregnant, who bought enough Midol each month to keep the pharmacist in business.

God forgive her, but she had actually invented a tourist with cramps to explain her absence last night, and prayed Mary wouldn't call her niece Leandra at the hospital and ask for details.

Once in the privacy of her bedroom, Ellen stripped off the party dress and tossed it on the bed. Everything she owned was packed and ready to be loaded onto the moving van that was due to arrive within the hour, and unless she wanted them to catch her in her underwear, she had to get dressed and fast. Her favorite outfit, ivory linen slacks with a hand-knit silk top, was draped over the back of the slipper chair near the window. All she had to do was brush her teeth, don her lucky bra and panties, and she was ready for anything.

Which, of course, was an even bigger lie than the pregnant tourist with cramps.

She noted the time as she fastened on her watch. Jamie McIntyre's C-section was probably over. If everything had gone according to schedule, she and Don were back in her room with their beautiful baby boy. Jamie and Don had gone through hell trying to conceive their second child. If ever a child was wanted, Baby Boy McIntyre surely fit the bill. Was he a fair-skinned blond like his mother, she wondered, or a ruddy redhead like his dad? Did he let out a yell when he first met the world beyond his mother's womb, or did he look around quietly as if to say "I've been here before"?

Hall should have called by now. Not that she had been expecting him to, not after the way she had walked out on him without listening to his apology, but a part of her had been waiting for the phone to ring just the same. It wasn't that she wanted to hear his voice. (She had heard his voice loud and clear last night when he murmured Annie's name, thank you very much.) But there was something sacred about their post-delivery ritual, something joyous and life-affirming and beyond the reach of everyday strife. She almost wished—

No matter. She would find out later. Maybe after the closing she would stop by the hospital and peek in at the newborn and wish his parents well. And if she happened to bump into Hall, maybe she would handle the situation a little bit better than she handled it this morning.

It will all work out, she told her reflection as she brushed her teeth. They were adults, weren't they? Even more important, they were friends, not just business colleagues. Just because their encounter this morning had been more uncomfortable than root canal without novocaine, that didn't mean it wouldn't all smooth out between them as soon as they resumed their normal routine. They were never meant to be lovers. They could put that notion aside right now. They were friends who got caught up in the emotion of the moment and took their friendship a step too far.

If she could just manage to forget that moment when he—

See? She could push it aside. Metaphorically stick her fingers in her ears and whistle so loud she couldn't hear him when he murmured Annie's name every hour on the hour.

Pretending was easy. She came from a long line of people who turned pretending into performance art. Her parents had pretended they were a normal family, and, after a major detour in her teens, she learned how to pretend they were right. No reason it wouldn't work with Hall. As long as their indiscretion remained their own business, they could simply pretend it had never happened and pick up where they left off. Maybe not tomorrow or the next day, but soon.

That was her inner optimist talking. Her inner pessimist still needed to be convinced that the world as she knew it wasn't coming to an end.

Smuggling a one-hundred-fifteen-pound dog into her motel room had been hard, but smuggling the same dog out again was proving to be impossible.

Deirdre O'Brien opened the door to her room, peeked out, then quickly closed it again. Unless she put a hat and coat on Stanley and called him "Dear," they weren't going anywhere. The same manager who had eyed her with such suspicion six hours ago when she checked in was berating two of the housemaids for not folding the bath towels properly. You wouldn't think an establishment that prided itself on its easy access to the local truck stop would be quite so fussy about towels, but she had heard him quite clearly. This was not a man who would take kindly to the sight of a dog the size of a baby elephant sharing the accommodations with a paying guest.

NO PETS meant no pets, even if the pet in question didn't see himself that way.

"Don't worry, Stan," she said to the dog, who was sitting at her feet. They were almost eye to eye. "As soon as the coast is clear, we're out of here."

Sneaking a boy into her dorm room at St. Adalbert's Academy had been easier than this.

But Stanley was a patient dog. He yawned, exposing some extremely large teeth, then settled down for a nap. He was a big dog but very well behaved. The woman at the shelter in Pennsylvania hadn't lied about that fact. "He has a problem with saliva," she had said to Deirdre, who was leaning toward a tiny mixed breed that would fit inside her tote bag, "but he's good as gold. Too bad he's the size of a small grizzly. Not many people have the kind of room he needs. We do our best for our animals, but I'm not too optimistic about Stanley's chances."

Deirdre asked what the woman meant by "Stanley's chances," and the woman told her quite bluntly that he probably wouldn't be around this time next month.

That was all she needed to hear. Deirdre mentally crossed herself and told the woman she had a big farm in western Massachusetts where Stanley could run free with her other dogs, Lassie and King. And don't forget her children. Two girls and a boy, ages six, eight, and almost ten. The woman's eyes misted over with happy tears, which inspired Deirdre to add a husband, a kid brother, and a grandfather who liked to sit on the front porch and whittle.

Give your audience what she wants and you'll have her eating out of your hand in no time.

The woman wasn't sure she should hand Stanley over without doing an at-home check, but when she saw Deirdre's Massachusetts driver's license, she surrendered to destiny, and moments later Deirdre was trying to squeeze Stanley into her Hyundai between the harp, the saxophone, and her father's old suitcase, the one with the travel stickers pasted all over it.

Stanley rolled with the punches. He didn't seem to care that she not only didn't own farmland in western Massachusetts, she didn't even have an apartment. He didn't get carsick. He wasn't a finicky eater. And, best of all, he was good company.

Maybe he didn't laugh at her jokes, but then neither did her last boyfriend, and so far Stanley was much better company.

Too bad Stanley was a dog, because in many ways he was the perfect man.

"Elly's going to love you," she said, reaching down to scratch behind Stanley's right ear. "Just make sure you bring your company manners."

At least, she hoped her sister would love Stanley, since she was going to ask Elly to take him in for the summer. The good people at the Crooked Isle Inn told her they had room for her and for her harp, but not for a one-hundred-fifteen-pound dog. She needed the job. She loved the dog. The only solution was to throw herself on her sister's mercy and pray Elly was still a soft touch for a hard-luck story.

Finally the manager finished lecturing the housekeepers. Deirdre shot Stanley a warning look as the manager's heavy footsteps moved past the door. Stanley's ears lifted at the sound, but, thank God, he didn't so much as grumble. She peeked out the door again. The housekeepers had dispersed and there was nobody in sight.

"This is it," she said, slipping the harness around Stanley's barrel chest and broad shoulders. "Out the door, into the car, then lie down until we hit the main street."

You could take the girl out of Catholic school, but you could never take Catholic school out of the girl. She could lie with the best of them, but she always felt guilty about it afterward. She pulled her last ten-dollar bill from the tiny pouch slung across her chest and left it on the dresser for the maid. It wasn't much, but it did help to ease her conscience.

Stanley must have been an undercover agent in another life, because he played his role perfectly. He darted from the motel room and leaped straight into the front seat of her Hyundai, where he promptly slumped down out of view.

"Good boy!" Deirdre said as she turned the key in the ignition. "Ellen is going to absolutely love you."

The engine sputtered. She turned the key again. This time it sputtered and coughed. The third time it sputtered, coughed, then dropped dead.

"Oh, God," she said, trying again. "Don't do this to me!"

Punishment, that's what it was. God's way of telling her it was time to mend her ways.

She finally managed to get it started just as two of the housekeepers popped out of an adjacent building. Of course Stanley chose that moment to sit straight up in the passenger seat and peer out the window at the astonished women. Deirdre clutched the wheel and prayed all the way across the parking lot, and she didn't stop praying until they reached the main road.

What was it her mother always used to say to her about telling lies? She couldn't remember, but she knew it was something Biblical, designed to scare her into walking the straight and narrow. She usually limited herself to white lies with an occasional dip into pale gray, but last night's desperation had pushed her straight over into the black. She should have slept in the car with Stanley or out on the beach. It was June, after all, and it wasn't as if she had never spent the night on a beach before. Instead she had bounced all over the place in search of Ellen. Her apartment, the hospital, back to her apartment again until she finally gave up and found herself handing over two twenty-dollar bills for a room at the Cozy Cottage Motor Court.

"You're just like Billy," Mary Pat always said, sounding more like their mother every year. "You wouldn't know the truth if it reared up and bit you."

No argument there. That was why she was an artist and musician while Mary Pat baked cookies and stifled her children's creativity.

"Never trust a woman who doesn't like dogs," she said to Stanley, who was busy slobbering on the passenger-side window. "A word to the wise."

The look on Mary Pat's face when she saw Stanley bounding full speed toward her would have been downright comical if Stanley had only managed to screech to a stop before he reached the woman. Unfortunately Stanley hit the brakes a fraction of a second too late and he careened into Mary Pat, who fell flat on her butt in the middle of the rainswept driveway.

So much for Stanley's chances of spending the summer at Mary Pat's cottage on the Cape.

At least Ellen liked dogs. Or so Deirdre thought. Ellen might be a workaholic without much of a social life, but she had a soft heart for hard-luck cases and Stanley certainly qualified.

"One look into those big brown eyes of yours, Stan, and she'll be a goner," Deirdre said as she rolled to a stop at the first traffic light. "Elly would never let us down."

The light changed. Deirdre let up on the brake. The Hyundai gave a mighty wheeze, then collapsed right there in the middle of the street like a beached pilot whale.

Deirdre tried to start the car, but instead of the welcome sound of the engine turning over, she was rewarded with utter silence. She climbed out and circled the vehicle, peering at the rusty back panel, the dent on the right fender, the crumpled rear bumper. Everything was in order. She considered lifting the hood and looking around, but why bother? It wasn't as if she had the slightest idea what any of that paraphernalia actually was, and, even if she could identify it, she hadn't a clue what to do with it.

For a main drag, Harbor Road didn't have a whole lot going for it. Not a gas station in sight. People traipsed in and out of the doughnut shop in the middle of the block. A few men were chatting in front of Custis Hardware while they sipped from paper cups. One of them gazed in her direction, then looked away. A woman with curly amber hair was arranging baskets of tulips in an eye-catching display in front of a place called Annie's Flowers. The woman turned and looked in Deirdre's direction, then started walking toward her.

"Car trouble?" she called out as she approached.

"I think it's terminal," Deirdre said.

The woman glanced both ways, then darted into the street. "Did you check the gas gauge?"

"Over a quarter tank," Deirdre said. "At least, that's what it said last night."

"I'm afraid that's the limit of my diagnostic abilities," the woman said with an easy laugh. "If you like, you can use the phone in my shop."

"To call the auto wrecker?"

"You should see my truck," the woman said. "The term *junker* would be a compliment."

Deirdre extended her hand. "Deirdre O'Brien."

"Annie Butler." She had a strong handshake. "Let's push the car over to the curb and then see what we can do."

"I'm not so sure we can—"

"Watch and learn," said Annie. She released the latch and lifted the hood. No sooner had she locked it into position than the three men from the hardware store ditched their cups of joe and galloped toward them like racehorses out of the starting gate. They were followed by two other men, who raced out of the doughnut shop as if they were on fire, and an old guy who screeched to a stop going the other way and leaped out to offer aid and assistance.

Annie made the introductions. Pete. Edmund. Kyle. George. Harold, two Arties, a Daniel, and a Lowell. Deirdre found herself wishing they had their names embroidered on their shirt pockets. So many new faces!

"This works better than cleavage," she whispered to Annie while the men held a consultation under the hood. "For a minute I thought it was raining men!"

The men decided that the Hyundai was definitely in big trouble and pushed the car over to the curb while Stanley supervised from the driver's seat.

"You'd better call Jack," Harold from the doughnut store said. "He's the best."

Deirdre looked to Annie, who nodded. "Definitely the best," Annie said. "Come on. You can call from my shop."

She glanced over at the Hyundai. "Do you mind if I bring Stanley with me?"

"Not at all."

"I have to warn you," Deirdre said. "He's even bigger than he looks."

"We have a yellow Lab at home, so I'm used to a lot of dog."

"No wonder my sister loves it here," she said as she liberated Stanley. "You're terrific."

"You have a sister in Shelter Rock?" asked Lowell. (Or maybe it was one of the Arties.)

Deirdre nodded. "She lives in the condo complex over by the beach."

"So why didn't you stay there?" Pete (or was it Edmund?) asked.

"I thought I'd surprise her," Deirdre said. She had lived in Massachusetts the first ten years of her life and was accustomed to the blunt curiosity of the native New Englander. "I popped by her place three times, then finally gave up around two and found a motel room. I guess she's out of town."

"Who is she?" Pete asked. "This is still a pretty small place. We probably know her."

"You probably do," Deirdre said. "She's Dr. Ellen Markowitz."

Deirdre didn't believe you could literally hear silence fall until the words "Dr. Ellen Markowitz" escaped her lips and a profound silence fell all around her like a box of rocks.

She forced a small chuckle and looked toward Annie. "Was it something I said?"

A few of the men exchanged looks. Oh, yeah. It was definitely something she said, but what?

Annie blinked the way you did when you were trying to recover your equilibrium, then gave Deirdre a slightly false smile. "Dr. Ellen's my obstetrician," she said. "I didn't know she had a sister."

"O'Brien and Markowitz?" one of the Arties asked Deirdre. "You married an O'Brien?"

"Maybe Dr. Ellen married a Markowitz," the other Artie offered.

"Dr. Ellen's never been married," Pete broke in. "Elaine was talking to her at the parade and she told her she'd been engaged once, but it didn't work out." He turned to Deirdre. "Right?"

It wasn't that the questions were tough to answer. Ellen was a Markowitz and Deirdre was an O'Brien. If you were looking for the simple answer, there it was. It was the background information that gave her pause. Deirdre was rarely at a loss for words, but this was Ellen's world and anything she said would reflect back on her sister. She could easily weave a pretty little story that would pacify their curiosity, but she knew instinctively that Ellen would hate that. She also had the feeling Ellen wouldn't much like it if she told the truth, either.

"Hey, guys!" Bless Annie for leaping into the fray. "This isn't *Meet the Press.*"

There was something in her tone of voice that gave Deirdre the feeling that she was warning the men away from pursuing other questions as well. Very interesting. Was it possible that her upright sister might have a few secrets worth gossiping about?

God, she hoped so.

Four

Claudia parked her Chrysler at the curb and walked up the long path to the front door of the house where she had spent the best years of her life.

Some of the saddest years, as well, but she wasn't thinking about them today. She was thinking about the day she and John brought their first child home . . . about how lovely Susan had looked as she floated down the staircase in her wedding dress . . . Eileen in her prom gown . . . the boys racing in and out in football gear and baseball uniforms . . . grandchildren spilling from the guest rooms, somersaulting across the yard, their laughter filling the house from basement to attic with the sound of life.

Such a big house, she thought, as she unlocked the door and stepped into the foyer. How would Ellen Markowitz ever manage to breathe new life into it all by herself?

She laughed at the thought and started toward the kitchen. She could just hear what John would have said to her. *Let go, Claudia . . . you've sold the house . . . let Ellen figure out how to live in it.*

But as she wandered through the kitchen, reliving the history of every scratch on the countertops, every dent in the floor tiles, the shelves her son Kevin had put up for her just one week before he died—well, it was hard to let it slip through her fingers without trying to hang on a little bit longer.

Ellen's heart sank to her knees when she saw Claudia's car parked in front of the house. She considered pulling into the driveway as she had originally planned, but it wasn't her house yet so she parked behind Claudia at the curb.

It was a wonderful house. One of those big sprawling two-story houses that had been built after the Victorian era but before the Levittown era of cookie-cutter construction. "There's a lot wrong with this place," Susan had warned when she first showed her the house. "I love my mother, but she did let things get a little out of hand." The roof needed work. The exterior hadn't been painted in forever. The only thing holding the windows in place was over forty years of caulking. The entire structure slumped a little on its foundation like a tired dowager at the end of a party, but to Ellen the imperfections only made it more beautiful.

Every room, every staircase, every corner of the house bore witness to family life. The history of the Galloways was everywhere you looked. The pencil marks on the wall near the kitchen door that charted the children's growth. The shelves Annie's late husband had put up not long before he died. Susan had made each room come alive in a way that might have unnerved a woman with family stories of her own. But Ellen didn't have any, at least none that she cared to dwell on. She gathered each and every story Susan told her about the Galloways, then tucked them away to bring out and examine once she could finally call that wonderful house her home.

She would miss the friends she had made at the condo complex, but it was time she made a real commitment to Shelter Rock Cove and the life she was trying to build for herself. Nobody in either of her families had ever owned a house before. Back home on the Upper West Side, she had never even given it a thought. She was descended from a long line of renters, people who were more than happy to hand a check over to the landlord on the first of every month in exchange for knowing that the busted pipes and clogged toilets were somebody else's problem.

As far as Ellen knew, she was the only one of the clan who had ever yearned for land. The only roots her aunts were concerned about were the ones the hairdresser touched up for them every six weeks. They were New Yorkers, born and bred, and they didn't need a mortgage to know they were exactly where they belonged.

It had never been that easy for her. From the very beginning she had been looking for something that nobody else in the family seemed to know was missing from their lives. What she was looking for was a sense of belonging, of knowing that her place at the table was secure.

She laughed as she switched off the engine. What table? It wasn't like her family ever saw each other. Not even during the high holy days. Her aunts had made an effort to keep everyone together the first few years after the accident that took the lives of her mother and unborn brother, but before long the attempt at maintaining the ties between them went the way of 8-tracks and disco fever. Now that the truth was out there and it wouldn't go away, nobody was willing to keep up the pretense of being a real family.

Her stepfather Cy threw himself into his medical practice, pouring his grief into a passionate commitment to his patients. Unfortunately that commitment came at the expense of the child he had raised as his own from the time she was six months old.

So there she was, almost thirty-five years later, sitting in front of a drafty old house on the Maine coast, praying the owner wasn't about to back out of the deal. She wanted that house more than she had ever wanted anything before in her life. She wanted to live some place where people had been happy, where a family had fought and loved and pulled together when the going got rough. She knew the Galloways and liked them. She knew the stories and the legends. She knew the kids and the grandkids and the ones who had moved on and, God help her, she envied them their good fortune.

She might have grown up as a doctor's daughter with all the privileges that entailed, but the Galloways had grown up with something neither her money nor her education could buy: a real family.

Claudia was upstairs in the room she had once shared with John. The room was empty. The floors had been swept clean. All six windows were open to the ocean breeze that swept across her garden, carrying with it the mingled scent of roses and the sea. She closed her eyes and breathed deeply, letting that unique combination imprint itself deep within her memory. To her it was the smell of love.

"Hello!"

She opened her eyes, startled from her reverie by the sound. Her heart lurched forward and she placed a hand against her chest as if to halt its progress. An old woman's gesture, from a time and place long past.

The walk-through wasn't until eleven o'clock. She had intended to slip in and out without seeing anyone.

"Claudia, it's Ellen Markowitz. I'm afraid I'm early for the walk-through."

Of course. The only other person in Shelter Rock with that accent was Annie's husband, Sam.

"I'm upstairs in the master bedroom," Claudia called from the landing. "Come join me."

Ellen looked so young and uncertain, standing there in the doorway. Not at all like the competent doctor with the white coat and take-charge attitude. Claudia reached out her hand.

"Don't you look lovely," she said, drawing the young woman into the room. "So slim and elegant in those beautiful trousers."

Ellen's cheeks reddened very slightly. "I apologize for showing up early, Claudia. If you'd like to be alone, I—"

"Of course not," said Claudia, brushing away the thought. "I've been alone here for more years than I care to count."

"It's a wonderful house."

"I wish you had seen it in its day. I'm afraid I haven't kept it up the way it deserves."

Ellen tilted her head and took a long, deep breath of the perfumed breeze. She looked at Claudia, who nodded.

"I know," she said. "It's something very special."

"It must be hard," Ellen said softly.

"It is. My children have been urging me to sell for years." The thought of change terrified her, and she clung to what she knew like a drowning woman. *When it's time for me to move, I'll let you know,* she had informed them, *and not one single day before.*

She didn't tell them about the nights when she made a wrong turn going from bedroom to bathroom and nearly tumbled down two flights of stairs. She didn't tell them about the day she left the gas on under a pot of soup and went off to Cappy's with Roberta. Instead, she buried the scorched pot in her garbage pail, then bought a night-light, but not before she thanked God from the bottom of her heart for sending her home early with a headache before a fire broke out.

Who would have imagined that a tiny patch of ice by her mailbox would be, quite literally, her downfall? She had hurried down the driveway to pop a Christmas card in the box before Jeannie the mail carrier arrived, and she was just about to raise the flag when she heard the sound of a car horn and she turned to see who it was. She must have moved slightly, even though she had no memory of doing so, because one minute she was standing there by the mailbox and the next she was flat on the snowy ground with the remains of her independence scattered around her.

Oh, she had fought the good fight. Her beloved John would have been proud of her. Despite her children's urgings, despite her dear friend Warren's persistent badgering, she refused to put her home on the market. After one particularly grueling round of physical therapy, she had even turned on her daughter Susan and accused her of trying to score points at the real estate office where she worked. Susan didn't speak to her for weeks after that.

It was the second fall, a tiny tumble down the last two basement steps that changed everything. She agreed to move temporarily to an assisted-living facility while she recuperated from a second hip operation, and the weeks passed and then the months and one day she woke up and realized she would never move back home again. The truth was the idea of being alone in that big house scared her now. After so many years of living alone and coping with whatever came her way, Claudia Galloway had lost her nerve. She no longer trusted her body to do what she asked it to do without mishap. It was time.

And now she was strolling through the empty house where she had lived a very full life with the lovely young woman whose own dreams would fill the rooms before the day was over.

"I knew it was a big house," Ellen said as they stepped out onto the front porch, "but I'm not sure I realized exactly how big."

"I'm sure it won't stay this empty for long. Now that you and Hall are—"

"Excuse me?"

The poor child looked shocked. "I'm sorry," Claudia said. "I thought you and—"

"No." She plunged her hands deep into the pockets of her trousers and fixed Claudia with a steady gaze. "You thought wrong."

"I'm—I'm so sorry. You two made such a lovely couple yesterday at the christening party. And Susan told me this morning that you—"

She stopped abruptly at the look of horror on Ellen's face and quickly regrouped. It was crystal clear that her nosy daughter had been wrong and there was nothing whatsoever between the two physicians.

"I'm sorry," she said. "I hope you'll forgive my mistake. I would blame it on my age, but I've always said more than I should."

"No apology necessary," Ellen said, that stricken look still lingering in her eyes. "It's already forgotten."

Claudia made some excuse about not wanting to be there when her daughter arrived for the walk-through because she didn't want Susan to think she was checking up on her. They both knew it was a polite way to escape what had become a very uncomfortable situation.

No sooner had her Chrysler vanished around the corner than Susan's SUV appeared at the opposite end of the street. Ellen was beginning to think she was trapped in some kind of

Yankee version of a French farce except for the fact she wasn't laughing.

"You're getting cold feet, aren't you?" Susan said as she climbed the front steps to the porch.

"What makes you say that?" And they said New Yorkers were blunt? Mainers put them to shame.

"All first-timers get cold feet. It comes with the territory."

She sighed. "Not exactly cold feet, but I will say this house looks a lot bigger than I remembered."

"It's huge," Susan said. "I warned you that you were taking on a lot of house for one person."

"How did your mother manage this place all those years? She must be a human dynamo."

"She had six kids, remember. Child labor laws don't count if you're family."

They talked about cleaning services and snow removal and landscapers. They checked the heating system, the cooling unit, all of the appliances. They ran water in each of the sinks, flushed all three toilets, inspected the basement for surprises.

Susan checked the list she had sticking out of her tattered notebook. "I think that's everything. Next time you walk through that door, you'll be the new homeowner."

Ellen took a last look at the huge expanse of empty space, then stepped out on the front porch while Susan locked up.

"I think I'm having an out-of-body experience," she said when Susan joined her. "I can't believe I'm about to buy a house."

"You won't regret it," Susan said as they walked down the driveway toward their cars. "I'm sure your financial adviser has told you everything you need to know about the benefits of home ownership."

Ellen just smiled. This was more than buying the roof over her head, more than another deduction on her income taxes. Susan had grown up in that house, in the middle of a loud and loving family, and she had gone on to create a loud and loving family of her own. She couldn't possibly understand how deeply Ellen envied her.

They chatted for a few minutes at the foot of the driveway, then Ellen glanced at her watch. "I'd better head for home. My next-door neighbor is supervising the movers."

"Go," Susan said. "I'll see you at Ed's office at one."

Ellen grinned. "I'll bring my checkbook."

"Good girl," Susan said. "That's what we like to hear."

Ellen breathed a sigh of relief as she slid behind the wheel of her car. Forty-five minutes and not one single reference, veiled or otherwise, to Hall.

Finally the day was starting to look up.

Deirdre prowled around the flower shop while Annie phoned for a tow truck. The store was an explosion of color that made her head spin. Hollyhocks. Larkspur. Pale gray roses and deep velvety red American Beauties. Delphinium. Bird-of-paradise on the coast of Maine! The magnificent blooms vied for space with lush greenery, one-of-a-kind toys, framed watercolors, note cards, quilts, handwoven scarves in shades of amethyst and sapphire and pearl, small alabaster and soapstone sculptures, stained-glass pieces, handmade lace that begged you to drape it across your naked body. Deirdre was flung instantly into a blissful state of sensory overload. Stanley seemed enchanted by the scent of lilacs and freesia in the air. He stood in the middle of the store, nose pointing toward the ceiling, and then sniffed lustily.

"A Hyundai," Annie said, glancing over at Deirdre, who nodded her head. "Massachusetts plates . . . oh, for heaven's sake, Jack, I'm sure Scott will find it with no trouble." She hung up the phone. "You'd think he was searching Manhattan for it."

Deirdre forced herself to turn away from an exquisite sculpture of a man cradling an infant in the crook of his powerful arm. "Your store is incredible, Annie. Not too many places offer both roses and pieces like this."

"That's one of mine," the woman said with an understandable note of pride. "I'm glad you like it."

"I love it."

Annie quickly pointed out two more of her pieces scattered in among the flowers, plants, and stained-glass lamps. "I'm usually in my studio in the morning," she said, "but we had to adjust our schedules today so Claudia could get to the closing. My husband is watching the babies while I open up."

Deirdre nodded as if she knew who Claudia was.

She offered Deirdre a cup of coffee, which she accepted with almost pathetic gratitude.

"Delicious," she said, taking a big gulp. "I just might live."

Annie poured herself a glass of milk. "I suppose you're here to help Ellen with the move."

"What move?"

Annie laughed. "Very funny. Do you need more sugar?"

"I'm serious," Deirdre said. "Ellen's moving?" That would explain why she hadn't been around.

"Today." Annie looked just the slightest bit less sunny than she had a minute ago. "You really didn't know?"

"Not a clue," Deirdre said as Stanley sidled up to her for a head scratch. "Is she leaving town?"

"Actually, she bought my former mother-in-law's house."

"You're kidding." Talk about a small world.

"You probably saw it. It's the big white frame house on the hill. It overlooks the beach near the marina."

"You're in luck, Stanley," she said. "Sounds like Aunt Ellen will have plenty of room for you."

Annie had one of those faces that displayed her emotions like a highway billboard. She was clearly beginning to wonder if she had a lunatic on her hands.

"We love each other to bits, but we're not a close family," Deirdre offered by way of explanation for her lack of up-to-the-minute data on Ellen's life. "There's a married sister, a doctor sister, and a spontaneous sister. Guess which one I am."

"Got it," Annie said, her smile returning. "I'm sure Ellen will be glad to see you."

"Oh, she'll be glad to see me. It's Stanley I'm not so sure about." Actually she wasn't all that sure Ellen would be that glad to see her, either, since Ellen was the type who waited to be invited before she showed up on your doorstep, but that was probably way more information than the poor woman needed to hear.

"Stanley's definitely a lot of dog," Annie said, offering her hand for his sniff of approval.

Deirdre asked about her children and was listening, with unabashed delight, to the story of how Ellen delivered both of Annie's daughters when the front door jingled.

"Scott!" Annie's smile widened. "Thanks for getting here so soon."

Deirdre turned around and saw a tall, muscular male form backlit in the doorway.

"I found the Hyundai," Scott said in a distinctly Massachusetts accent much like her own. "All I need now is the owner."

"And that would be me," Deirdre said, stepping forward.

He turned and before she could say another word he was out the door and heading across the street to where she'd left her car.

"Is he always like that?" she asked Annie.

"Afraid so. He's a great mechanic, but not much when it comes to conversation."

Or manners, either, she thought, but wisely kept the opinion to herself. She thanked Annie for the help, then, grabbing Stanley's leash, hurried after Scott the moody mechanic.

He was peering under the hood when she reached the car.

"It won't start," she said.

He mumbled something.

"It began acting up yesterday afternoon when it stalled out twice at stoplights."

No response.

"So what do you think is wrong?"

He fiddled with something grubby and metallic. "What do you think is wrong?"

"You're the mechanic. You tell me."

"How did it sound?"

"It didn't. It wouldn't start."

"When it was trying to start. Did the engine catch?"

"I don't remember."

"Did it try to turn over?"

"I think so."

"You're not making this easy for me."

"Am I supposed to?"

He looked up at her and for a second she thought she saw the beginnings of a smile. "Wouldn't hurt."

"Sorry," she said. "I really wasn't paying that much attention to the car this morning. I was too busy trying to smuggle Stanley out of the motel without getting caught."

"I take it Stanley's not your husband."

"This is Stanley," she said, gesturing toward the dog. "Better than most husbands I've known."

It was probably the best straight line she had ever put out there, and he didn't even bite. She wasn't sure if she was disappointed or deeply impressed.

He lowered the hood. "I'm going to tow her into the shop. Give me a phone number where you can be reached, and I'll call you when I know something."

"You can call me at my sister's," she said and recited Ellen's number. "That's where I'll be until you get the car fixed."

"Hope you two like each other, because it's going to be a bitch to get parts."

"It better not take too long because I have to be in Bar Harbor this weekend."

"Vacation?"

"Work."

"Waitress?"

"Musician." She paused a second, then decided what the hell. "I'm a harper." She use the term preferred by those who played the Celtic harp.

"You play the harp?"

"Somebody has to."

He grinned and she found herself smiling back at him. "You don't look like a harpist."

"Right," she said, leaning against the side of the Hyundai while Stanley sniffed the unfamiliar smells all around him. "And you've seen enough harpists to know what we're supposed to look like." She had been working very hard on both angelic and ethereal.

"You look more like a blues singer than a harpist."

"You're good," she said. "I spent ten years of my life singing the blues." In many more ways than just the obvious, but she wasn't about to tell him that.

"I'm waiting for the punch line."

"That is the punch line," she said. "I sang in every smoky, forgettable bar from Bangor to Key West until I finally got it through my thick skull that it wasn't going to happen for me."

A moment of silence, please, for her dead career.

Scott the Mechanic wasn't big on sentiment. "Yeah, well, this car isn't going to happen if I don't get her back to the shop." Just like that he turned and started doing whatever it was that had to be done to hook the car up to the tow truck.

Most people would have asked how she made the jump from blues singer to harper. It wasn't exactly your normal career track, not even for a musician. Clearly even Stanley had more intellectual curiosity than this auto mechanic. Good thing he had his name embroidered on his shirt pocket, or he'd have trouble remembering it.

Now, that was going too far. For all she knew he could be a rocket scientist turned auto mechanic. The Northeast was littered with former scientists and engineers whose companies went belly-up when the stock market went sliding downhill. Scratch an adult-ed teacher or real estate agent and you just might find an MBA who was looking for a steady paycheck.

He looked like a mechanic, though. A little rough around the edges, but in a sexy kind of way. His hair was too long for fashion, too short for a political statement. He wore a beat-up Timex on his left wrist. The crystal boasted a long diagonal scrape. No wedding ring. A silver Saint Christopher medal hung around his neck. He had mechanic's forearms, muscular and well-developed, the kind you got from hard work, not daily visits to the local Gold's Gym clone. She could imagine him in one of those smoky bars she used to sing at. He'd be a Sam Adams type. No glass for him. He'd drink straight from the bottle. He'd be leaning against the wall, eyes narrowed slightly against the cigarette haze, his attention wandering until she took her seat on a small stool in the center of the tiny circle of stage and started to sing for him. Then he would climb up into the tow truck and drive off without her.

"Hey!" she cried out as he started the engine. "Where the hell do you think you're going?"

He looked at her through the open window of the tow truck. "I'm taking her back to the garage."

"You were going to leave me here?"

"That was the plan."

"Well, you need a new plan. I'd like a lift to my sister's place."

"Fine," he said, sounding less than enthusiastic about the idea. "Hop in."

She and Stanley ran around to the passenger-side door and flung it open.

"Wait a minute," he said. "You're not bringing that dog with you."

"What do you suggest I do with him? Tell him to hitch a ride to Ellen's?"

"There isn't room for three of us in the front seat."

"Then he can sit in the backseat." She took a second look. "Except you don't have a backseat."

"Put him in your car," he said.

"Why don't I let him sit up here with you and I'll sit in my car." Stanley would be terrified alone in the car while it was towed down the street at such a crazy angle.

Was she imagining things or did Scott the Mechanic turn pale at the suggestion?

"Are you afraid of dogs?" she asked.

"Hell, no." His expression softened just the slightest bit. "Are you sure that's a dog? I've seen smaller bears."

"He's harmless," she said, her own expression softening in response. She bent down and wrapped her arms around Stanley's massive neck and pressed a kiss to the top of his silky head. "See? My Stan wouldn't harm a fly."

"Get in," Scott said. "But the dog sits next to the window."

Five

Ellen's cell phone rang as she pulled away from Claudia's house. The moving men were hung up on a delivery and wouldn't be able to get to her until mid-afternoon. It was a few minutes past noon. She still had time before she was due at the lawyer's office for the closing. She downshifted from a building excitement to mild disappointment, then turned the car around and headed for the hospital to check on the McIntyre baby, who, if everything had gone well, would be over four hours old.

Hall's Rover was parked in his assigned spot. She slid into her spot next to him. No time like the present, she thought as she dropped her keys into her purse, then ducked into the hospital. Sooner or later she was going to have to show her face around Shelter Rock Cove, and this was as good a time as any to start.

She thought Marie's smile was a little snarky as she passed the reception desk, but Leandra's greeting seemed normal enough. Ellen waved at both women and kept walking, head held high. Let them think what they wanted. As long as they didn't have pictures, she was in the clear.

"Morning, Doc." Sarah from Admissions popped out of the

elevator as Ellen was getting in. "Beautiful day."

"Oh, it definitely is." Was it? She hadn't a clue. She could have driven through a June snowstorm for all she could remember about the weather. She smiled politely as the elevator doors slid shut, then leaned against the wall, weak with relief. If a comment about the weather was going to throw her into a tailspin, she was in big trouble. "Get it together, Markowitz," she ordered herself. Personal problems had no place at work.

Maternity was on the third floor. The elevator doors opened, and instantly she was swept up into the world of miracles. God, how she loved everything about the maternity wing. The pink and blue and green and yellow and lavender murals on the walls. The soft rosy carpeting underfoot. The way the rest of the world and its troubles dropped away the moment you entered this world.

"Hi, Dr. M." Jeannie, the day shift head nurse, looked up from the computer terminal. "Thought today was moving day."

"It is," Ellen said. "I had a few minutes, so I figured I'd stop by and see how the McIntyres are doing."

Jeannie laughed. "I thought we were going to have to call out for a bigger crib. He's in number three. You can't miss him."

If Jeannie had heard any gossip, she was doing a great job of hiding it. Ellen thanked her, then zipped around the corner to the nursery.

Simon McIntyre was a bruiser. There was no other way to put it. As big and rosy and perfect as it was possible to be, and the sight of him, sound asleep in the third crib from the left, brought tears to Ellen's eyes. They always did. Every single time. It didn't matter if she helped deliver them or not. The miracle of conception and birth had the power to bring her to her knees. She knew you were supposed to divorce your emotions from your job, but she had never quite mastered that skill. How on earth could you keep your heart from becoming involved when your job was helping to bring a new life into the world? To be there at the moment a family was born.

"Simon Andrew. I left you a note."

Hall was standing behind her. She met the reflection of his eyes in the nursery window.

"I haven't stopped in at the office yet."

"Nine pounds, two ounces. Twenty-four inches long."

"Jamie?"

"Happy. Relieved. Sleeping." He hadn't moved an inch closer, but her awareness of him, his body, was unbearable. "Frank almost keeled over, but she told him to get a grip and by God he did."

She laughed despite herself. "If I had a dollar for every husband who almost keeled over, we could open a second maternity wing."

We. Now where did that come from? She meant their partnership, of course. She considered hammering that point home, but it might sound a bit defensive and that was the last thing she wanted.

"Ellen." His voice was low, his tone urgent. "We need to—"

"I'd better get moving," she said. "The closing's at one and I need to check messages."

She started toward the elevator with Hall in lockstep next to her. Jeannie looked up as they passed the main nurses' station, and it seemed to Ellen that she and the other nurses seemed unusually interested in watching their progress.

Hall was his usual easygoing self. He smiled at the nurses and told Jeannie that he was going to stop in at the office but would be back on the floor within a half hour. The two younger nurses exchanged glances. Ellen arched a brow in their direction, and they quickly feigned interest in the water cooler.

"Just let it roll off your back," he advised as they waited for the elevator. "Don't give them more fuel for the fire."

She pressed the Down button a second time. "I gave them all the fuel they needed when I—"

"Morning, Joe." Hall smiled over her head. "See you at tomorrow's staff meeting?"

She turned and saw Joe Wiley, the hospital's chief of staff, standing behind her. Her knees began to knock.

"I'll be there," Joe said, nodding a friendly good morning to Ellen. "Not very good form to ditch a meeting you're slated to chair."

Ellen was extremely fond of the older doctor. He had welcomed her into the fold with warmth and respect, and that welcome had set the tone for the rest of his staff. Joe Wiley was in his early seventies, and as vital and sharp as most forty-year-olds. He had cut back on his workload in the past year, and rumor had it he was easing toward retirement. She couldn't imagine Shelter Rock Cove Hospital without his gentle competence. He was a good man who adhered to a high standard of behavior and expected his doctors to do the same. The thought of disappointing him in any way made her feel physically ill.

The three of them chatted for a few moments about the weather, about their respective golf games, about the latest fund-raiser that kicked off during the Memorial Day festivities. The elevator doors opened and they were faced with a contingent of giggling kindergarteners and their harried teachers.

"Go ahead," Joe said with a shake of his head. "I'll wait for the next one."

She and Hall squeezed into the car and she pressed 1. Hall's white coat and stethoscope slung around his neck garnered lots of giggles and silliness. One little girl with red hair like Ellen's tugged at his hem and asked, "Are you a doctor?"

"Yes, I am," he said with great solemnity. "Are you a doctor, too?"

The little girl dissolved in a fit of giggles, which seemed to be contagious.

"Are you a nurse?" a little boy with a thick shock of dark hair asked Ellen.

"No, I'm not," said Ellen, emulating Hall's solemn manner. "I'm a doctor."

"You are not," said the little boy.

"Alex!" One of the teachers stepped forward. She made an *I'm sorry* gesture in Ellen's direction. "Apologize to Dr. Markowitz." You had to love small towns. Somehow they all knew her name, even women she had never laid eyes on before.

"You can't be a doctor," Alex continued. "Where's your white coat and your stesscope?"

"I'm in disguise this morning," Ellen said, her lips twitching with a smile. "Tomorrow morning I'll wear my white coat and have my stethoscope with me."

"Good job," Hall said as they exited the elevator at the first floor. "I was about to give him the lecture on equal opportunity doctoring."

"Poor kid wouldn't have known what hit him. I've heard that lecture and it's a barn burner."

"Barn burner? Since when does the city girl use terms like *barn burner*?"

"You'd be surprised how much I've learned since I moved to Maine." Damn. She hadn't meant to sound defensive. He was the one who should be sounding defensive.

"We have to talk about last night."

"No, we don't," she said as they approached their office.

"I'll come by your place later. Maybe bring a pizza."

"You're not invited. I'm moving today, remember? I have things to do."

"You're making this a hell of a lot harder than it has to be, Ellen."

She stopped in her tracks. "I really don't want to have this conversation, Hall. I'm not making anything harder. You want easy? I'll give you easy. It never happened."

She pushed past him and into the small office suite they shared at the hospital. They rarely saw patients there, preferring to use the more spacious accommodations at the Medical Arts Building. This was mostly a place to catch up on paperwork, make phone calls, and occasionally decompress between deliveries or surgeries.

Janna, their office manager, hung up the telephone as they walked into the room, and instantly Ellen knew she had heard the gossip. The air was charged with questions.

"I thought you were off today, Dr. M."

"I am," she said. "I'm just here for messages."

"Okay," Janna said, obviously trying very hard not to glance over at Hall to gauge his mood. "I won't forward any calls."

Ellen nodded her thanks, then disappeared into her tiny hole-in-the-wall office. She didn't usually close the door behind her, but she made an exception this time.

For a woman who was trained in the sciences she had a remarkable ability to discount reality when the spirit moved her. Last night was the perfect case in point. She knew how to weigh the pros and cons of a subject. She knew how to analyze, dissect, and evaluate. She knew all about odds, percentages, and bad risks. And despite all of that, she had slept with him anyway.

She picked up the phone and pressed 8 for messages. Two cancellations. One request to have patient records transferred to Vincent Marino's office in Brunswick. It hadn't taken long for the word to get out. Admittedly the patients involved were older women who had been less than pleased to find themselves under the care of a young female physician from New York City. Still, the timing was certainly no coincidence.

She sank into her chair and placed the phone back in the console. The unfairness of the situation wasn't lost on her. It had settled deep in the pit of her stomach like a burning stone, and more than anything she wished she could wipe the slate clean and start again.

"Liar," she muttered. The only part she wanted to erase was that moment when he called out Annie's name. The rest of it . . . oh God, she would remember it forever.

"Oh, damn," she muttered, fumbling around in her top drawer for the paper napkins she stowed in there for emergencies. She wasn't one of those women who cried over romantic misadventures. She saved her tears for more important things, like birth or death or the New York Jets' playoff chances.

She didn't find the napkins, but tucked beneath the corner of her Rolodex was one of Hall's note cards. Scrawled across it in his distinctive script were the words *Simon Andrew McIntyre. 9# 2oz—24 in*.

As if on cue, her door opened and he stepped into the office.

"You found it," he said.

She nodded, not trusting herself to speak.

"I wanted to call you, but—"

Damn those ridiculous tears. She should be hurt or, even better, angry as hell with him, not filled to overflowing with wild sweet emotion at the sound of his voice.

"I know you're hurt." He waited for her to say something, and when she didn't he continued. "I don't know if I'd believe this if someone told it to me, but there were only two people in that bed last night, Ellen."

"Right," she said, suddenly finding her voice. "You and Annie Butler."

"I don't know why it happened. Blame the booze. Blame the years I spent wanting someone who never wanted me. Blame me! I don't give a damn who or what you blame, but know this: It was you last night, Ellen. Nobody else."

She opened her mouth to speak when Janna rapped on the door, then peeked inside. Her cheeks were bright red, and Ellen had the horrible notion that the woman had heard much more than she should have.

"Sorry to interrupt," Janna said, "but your phone seems to be off-hook and—"

"It can wait," Hall said. "We're in conference."

"Well, no, it can't wait, Dr. Talbot," Janna said, a testy note creeping into her voice. She looked toward Ellen. "A Deirdre O'Brien is calling from the police station. She says she's your sister?" Janna ended the sentence on a question, and who could blame her.

"Sister?" Hall said. "You don't have any sisters."

"Put her through, please, Janna."

"One second," Janna said, then disappeared.

"You have a sister?" Hall looked dumbfounded.

"Two," Ellen said. "They're my half sisters. Didn't you ever wonder where the O'Brien came from?"

The phone rang and she grabbed for it.

"Deirdre . . . Deirdre . . . will you calm down? Take a deep breath . . . that's better . . . Stanley? . . . you're joking . . . you're not joking . . . okay, okay . . . put Harry on and I'll take care of everything . . . hi, Harry . . . yes, she's my sister . . . I'm sorry about the dog . . . no, there's no problem . . . I'll swing by on my way to the closing . . . absolutely . . . thank you."

Hall was leaning against her desk, staring down at her as if he'd never seen her before. "You have two sisters and you never told me."

"You never asked."

"Why didn't you introduce me to them?"

"If you want to drive over to the police station with me, I'll introduce you to Deirdre. Harry is holding her for unlawful entry."

"You've been here more than three years. You could have found a—"

"We're not that close, okay? I don't know what Deirdre's doing in town, but you can bet it isn't just to help me unpack. Now, if there isn't anything else, it's time for me to pick up my sister from the police station and close on my new house."

She pushed back her chair and stood up.

"You're sitting on my purse."

He rose to his feet, all elegant lines and graceful movements. She had never seen him sweat. His clothes never wrinkled. For a second she almost hated him for being everything she had always wanted to be but never would.

Her purse wasn't there.

"Oh, damn," she said. "What did I do with it?"

The office was ten by ten. You couldn't lose a flea in there. She looked under the desk, behind her chair, near the filing cabinet.

"Maybe you left it in the car."

"I didn't leave it in the car."

"Down in maternity?"

"I don't know . . . oh, damn . . ." She was losing control. She could feel it slipping away from her.

She didn't remember moving toward him. She didn't remember seeing him move toward her. But somebody must have done something because it seemed as if she blinked and they were in each other's arms and they were kissing as if they had invented the sport, as if their lives depended on it.

There was no champagne this time. No moonlight. No easy excuse for the flood of sweet longing that lifted her and set her free. Only the one she wasn't ready to hear.

"No!" She pushed him away, her hand shaking from the violence of the emotions his kiss unleashed. "I have to go."

"We still need to talk."

"You need to talk, but I don't. I need to spring my sister from the police station." And she needed to get as far away from him as possible before she made the biggest mistake of her life all over again.

He bent down and plucked her purse from the floor near the wastebasket. "Here," he said.

She grabbed it from him and tucked it under her arm.

"We're going to talk about what happened between us, Ellen."

"Not if I can help it," she said.

For the second time that day she left without saying goodbye.

Damn her. He wouldn't have figured her as the type who
excelled at dramatic exits, but then the last twenty-four hours
had been filled with surprises. She knew he wouldn't follow
her again, not with Janna on alert out there in the waiting
room. The Ellen Markowitz that Hall thought he knew was
easygoing and laid-back, slow to anger and quick to forgive.
This highly charged, passionate woman was a stranger to him.

He was neither spontaneous nor impulsive by nature. He
made his decisions by following the rule of logic he had been
following since childhood. Even his mistakes, and there had
been many, were mistakes of the head as well as the heart.
The women he had married were all bright, witty, well-
educated women with high standards of excellence. That the
marriages ended was his fault and his alone.

He knew that. He could follow the threads of logic back to
the beginning and see where he had made his mistakes, identify the moment when he should have chosen another path. It
all made a kind of emotional sense and that knowledge com-
forted him each time he found himself alone once again.

Last night with Ellen was unlike anything he had ever experienced before, and he was old enough, and experienced
enough, to know it went far beyond great sex. Something deep
inside his heart had cracked open when he touched her, elaborate defenses that had been part of his heart for so long he
had forgotten they existed until they started to fall. Last night
they all came tumbling down, and now he was left to sift
through the wreckage.

Years ago, before responsibility in the form of four daughters came his way, he decided that jumping from an airplane
sounded like a good idea. He showed up at the local airfield,
took the necessary instruction, then stood there while they
strapped and buckled him into the harness and loaded him into
the small plane that would take him up. The higher they

climbed, the less he felt like hurling himself through the open door into space, but when you're nineteen and looking to impress your friends, you did it anyway. So when they pointed to him and said, "Go!" he did and fell face first into the sky. The split second the chute opened, jerking him up into the clouds, was the single most exhilarating, terrifying, life-affirming moment he had ever known until last night.

He never thought he would feel that same wild exhilaration again, never thought he would free fall without leaving the ground. Hope and despair and the sharp claws of desire: It was as heady a mix today as it had been when he was nineteen, and he still was at its mercy.

Six

"You found it?" the desk sergeant asked as Scott handed him an invoice.

"Have I ever let you down?"

"You've only been here a few months, Peretti. Give it time."

"Next time try to mention a street name or two," he said, nodding to the town assessor as she walked by. "Might help."

"Gotta keep you on your toes."

"Regular crime wave around here. Two grand-theft auto on the same weekend. What's going on?"

"Prom night. Mayor Bourke's kid borrowed the car, then forgot where he put it."

"How'd it end up in Lincolnville?"

"Who the hell knows? Somebody walks by, sees the keys, next thing you know they're doing eighty on the parkway. Good thing we found it. He's supposed to sign us a pay raise next week. Gotta keep him happy."

"I parked it next to your beater," Scott said, waiting for the signed copy to take back to Jack at the garage. "Think you'll be able to tell the difference?"

The sergeant, an old-timer named Bailey, gave one of those

dry harrumphs that passed for a laugh Down East. "Ay-uh," he said, scribbling his name on the bottom of the carbon set. "Not much chance of mistaking a Lexus for a Dodge."

"Keep 'em coming," Scott said, folding the signed paper and sticking it in his back pocket. "Beats hell out of rotating Jim DeTrano's tires."

A dog's bark sounded from somewhere in the back of the station.

"Sweet Jesus," Bailey said. "That damn dog won't stop his caterwauling."

It couldn't be.

"You're into arresting dogs these days?"

"Sounds like a dog, but I'm not convinced. You should see this thing. Looks like a linebacker for the Pats."

"Stanley."

"Yeah," Bailey said. "You know him?"

"What the hell is he doing here?"

"Unlawful entry. The owner, not the dog."

"Small, round, lots of red hair?"

"And the temper to go with it. Said she's Dr. Ellen's sister, but we weren't buying it."

"Is she?"

"Yep. The doctor's on her way over to spring her."

"Where're you holding her?"

"Out back with the dog. Terry's keeping an eye on her."

The back door was closer to the parking lot. Why not save a few steps?

"Ouch!" a familiar voice yelped. "Don't you look before you swing open a door?"

"Sorry." He joined her on the landing. "It never occurred to you somebody might actually use the door?"

"A lot of things have never occurred to me." She squinted up at him, shielding her eyes against the sun. "Getting arrested, for one."

He leaned against the railing and watched as Stanley sniffed his way around Bailey's parked car. "Did they really arrest you?"

"I think so. They read me my rights. For a second I thought I was auditioning for *The Practice*."

"Better that than *Six Feet Under*."

She didn't laugh like a harp player. She laughed like a blues singer, full and rich and uninhibited. The sound surprised him. The fact that he noticed surprised him even more.

"I didn't think you had a sense of humor," she said as Stanley bounded over to see what was happening.

He tensed a little as Stanley nosed around his leg. Actually he tensed a lot. The dog hit one of those low notes deep in his throat that sounded like the last rites to him.

"Stanley!" She placed her hands under the dog's muzzle and tilted his face toward her. "What's the matter with you? Don't you recognize Scott the Mechanic?"

"Gotta go." Scott the Mechanic was no fool. Better make a break for it while the woolly mammoth was occupied.

"Chicken!" she called out as he jogged across the parking lot toward the tow truck. "He wouldn't hurt a fly."

The rich notes of her laughter seemed to follow him to the truck, and it was a long time before the sound faded away.

Ellen glanced at her watch as she raced up the front steps of the police station. Twenty minutes after twelve. That meant she had exactly forty minutes to bail her kid sister out of jail, deposit sister and Stanley the mystery dog at the condo for safekeeping, then race to the attorney's office to close on the house. She probably shouldn't have driven around the block twice before she parked her car, but the encounter with Hall had left her so flustered she needed time to pull herself together.

Cautious, careful Ellen Markowitz—what in hell was happening to her?

She greeted Bailey, who was gulping down a take-out lobster roll from Cappy's.

"Please don't tell me she's in lockup," she said as she signed the paperwork he slid toward her. "She'll add it to her résumé."

Bailey, whose wife had been one of her first patients, snorted. "She's sitting out back with that giant dog of hers. Terry's keeping an eye on her from the office window, but I didn't think she was much of a flight risk."

"Sorry for the trouble, Bailey. I should have told Mary to

let her in if she showed up again. It's my fault."

"You didn't threaten Casey and Rita with passive resistance."

"Oh, God." Her head started to pound with the beginnings of a migraine. "Tell me you're joking."

"Wish I could, Doc. She said if they didn't let her take the dog with her to the station, they'd have to carry her out."

"So they let her take the dog?"

Bailey shrugged. "Rita's pregnant and Casey has a bad back. They figured it was easier that way."

Her first, selfish reaction was one of relief. Her sister's almost-arrest would take everyone's mind off the fact her car had been parked in front of Hall's house all night. Wasn't that what family was for?

She hurried down the hallway to the rear exit, pushed open the door, and let out a shriek of alarm as a solid wall of brown fur launched itself in her direction.

"Down, Stanley!" Deirdre's voice sounded from behind the wall of fur. "You're scaring Aunt Ellen."

Aunt Ellen?

Stanley was clearly thrilled to meet her. He expressed his enthusiasm by placing a furry paw on each of her shoulders and proceeding to slobber all over her chin.

"Deirdre! Do something!" she said. It was hard to sound stern when you were laughing into a giant dog face.

"He loves you! I knew he would."

"He's slobbering all over my shirt."

"Tell him he's a good boy. That's all he wants. Then he'll calm down."

"Good boy," Ellen said, sagging under his weight. "Good Stanley!"

Darned if her sister wasn't right. Stanley yipped twice, then galloped off down the steps as if he had an appointment with the nearest tree.

And speaking of her sister, there Deirdre was, all flowing hair and flowing skirt and big wide sunny smile, looking not a day over twenty-two.

"Dee!"

"Elly!"

Oh, how wonderful she felt. Soft and warm and smelling

of lavender and Stanley. A rush of affection, unexpected and powerful, flooded her.

"How long has it been?" she asked, pushing away just the tiniest bit so she could see her sister's face.

"Two years," said Deirdre, her deep blue eyes twinkling with delight.

"It couldn't be! We were in Boston. I had the conference and you—"

"Two years," Deirdre said again, laughing. "That was the weekend I broke up with Antonio. You took me to the Ritz-Carlton and I cried into my champagne cocktail."

"Antonio!" Her laughter mingled with Deirdre's. "The poor little rich boy from Venezuela."

"Except he wasn't rich," Deirdre said with a sigh. "Poor and gorgeous."

"There are worse things."

"Like poor and not gorgeous."

"You haven't changed a bit," Ellen said. "Still looking for Prince Charming with the soul of a poet and a Bill Gates bank account."

"In case you haven't noticed, Prince Charmings are in short supply. I'd settle for the bank account."

"I thought you were the family romantic." God knew she dressed the part with the pre-Raphaelite curls tumbling down her back, the off-the-shoulder blouse and long, flowing skirt.

"It's the harp," she said. "Fools 'em every time."

"When did you start playing the harp? The last I heard you were still singing in blues clubs."

"Like I said, it's been a long time, Elly. A lot's happened."

"There's an understatement for you."

Deirdre's face lit up. "Do I smell the unmistakable aroma of romantic turmoil?"

"No, no," she said quickly. Probably too quickly. "It's just been a crazy day. I have the closing in less than half an hour."

"I don't blame you for moving," Deirdre said, linking her arm through Ellen's. "That old bat next door is a horror show."

"Mary's wonderful. You just took her by surprise."

"She called the cops on me." Deirdre's expressive voice was filled with indignation. "Can you imagine! All I was doing was waiting for my own sister, and she picks up the phone and calls the police."

"Don't blame Mary for that," Ellen said. "I should have told her it was okay to let you in if you came back."

"She acted like she didn't know you even had sisters."

"Listen," Ellen said with a showy glance at her watch. "Let me get the closing out of the way and then we can catch up with each other. I signed all the paperwork inside, so you're free to leave. Why don't you and the—Stanley go over to the condo and wait for me there."

"Great idea," Deirdre said, "but no car, remember?"

"You rode the dog here from Boston?"

"Love that New York humor. The car broke down near the doughnut shop. A woman named Annie Butler rescued me. She took Stanley and me into her shop and called for a tow truck."

"You were in good hands," Ellen said, pushing thoughts of the night before away. "Annie's a terrific woman."

"I left one of my bags with her. Do you think we could—"

Ellen took another, closer look at her watch. "Dee, we can't anything. It looks like you and Stanley are going to have to come with me to the closing."

"Sounds terrific!" Deirdre said. "Just one adventure after another today."

She didn't know the half of it.

ACROSS town Claudia leaned forward to peer at Susan's watch.

"It's not like Dr. Markowitz to be late," she said.

"She is an obstetrician," her daughter reminded her, "and we both know babies don't follow timetables."

"She should have asked that nice Janna to call and let us know."

"I didn't say she's delivering a baby. I just reminded you that things happen."

"You distinctly said—"

"Ma, it's only three minutes after one. Cut her a little slack, will you? The lawyers aren't even here yet."

"Perhaps she changed her mind about the house. She seemed a little iffy this morning."

"This morning?" Suddenly she had her daughter's full attention. "You saw Ellen this morning?"

In for a penny, in for a pound. "At the house. I wanted to say goodbye."

Susan's cheeks reddened just enough for a mother to notice. "I would have taken you over if you'd asked."

"I didn't want you to take me over," she said. "This was something I wanted to take care of on my own."

"There aren't any surprises coming at closing, are there? I mean, you didn't try to raise the price on her, did you?"

"She said that?"

"No. She didn't even mention she'd seen you. Then again she probably had other—" Susan's lips clamped down on the end of the sentence.

"I hope you weren't going to bring up that nonsense about Dr. Ellen and Hall again. I mentioned it to her, and let me tell you, she put me in my place in no uncertain terms."

Susan groaned louder than she had when she was in labor. "Ma, have you entirely lost it? Why on earth would you mention Hall to Ellen?"

"Be that as it may, the point I'm trying to make is that you were wrong. She isn't seeing Hall. Certainly not the way you implied on the telephone this morning."

Susan leaned forward and banged her forehead against the tabletop three times in rapid succession.

"Really, Susan. You were more mature when you were six."

"I thought your generation was uptight about sex," Susan said. "You sure as hell never talked about it with me."

"It's a different world," Claudia said, trying very hard not to let her oldest daughter prod her into a full-blown battle. "Women marry later, if they marry at all. It's unrealistic to imagine they'll go to their graves as virgins."

"Jesus, Mary, and Joseph!" Susan fanned herself with the printout of the title search. "Why weren't you this progressive when I was seventeen?"

"I'm glad you're finding this so amusing, Susan. You should be thanking me for providing you with the true story so you can nip any vicious gossip in the bud."

"And the true story is?"

Claudia hesitated, then regrouped. "That there is nothing of a romantic nature between Dr. Ellen and Hall."

"I don't know how to break it to you, Ma, but that doesn't mean they didn't screw each other's brains out last night."

"I'm too old to be shocked, Susan, if that was your intention."

Susan drew in a long breath. "So how do you know what didn't go on between them last night?"

"She told me."

"You mean, she walked up to you and said, 'Oh, by the way, Claudia, Hall and I didn't—let me edit myself—make love last night.' "

"In a manner of speaking, that's exactly what she did."

"With no prodding from you."

"Really, Susan, you're too young for these senior moments. She commented on the size of the house, and I simply mentioned that now that she and Hall were seeing each other, it might not seem that large much longer."

"You really said that?"

"I was making conversation with her."

"Ma, you have bigger cojones than the entire batting order of the Red Sox combined."

"Thank you," Claudia said as she powdered her nose.

Susan had a hard time keeping her mind on the proceedings. Jack was going to have a field day when she told him what she had done. Once again she had gone out of her way to make sure her mother knew exactly what had happened between Hall and Ellen last night. The fact that she wasn't one hundred percent certain herself hadn't slowed her down any. No, she had been determined to make sure her mother believed Hall and Ellen were sleeping together.

Her gaze kept wandering to Ellen, who was busy signing her name to a mountain of official documents and checks.

She looked different. No doubt about it. More womanly, somehow. The slender angles of her body seemed softer, as if the edges had been rounded off. Susan wasn't sure if it was the look in her eyes or the half-smile on her lips as she read the mortgage agreement, but that wasn't the same woman she had chatted with yesterday afternoon at the christening party.

Was Hall that good in bed? She'd been friends with him since grade school, and there had never been even the slightest physical attraction between them. Still, every other female in Shelter Rock Cove treated him like a rock star with a speculum. Did his intimate knowledge of the female anatomy give him super powers in the sack? Her Jack only knew trannys and valve jobs, and she had always found him pretty amazing between the sheets. Hall must be—

Heat moved upward from her chest, flooding her cheeks with color. He was her best friend. You weren't supposed to think about your best friend that way. Whatever he and Ellen had done last night was their business. Not that she would complain if he wanted to share a few of the juicier details, but to her regret Hall had never been one to kiss and tell.

Claudia glanced over at her, then gestured toward the lawyer's assistant who was standing near the door. "Would you be a dear and raise the air-conditioning? My daughter's having a hot flash."

"I'm not having a hot flash," she said through clenched teeth.

"No reason to be embarrassed," her mother went on. "It's just another season of life." She turned her attention to Ellen, who was obviously trying very hard to stay out of the conversation. "Perfectly normal, isn't it, Dr. Ellen?"

Ellen looked up from her paperwork, and you could see her sifting through possible responses for the one least likely to backfire on anyone there.

"Menopause is a perfectly natural transition," she said carefully, then winked at Susan, who laughed despite herself. "But that doesn't mean I wouldn't mind a little more air-conditioning."

Ellen Markowitz was a terrific woman. She was sexy, vibrant, fiercely intelligent, and she was every bit as dedicated to her work as Hall was. He could do a lot worse.

Too bad Ellen could do a lot better. Susan wouldn't be at all surprised if her best friend, the beloved Dr. Talbot, had the words *Proceed with Caution* tattooed on his butt. When it came to love, he was the worst bet in town. Ellen Markowitz had never seemed the gambling type, but desire and caution rarely walked hand-in-hand.

Let Claudia believe whatever she wanted to, but it was crystal clear to Susan that something was definitely going on, and damned if she wasn't just the tiniest bit jealous.

Seven

"This is a big moment," Deirdre said as they followed Stanley to the front door. "Maybe you want to be alone." She was carrying three pizzas for the moving men and a container of mocha fudge.

Ellen, who was in charge of the beer and soda, laughed as she fumbled around with the keys. "What I really want is to be able to figure out which one of these is for the front door."

"Try the one with the yellow yarn threaded through it," Deirdre suggested. "It has a certain presence."

Leave it to her sister to see presence in a house key.

Deirdre was right. The key worked.

"There are eight keys here, three of them with yarn threaded through them. How did you know to pick the yellow one?"

"It's a gift," she said as Ellen swung open the door and Stanley raced inside. "Some people deliver babies. I can tell you which key to use." She stepped into the foyer and let out a long, loud whistle. "Why didn't you tell me you'd bought a hotel?"

"It is huge, isn't it?"

"Are you planning on taking in boarders?"

Ellen laughed, but Deirdre's words struck a nerve. "You think it's too big for one person?"

"I think it's too big for the Sixth Fleet, but don't go by me. I'm a city girl. I'm used to being able to wash the dishes while sitting in bed. This is probably small by Shelter Rock standards."

She started toward the kitchen. She had to remind herself that Deirdre didn't have that internal censor that kept most people from saying what they were really thinking. "Actually it's pretty big by Shelter Rock standards, too."

Deirdre trailed behind her. Her long skirts made a lovely hushed sound against her legs as she walked. Ellen couldn't remember the last time she had worn a skirt that flowed and whispered. Maybe back in college. Maybe never.

"Wow!" Deirdre handed Ellen the pizzas, then executed a dancer's turn. Her skirt billowed like a sail. "This looks like the set for one of those old films you see late at night on AMC."

Ellen grinned as she placed the pizza boxes down on the granite-topped island. "It's something, isn't it?"

"Cabinets with frosted-glass fronts, big old-fashioned windows—oh, my God! A stone fireplace! Exactly what you always wanted."

"You remembered that?"

"Sure. I wanted a mansion with hot and cold running servants, and you wanted a country kitchen with a stone fireplace and copper kettles hanging from hooks overhead."

"I ordered the kettles last week from Williams-Sonoma. They should be here any day."

"That's it," Deirdre said, running her hand across the rough coolness of the granite countertop. "I'm moving in with you."

Ellen waited a beat too long. She wanted to say, "What a great idea! There's plenty of room!" but somehow she couldn't quite push the words out in time.

"Don't worry," her sister said with a little laugh. "I'm only teasing. You know me. I can't stay in one place too long or I start getting itchy and wondering what's waiting around the next corner."

"Just like Billy."

"Yep," said Deirdre, with that same odd little laugh. "Like father, like daughter."

A long silence fell between them. Ellen had turned away from Billy O'Brien many years ago. A handful of teenage summers hadn't been enough to change all that had come before. Billy was a charming stranger to her and nothing more. She liked him. He amused her and made her laugh. In a way she even felt sorry for him, for when he chose his wife over Ellen's mother, he changed all of their lives forever.

The only sound in the cavernous kitchen was the scratching of maple tree branches against the window.

"So how is he doing?" Ellen asked finally. "Is he still in Ireland?"

"Last I heard. He goes off for a while and then shows up on Mary Pat's doorstep looking for a place to crash between gigs."

"I thought Ireland was the real thing. The last time we talked, he told me he planned to stay over there."

"Right," Deirdre said. "You still don't take him at his word, do you?"

"Did that record deal ever pan out?"

"Close but no cigar. Story of his life."

"He's so talented," Ellen mused. "I don't understand why it never happened for him." Billy O'Brien had one of those Irish tenor voices that could make grown men fall down weeping and send grown women racing into his arms. Long ago and far away, her mother had been one of them.

"Same reason it hasn't happened for me," Deirdre answered. "Because they're all dumb bastards out there who wouldn't know talent if it bit them in the ass."

They locked eyes over the pizza boxes, then dissolved into gales of raucous laughter that drowned out the sound of the front doorbell.

However, nothing could drown out Stanley. His persistent howling finally penetrated through the laughter, and the two women went into the hallway to investigate. They were just in time to see Annie Butler dashing across the driveway to her minivan.

"Annie!" Ellen pushed open the screen door and darted after her.

Annie spun around, and, as always, Ellen was struck by her loveliness. If a woman could radiate happiness, Annie Butler did exactly that. She was a walking testimonial to marriage and motherhood.

"You two were laughing so hard in there that I figured I'd come out here and call you from the cell phone!" She looked down at the giant dog dancing around her feet. "Hi, Stanley! Good to see you again."

Deirdre, barefoot and nibbling a slice of pizza, wandered down the driveway to join them. "We have plenty," she said to Annie, "if you want to join us."

Ellen felt a little pinch at the back of her neck, a sure sign that a tension headache was beginning to build.

"That's sweet of you two, but I have to get back to the store." She turned and slid open the side door and reached inside. "I have your bag, Deirdre." She handed over a scuffed garment bag, then reached back into the van. "Just wait until you see what I've got for you, Ellen!"

First out was an enormous arrangement of hollyhocks from Janna and the rest of their assistants at the office with a note that read "Happy Homecoming!" Then came a basket of daisies from Sweeney, whose Artists' Co-op shared space with Annie's flower shop. An impressive spray of bird-of-paradise and ginger blossoms from her banker. A basket of daisies from Claudia with a handwritten note wishing her many years of happiness. One from Susan wishing her the same. A tasteful bouquet of glads and lilies from her stepfather, Cy. A knockout arrangement of delphinium, snapdragons, jonquils, and love-lies-bleeding from Mary Pat.

"Mary Pat?" Deirdre glared at the showy card attached to the basket. "How did she know you were moving today?"

"I probably mentioned it to her once and she wrote it down in her Filofax."

They both knew that flowers from Mary Pat meant about as much as a hello from your friendly neighborhood meter reader. Mary Pat did the right thing because it was expected of her. Sentiment of any kind didn't enter into that arrangement, except maybe the slightest touch of pity.

"Now, wait until you see this," Annie said, reaching deeper into the minivan. "It was the talk of the shop this afternoon!"

Deirdre let out a long slow whistle as Annie handed a bouquet of three dozen red roses to Ellen.

Ellen's face turned as red as the blooms. She could barely wrap her arms around them. Her powers of speech vanished as the scent filled her brain.

"Who sent them?" Deirdre demanded, poking through the flowers. "Is there a gift card?"

"No card." Annie's smile grew wider. "The buyer wishes to remain anonymous."

Deirdre wasn't about to be deterred. "You can tell me. I won't tell a soul."

Ellen remained speechless. Annie looked at her closely, then slid the minivan's door closed. "Sorry," she said. "I took the Florist's Oath."

"The Florist's Oath?" Deirdre asked, laughing.

"Thou shalt not divulge the name of he who wishes to remain anonymous."

"And what happens if you break the oath?"

"Too terrible to contemplate." She gestured toward the mountain of blooms at their feet. "Why don't we get these inside before Stanley decides to water them?"

The dog was circling Mary Pat's arrangement with great interest.

Finally Ellen found her voice. "We can manage, Annie. I know you need to get back to the shop." She already knew from past experience that Annie wouldn't accept a tip, so she made a mental note to double up the next time one of her teenage workers made a delivery.

"Why don't you like Annie?" Deirdre asked after the minivan disappeared around the corner.

The question brought Ellen up short. "Who said I don't like her?"

"You made it pretty clear you didn't want her hanging around."

"Annie has a store to run and an infant, a toddler, and a husband waiting for her at home. The last thing she needed was to waste time lugging flowers into the house for me."

"I like her," Deirdre said. "I'm sorry she didn't stay awhile."

"I like her, too. In fact, I delivered both of her babies."

"Wow. I'm surprised you seemed so uneasy with her."

"I wasn't uneasy; I was surprised." And embarrassed, but she didn't tell Deirdre that. If Annie had the slightest idea what had really happened last night—it just didn't bear thinking about. "Believe it or not, I don't receive a truckload of flowers every Monday afternoon."

It took two trips, but they managed to get the flowers safely inside before Stanley did something unspeakable to them.

"So much for counter space," Ellen said as she surveyed her bounty.

"I'm impressed," Deirdre said. "You must be the most popular gyno in Shelter Rock." She fingered the bloodred roses. "So who's the mystery man?"

"Who says it's a man? Maybe they're from a grateful patient."

"Patients don't send three dozen American Beauties."

She shrugged as if it didn't matter a bit to her.

"Come on! You must have a clue."

"Not a single one."

"You don't really think I believe that, do you?"

"Probably not." She paused for a second at the sound of a truck in the driveway. "Grab Stanley and put him in the backyard. The moving men are here."

And not a moment too soon.

So far it wasn't going at all the way Deirdre had expected it to. Two years ago, during their boozy lunch at the Ritz-Carlton, Ellen had been all warmth and solicitude as she listened to Deirdre unburden herself about the treacherous Antonio. "Stay with me tonight," she had said, offering to share her suite with her falling-apart sister. Her focus had been on Deirdre. She couldn't do enough to make her smile.

Today she had to get herself arrested in order to get her sister's attention, and even then she hadn't kept it for very long. Annie Butler showed up with a truckload of flowers, and Deirdre could see Ellen close in on herself like she did during the last summer they were all together. She would smile and say all the right things, but you just knew she was some place else.

Something was definitely up with her, and Deirdre was reasonably sure it had to do with a man. The clues were all there. She didn't come home last night, and today a mystery man showered her with three dozen pricey long-stemmed roses. Red ones, at that. One of the few romantic clichés no woman on the planet ever grew tired of.

Since being dumped by that scum of a fiancé a few years ago, her sister had been close-mouthed about whatever was or wasn't going on in her bedroom. Not that Deirdre blamed her for that. She was the same way. People invariably got the wrong idea when you talked about your love life. They either figured you were getting too much or not half enough, and either way you ended up having to explain yourself to someone who didn't deserve to know. Besides, you needed close girlfriends to share that kind of thing, and Deirdre hadn't had a best friend since eighth grade. Billy's singing career had kept them moving around from place to place, and it was hard to keep making new friends, knowing you were going to have to say goodbye before you had a chance to share your secrets.

"You're lucky you have Mary Pat," her mother used to say as they packed up for yet another move. "That's why God made sisters, so you'll always have your best friend close by."

And her mother really believed that crap. That was what made it so sad. Billy might have begat himself two more daughters, but in Mary Pat's mind she was still an only child. It made their mother's Disneyland take on sisterhood downright laughable.

The closest Deirdre had ever come to that kind of connection with another human being was during those first few summers after Ellen's mother died when Billy decided it was time for his three girls to get to know each other. Yeah, there was a bright idea. Try throwing a mystery sister into the already volatile mix of two teenage girls in an unhappy home and see what happens.

Mary Pat never came around. She had been old enough to understand that there was trouble between her parents, old enough to know her father loved somebody else. She hated Ellen, whose very existence had ripped the heart out of her family.

After the shock and the anger began to wear off, Deirdre

and Ellen had found themselves growing closer. They looked alike, although Deirdre was shorter and rounder than her willowy half sister, and both shared a love of Chinese food, blues music, and bad television. While Mary Pat locked herself in her room to write long, impassioned letters to the boy who would soon become her husband, Deirdre and Ellen sprawled on the sofa and watched old movies while they talked about the future. Ellen had hers planned out to the last detail. She was going to become an OB-GYN like her stepfather. She had her schools picked out. She hoped to do her residency at Mount Sinai in Manhattan, then open up a private practice on the Upper West Side, where she grew up.

They were only six months apart in age, but Deirdre remembered feeling like a little girl as she listened to Ellen talk about her plans. When Ellen asked what she was going to do after high school, the best Deirdre could come up with was "Maybe bum around Europe for a while and see what happens."

"I thought you were going to study music."

"Yeah, well, we'll see what happens."

Ellen believed in thinking ahead. Even her plans had plans. She had been raised to believe that anything was possible if you set your goals high and worked toward them, and from the look of things today that was exactly what had happened. Okay, so maybe this wasn't the Upper West Side, but she had tried that and discovered it wasn't quite what she wanted. Shelter Rock Cove was. All you had to do was watch the way people treated her, and you knew she was somebody special around here. She had her job. She had her new house. She had some guy who liked to send her roses.

Deirdre sat out on the back porch with Stanley, listening to the sounds of the moving men unloading Ellen's furniture. Ten minutes should about do it. She had peeked into the truck, and, as far as she could tell, her sister didn't have all that much. A plain double bed with a pine headboard. A soulless chest of drawers. One of those couches that looked better than they sat. No quilts. No family photos. No signs of life. If Deirdre had a doctor's income, she would have the stuff to go with it. Plush sofas. A big wide bed with a brass headboard. Antique quilts and big puffy down comforters with satin duvets. One of those giant TVs that hung from the wall and practically invited you to walk straight into the screen and join the party. Pictures everywhere, all beautifully displayed in handcrafted frames. And she would have clothes, too, great stuff from funky boutiques and maybe a couple of knock-'em-dead audition dresses from Saks.

A lot of time had passed since those long-ago summers with Ellen and Mary Pat. She hadn't realized just how much until now. The Ellen she once knew was long gone, vanished the same as the girl who had dreamed about bumming around Europe and becoming a star. They had nothing in common except Billy O'Brien and a few old memories that were growing older by the day.

But what the hell. Despite her practical nature, Ellen was a soft touch when it came to kids and animals. When Deirdre explained the situation, Ellen was bound to suggest Stanley stay there with her until the gig in Bar Harbor ended. And if she didn't—well, Deirdre would jump off that bridge when she came to it.

Everyone in Shelter Rock Cove agreed that Hall loved his four daughters. His reputation as a doting father had been secured years ago when Kate gave him a buzz cut one afternoon while he napped on the back porch, and he shrugged it off and didn't even resort to wearing a Red Sox cap until it grew out.

On days like this, however, even his renowned stores of paternal patience began to wear thin. He wasn't sure if it was because he was older or that his two youngest daughters were more skilled at pushing his buttons, but whatever the reason, he was on the verge of grounding them for life.

"Willa! Mariah! If you two don't stop whatever you're doing back there, you can forget about the Ice Cream Palace."

"We're breathing," Mariah said with one of those strangled giggles he had come to recognize as pure trouble. "You want us to stop breathing?"

"We're sitting," Willa said, her words practically lost in her laughter. "You want us to stop sitting?"

He shot them a look through the rearview mirror. The two little girls, who seemed to be growing up right before his eyes, were collapsed into giggling blond heaps. He loved them. He would give his life for them.

And they were driving him nuts.

"We don't want to go to Dr. Ellen's house," Mariah announced.

"Yeah," said Willa. "We're hungry. Can we go to the Ice Cream Palace right now?"

"No, we can't. We're going to stop by Dr. Ellen's new house for a few minutes, then we're going to Cappy's for supper."

Mariah shrieked in protest. "But you said we could go to the Ice Cream—"

"After supper."

"That's not fair," Willa said. "You promised!"

A new chorus of wails erupted from the backseat, reminding him that, as bad as this was, it would only get worse because adolescence wasn't far away. No wonder Yvonne asked him if he could take the girls for a few days. He wouldn't have been surprised if she had begged her boss to send her on that field trip to Providence. If she had been thinking clearly, she would have sent the girls to Providence and locked the doors behind them.

"Settle down," he said as they turned onto the street where the Galloway family had once lived. "I expect you two to behave yourselves while we're visiting Dr. Ellen."

More giggles, but slightly subdued. He was crazy enough to consider that progress.

Good thing they weren't old enough to ask him why he was dragging them over to Ellen's new place, because he still hadn't come up with a reason. At least not one that wasn't as phony and transparent as hell. He needed to see her. He needed to prove to her that the damage he had done to their friendship wasn't irreparable. The house was bound to be swarming with people—residents of Shelter Rock Cove loved group projects like moving day and yard sales—and his presence would be a lot less gossip-worthy with Willa and Mariah by his side.

Shameless manipulation? Damn right. They had to pick up where they had left off and do it as soon as possible or the gossips really would have a field day with the evidence they had gathered. Right now they would be far more interested in

Ellen's mystery sister, who had managed to get herself arrested her first morning in town. As far as he was concerned, that kind of news beat the hell out of a sleepover any day.

The Galloway house dominated the hill overlooking the beach. Around 1898 a wealthy shipbuilder named George Laidlaw purchased the hill and the surrounding land, then set out to construct a compound of houses for his children and their children. He had managed to oversee the completion of the main house, a quirky Queen Anne with gingerbread trim and turrets, and was set to commence work on the second when influenza claimed him and his beloved wife, Edna. Their children fought bitterly over the properties, and ultimately the land and the house fell into the hands of creditors who ended up dividing the property into smaller parcels.

By the time the Galloways came along in the 1950s, Laidlaw Road boasted six houses and arguably some of the best views of the ocean in the area. The Laidlaw house soon became known as the Galloway place as Claudia and John began to fill the empty rooms with the laughter of children. Before long the children brought their friends home, and the Galloways' place became a second home to half the kids in town.

Hall was one of them. The family had welcomed him into their midst as one of Susan's friends, and then before long he was part of the clan. Or at least it had felt that way to him. For all of her faults, Claudia had an unerring instinct for lost souls, and she recognized in him the need for family.

The years passed. The kids grew up and moved out. John Galloway died and Claudia held on to the house as the next generation, in the form of grandchildren, once again filled the rooms with laughter. But not even Claudia could hold on to the past forever, and now the house belonged to Ellen.

The driveway was jammed with cars. He recognized Annie and Sam's minivan. Sweeney's Harley. Two rescue vehicles. One police car. A slew of Buicks and Chryslers. The residents of Shelter Rock Cove believed many hands made light work of just about any job that came along. Ellen had been part of the town for only a little more than three years. It usually took ten or more before a newcomer was accepted. This display of affection was proof positive that they considered her a keeper.

"Daddy! Look!" Willa screamed from the backseat. "A dog!"

He parked at the end of the driveway and turned off the engine as a woolly mammoth galloped across the yard toward them. His first instinct was to lock the doors and pray, but his daughters had other ideas.

"Stay put," he ordered them as Mariah reached for the door handle. "You're not to get out of this car until I tell you."

Another reason to thank Detroit for remote door locks.

He opened the door and stepped out as a small red-haired woman rounded the corner of the house. Her skirts billowed as she ran; her long curly hair seemed to do the same. She was shorter than Ellen and more voluptuous, but there wasn't the slightest doubt that this was her sister.

"Stanley!" she called and the giant dog screeched to a stop a few feet away from him. "Sit down! Good dog! Good boy!"

Stanley sat down on the grass, and his tail, which was easily the size of a small child, thumped the ground wildly as they both watched the woman approach.

"Isn't he wonderful!" she exclaimed as she gave the dog a huge hug. "What a good, obedient boy you are, Stanley!"

Hall laughed and gestured toward his car. "Maybe he can give lessons to my kids."

The woman looked up at him—she had wonderful blue eyes, dark and expressive—and smiled a very Ellen smile. "He's great with kids. Feel free to spring them. Just ask them to go slow at first until he picks up their vibe."

He tried to imagine Ellen saying "picks up their vibe," but the thought made him laugh again. "I'm Hall Talbot," he said, extending his right hand. "Ellen's partner."

"Deirdre O'Brien," she said, clasping his hand. "The sister she never talks about."

"I'd know you anywhere."

"Well, I wouldn't know you," she said, flashing that Ellen smile. "She told me you were brilliant and that you liked to get married a lot, but somehow she forgot to tell me you were gorgeous."

"Let's go up to the house and give her hell," he said as Deirdre tossed back her head and laughed one of those great full-bodied laughs most women managed to suppress.

"I think you should spring your kids first," she said, waving at the two little faces pressed against the window. "Stanley would love to play with someone his own size."

His girls loved her instantly, almost as much as they loved Stanley. They managed to curb their enthusiasm long enough to allow the dog to sniff their hands and process the scent, then they fell on him like he was their long-lost canine brother.

"He's a great dog," Hall said as they started up the walkway toward the front door with the girls and Stanley right behind them. "What kind is he?"

"What kind isn't he?" Deirdre shot back. "The woman at the shelter figured Great Dane, maybe a little Newfie and Bernese mountain thrown in for good measure."

"How old?"

"Maybe two or three. He's had a tough life. People don't know what they're getting into when they take one of these big guys home. That's why so many of them end up back at the shelter."

"That's where you found him?"

She nodded. "In western Pennsylvania. He was down to his last two days. I've always been a sucker for a hard-luck story, so . . ." She shrugged. "You know how it is."

"Your sister's the same way."

"That, my dear Dr. Talbot, is exactly what I'm counting on."

She didn't explain and he didn't ask. Actually he would have liked to ask, but it really wasn't any of his business what went on between the O'Brien sisters. Or were they the Markowitz sisters? And didn't she say there was a third one out there somewhere? Where did they come from and why hadn't Ellen ever mentioned them before?

Come to think of it, there were a hell of a lot of questions he'd like to ask of the woman he had once believed had no secrets at all.

Eight

Not long after she moved to Shelter Rock Cove, Ellen dreamed she was at a cocktail party. Everyone she knew in town was there. The men were garbed head to toe in Armani, while the women dazzled in Versace and Chanel. Except for Ellen, who happened to be stark naked, sipping a Cosmo and trying very hard to escape notice.

Which pretty much summed up the way she felt when Deirdre burst through the door with Hall Talbot in tow and announced, "Where have you being hiding him, El?"

Conversation in the room stopped dead, and suddenly it was her dream all over again as everyone turned to gauge her reaction. It wasn't a cocktail party and nobody there was wearing Armani, but she felt naked just the same. She rarely found herself at a loss in social situations, but what on earth was the proper response when everyone in town knew you had slept with their favorite son? The guy who loved somebody else.

Bless Stanley's impeccable timing. He pushed past Hall and Deirdre and bounded into the room, followed by Mariah and Willa Talbot, who looked like small blond whirlwinds. Deirdre, of course, was oblivious. She didn't understand small

towns and, thank God, hadn't a clue what had happened between Ellen and Hall last night.

Ellen knew she couldn't blame her friends for what they
were thinking as their gazes bounced between Hall and herself.
She would be thinking it, too, if the shoe was on some foot
other than her own size 8AA.

Stanley thundered by, nearly knocking her off balance with
an enthusiastic wag of his tail. He was followed by Hall's
daughters, who waved to her as they raced in hot pursuit. The
silence deepened and she knew that if she didn't do something—and fast—she would only make things worse.

Plastering a big smile on her face, she waved at Hall, then
motioned to Deirdre. "Scott called," she said, loud enough for
everyone to hear. "You left your harp in your car."

Deirdre grabbed Hall by the hand and pulled him over to
the bottom of the staircase, where Ellen was standing.

"Let me borrow your wheels," Deirdre said to Ellen, "and
I'll drive over to pick it up. I think he has my wallet too."

"He's bringing it over," Ellen said, trying very hard to act
casual. "He'll probably bring your wallet with the harp."

"Geez!" Deirdre dragged a hand through her mane of curls.
"You wouldn't think anyone could lose a harp, would you?"

Hall's left eyebrow lifted just enough for Ellen to notice,
and some of that naked-among-the-Armani feeling started to
fade. She wouldn't have to explain Deirdre to him after all.
He was already beginning to figure her out for himself.

Deirdre dashed off toward the kitchen.

"She's a musician," Ellen said.

Hall nodded. "That explains a lot."

"She never met an impulse she didn't follow."

"Unlike us scientific types."

"Don't start. The last thing I want is to—"

He grabbed her hand and started for the side door that led
into Claudia's old vegetable garden.

"Hall." She considered literally digging in her heels, but
from the look in his eyes, he just might toss her over his
shoulder and the entire population of Shelter Rock Cove would
need simultaneous defibrillation. "This will only make things
worse."

He ignored her and she had no choice but to keep that

stupid smile plastered on her face and act like this was business as usual.

"You fool!" she exploded as soon as they were alone in the garden. "Didn't we give them enough to talk about last night?"

"If you keep on avoiding me, they'll never stop talking."

"I'll bet they don't think we're just talking out here."

"And they'd be wrong," he said. "In fact, I just saw Sweeney watching us from the window. They'll have a full report before I finish this sentence."

"See? It's a nightmare. Every single one of them thinks we slept together last night."

"We did," he said.

"I don't want them to know that."

"Regrets?"

"Of course I have regrets. I don't know what I was thinking last night. I wish—" She stopped. "Damn it, Hall. You know what I'm saying."

"You think I don't have a regret or two about what happened?"

"I know all about your regrets."

"No, you don't."

"I think I do."

"You think I was wishing you were Annie."

"That's exactly what I think."

"Despite what happened, you were the only woman in my bed last night, Ellen. If you believe nothing else I've ever said to you, I want you to believe that."

"What difference does it make?" She met his eyes. "It was a one-night mistake. We were lonely. We had a little too much to drink. We're good friends who took it too far. It won't happen again."

"Would it be so terrible if it did?"

"Terrible? No, it wouldn't be terrible, Hall, it would be disastrous. It would be the end of my career in Shelter Rock. I've spent over three years building a reputation for myself, and I came close to destroying everything last night."

"I didn't know I had that kind of power."

He sounded hurt, angry, and bewildered simultaneously. The combination was almost her undoing, but she held tough.

"You don't," she said, not unkindly, "but I'm trying to

build that kind of power with the young girls in this town. You saw them inside, Hall. They're starting to look up to me."

"And that means you have to join a convent."

"Of course not. But it does mean I have to take some responsibility for the choices I make."

"So let me get this straight: It isn't that we slept together, it's that you left your Cruiser in my driveway."

"You know what I'm talking about."

"I'm not sure I do."

"You've heard me talking with the girls at the health center workshops. I tell them to be careful, to exercise restraint whenever possible, to try to think with their heads and not their hormones, and then I go and do exactly the opposite and leave a trail of breadcrumbs behind."

He was quiet longer than was comfortable.

"You're right," he said at last.

"About what?"

"Everything. We made a mistake. It won't happen again."

She felt disoriented. What had happened to the high drama of a few moments ago when he grabbed her hand and dragged her out into the vegetable garden? She opened her mouth to protest, then caught herself. He agreed with everything she said. They were on the same page. Too bad if it didn't make her feel quite the way she had expected it would.

Too bad about the whole damn thing.

Susan and Annie were sitting on the kitchen counter nibbling on tiny egg rolls some kind soul had brought to the house-warming.

"She's going to need furniture," Susan said, looking out toward the front room.

"Lots of furniture," Annie said. "It's a great house, but I'm not so sure it's the right one for her."

"Wash your mouth out. I haven't deposited my commission check yet."

Annie laughed and popped another egg roll in her mouth. "It's just that this is such a family house. I can't imagine how she'll feel, all alone in this big place."

"It's not like she's home all that much," Susan said. "Hall

says she just about eats, sleeps, and breathes her job."

"You won't hear any complaints from me," Annie said. "She's a wonderful doctor."

Susan tilted her head toward the vegetable garden. "So what do you think is going on out there?"

Annie sighed deeply. "Wouldn't it be wonderful if they were—"

"No!" Susan winced at the fierce sound of her own voice. "I mean, I can't imagine the two of them together."

"They work well together."

"That's different. She isn't his type at all."

"Well, so far he hasn't had a great deal of luck with his type, has he? I think they'd be a great couple."

"No chemistry," Susan said.

"You were there yesterday at Kerry's christening party. You saw the way they were looking at each other. We all did."

"Oh, please." Susan made a face. "Everyone gets sappy at a christening. God, I almost made a pass at Jack."

Annie gave her a gentle elbow in the ribs. "You know you love your husband."

"That doesn't mean I don't sometimes—" She caught herself. "Oh, forget I said anything. You're still a newlywed. You wouldn't understand."

"Your brother and I were married a long time, Suz. I think I remember how it felt."

"Not you," Susan said. "You and Kevin were always—"

Annie shook her head. "Not always. You know that. We had a lot of rough times."

Funny how many tricks your memory could play on you. In the years since Kevin's death, Susan had somehow managed to erase her beloved brother's many flaws until only a saint remained.

"Ellen's car was in Hall's driveway all night," Susan said.

"Tell me something I don't know." Annie laughed softly. "Tell me something the entire town doesn't know."

"She's always been very discreet about her love life."

"Maybe she still is. Maybe he borrowed her car. Maybe she was home alone all night."

"You don't believe that any more than I do."

"No, I don't," Annie admitted, "but I know what it's like

to be the number-one topic of conversation around town, and I wouldn't wish it on anyone I cared for."

"She always seemed so open and forthright. I mean, where did that sister come from? I never heard her mention a sister before, did you?"

"Further proof that she keeps her private life private. It isn't a crime, you know."

"You used to be more fun," Susan grumbled. "Scruples never used to hold us back when it came to good dish."

"Maybe when we were thirteen," Annie said. "They're two wonderful people, Suz. Let them live their lives. Let—" She stopped mid-sentence and shook her head.

"What?" Susan prodded. "Go ahead. Finish what you were going to say."

"Not this time," Annie said. She hopped down from the counter. "I really should be going home. Sam's a great father, but I'm still the only one who can breast-feed."

"Thanks," Susan said.

"Thanks for what?" Annie asked as she pulled her car keys from her purse.

"For what you didn't say."

"I may not always not say it."

Susan grinned. "I know. But thanks just the same."

She waved goodbye to Annie, then settled down to wait. They couldn't stay out there in the garden all evening.

Deirdre didn't mean to eavesdrop, but the only thing separating the vegetable garden from the backyard was a flimsy vine-covered trellis and a row of rosebushes about to bloom. She probably should have clapped her hands over her ears or joined Stanley and the kids, who were playing fetch, but she was riveted to the spot.

Not that they were saying anything. In fact, they hadn't uttered a sound in at least two or three minutes. A lovely warmth spread through her chest. Of course! Where there was heat, there was also passion. It wouldn't surprise her one bit to find them wrapped in each other's arms, completely oblivious to the world around them.

Oh, why not? Just one peek wouldn't hurt. They weren't

locked away behind closed doors, after all. They were out there in the garden where anyone could see them. God knew she had noticed more than one nosy face peering through the window while she had been sitting there on the back steps. She stood up, brushed off her skirt, then tiptoed closer to the trellis.

"Deirdre!"

She practically jumped out of her clothes at the sound of Ellen's voice behind her.

Ellen looked a little puzzled, but if her sister had any idea what she had been up to, she didn't let on. Hard to believe there was any O'Brien blood in Ellen's veins. Any O'Brien worth her salt would have blocked her way and demanded an explanation.

"Stanley," she said. "He was here a second ago."

Ellen jerked her thumb over her left shoulder. "He's with the kids."

"Okay. Thanks. I'll go see if everything's okay."

"Scott came by," Ellen said. "He dropped off the harp."

Her heart did a little two-step. "Hey, terrific! Let me go thank him and—"

"He dropped off the harp, then took off. I asked him in for a while, but he isn't exactly the most social man in town."

The two-step skidded to a stop.

"Wife?" He didn't look married. His hair was too scruffy. His shirt had that straight-from-the-dryer look. And he didn't wear a ring.

"Not that I know of. Actually I don't know much of anything about Scott."

"I didn't think anyone in this town managed to fly beneath the radar."

"He's fairly new here."

"A real Yankee loner?"

Ellen thought for a second. "I suppose so. I've found him to be polite but distant. Not exactly what you would call a people person."

"Good thing he's a mechanic and not a doctor."

"Good thing for all of us."

Her sister really was lovely when she smiled. She had the O'Brien crinkle, a starburst at the outer corners of her deep blue eyes, a feature which was shared by Billy and all three of his daughters. Deirdre felt an odd tug of tenderness mingled with a tinge of guilt for eavesdropping on her.

"Your harp is getting a lot of attention," Ellen said as they made their way back inside.

"I've been thinking about sending the harp up to Bar Harbor without me. Might do wonders for my career."

"Sweeney and a few of the others asked me if you would consider playing something."

"How do you feel about that?"

"I'd love it." Again that wonderful crinkly-eyed smile. "I think it would be a great way to make this house feel like a home."

That was just about the nicest thing anyone had ever said to her, and the fact that it was her sister who said it made it twice as nice.

It also made her feel guilty as hell for showing up at Ellen's unannounced, uninvited, and with a one-hundred-fifteen-pound dog in tow. The least she could do was sing for her supper. Too bad Scott the Mechanic hadn't bothered to hang around a few minutes. She knew she had sounded like a flake that morning when he towed her car into the shop. She would have liked to show him that her harp was more than the latest fashion accessory among the music crowd.

The thought made her almost laugh out loud. Oh, yeah, Scott the Mechanic definitely looked like the kind of guy who would get off on harp music. He probably couldn't wait to put as much distance as possible between him and the possibility of having to listen to her play.

Well, too damn bad, Scott the Mechanic. She hoped nobody else in the room felt that way.

Hall wanted to escape before the harp music started. Once Ellen's sister hit the first note, he would be honor-bound to stay for the entire performance, and that wasn't exactly at the top of his list of things he felt like doing. He would round up Willa and Mariah, say goodbye to Ellen, then head for Cappy's before it got any later. He went out back to collect his daughters only to find they had slipped into the house to watch Deirdre unpack her harp.

"That doesn't look like a real harp," Mariah said, eyeing the wooden instrument. "It's tiny."

"Not too tiny," Deirdre said, crooking her finger. "Come here and see."

Mariah cautiously approached. This time last year she might have popped her thumb into her mouth in a reflexive gesture left over from babyhood. This year that was nothing but a distant memory. Time was slipping by more quickly every day.

"Go ahead," Deirdre said as Willa, not one to be left behind, joined her sister. "Try to pick it up."

They tried and failed.

"See?" Deirdre eased the base of the harp into what looked like floor protectors. "Angels must have very strong muscles under those pretty robes they wear."

"Do you have muscles?" Willa asked.

Deirdre grinned and flexed a bicep. "You would, too, if you were a harper."

"I play the piano," Mariah confided.

"You do not," her sister said. "She's still learning 'Twinkle, Twinkle, Little Star.' "

"I can show you how to play 'Twinkle' on the harp, if you'd like." She looked over their heads at Hall, who saw his last chance at escape slipping away from him.

"It's getting late, girls," he said. "If we're going to grab fish 'n' chips at Cappy's, we'd better leave."

"We don't want to go, Daddy," Mariah said. "We want to stay and hear Deirdre play the harp."

"I thought you wanted ice cream." *Good going, Father of the Year. You're playing the ice-cream card a little early tonight, aren't you?*

Willa wrinkled her nose. "I'm not hungry. I had egg rolls."

"Me, too," said Mariah. "And some pizza."

Where had he been when they were giving out the pizza and egg rolls?

She positioned both Mariah and Willa to her left.

"There's room for one more," she said to Susan's son, but no self-respecting son of an auto mechanic would be caught dead near a harp, no matter how beautiful it was. And this was definitely one of the most beautiful musical instruments he had ever seen.

Years ago he had had the privilege of hearing Segovia in concert, and the sight of the master cradling that luminous guitar had affected him profoundly. The shimmering gloss of the wood, the graceful curving shape, it stole your breath before a single note sounded. He felt that same exhilarating rush of emotion as he watched his daughters brush the strings under Deirdre's patient tutelage.

"Keep your pinkies tucked out of the way," she told them. "Backs nice and straight. Elbows parallel to the floor, just like this." She gently nudged Willa's elbows up a tiny bit and the difference was amazing. Mariah, never willing to be bested by her sister, instantly upgraded her posture and made sure her own elbows were locked in place.

"Okay," Deirdre said, "now, here we go."

The girls' faces beamed with delight as the sweet, pure notes filled the room. Sweeney called out "Brava!" which made Hall's daughters giggle and duck their heads. After another try, Deirdre whispered something to the girls and they hurried back to his side.

"Did you see us?" Mariah asked, breathless with excitement. "Did you see us play the harp?"

"I sure did," he said, ruffling her hair with a gentle hand. "You were terrific!"

"Me, too," Willa demanded. "I was better than Mariah."

"You were both terrific," he amended. Nothing wrong with his kids' self-esteem.

The low-grade chatter in the room silenced as Deirdre leaned into the harp. Or did the harp lean into her? It was hard to tell. She was all graceful curves, and so was the harp as she wrapped her arms around it in a lover's embrace.

In retrospect it was the wrong thing to do. If he had given it even a second of thought, he would have found a way to protect himself, but as the first achingly pure notes blossomed, he looked across the room at Ellen. She was sitting on the arm of the sofa a few feet away from her sister. The resemblance was striking. The auburn curls. The flashing blue eyes. The elegant hands. Except where Deirdre was small and round, Ellen was tall and willowy.

Ellen met his eyes and the night before rose up between them. Her cheeks reddened slightly, as if she knew what he was thinking, as if she was thinking it, too, and they both looked away. Better to concentrate on the sister with the harp.

He couldn't recall ever seeing a harp quite like that before. It wasn't the tall and elegant instrument played by a woman in a flowing gown on a concert stage, the kind that made you think of heavenly choirs and hosts of angels on high. There was nothing either celestial or angelic about it. Both the harp and the harper were born of this earth.

A Celtic harp, Deirdre had explained earlier, its magic born of an ancient oral tradition of storytelling whispered and sung by minstrels who roamed the Irish countryside. It wasn't hard to imagine her on an emerald green hilltop, offering up her music to the old gods.

He couldn't help wondering about the man who had fathered two such different women. Deirdre was both fey and dramatic. Ellen was calm and precise. An artist and a scientist. Was it nature or nurture that had molded their personalities, a trick of genetics or the lives they had led?

Yesterday he would have asked Ellen about it and not thought twice. He had assumed he knew all there was to know about her background. After all, it had been on all of her paperwork, on her degrees, her medical license, everything. Ellen O'Brien Markowitz. The O'Brien, he had assumed, was a gesture toward a close friend of the family or maybe a married Markowitz. He had known enough strangely named infants in his time to not blink an eye at an odd combination.

Yesterday he would have walked into her office and asked her flat out about the sister, the parents, the name, the whole nine yards. Now he had to wait and wonder if Ellen would ever tell him her family story or if last night had marked an end to their friendship. An end to those late suppers at Cappy's, those afternoons on his back porch when they dropped their guard and let their fears escape into the darkness. She knew he prayed before each delivery. He knew that she cried after every birth. They had done both on more than one occasion, over more than one woman who battled disease and ultimately lost.

The music washed over him, clear and haunting and painfully beautiful, cutting deep into the place he hid from the world. Each successive note cut deeper than the one before until it hurt to draw a breath.

"Daddy?" Mariah whispered in what he thought of as her worry voice.

He drew her against his right side and stroked her soft blond hair. Willa reached for his left hand and rested her head against his leg.

He had everything a man could want. Four happy, healthy daughters. Work that mattered. Friends and family who loved him. Over the last few years the gnawing emptiness he had filled with doomed marriages had begun to disappear, so slowly at first that he didn't notice it until this morning when he felt the familiar ache reappear inside his chest. The difference was Ellen.

Ellen had come along and filled those empty spaces with her enthusiasm and her dedication and her friendship. She was the one he went to for counsel or advice or a much-needed kick in the ass. She never pulled her punches. She never softened the blows. She said what he needed to hear when he didn't particularly want to hear it. She was a gifted doctor. A beautiful woman. A passionate lover. And up until this morning she had been his friend.

As wonderful as last night had been (and he was old enough to know wonderful when he found it), he would trade away the memory if it meant they could go back to where they had been less than twenty-four hours ago.

He came back.

Deirdre glanced up after a particularly showy glissando and saw Scott the Mechanic standing in the open front doorway and she started to melt. She felt like one of those fast-burning candles they used to display in old Italian restaurants, the kind that melted down the side of an old Chianti bottle and became part of the decor. She was melting right there in the middle of one of Turlough O'Carolan's planxties, an ode to a wealthy patron in need of a few musical strokes to enhance his standing.

The man might as well have *bad boy* embroidered on the pocket of his shirt because there was no doubt in her mind that he had been born to break hearts. He had that untouchable look to him that all bad boys had, that run-while-there's-still-time aura that most women found irresistible.

Most women? Who was she kidding? Bad boys were catnip to her, they were better than a five-pound box of Godiva and a bottle of Veuve Clicquot.

God, what was wrong with her? She had sworn off this kind of romantic nonsense two years ago after Antonio. Every woman needed to experience at least one wildly passionate love affair that ended badly so she would know what she wasn't missing. Deirdre should have known that three would be pushing her luck. First there was Paul, the actor she had met in London. Paul of the wide shoulders . . . and the enormous ego that had required as much care as a Thoroughbred pony. She had found him in bed—her bed!—with a twenty-year-old Academy student, and for a few moments there she had almost convinced herself they were just rehearsing.

And she could write a book about Matthew, the pro baseball player she had met down in Houston in another lifetime. For a little while she had actually believed she might have hit the jackpot, but then he got himself traded to Toronto and forgot to tell her. Chalk up another loser for the little lady.

And who could forget Antonio? She could still see herself sobbing all over Ellen at the Ritz-Carlton while she tried to figure out why great sex never seemed to make up for the lack of everything else. For a little while it had come darned close, but you still had to do something with the other twenty-three hours of the day. That was what always seemed to get her into trouble.

Sorry, Scott the Mechanic, she thought as he watched her from the doorway. Next time she found herself crazy enough to consider dating again, she was going to steer clear of bad boys. Next time—if there was a next time—it would be a churchgoing, Bible-studying, loves-his-mama type or nobody at all.

*   *   *

$\mathcal{D}$eirdre's music filled the house. It spiraled up the staircase. It spun down the hallways. It burst through the windows, then back in again. It turned the house into the home she had dreamed about since she was a little girl. And always, always, it found its way straight into Ellen's heart.

This was her dream. A big old house bursting at the seams with friends and family and music and laughter. Now if she could just figure out a way to make it last, she would have it made.

Why hadn't she realized before how gifted Deirdre was? Ellen had seen her perform quite a few times over the years, and her smoky, bluesy voice had never failed to delight even though it never made her a star. She had listened to her play the piano, the tenor sax, and the glockenspiel, and she still hadn't suspected her sister could weave this kind of magic spell.

But this was different. It was as if everything Deirdre had done up until that moment had all been preparation. The lessons. The cabarets. The down-on-their-luck lounges. All of Deirdre's experience, her heartbreaks, her longing—every single morsel of it spilled out into her songs, into her music, and drew her listeners closer.

The children were enchanted. Hall's two girls sat at Deirdre's feet, watching her with a kind of awe that put a lump in Ellen's throat. Even Susan's son had stopped fidgeting and tapped his foot to the jig Deirdre was playing. The girls from the youth club swayed gently, arms wrapped across taut middles, dreaming to the music. Susan's eyes were glossy with tears, and even Sweeney, queen of hard rock, looked as if she might be crying. Scott from Jack's garage had appeared at the front door a few minutes ago, and he stood there now, transfixed by the music. Pete from the hardware store, Fred, the two Arties, there wasn't a soul in the room untouched by the beauty of the harp's vibrant sound.

She met Hall's eyes across the room. God, how she had missed him today. The quickly shared observations. The laughter. Knowing that there was one person who cared for the women who walked into their office as much as she did, who was ready to fight as hard to keep them well, who would do anything to help them safely deliver a brand-new life into a very tired old world.

Was she going to sacrifice the deep joy of his friendship because she had been unable to capture his complete attention in the bedroom? Today she had had a glimpse of what life would be like without that friendship, and she wasn't willing to let that happen again. He was too important. His opinions, his ideas, his bad jokes, his tender heart.

As long as they were careful, one day the gossip would fade. Susan would quit shooting her that curious look. Ceil would stop whispering behind her hand over there near the nachos. The men would lose interest in nudging each other every time Hall glanced her way. The town would move on to other issues, like the new road proposed for south of town or maybe the Labor Day fair, and she and Hall would find their way back to friendship.

And it would be enough for her. Like it or not, it would have to be.

Nine

Deirdre finished playing the last notes of "MacAllistrum's March." She always added a gliss right there at the end, one of those quintessential harp flourishes that audiences loved. The room burst into stomps and cheers, and for a second she felt the way she used to feel when she played a great set. Powerful! Invincible! Like all of her dreams were about to come true. Of course, that was back when she believed she was on the first rung of the giant ladder of success and all she had to do was keep on climbing until she reached the top.

Nobody tells you when you're starting out that the giant ladder of success only has two rungs. The first rung is easy enough to climb. A little guts, a little talent, some persistence, and you can manage to hold on. It was that second rung that was the real bitch. So far up there, so damn hard to reach, that most people spent their whole lives struggling to make it and forgot to enjoy the view while they were climbing.

That was Deirdre for most of her life. Struggling to make it to that second rung while everything else went to hell at her feet. She was a bottom-rung artist, and nothing short of a Saturn 5 would ever put her in position to land at the top. Like father, like daughter. Billy was a bottom-rung performer, too.

Great looks, great voice, great performer. But the magic, that indefinable something that sets stars apart from mere mortals, just wasn't there.

Yet nobody in that room seemed to know that. They were looking at her as if she was one of the Chieftains and her harp a direct descendant of Turlough O'Carolan himself, and she was the only one who knew what a fraud she really was.

Ellen's eyes were wet with tears. The sight of her sister's face transformed by emotion was almost Deirdre's undoing. Come to think of it, they all seemed a little teary-eyed and emotional. She wouldn't have minded a little sobbing, maybe a few of those "bravas" that the two little girls were given, but tears were good. She could handle tears. She glanced toward the front door, hoping to see Scott the Mechanic's handsome mug streaked with a few manly tears shed over the beauty of her music.

He was gone. She glanced around the room, poking into the corners, peering back toward the kitchen. Not a sign of him. He must have sneaked out while she was playing. How rude was that? She had wanted to impress the hell out of him with her musical talent, and he hadn't even hung around to listen. He probably heard those first few girly notes from her harp and ran back to his truck as if a squad of Mary Kay ladies were hot on his heels.

Wimp.

They were used to Scott by now up on Captain's Lookout. They nodded in his direction as he reached the top, then went back to looking at the stars. He set up near the western edge of the Lookout, not a prime spot but not bad for somebody who had only joined them eight months ago. Stargazers were a funny group, people who came alive when the sky went dark. They were loners, most of them, whose lives were bounded by the rings of Saturn and the arms of Orion.

Nobody asked any questions. Nobody wanted to know your life story. They just shoved over a little and shared a piece of the sky.

He cleared away some small rocks with the side of his foot and set the tripod down, making sure it was balanced and secure, then screwed the telescope into the armature. The moon was full tonight and he never tired of losing himself in her voluptuous beauty. He had been fifteen the first time he peered at her through a telescope, and the impact on him had been right up there with his first sight of a naked woman. The sense of wonder had never fully left him.

He needed some of her magic tonight, some of that healing wonder, because the memories had come roaring back at him like an angry sea.

Who the hell knew she was going to put on a damn harp concert right there in the middle of Dr. Ellen's living room? He had driven back to the big house on the hill to give her back her wallet. That should have taken what—two minutes? But she was doing something with the strings of her harp, and there were lots of people milling about, so he figured he would hang around while she played some of that watery music harps were famous for, then hand her the wallet before the last note faded away.

Except it didn't work out that way. He had hesitated too long. Too late to hand her the wallet. Too late to leave without looking as if he was making a statement. Music didn't do it for him. It never had. It didn't matter if it was a Beethoven symphony or a little Brubeck, it was nothing more than background noise to him.

But just when he was ready to tune out for the duration, she placed her hands on the strings and broke his heart. Simple as that. The first notes hung in the air for a second—he could swear he had been able to see them—then zeroed in on him. There was nothing he could do. It was deer season and he was Bambi's big brother.

Megan would have loved that. She used to laugh about his tin ear for music. The sound of an air wrench gave him as much pleasure as a concerto gave his wife. Sometimes, just to see her amber eyes dance with laughter, he would throw back his head and sing the first song that came into his head. An old Sinatra number. Maybe a little Elvis. Some Bon Jovi. Anything to make her laugh, to make her look at him as if he were the sun and the moon.

Fuck it. He popped the lens cap off the telescope and slipped it into his pocket. Megan was gone. Colin was gone.

Memories were a waste of time. All they did was break what was left of your heart.

You learned to deal with pain, to compartmentalize it, to accept it as the new normal, and you were doing pretty good at it until a woman with long red hair breezes into town with a bad car, a big dog, and a goddamn harp of all things and you lose it right there in the doctor's doorway.

He knew he should have tossed her wallet to someone before he split, but when the pain hit all he could think of was getting out of there. At least he made it to the truck before the dry heaves caught him. It didn't take much these days to make him grateful.

He bent at the knees and pressed his right eye against the viewer. Ah, Jesus, there she was. Luna rising overhead, glowing and female. He never understood it when people called the moon barren. The moon he saw through his telescope was ripe and fertile.

"She's bright tonight," one of the regulars said, his voice lifting softly in the warm air.

He swung around away from the light, focusing in on a web of stars near Cassiopeia. A small grouping of mag 3s called the Cradle. Legend had it that was where the children of the gods slept sweetly in a cradle of stars, warm beneath a blanket of clouds.

He liked to believe that was where they were right now, his wife and his son watching him, watching them.

"You really need some furniture," Deirdre said as they finished up the last of the dishes. "I mean, a kitchen table might be a nice touch."

"I didn't need a kitchen table in my old place," Ellen said, hanging the dish towel on the rack beneath the sink.

"You ate on the floor?"

"I had one of those built-in breakfast nooks."

"How about some radios?"

"They're on my list."

"And what about a television?"

"I have a television. It's up in my bedroom."

Deirdre made a face. "That little thing? You could only see half of Pamela Anderson on that tiny screen."

"Half of Pamela Anderson is twice as much as I need to see."

"I thought you liked television."

"I do," Ellen said, "but it's not high priority. I'm not around that much to enjoy it."

"Population explosion in Shelter Rock Cove?"

"You're laughing," Ellen said, "but you'd be surprised. I'm beginning to think this is the new Fertile Crescent."

"Let's hear it for celibacy," Deirdre said with a self-mocking laugh. "At least that's one problem I won't have."

Ellen wasn't about to touch that statement. "How does sitting out on the back porch sound to you?"

"If you throw in some of the leftover pizza and a bottle of Sam, I'd say it sounds great."

Stanley pushed up against Ellen's leg, and she reached down and stroked him behind his silky ears. "You really are just a giant baby, aren't you?"

"He likes you," Deirdre said.

"He seems to like everyone. I can't believe somebody gave him up for adoption."

Deirdre crouched down and cradled the dog's massive head between her hands. "They loved him at the shelter. He would let the little dogs climb all over him like he was a hiking trail."

"And still they were going to—"

"Simple economics," Deirdre said with a shake of her head. "Stanley took up a lot of space and ate a lot of food. If I hadn't come along—"

"But you did." She kissed the top of Stanley's head, then laughed as he looked up at her with adoring brown eyes. "So when are you going to ask me, Dee?"

"Ask you what?" Deirdre did an admirable job of feigning ignorance.

"To dog-sit Stanley."

"I wasn't going to—"

"Oh, come on," she said, laughing. "You know you were counting on me to come through. That's why you stopped by."

Deirdre looked a little bit sheepish but not terribly embarrassed. "I was hoping," she said, "but I wasn't counting on it."

"What if I hadn't been here? Please don't tell me you were going to show up at that posh place in Bar Harbor with Stanley in tow."

Deirdre shrugged her shoulders. The movement made her entire ensemble ripple and flow like her music. "I figured I'd worry about that if it happened."

There were times Ellen found it hard to believe they shared a gene pool.

"Remember the time Billy piled us all into that rented car and drove us out to see his friends in the Hamptons?"

"Eight hours trapped in that Chevy with Mary Pat moaning about her boyfriend, and when we got there we found the house had been rented for the summer to some movie people."

"At least they let us use their bathroom," Ellen said.

Deirdre started to laugh. "And that gave Billy time to try to hit them up for a job."

"I was so embarrassed I wanted to say I was a hitchhiker and not related to Billy at all."

"How about now?" Deirdre asked as they carried pizza and beer out to the back porch. "Still feel that way?"

Ellen settled herself down in one of the cushioned chairs and put her feet up on the railing. "I don't really know how I feel about Billy," she said after a bit. "Being fourteen is bad enough, but imagine being told that your father wasn't the kindly Jewish doctor you had known all your life—the one you even thought you looked like, the one you wanted to *be* like—but a charming Irish Catholic musician with a roving eye. . . . Let's just say it's not my favorite memory." Twenty years had gone by since the night her world was turned inside out, and she still hadn't found a way to accept the fact that the people she loved most in the world had deceived her.

"That was a long time ago," Deirdre pointed out. "You're not fourteen any longer."

"A part of me is," Ellen said. "I think a part of me is always going to be that fourteen-year-old girl who had the rug pulled out from under her."

"Don't forget that same rug was pulled out from under Mary Pat and me." Deirdre took a long pull of Sam. "It's not much fun to realize your father screwed around on your mother for most of their married life. Doesn't exactly give a girl a lot of faith in the sanctity of marriage."

Ellen didn't know her sister well enough to read her tone of voice, and it was too dark out there on the back porch to see her face. "Your mother stayed with him."

"Longer than she should have," Deirdre said. "I'm glad for every one of the five years she had with Tommy."

"I don't think Mary Pat would agree with you."

"Mary Pat sees what she wants to see. I think she still blames you for everything that went wrong between Billy and Ma."

"Me? My mother I could understand, but why me?"

"Because your existence changed everything. After your mother died and Cy told you he wasn't your biological father, that gave Billy the right to do what he had wanted to do from the day you were born: claim you as his own."

"Give me a break." Ellen took a sip of iced tea. "This is Billy O'Brien we're talking about. He only wants what he can't have. As soon as I landed on his doorstep that first summer, he was ready to send me back to Cy on the next train."

"You were a bitch," Deirdre said, laughing softly. "A flaming, first-class bitch on wheels."

Ellen grinned into the darkness. "I was, wasn't I?"

"You walked in the door, threw your bags on the floor, and said you hated all of us."

"Please tell me I wasn't that bad."

"You were that bad. I thought you were the most exciting thing to happen to this family in years."

"Right," said Ellen. "I'm sure you were thrilled to meet me."

"No," said Deirdre. "I pretty much hated you as much as Mary Pat did at first, but you were from New York, you had great clothes, and you knew all the latest dances. I caved before that first week was over."

In some ways it was inevitable that they ended up bonding together the way they had. They were only six months apart in age and both shared a burden of responsibility neither one deserved. Ellen's mother had used her pregnancy to try to force Billy into divorcing his wife while Deirdre's mother had used her pregnancy as a means to keep him from leaving. Two weeks after Ellen was born, Billy told Sharon Cooper that he couldn't leave his wife alone with two children.

Six weeks later Sharon married Cy Markowitz, and it wasn't until Sharon's death the year Ellen turned fourteen that the name Billy O'Brien was mentioned in their house.

"We did have fun for a while there, didn't we?" Ellen said as the sweet smell of roses and sea air enveloped her.

"We had some great summers," Deirdre agreed. "Right up until you started med school."

"Things changed, Dee. If you want to make it through med school, you have to commit to it totally."

"Unlike music."

"I didn't say that."

"You should have. I've never committed totally to anything in my life except looking for a good time."

"I've always envied that."

"Yeah," Deirdre said. "Sure you did."

"I'm serious, Dee. I wish I had some of your ability to say to hell with everything and follow my heart."

"I could give you Antonio's number."

Ellen tried to make a joke, but the words wouldn't come. Sitting there with her sister in the moonlight on the back porch of her new house in a town she had grown to love, she was so filled with emotion that she couldn't speak.

They were quiet for a few minutes. Stanley, who lay at their feet, grumbled softly in his sleep.

"You slept with your Dr. Talbot, didn't you?"

"Last night," Ellen said.

"That's what you were fighting about in the side yard."

"We weren't fighting."

"It sounded like fighting to me."

"You eavesdropped?"

"It's an O'Brien family trait. I'm surprised you don't recognize it."

"Do you peek inside medicine cabinets, too?"

"You're trying to change the subject. Why were you fighting with Hall Talbot? Was he hopeless in bed?"

Heat, unexpected and delicious, ignited her body from head to toe at the memory of just how hopeless he was. "There's a small problem."

"Uh-oh."

She laughed despite herself. "Not that. Unfortunately the good doctor happens to be in love with someone else."

"So why wasn't he sleeping with her?"

"Because she's married. Because she loves her husband. Because she just had her second baby and—"

"Annie Butler."

"How on earth did you figure that out?" Deirdre's sixth sense had always unnerved her.

"I haven't a clue." Deirdre rearranged herself on the chaise. "Does Annie love him?"

"Only as a friend. She's madly in love with her husband."

"Did they ever—"

"Never! I'm not even sure she knows how he feels about her."

"He doesn't look like the kind of man who'd go around carrying a torch for anyone. The man is beyond gorgeous."

"If you like that sort of thing."

They both dissolved into laughter loud enough to draw an annoyed grumble from Stanley, who buried his nose beneath his front paws.

"So what's the problem?" Deirdre asked, propping her feet up on the railing next to Ellen's. "It's not like you're in love with him." She paused. "You aren't, are you?"

"No, no," Ellen said, wishing the topic had never reared its ugly head. "Of course not. Like I said, he's in love with someone else."

"So?"

"That wouldn't bother you?"

"It would if I was in love with him, but since you say you aren't, I don't see the problem."

"Neither one of us is looking for that kind of involvement."

"So you had a one-nighter. Big deal."

Ellen flinched. "You make it sound kind of tawdry."

"Do you like 'fling' better?"

Ellen looked up at the stars and sighed. "Mistake," she said at last. "A big fat mistake."

*   *   *

It took four bedtime stories and a stern admonition before Mariah and Willa finally settled down for the night. Hall lingered in the doorway for a long while, watching them as they slept, spoon-fashion, in the same double bed their big sisters Kate and Elizabeth had once shared when they were the same age.

All he did was turn his head for an instant and they were practically grown, away at college and living lives he would never fully know. It would happen with Mariah and Willa, too. One morning he would wake up and they would have boyfriends and driver's licenses, and moments like these would be nothing more than a distant memory of a time long past.

Unfortunately with memory came regrets. Lots of them. Three failed marriages was a good place to start. He had read somewhere that the greatest gift a man could give his children was to love their mother. He had cared deeply for each of his wives. He had been faithful and he would have stayed faithful if they hadn't seen right through him. They wanted to be loved the way a woman deserved to be loved, and that was the one thing he couldn't provide. His feelings for Annie Galloway always got in the way. Years and years of watching her from across the room, knowing things about her marriage that he had no business knowing, quietly biding his time after Kevin's death, waiting respectfully like the good family friend that he was for the right day, the right moment, to tell her how he felt.

Except that moment never came. Sam Butler moved into town and stole her heart, and Hall was left standing on the sidelines once again, wondering where he had gone wrong.

But there was something to be said for small towns. You couldn't avoid life if you tried. It was out there waiting for you in front of the post office, or on Ceil's line at Yankee Shopper, or across from you at Susan's dinner table. He saw Annie every day, watched her grow big with her first child, came to understand that she had found the real thing with Sam Butler. And somewhere along the way he let her go. He couldn't say exactly when it had happened, but one morning he woke up and she wasn't his first thought or even his fifth. He could bump into her at Cappy's or see her leaving Ellen's office with a belly swelling with her second daughter and only wish her well. The ache of love, of longing, was finally gone.

He wandered out onto the deck and settled down on the old swing. A full moon rode high in the star-spangled sky. Ellen loved nights like this, when the sky was bright and the breeze off the ocean carried the scent of flowers. She loved cats and dogs and birds and babies, peach pie and lobster and sweet corn dripping with butter. She loved summer nights, snowy winter afternoons, long books, and short movies. She loved the women who put themselves in her hands, the young girls looking for direction, the babies who turned couples into families.

He had handled things badly at the house. Out there in the garden he had veered wildly from desire to regret to anger and back again, all over the emotional map. Her defenses had popped up faster than he could knock them down. Public displays of private emotions weren't her style—or his, either, under normal circumstances. But he had the sense that she was pulling away from him and that if he didn't get through to her now, all that would be left was polite conversation.

He glanced at the time on his cell phone. Three minutes after eleven. Her sister was there. They were probably tired. Maybe he should wait until tomorrow and—

Screw that. Waiting didn't get you anything but older. He punched in her speed-dial code.

One of the many items Ellen needed to buy was a bed for the guest room. Deirdre said she would be fine sleeping on the sofa, but Ellen insisted she share the bed with her.

"I don't know how to break this to you," Deirdre said as she settled back against the pillows, "but Stanley likes to sleep with me."

"You slut," Ellen said, grinning at her sister.

"Any port in a storm." Deirdre stifled a yawn. "He's big, he's strong, and he doesn't snore. Find me a man like that and I'll marry him."

Ellen switched off the bed lamp and opened the curtains wide to let in the evening breezes. How it must have hurt

Claudia to leave this wonderful house. The heady mix of ocean breezes and beach roses made her shiver with pleasure.

"You'd better climb in before Stanley does," Deirdre said, sounding half asleep. "Once he claims his turf, you might find yourself on the floor."

"I—" The cell phone on Ellen's nightstand bleated. "Oh, damn." She grabbed for it and pressed the On button. "Dr. Markowitz."

"Dr. Talbot here."

"What's wrong?" She peered at her clock. "It's almost eleven—"

"I know what time it is. We need to talk."

"I think we talked enough this afternoon."

"That wasn't talking. That was arguing."

"This really isn't a great time."

"Don't mind me," Deirdre called from the depths of her pillow. "I'm going to sleep."

"I'm going downstairs," she told Deirdre and a minute later settled herself on the deck. "Make it quick. It's freezing out here."

"Put a blanket on."

"I don't keep blankets on my deck, Hall."

"Look under the chaise cushion," he said. "Claudia always kept a blanket hidden there."

He was right. The lightweight throw felt wonderful against her bare skin. "So what do you want?" she asked, curling herself into the corner of the swing. "I have early rounds tomorrow morning."

She heard him pull in a deep breath. "I don't want to lose you, Markowitz."

Her own breath caught in her throat. "Am I going someplace?"

"Your friendship is too important to me."

She experienced an odd blend of disappointment and joy that left her feeling as if she had just stepped off one of those whirling teacup rides at Disney World. "I feel the same way."

"They'll be watching us tomorrow."

"They'll be watching me."

"Both of us," he said. "We can get through this if we put up a united front."

"You're homegrown. They have to forgive you. Me, they can ship back to New York."

"Is that what you want to do?" he asked. "Go back home to New York?"

"This is home now," she said. "I'm not going anywhere."

"I wish I could make it all better for you, Markowitz. I wish—"

"Yeah, yeah." She wiped the back of her hand across her eyes. Why didn't she ever have a Kleenex with her when she needed one? "If wishes were horses . . ." She covered the phone, then sniffled loudly. "Why don't we pretend it never happened."

A beat of silence passed before he responded. "You mean when I—"

"The whole thing," she said. "Erase the whole mistake."

"Is that what you want?"

"Yes," she said fiercely. "That's exactly what I want."

"You want us to go back to being friends."

Damn those stupid tears.

"Ellen?"

"Yes," she said. "We'll go back to being friends."

Just like the night before had never happened.

Ten

"Knock it off, Stanley!" Deirdre buried her head under her pillow. "It's the crack of dawn."

Stanley barked again, more urgently this time, and from somewhere in the distance she heard a buzzer. She opened her eyes, groaned, and quickly closed them again. The room was flooded with full sunlight. It took her a second to remember where she was, and once she did she made a note to remind her sister to buy some blackout curtains.

She squinted at the clock on Ellen's nightstand but couldn't make out the numbers through the glare. The buzzer sounded again, followed by three short knocks on the door. Stanley threw back his mighty head and thundered off a rolling bark that they could probably hear across town. She had a vague memory of Ellen bustling around the room at dawn, followed by the sound of her car roaring to life, so there would be no help on that score. It was becoming clear that sleep would not be an option until she got up and answered the door.

Maybe it was the furniture fairy delivering some presents, she thought as she followed Stanley down the staircase in her ratty old Caesar's Palace T-shirt and bare feet. A lovely guest bed. Some dressers and lamps. A kitchen table. A sixty-inch flat-screen plasma television with cable and TiVo.

"It's awfully early," she said as she swung open the door, "but since you insist—" Her words stopped abruptly as she found herself looking up at a smiling Scott the Mechanic. "You could have left my wallet here last night."

"I felt funny handing it to someone else."

She stifled a yawn. "So why didn't you hand it to me?"

"You were playing that harp."

"So why didn't you wait?"

He handed her the wallet. "You're good. Damn good."

She was pleased despite herself. "Like you know harps."

He turned and started down the front porch steps toward the tow truck idling in the driveway.

"Wait!" she called out, running down the steps after him. "I didn't mean that the way it sounded."

He stopped and turned to face her. Nobody had ever looked at her quite that way before. She couldn't begin to figure out the expression in his eyes.

"Okay," she said as Stanley galloped past her. "I'm lying. I meant it exactly the way it sounded and I'm sorry."

"I was going to tell you I ordered the parts for your car, but thanks for the apology." Who knew he had such a terrific smile?

"I'm withdrawing the apology," she said as an answering smile spread across her face.

"Too late. Once an apology is accepted, it can't be withdrawn."

"Like there's a rule out there about apologies."

"There's a rule out there about everything if you know where to look."

Scott the Mechanic was growing more interesting by the second. "How many parts did you order?"

"Three," he said. "If you want to stop by later, maybe we can give you an estimate."

"Why not now?"

"The parts place hasn't come up with a quote."

"You ordered something, but you don't know how much it's going to cost?"

"Hell, I don't even know if they can find the parts."

Her smile vanished. "Oh, God, don't say that. You have to

find the parts. I'm leaving for Bar Harbor on Saturday morning."

"I scanned four states for parts, and only one source said they might have what we need."

This was quickly turning into a nightmare. "Listen, I probably shouldn't say this, but I don't have a whole lot of extra money for car repairs."

"You mean your other car isn't a Lexus?"

She rolled her eyes. "My extra car isn't even a car. It's a bicycle."

"Somehow I don't see you biking to Bar Harbor."

"Especially since I left my bike in Boston with friends." He didn't have to know it was a ten-year-old three-speed with a dented front fender.

"I'll make some more calls."

"I'd really appreciate it."

They stood there looking at each other for what seemed like a very long time. There was nothing left to say. She had her wallet. He understood her situation. Neither one was the type to make small talk about the weather. Still they stood there quietly, taking each other's measure. She couldn't get a reading on him. The externals were all very pleasing—great smile, great shoulders, great voice—but she couldn't seem to get a feel for the man behind those deep green eyes. She usually had a pretty easy time picking up a man's vibe, but Scott the Mechanic seemed to have the emotional equivalent of a Star Wars system keeping her at bay.

Which made him way too interesting for her own good.

She wrapped her arms across her chest, suddenly aware that she was standing there in full sunlight wearing nothing but a sleep shirt and a pair of bikini panties. "I'd better get back inside," she said, edging away from him. "God knows what Stanley's doing in there."

The man knew how to play silence for all it was worth. She had to pinch the inside of her arm to keep from filling the void with mindless chatter. She knew all about the art of the well-timed exit, and this was about as perfect a time for one as she was likely to encounter, but the thought of walking away from him in full sunlight in nothing but that stupid T-shirt held her in place.

"Don't let me keep you," she said. "I know you have things to do."

"You said you were leaving."

"I decided to stay here and wave goodbye."

"I can't see anything, if that's what you're worried about."

"That means you looked."

He nodded. "I looked."

"Sorry to disappoint you."

"I'm not disappointed."

Who would have guessed he had even noticed? "Humor me," she said. "Allow me to keep my cellulite a family secret."

Men hated the word *cellulite*. If you ever wanted to deflate a man's ardor, whisper it in his ear. She had used it a time or two to great effect.

But Scott the Mechanic was made of stronger stuff. He didn't even blink at the word *cellulite*. "I meant what I said before. You have a lot of talent."

"Bet you say that to all the half-naked girls."

"Only the talented ones."

"I'm not sure how to take that."

"Try taking it the way it was meant." He climbed into his truck, threw it into gear, and headed back to town.

Leave it to a mechanic to recognize a great exit line.

"I have good news for you," Ellen said as the young girl and her mother took their seats in her office. "Tori isn't pregnant."

Tori, sixteen and terrified, burst into tears of relief. Her mother, Amanda, forty and equally terrified, didn't believe it. "But the test," she said. "I saw it myself. There was a big plus sign right there."

"Home pregnancy tests are wonderful tools," Ellen said, closely watching her young patient as she spoke, "but they are occasionally inaccurate. This was one of those times."

"How can we be sure?"

"We are sure," Ellen said. "The test we ran is in perfect agreement with my findings during the exam. Tori is definitely not pregnant."

"Oh, God." Amanda Dietrich buried her face in her hands for a moment. "Thank God, thank God." She turned to her daughter. "If you so much as go near Jimmy Welles again, so help me I'll—"

"I think we all need to talk," Ellen broke in. "We need to discuss Tori's world the way it is, not the way we wish it could be." She focused in on the young girl, who was looking at her with a combination of respect and terror that tugged at her heartstrings. There wasn't a single one of them who didn't have the power to break Ellen's heart with their innocence and their problems. "You took an enormous risk when you had unprotected sex, Tori."

"It was the safe time of month, Dr. Ellen. I figured it out."

"Some times of month are safer than others," Ellen said, "but the cold truth of the matter is that no time of month is completely safe." She leaned back in her chair and kept her gaze focused on the young girl. "How long have you been sexually active?"

"Since she was fourteen," Amanda spoke up. "I tried to reason with her, but she's always been headstrong."

"Have you two talked about the Pill?"

Tori sat up a little straighter. "That's foolproof, isn't it?"

Sorry to shoot you down, Tori. "Nothing is foolproof," Ellen said, "except abstinence, but, taken properly, the Pill will afford you better than ninety percent effectiveness."

"That leaves a big margin for error," Amanda noted.

"Which is one of the reasons why I would also strongly urge the use of a condom as well."

Tori slumped back down in her seat. "They're gross."

"They're necessary," Ellen shot back. "Sex carries risks other than pregnancy, Tori." She launched into her STD speech, the one that would have sent her spiraling into a permanent state of celibacy if she had heard it at Tori's age. But the world had changed dramatically in the last two decades. AIDS was only being whispered about when she was in her teens. The widespread reality of its horror had yet to be understood.

She paused for a moment and waited while mother and daughter digested some of her message.

"So you're saying no matter what, I have to use condoms?"

"That's what I'm saying. The Pill can protect you from an

unwanted pregnancy, but it won't protect you from sexually
transmitted diseases."

"I thought it was like penicillin or something."

She met Amanda's eyes. "I think the two of you would
benefit from attending our Wednesday workshop on teenagers
and sex. It will help you understand the various options."

"I'm not sure I want my daughter on the Pill at sixteen."

"I can understand your concerns," Ellen said, "and I'm
happy to discuss them." She provided some facts and figures,
the prohibitions, and handed each of them a series of booklets
that detailed the various forms of birth control.

"Where is this Wednesday workshop?" Amanda asked.
They both ignored Tori's eye-rolling commentary.

"The community room at the hospital," Ellen said. "It begins at seven-thirty and ends at nine. It's a very straightfor-
ward, blunt presentation. I think you should know that going
in."

"Maybe that's what we need," Amanda said, slipping the
brochures into her handbag. "Tori has been very lucky so far,
but we all know that won't last forever."

They chatted briefly, then Amanda and Tori left. Why did
these mother-daughter encounters take so much out of her?
There was so much she had wanted to say to Tori about sexuality and its place in her life, but her mother had set the
boundaries and it was Ellen's job to abide by them. They were
skidding downhill toward disaster quicker than either one realized, and unless both Amanda and Tori faced up to reality
immediately, the next pregnancy test would yield a very different result.

Right now that was where Amanda's attention was focused,
but there were other risks, life-threatening ones she needed to
consider when she thought about her daughter's sexuality. Tori
was less than two years away from being an adult in the eyes
of the world. The choices made now would affect the rest of
her life. Wednesday's workshop could be of enormous value,
but that would require an admission from both of them that
they needed help.

The odds of that happening seemed very slim to Ellen.

She poured a glass of ice water from the carafe on her desk.
The cool liquid helped to revive her spirits. There had been a

few moments during the consultation where she had been forcibly struck by the gap between her advice to Tori and her own actions. The discussion of condoms had hit a nerve as she tried to recall what precautions she and Hall had taken the night they made love. It was such a blur of emotion that she wasn't sure they had taken any at all. She remembered hearing that Hall had had a vasectomy not long after she came to work with him, but that didn't let either one of them off the hook. Not in this day and age.

Amanda Dietrich faced a tough battle with Tori. Desire was a powerful force. It could turn educated, accomplished adults into fools, and yet they expected young girls to handle those powerful, complicated emotions with little or no guidance.

Janna poked her head into the room. "Frieda Langley is in Room three."

Ellen glanced down at her schedule. "I thought Lois Bannion was my two o'clock."

"Mrs. Bannion canceled, Doctor. I moved Langley up an hour."

She took another look at the schedule. "Did you move Gelardi up an hour too?"

Janna looked uncomfortable. "Gelardi canceled."

"Did she reschedule?"

Janna shook her head. "You know Gelardi. All those club meetings, her grandchildren. I'm sure she'll make an appointment soon."

Bless Janna. It was clear she knew exactly what was going on beneath the surface, and this was her way of letting Ellen know she was behind her. Janna went back to the reception desk as Ellen headed toward Room 3 and Frieda Langley.

Hall was exiting the room they used for colposcopies and other minor office procedures. His head was bent over a sheaf of papers, and he looked up as she approached.

"Hey," he said. "Good day?"

"Good question," she parried. "I'll let you know at five."

His gaze was so warm, so intimate, in a way that went far beyond the sexual. The look in his eyes felt like an embrace.

"We've had five cancellations," he said quietly.

"Five?" She forced her voice down to a more office-friendly decibel level. "I know about Bannion and Gelardi."

"Weinstein, Baker, and Dinofrio."

"Ouch," she said. "This isn't looking very good, is it?"

"We both knew there might be a little fallout."

"I'd better get to three before I give them more to talk about."

"Have dinner with me tonight."

She burst into laughter. "Oh, there's a great idea for you."

"I'm serious. I'm having dinner with Susan and Jack at Cappy's. Why don't you and Deirdre join us?"

All platonic. All aboveboard. She had no business being disappointed.

"I don't know," she said. "I'm not sure if we—"

"This is a small town. We can't avoid each other forever. Sooner or later we're going to have to get back to normal. Sooner sounds good to me."

"You're right," she said. "Name the time."

"Seven. We'll try for one of the dockside tables."

"Perfect," she said, smiling up at him. "We'll be there."

Take that, Mrs. Gelardi.

Jf you wanted to make a statement to everyone in town, Cappy's was the place to do it. Cappy's was town center, favorite restaurant, and scenic attraction all in one. What had started out fifty years ago as a summer-only lobster joint had evolved over time into the place you went when you wanted good food and you didn't want to be alone. And the fact that it was situated dockside with a view of the entire sweep of picturesque Shelter Rock Cove didn't hurt, either.

"I thought you were bringing the girls," Susan said as Hall joined her at the dockside table that evening. Charlie, her youngest, was sitting across the way with his friend Steve Winstead and the boy's family.

"Yvonne came home early," he said, "so I invited two other sisters to take their place."

"Ellen and the harp player? Why did you do that?"

He had to hand it to his old pal. You never had to worry that Susan was hiding her real feelings. She usually gave them to you right between the eyes.

"What's the problem?" He sat down opposite her. "You

liked Ellen enough yesterday when she handed you all that money for Claudia's house."

Susan began shredding her paper napkin, a sure sign something was bugging her.

"Knock that off," he said, grabbing for what was left of the napkin. "You're getting more like your mother every day." Claudia Galloway was notorious for shredding anything she could get her hands on when she was under stress.

"You don't have to insult me."

"That's more like it," he said. "Why the sudden problem with Ellen?" Was this the same woman who had convinced him to stop by Ellen's for the impromptu housewarming?

"I don't have a problem with Ellen," she said, maybe a little too quickly for his taste. "I thought it would be the three of us, that's all. Just family."

He looked around. "Where's Jack?"

"Stuck at the shop. He said he'll meet us here. Scott'll drop him off."

"If you have anything to say, Susie, this might be a good time to say it."

She leaned across the table and fixed him with a fierce look. "What the hell are you thinking?" she demanded. "I can't believe you're starting something up with your partner."

"Not your business," he said evenly. "That's why it's called a private life."

"Bullshit." Nothing like a good old Anglo-Saxonism to clear the air between friends. "You were born here. You know nothing stays private for long. I mean, didn't you cause enough talk after the christening? Mary Gelardi is thinking of switching to Hank's medical group at the hospital."

She already did, Susie. "Hank's a fine doctor. So are his associates. She'll be in good hands."

"That's all you have to say?"

"That's all I'm going to say."

"You know what this is about. You're still rebounding. Every time you're around Annie, you—"

"I think you'd better stop right there, Susan."

She leaned back and looked at him. It was clear she wasn't happy about it, but she let the subject drop.

They pretended rapt interest in reading Cappy's menu,

which hadn't changed since before either one of them was born. He was beginning to wonder if he shouldn't call it a night and head Ellen and Deirdre off at the parking lot. They could always drive over to the Barnacle. The food wasn't as good as Cappy's, but the company might be a lot less unpredictable. He was about to push back from the table when Ellen and Deirdre joined them.

Susan's smile looked sincere enough, but he didn't trust her not to make his life a living hell.

"Sorry we're late," Ellen said. She glanced at him, then aimed her smile in Susan's direction. "I shouldn't have stopped to change." She was wearing jeans and a crisp white shirt with the cuffs rolled back. He was so accustomed to seeing her in a lab coat or scrubs that the sight of her in civilian clothes always took him by surprise.

"Don't let her take all the blame," Deirdre said, sitting down next to him. "I couldn't lure Stanley back into the house." Ellen's sister was wearing jeans, too, but hers were soft and faded and her blouse reminded him of those peasant getups they wore in the late sixties.

The sisters launched into a story about Stanley that quickly had Susan laughing, and Hall felt himself begin to relax. Hallie, their waitress, lit two citronella candles on either end of the table, then brought them pitchers of iced tea and lemonade. She suggested sharing a bucket of steamers while they waited for Jack, but Susan shook her head.

"To hell with Jack," she said with a raucous laugh. "Let's order!"

"That was easy," Ellen said as Hallie hurried away. Three lobster specials, one cheeseburger medium rare, all with fresh corn and a side of cole slaw.

"Do you know what this would cost in Boston?" Deirdre asked. "I feel like I'm stealing."

The three women launched into a lively debate on the relative merits of small-town Maine over big-city Boston, which gave Hall the chance to sit back and enjoy watching Ellen. She had beautiful hands. A surgeon's hands. Strong but graceful, blessed with long, tapering fingers. Her nails were filed short and coated in clear polish. She wore very little jewelry. Earrings. A watch. No rings or bracelets or necklaces. Her mane of wild auburn curls was ornamentation enough. He loved the way her curls reflected the glow of the setting sun, like tamed fire wreathing her lovely and animated face.

She caught him looking at her and glanced quickly away. Susan clearly noted the byplay but said nothing. Deirdre, who had been entertaining them with a very funny story about a club she had played in Cambridge, suddenly fell silent. Her attention was focused somewhere over Hall's right shoulder, and he turned to see Jack walking toward them with his new mechanic right behind him.

Scott the Mechanic tried to escape, but Susan wouldn't let him. "Shove over, everybody," she said, and they made room at the picnic bench for one more.

Deirdre smiled at him over her mound of lobster. He flashed her what she assumed was a smile, but it vanished so quickly she couldn't be sure. It was clear he would rather be any place but where he was, and she couldn't help feeling a little bit sorry for him. Not too sorry, mind you, because she knew the type. Give them an inch of sympathy and next thing you knew you were handing over your checkbook and the keys to your car.

Come to think of it, he already had the keys to her car. The idea struck her as hilariously funny and she started to laugh. She tried to muffle the sound behind her lobster bib, but it was too late. All eyes were on her.

"J-just ignore me," she said, laughing merrily. "This happens whenever I eat lobster."

All eyes then shifted to Ellen, who shrugged. "Don't ask me. She's only my sister."

Bless her! That was exactly the right thing to say. The table broke up with laughter, and the conversation picked up where it had left off. Only Scott sensed something besides lobster was going on.

"So what's the joke?" He cracked the back of his lobster, then reached for the pick.

"I don't think you'd like it."

"Try me. I have a pretty decent sense of humor."

She dipped a nugget of claw meat into the drawn butter.

"It has to do with bad boys, car keys, and sympathy."

She wasn't sure if his expression was deadpan or deeply nuanced. Either way she didn't know what on earth he was thinking.

"No comment?" she asked, popping the meat into her mouth.

"Nope."

"You're not curious?"

"Should I be?"

How a man could smell so good after spending the day under a Hyundai was beyond her, but he did.

"I thought only New Yorkers answer a question with another question."

"Who says I'm not a New Yorker?"

She started to laugh again, but this time he laughed with her. "I grew up close enough to Boston to recognize a Southie when I hear one."

"Most people think I sound like I'm from Brooklyn."

"Only people who've never actually been to Brooklyn."

"Or people who've never actually known a Southie." Jesus, he really did have a great smile.

"It's all in your diphthongs," she said, even though there wasn't a diphthong within fifty miles. "If there's one thing I know, it's my diphthongs."

Oh, God. What if he thought a diphthong was something from the Victoria's Secret catalog. If you had to explain a punch line, it was all over.

"You're not trying to work it into a sentence, are you?" he asked as he slathered butter on an ear of deep yellow corn.

That smile was definitely a killer.

"You mean I don't have to?"

"Not for me."

Bad-boy looks. Good-boy vocabulary. This was getting dangerous.

Deirdre and Scott Peretti?

Ellen was so busy trying to eavesdrop on her sister and the mechanic that she lost track of the other conversations at the table. So that was what he sounded like. She hadn't heard Scott utter more than ten words since he first moved to Shelter Rock Cove a few months ago, but he had been making up for lost time since he sat down next to Deirdre.

In fact, all three of the men at the picnic table seemed fascinated by her sister. Hall had a huge smile plastered across his face each time he looked at Deirdre, and even Jack, who didn't have a flirtatious bone in his body, was practically twinkling in Deirdre's direction. It was the clothes. Ellen was sure of it. All a woman had to do was wear something that looked as if it just might slip off any moment, and you had them eating from the palm of your hand. She was considering the wisdom of an off-the-shoulder lab coat when her pager went off. She unclipped it from the waistband of her jeans and checked the code, then whipped out her cell phone.

"I have to leave," she apologized as she rose from the table. She slipped some money under Deirdre's iced tea glass to cover the bill.

"Patsy Wheeler?" Hall asked quietly.

"Her husband brought her into emergency." She wanted to say more, but it was inappropriate with everyone listening.

"I'll go with you."

The first time he joined her on an emergency call, she had been highly insulted. She had called him out into the hall and read him the riot act about his lack of faith in her abilities, telling him she would pack up her office right that minute and leave if this was the way things would be between them.

She had grown up in the world of big city hospitals, of pecking orders, and territorial disputes. The world in which she had trained was built on a foundation of politics and funding, and she had brought that protective attitude with her to Shelter Rock Cove. Not that it was any different in Maine. Doctors still battled for position and funding for their particular specialties, but not Hall. It had taken her a while to fully understand that when he said he wanted to join her on a call, it wasn't because he didn't trust her. It wasn't about her at all. It was about the patient. Odds were he had grown up with the woman or played ball in her yard as a boy. They weren't patients to him. They were women with histories, families who loved them. He had been a part of it all, and he wanted her to be part of it, too.

She pulled her car keys from the back pocket of her jeans. "Let's go."

"Did you forget someone?" Deirdre muttered as Hall and Ellen drove away in their separate vehicles. What kind of sister would leave her penniless sibling alone in the middle of nowhere with a group of lobster-eating strangers and their offspring?

"She's the best thing that ever happened to him," Jack said. "I haven't seen him look this happy since—"

"So does anyone want more ice cream?" Susan interrupted, a bright smile plastered on her face.

"Not me," Scott said.

"Me, neither," said Deirdre, "but I could use a lift back to Ellen's place."

"No sweat," said Jack. "We'll—"

"I'll drive you," Scott said. "It's on my way."

"No, it's not," Jack argued. "You live out beyond the Ridge."

"Jack, for God's sake, quit being a horse's ass and shut up." The smile was falling apart at the seams. "He wants to drive her home. Let him."

With that the woman burst into tears.

They waited to see if Jack had anything to say about it, but he was staring down at his wife as if she was a premenopausal mermaid who had just washed up on shore with a missile launcher under her fin.

And people wondered why Deirdre had never married.

Eleven

"You know how much this baby means to us." Patsy Wheeler reached for Ellen as they prepped her for the procedure. "I don't care if I have to lie flat for the next five months."

Ellen gripped the woman's icy hand and held tight. "We're doing everything possible to make sure you maintain this pregnancy, Patsy." She was struck by how empty the words sounded. How many times a week did she utter the same sentence, trying hard to stand clear of the fear and worry in a woman's eyes as she looked to Ellen for answers. Early on in her training she had been warned of the danger to be found in identifying too strongly with a patient, of allowing emotion to get in the way of clear-eyed diagnosis and treatment.

It was a difficult tightrope walk. She cared about the well-being of all her patients. She wished them all happy babies and loving relationships and long healthy lives. But there was always one who touched your heart in a special way, whose situation resonated more strongly than usual. Maybe she reminded you of someone you loved. Maybe you saw yourself in her eyes or heard your own life in her stories. Sometimes you didn't understand why a particular patient touched you so deeply, and that was the way it was for Ellen with Patsy Wheeler.

She didn't meet Hall's eyes. She knew her own sadness would be reflected in them and that was the last thing their patient needed to see. Patsy Wheeler was forty-two years old and pregnant with her first child. After years of trying to conceive, she and her husband had finally hit the jackpot, and Ellen had celebrated right along with them.

Unfortunately it seemed their elation might be short-lived. Patsy Wheeler's cervix, which had been compromised by two punch biopsies over the years, was beginning to dilate months earlier than it should. Ellen would add a few stitches to strengthen the cervix and, please God, enable Patsy to carry the baby closer to term.

"Do you mind if I stick around?" Hall asked as they stepped out into the hall so Patsy and her husband Doug could be alone for a few minutes.

"I'd like that," she said. There was nothing difficult about the procedure, she had performed over one hundred of them, but the fact that he cared enough about Patsy to stick around mattered deeply to her. They had both grown up as the child of a physician. Hall understood the ways in which that shaped a young person, the dreams it could awaken.

Her clearest memories of childhood were the sound of the phone ringing at odd hours of the night, the image of Cy, his cheek still creased from sleep, as he grabbed his bag and headed out into the dark city. He would come home hours later, rumpled and tired but exhilarated, to her mother's punishing silence. Sharon had never asked questions about Cy's life beyond their six-room apartment on the Upper West Side. It had taken Ellen a very long time to understand the irony involved in being the childless wife of a successful obstetrician who helped create miracles for everyone but the woman he loved.

Ellen had been hungry for information. She wanted to know about his patients, his routine, the way he felt when a tiny human being saw the world for the first time. Sometimes he came home steeped in sadness, and she would sit quietly in the living room, watching him as he looked out the window at the city traffic below. For as long as she could remember she had wanted to follow in his footsteps. She had wanted to care that deeply, work that hard, know the joy he felt when a new life entered the world even at the risk of the unbearable sadness that was also a part of the equation.

To connect with him, make him finally see her.

The words *You're just like your father* had been music to her ears.

Until the day she learned he wasn't her father at all.

"Thanks for the ride," Deirdre said as they turned the corner onto Ellen's block. "First my sister walks out on me and then—" She stopped mid-sentence and looked at Scott. "What on earth happened back there with your boss's wife anyway?"

"I figured it was a woman thing."

"Maybe if the woman is an alien," Deirdre said. "Is Susan usually like that?"

"She's never pitched a fit at the garage, if that's what you're asking."

"Is she moody? Emotional? Prone to screaming fits?"

"I never noticed."

"Oh, come on! Even a man would notice if a woman's head did a 360 while you were talking to her."

He laughed out loud. "Yeah, that might grab your attention."

"Are they happy together? Does he play around?" A thought occurred to her. "Does *she* play around? Maybe—" Another thought occurred to her. "Is there anything between her and Hall Talbot?"

"You have one hell of an imagination."

"He's very good-looking."

"Something else I never noticed."

"You must hear a lot of gossip working at the garage all day."

"Yeah, that's pretty much all we do. Swill beer and shoot the breeze."

"Don't get defensive on me. I'm searching for information."

They had come to a stop in front of Ellen's house, but neither made a move to call it a night.

"Why are you searching for information?" he asked. "Because you want to know if your sister has any competition with Talbot?"

Surprise almost blew her out the passenger door and onto the driveway. "Was I the last one to find out?"

"Depends when you found out," Scott said, leaning back in his seat. "It only happened Sunday night."

"Garage gossip?" she asked with an edge to her voice.

"Observation," he shot back. "Her car was parked in front of his house all night."

"And you make a habit of driving around town checking out parking arrangements?" She regretted her words immediately. "Sorry, but that's my sister we're talking about." She knew more about the secret life of the kiwi bird than she knew about Ellen. Her fling with the doctor notwithstanding.

"This isn't Boston. When you own the only bright red Cruiser in town, people notice where it's parked."

"And I suppose people don't just notice these things. They talk about them, too."

"Other people. Not me."

"You're a regular Boy Scout."

"And you're a real bitch."

She flinched. "I guess I deserved that."

He didn't answer. She felt an uncomfortable blend of regret, embarrassment, and tenderness that made her wish she had stayed home with Stanley.

Time to cut her losses.

"Thanks for the ride," she said once more, fumbling for the door handle. "Let me know when my car's ready and I'll—"

"Don't get out."

She swung open the door. "Listen, I think we've said about as much as—"

He pointed toward the side garage window, illuminated by the headlights. "Somebody broke in."

Doug Wheeler was the only person in Surgical Waiting. He jumped up the second Ellen appeared in the doorway.

"Everything went as planned," Ellen said quickly, glad to

put him at ease. "Patsy will be back in her room in a few minutes."

The look of relief on his face made her smile.

"The baby?" he asked.

"Fetal heartbeat is strong. The sonogram looked good. Patsy's in excellent physical condition." It was a question of buying as much time as possible for the baby to develop properly. She laid out a plan that included bed rest and medical supervision, but it quickly became clear that the poor man wasn't tracking well at all. "I'll write this all up for you, Doug. They'll be bringing Patsy back to 3D. Go wait for her."

"Thanks, Dr. Ellen. We—" His voice broke and she reached over and patted his arm.

"Go visit your wife," she said. "That's an order."

He managed a smile, then took off down the hall at a run.

David Letterman flashed his own gap-toothed smile from the television mounted to the wall across the room as Ellen gave in to an enormous yawn. The temptation to lie down on one of the leatherette couches and drop into sleep was almost overwhelming, but she resisted. She would be back here again in less than seven hours to perform a laparoscopy on Lucy Hunt, a seventeen-year-old girl with chronic abdominal pain. Ellen suspected adhesions from a childhood appendectomy, but she wouldn't know with certainty until she went in with the scope.

Hall had said he would wait around, but she wouldn't blame him if he had abandoned ship and headed home. She would change, pop into the office to see if he had left a note on her desk, then drag herself home before it got any later.

"Hey, Doc." Mary Ann Ippolito, head surgical nurse, greeted her as they approached the elevator.

"You're here late, M.A." This time she stifled her yawn.

"Claire started maternity leave and Ginny called in sick. Leave it to the old girls to pick up the slack." Mary Ann had been with the hospital since the day it opened in 1965. She was as much a part of the place as the bricks and mortar. There wasn't much that escaped her notice. "I saw Dr. Talbot a little while ago."

Ellen nodded in what she hoped was a casual fashion. "He was consulting with me on Wheeler."

"I hear you were both at the Butler christening this weekend."

"Absolutely! I was delighted to play a small part in the birth of their little girls." *Try to parse that sentence for gossip, M.A., I dare you!*

Mary Ann was the past master of the poker face. Whatever she knew, or thought she knew, wouldn't reveal itself until she was good and ready. That was how she had earned the nickname the Cobra from cowed underlings. You never knew when she was going to strike until it was too late.

Jenny, a night clerk from radiology, joined them and the conversation veered toward the weather and last week's Memorial Day Haddock Fry. Ellen silently blessed the young woman for showing up when she did. She was tired and feeling more than a little bit prickly. One raised eyebrow from Mary Ann and she just might tell the lot of them to worry about whose car was parked in their own driveways and leave her alone.

She parted company with them on her floor, then slowly walked the dimly lit hallway to the tiny office she shared with Hall. A thin pool of yellow light spilled under the door and she smiled. He had waited for her after all.

"We're not out of the woods," she said as she stepped inside, "but things are looking a lot better than they were a few hours ago."

She glanced around. The light on Janna's desk was lit, but there was no sign of him. She peeked into his tiny office. He wasn't there, either. She pushed open the door to her office, then stopped in her tracks. His long, lean frame was draped across two hard-backed chairs. His arms were crossed over his chest. His head rested against his right shoulder. He wasn't exactly snoring, but it was close.

A twisting sensation settled behind her breastbone, an odd blend of tenderness and raw desire. Was it possible to want to jump a man's bones and tuck him in at the same time? She felt stripped bare, more naked than when she lay beneath him in his bed. The sensation was painful. She wanted to back away from it, push it aside. Whoever first noted that sex was the best way to ruin a friendship deserved the Nobel Prize in Romance.

They were never going to find their way back to where they had been. Even if they said to hell with the town and its opinion, Annie Butler's shadow would always come between them. Ellen had been around long enough to know a man didn't stop loving one woman just because he had sex with another. They weren't hard-wired that way. Good sex and true love sometimes walked off into the sunset together, but mostly that happened in fairy tales. In the real world good sex and true love weren't even on speaking terms, at least not most of the time. If you ever managed to get the two of them in the same man at the same time, you had better check your pulse because odds were you were dead and this was heaven.

She placed a hand on his shoulder. "Hall, it's late. Time to go home."

He had the doctor's ability to wake up instantly, clear-headed and alert. He swung his legs to the floor and stood up. "How did it go?"

"So far, so good. I'm putting her on complete bed rest."

"Home or hospital?"

"We'll try home first. If it proves too stressful, I think her insurance will cover in-hospital care."

"Have Janna check into it. She has the revised plans on file."

Somewhere down the hall a telephone rang three times, then stopped.

"Amanda and Tori were in this afternoon. Tori was afraid she was pregnant again."

"Did you recommend the Pill?"

"I recommended abstinence, but I don't think she was listening."

"Once that genie's out of the bottle . . ."

"I know, I know." She dragged her fingers through the riot of curls and waves that served as a hairstyle. "I recommended the Pill and a condom."

"The suspenders-and-belt system of birth control."

"No," she snapped, "the birth control and AIDS system of survival."

He met her eyes. "What's wrong, Elly?"

"You know what's wrong."

"No, I don't think I do. Talk to me."

She met his eyes. "Did we use protection Sunday night?"

"I—" He stopped cold. "Jesus," he said, "I don't remember."

"Don't look so guilty. I was there, too, and I don't remember, either."

They had both been tested within the last year as part of a local drive to help erase the stigma surrounding AIDS testing, so that wasn't an issue.

"Are you on the Pill?" he asked.

She laughed out loud. "The only reason for me to be on the Pill would be to help keep the pharmaceutical companies in business." And there was the matter of the small blood clot in her left leg two years ago that warned her away from hormonal solutions. She looked at him. "Besides, you had a vasectomy."

"No, I didn't."

"Very funny. I remember exactly when you had it. I was leaving that afternoon for the seminar in Denver and you had a three o'clock with Rosenberg up in Bangor."

"It didn't happen."

Your blood really could run cold. Who knew?

"What do you mean, it didn't happen?"

"It didn't happen. I canceled."

"You canceled? Why did you cancel?" *Why didn't you tell me?*

"Rosenberg asked a few questions about my motivation and ended up suggesting that I postpone the procedure."

"Tell me you're joking."

"Wish I could, Elly, but that's the truth."

Neither one of them needed to have it spelled out for them.

"I can't believe this is happening," Ellen said, sinking down onto one of the hard-backed chairs he had been sleeping on.

"Nothing's happened yet," he said, resting a hand on her shoulder. "The odds are against it."

Her laugh held a tinge of hysteria. "You sound like every sixteen-year-old girl who ever passed through my office. It can't happen the first time. . . . It can't happen if you're standing up. . . . It can't happen when you have your period or you're nursing or a thousand other reasons, but it happens anyway. It happens all the time, every single day, to thousands of women who didn't think it could possibly happen to them."

He crouched down in front of her until their eyes were on a level. "I'm in this with you."

"I know," she said.

He hesitated for a moment. "You're still within the seventy-two-hour window for more extreme forms of birth prevention."

She shook her head. "I'm not a good candidate, remember?"

"Then we'll wait and see where we stand."

"On quicksand."

"You haven't lost your sense of humor."

"They say it's the last thing to go."

"We'll get through this," he said, stroking her hair with a gentle touch she felt straight through to the soles of her feet.

"I hope you're feeling lucky enough for both of us."

"Always," he said. "We're friends, remember?"

She remembered. She remembered all of it.

They left the hospital together. He waited while she started her car, then he climbed into his Rover, waiting again for her to exit the parking lot before he fell into line behind her. She made a right at the traffic sign. He made a left. She wished the whole town could have been there to see them go their separate ways, but Murphy's Law was in full effect. Live your life like a cloistered Jewish nun, and there was nobody around to bear witness, but kick up your heels for even one second and the whole town turns out with their camcorders.

The night air was cool and scented with pine. When she first arrived in Maine, she had brought with her a boatload of preconceptions about what she would find, and in most cases she wasn't disappointed. It was every bit as beautiful as she had imagined. The coves and harbors were picture-postcard perfect. The towering pines. The lobster shacks and the secluded islands. The odd blend of tourist excess and Down East asceticism that suited her down to the ground. Maybe the accents weren't as over-the-top as she had hoped and the welcome was a tad reserved, but those were small things in an otherwise perfect landscape. Cy had warned her that native New Yorkers never felt truly comfortable beyond the five boroughs—with the exception of Florida, the unofficial sixth borough—and that she would find herself back home on the

Upper West Side before her first year was over. He found it difficult to believe that she considered Shelter Rock Cove home now. He was probably still reeling over her decision to buy a house.

Like Cy, Billy O'Brien had never owned a house, either. He had never owned anything in his life except his music and the clothes on his back. Billy lived the classic life of the traveling minstrel of Irish legend, never staying long enough in any one place to leave a mark behind. Deirdre and Mary Pat's mother had brought up her children in a series of small apartments in a series of cities and towns and done it well with little help from her wandering husband.

She wondered if her own mother had ever dreamed of a home in the suburbs. Maybe a split level in Westchester County or an elegant colonial in one of the Five Towns on Long Island. She knew so little about her mother. Sharon Cooper Markowitz never spoke about her past, never talked about a future. As far as she could tell, her mother's life had begun the day she slipped into a white dress and married Cy beneath the chuppa.

She tried to imagine her mother as a woman of sixty but couldn't. Sharon was forever thirty-six, a beautiful woman who would always be just out of her daughter's reach.

What she wouldn't give now to be able to rest her head in her mother's lap and pour out her worries. This afternoon she had found herself envying Tori Dietrich. Amanda might be a bit of a flake, but she loved her daughter deeply. Tori might not always make the right decision, but there was no doubt that Amanda would be in her corner come what may.

Deirdre and Mary Pat had been lucky that way, too. Their mother had been fierce in her defense of her daughters, doing everything she possibly could to protect them from their father's wandering eye. Jeannie O'Brien had been cheerleader, guardian, and role model all wrapped up in a tiny five-foot-two-inch package of fierce maternal love. She had met Jeannie only once when the woman came to fetch Mary Pat early from one of Billy's summer holidays with his three girls. Billy's wife had been excruciatingly polite to Ellen, but her true feelings had been abundantly clear just the same. Ellen was the outsider, the enemy, the one who didn't belong.

The one who just bought a house but was still looking for a home.

"Oh, no," Deirdre said as she fiddled with the staple gun. "I think I hear Ellen's car."

"Almost finished," he said, stretching the screen taut across the window. "I want you to put two staples right down there in the left-hand corner."

She positioned the staple gun. "There?"

"About a quarter-inch to the right . . . okay . . . right there!"

She squeezed the trigger. "Wow! That thing has some kickback."

He gave her a look over his shoulder. "If you can lug that harp around, you can handle a staple gun. I need two more . . . over there near my left thumb . . . Hey, not too close. . . . Okay, right next to each other. . . . There you go."

It wasn't rocket science, but Deirdre felt a sense of accomplishment just the same. At least now the first thing Ellen saw when she climbed out of her Cruiser wouldn't be a broken window courtesy of Stanley, the escape artist. The break-in had turned out to be a break-out instead. Apparently Stanley had thrown his weight against the garage window and landed in the hydrangea bushes. They followed the trail of broken blossoms down across the driveway to the steps that led down to the beach, where they found Stanley cavorting in the surf. At the moment Stanley was sitting in the driver's seat of Scott's truck, probably contemplating a getaway.

"She's pulling into the driveway," Scott said. "Want me to take off?"

"No! I want you to protect me."

"She has a temper?"

"We'll find out."

She heard the sound of Ellen's footsteps crunching across the gravel.

Then silence.

Then the sound of her footsteps walking away.

She darted off after her sister. "Ellen! Ellen, wait! I can explain."

The woman walked faster than Deirdre could run.

"Was I robbed?" Ellen called over her shoulder.

"No, you weren't robbed."

"Was anyone hurt?"

"We're fine."

"And Stanley's okay?"

"Stanley's fine."

"Good. I'll see you in the morning."

Ellen dashed up the front steps. A second later the door clicked shut behind her.

"She's mad?" Scott appeared behind Deirdre.

"I have no idea." Her voice broke on the last word. "Oh, damn. How stupid is this." A broken screen and a curt sister shouldn't bring a grown woman to tears.

"You two don't really know each other very well, do you?"

She sniffled and shook her head. "It shows, does it?"

"Go in and talk to her."

"You heard her. She said she'll see me in the morning."

"I have four sisters," Scott said. "She doesn't mean it. Trust me."

"And I have another sister you've never met and believe me, if she said it, she'd mean it."

They walked back down the driveway to his truck and opened the door so Stanley could come out.

"C'mon, Stan," Deirdre said, stifling a yawn. "We've all had enough excitement for one night."

Stanley's tail thumped against the upholstery. He didn't move an inch.

"Okay, pal," Scott said, scratching the dog behind the left ear. "Fun's over for tonight. You'd better do what she says."

Stanley studied Scott for a moment, then leaped from the truck, tail wagging wildly.

"Thank you for everything," Deirdre said as she clutched Stanley's collar to keep him from running back down to the beach. "I doubt if you expected to spend your evening repairing a window for a total stranger."

"Glad I could help."

She was almost used to the awkward silence that seemed to blossom between them every time they said goodbye. She had the crazy urge to fling herself in his arms and plant a big kiss on his mouth. That would loosen him up and get them over these uncomfortable leave-takings. A few years ago she would have done it with no regard for the consequences. His reaction would have been secondary to the momentary buzz that came with doing the unexpected, to seeing the look of surprise on his face when she broke the rules.

She could still do it. He wouldn't stop her. He might even like it. Maybe he would kiss her back, pulling her closer to him so she could feel the heat rising from his body.

And then what? That one perfect moment would be followed by moments so utterly imperfect that you ended up wishing you had never set the whole damn thing in motion.

She settled instead for good night.

Twelve

Ellen was still awake when Deirdre came to bed. She had been lying there listening to Stanley's snoring, wondering how on earth her life could have changed so completely in such a short span of time. If somebody had told her last week that in the space of three nights she would share beds with Hall Talbot, her younger sister, and a one-hundred-fifteen-pound dog of dubious origin, she would have calculated the odds as significantly higher than her chances of winning the lottery.

And she would have been wrong.

"You don't have to tiptoe around, Deirdre," she said into the moonswept room. "I'm awake."

"Sorry," Deirdre said. "I didn't mean to wake you."

She angled herself up on one elbow and pushed her hair off her face. "You didn't. I can't sleep."

Deirdre stripped off her floaty top and tossed it onto the bed where it drifted across the sleeping Stanley. "Did you try warm milk?" she asked as she skimmed off her faded jeans.

"I'd rather stay awake for the next ten years."

Deirdre stripped down to her skin, then shimmied into the enormous T-shirt she liked to sleep in. "Scott fixed the window," she said, stifling a yawn. "It's good as new."

"Do I want to know how it happened?"

"No, but I might as well tell you: Stanley made a jail break."

"Through the garage window?"

"Impressive, huh?"

"I'm not sure that's the word I'd use."

"I know you're probably wondering how you'll be able to keep him safe while I'm up in Bar Harbor, but I swear to you I'll figure something out."

She could almost see her nerves shredding, one by one. "You're telling me Stanley's going to keep breaking out?"

Deirdre sat on the foot of the bed next to the sleeping dog. "Sounds like this might be the right time for a little creative obfuscation."

"Yes or no."

"Yes, probably, but I'll get it all worked out before I leave on Friday, I swear to you."

Classic Deirdre. Her sister had never been able to see beyond the boundaries of her own immediate needs. "You know what? Stanley is your problem."

"You don't mean that," Deirdre said finally. "You love Stanley."

"I'm fond of him," Ellen said, "but I'm not the one who adopted him."

"I told you how that happened."

"Right," said Ellen. "You saved his life and that's a great thing, but now what?"

Deirdre stroked the dog behind his left ear and he sighed blissfully. "And now he's my dog."

"Your responsibility," Ellen said. "You seem to have forgotten that part of the equation." She was only six months older than Deirdre. Why did it feel like six lifetimes?

"If you don't want to watch him while I'm in Bar Harbor, why didn't you just say so when I still had time to find somebody else?"

"Because I didn't think it through, either. I can't stay home with him all day, Deirdre, and apparently he's not going to be too happy being alone."

"Well, I can't take him with me."

Again, classic Deirdre. Or was it classic Billy O'Brien she

was hearing? Their father had never met an impulse he didn't embrace wholeheartedly, damn the consequences. Okay, so maybe she would have done the same thing in Deirdre's shoes. That wasn't the case. But at least she wouldn't have expected other people to work out the details. Deirdre's desire to save Stanley from being put to sleep was admirable, but Ellen couldn't help wishing her sister had projected herself ahead a week or two before she claimed him as her own.

Stanley sighed another one of his big doggy sighs of pleasure and Ellen's heart melted.

"Maybe he could stay in the yard. God knows it's big enough."

"What if it rains?"

Ellen considered the question. "How about a doghouse? I saw a few for sale at the lumber yard. They might have one big enough for Stanley."

"You wouldn't make him spend the night outside, would you?"

"No, I won't make him spend the night outside. I'll sleep in the doghouse and he can have my bed. How's that sound?"

"Like you wish you were an only child again."

"The thought has passed through my mind."

"Hey, it's not like I blame you or anything. I know you didn't ask to run a hotel for wayward harpers and their delinquent dogs."

"I'm glad you're here, Dee. I'm even glad Stanley is here. But I have obligations to my patients, and they come before anything and everything else." That had been complaint number eight on Bryan's list of reasons why he was breaking their engagement. *You're obsessed with your work, Ellen. . . . You might as well give up your apartment and live at the hospital.*

Maybe that was why she had no furniture to speak of, no drapes, no curtains, no little tchotchkes on the shelves or plants on the windowsills. Her real life was lived at the office, in the delivery room, in the hallway between the OR and the lounge. Home was where she went when she had no other place to go.

Deirdre looked chastened, which wasn't at all what Ellen had intended. Or maybe it was. She was so tired she could barely remember her own name.

"I should have asked before," Deirdre said. "I hope your patient's okay."

Ellen explained the procedure she had performed on Patsy Wheeler. "We're trying to help her maintain the pregnancy as long as possible, but there are no guarantees."

"She has to stay in bed for the next five months?"

"That's the plan right now."

"God."

That familiar silence fell between them. *Look at us,* she thought as Deirdre smoothed her hand down Stanley's muscular back. *We share the same father and we don't even know how to talk to each other.* A weekend in Boston every few years and the occasional phone call didn't add up to very much.

"Don't be angry, Elly, but when I think of your work, all I come up with are a pair of stirrups and a nursery filled with those big smiling babies you see in television commercials."

"Right," said Ellen. "Add a bunny and Bambi and it's a Disney extravaganza."

"See? There you go getting all touchy. I'm not criticizing. I'm just telling you how effortless you make it look." She poked Ellen with one bare foot. "That's a compliment. I wish I'd had a doctor like you when I—" She shook her head and fell silent.

Ellen leaned forward. "When you what?"

"It's no big deal. Forget it."

"Were you sick, Deirdre? Is there something I can help you with?"

"I had an abortion last year," Deirdre said. Her dark blue eyes suddenly filled with tears. "Like I said, it's over. No big deal."

"Oh, honey." Ellen scrambled down toward the foot of the bed and placed a hand on Deirdre's shoulder. "I'm so sorry you had to make that decision alone."

"I wasn't exactly alone," Deirdre said. "Antonio had at least a small part in it."

"But I thought—"

"I know, I know. I thought so, too. But he showed up one day all full of apologies and—" Her shrug told the story. "I thought maybe the second time around would be the charm.

Shows you how smart I am." They had talked about traveling down to South America together or maybe sailing to the Bahamas. Then Deirdre missed a period and the house of cards came tumbling down. "I wasn't looking to get pregnant, but when I first realized I was late I felt . . . I don't know . . . a combination of shocked and scared and happy. I don't think I'd ever felt that happy before. I mean, Antonio had come back into my life and we were talking about a future together and for the first time in my life I thought maybe I was going to get it right. I had all these stupid dreams about what Antonio would say when I told him we were going to have a baby. . . ." She quickly wiped her eyes with the back of her hand while she talked. "You know the kind, where the guy stares at you for a minute like he doesn't know the language and then his face goes all soft and his eyes begin to sparkle like Ricky Ricardo when Lucy tells him she's expecting. He's singing that stupid song about having a baby and scanning the crowd for the lucky woman and all the time it's Lucy sitting there right in front of him."

"We used to love that episode," Ellen said, smoothing her sister's hair off her face. "I remember yelling at the screen, 'It's Lucy, you idiot! It's Lucy!' "

"That's the one. When Ricky looks at her and she nods and it doesn't register and then he looks at her again and—" Her voice caught and she coughed to cover it. "I thought it was the most romantic moment I'd ever seen."

"Don't laugh, but that scene pushed me toward obstetrics over oncology," Ellen said. "I wanted to experience that same feeling every day of my life."

Deirdre looked at her. "I'll spare you the details, but let's just say things were a little different when I told Antonio."

"He wasn't supportive?"

"He was gone before I finished the sentence. Turns out he has a wife and two children in Florida."

"Sounds familiar, doesn't it."

She hadn't meant to say it, but a lifetime of memories lurked behind those words. *Was that what you did when my mother told you she was pregnant, Billy? Did you run back home to Massachusetts and hide behind your wife and daugh-*

ter? It was hardly a coincidence that Deirdre showed up six months after Ellen was born.

Deirdre flinched slightly, but she offered up no defense for either Billy or Antonio.

"Why didn't you call me?" Ellen asked. "I could have helped you." Maybe they weren't the closest family in the world, but she was a doctor. An obstetrician, for God's sake. She would have been able to tell Deirdre everything she needed to know about the choices out there for her. Adoption, abortion, choosing to raise the baby as a single parent—she could have helped guide Deirdre through the maze. She did it every day of her life for other people. If only she could have been there to do it for her sister.

"Thanks," Deirdre said. "I managed."

"Did you tell Mary Pat?"

"And risk excommunication from the family? Not on your life."

"I wish you'd come to me."

Deirdre turned her attention back to Stanley. "Maybe I didn't want you to know I'd screwed up."

"Everyone screws up."

"You don't."

"I told you I slept with Hall."

"So?"

"So I screwed up."

"You made a mistake, but you didn't screw up. If you'd slept with him and didn't use protection, then I'd say you screwed up."

"Like I said . . ."

"Very funny."

"Not funny at all."

"You're serious?"

"As a home pregnancy test."

Deirdre peered at Ellen through the darkness. "Do you think you're—"

"Probably not." She hesitated. "Of course not." If only she sounded more certain.

"When will you know for sure?"

"Two weeks," Ellen said. "Not that I think there's anything to worry about." *Two long weeks.*

"No offense, but how in hell did you of all people forget to use protection?"

It was too late to say it was none of Deirdre's business. They wouldn't even be having this conversation if she had been able to keep her big mouth shut.

"I thought he'd had a vasectomy, but I was wrong."

"There's more to worry about these days than pregnancy."

Didn't she have this conversation yesterday with sixteen-year-old Tori Dietrich? "We were both tested awhile ago." And they had both been celibate since. She felt a rush of empathy for all of her patients who had endured her relentless grilling. It wasn't much fun being on this side of the discussion.

"And what's wrong with *him*? I suppose he forgot he didn't have a vasectomy, too."

"Deirdre, it wasn't the way you're making it sound."

"Does he know you're worried?"

"He knows."

"And—?"

"He says he'll be there for me no matter what."

A long silence fell between them.

"You always were the lucky one," Deirdre said.

"Katie Glassberg delivered her daughter," Hall said as he passed Ellen in the hallway two mornings later. "Eighteen inches long, six pounds eleven ounces, great lungs."

"Katie's okay?"

"Beaming," he said.

"How about the father?"

"He didn't show," Hall said.

"Did she call him?"

"I didn't ask. Her mother and sisters were there and a couple of friends."

"Good," Ellen said. "At least she wasn't alone."

"Lindstrom?" he asked, gesturing toward Room 2.

"She asked for an epidural when she hit two centimeters."

"No surprise there," said Hall. "I've seen her ask for painkiller during a consultation."

Ellen laughed. "Tedesco called. She was sent home with

Braxton-Hicks yesterday, but she thinks this might be the real thing."

"It's the full moon," Hall said. "Babies love being born during the full moon."

"The full moon was three days ago," Ellen said as she continued on her way to the delivery room. "I call this a downright epidemic."

He was still grinning when he reached the office.

"You're looking cheerful," Janna observed as he slipped into his lab coat.

"Katie Glassberg delivered her daughter," he said, checking his pocket for his glasses.

Janna beamed at him in delight. "A blonde like her mother?"

"Bald," Hall said with a laugh.

"Not even some peach fuzz?"

"Like a billiard ball."

Janna hurried off to write out a card to Katie and her new daughter while he headed into his office. At least Janna had stopped giving him the fish eye every time he spoke to her. She still cast the occasional speculative glance Ellen's way, but even that was beginning to wane. Gossip in Shelter Rock seemed to have the life span of deli cold cuts. By the end of a week both had pretty much run their course. The appearance of Ellen's flamboyant harp-playing sister Deirdre and her giant dog had gone a long way toward diverting attention away from the juicy topic of sex to the even juicier topic of other people's families.

He remembered it well, that feeling of being at the center of every conversation that went on in town. He had grown up with it, worn it like a medal, carried it before him like a shield. *Poor kid,* they used to say. *How can James and Felicia leave him alone that way?* You wouldn't think the only child of one of the wealthiest men in town would end up being pitied, but life never seemed to follow the script. His parents were a terrific couple, great dinner companions, swell letter writers, the kind of people you'd love to meet on a cruise ship and exchange home phone numbers with. They were warm and witty, generous to a fault, the most loyal friends you could ever ask for. Unfortunately they were also the lousiest parents on the planet. Not unkind. Never intentionally cruel. Just clue-less.

"We weren't planning on having children," they used to say to anyone who would listen. "If we hadn't drunk so much champagne at the Hawthornes' anniversary party, Hall wouldn't be here at all."

On good days he was their little surprise. On not-so-good days he was the biggest mistake of their lives.

He tried to capture their interest with his accomplishments, offering up A-plus report cards and awards of excellence to the gods of parental indifference. He lettered in track, bulked up enough to play quarterback on the football team, won a full scholarship to Harvard Medical School, then relinquished it to someone who needed the money instead.

His parents smiled absently and murmured, "That's nice, dear," then booked their semiannual cruise to Bermuda.

He had made plenty of mistakes in his life, but at least he had managed to get it right with his daughters. He had no patience with the latest slang or the newest music. He had issued a global ban on tattoos and body piercing and—God help them all—thongs on the beach. His two oldest girls said he was stuck back in the twentieth century and needed to catch up with the times, but they laughed when they said it in a way that told him he was on the right track. He knew how to love, how to be there when they needed him, how to listen when they wanted to talk, and how to talk when they needed to listen. And he could recite *Green Eggs and Ham* from mem-ory.

He had done it well four times and considered himself blessed to have four bright and beautiful daughters. That was enough glory for any man.

But what if Ellen turned out to be pregnant? What if they had made a baby together Sunday night in his big wide bed with the moonlight spilling across her lovely face? What if—?

Hell, no.

Five would be pushing his luck. You didn't need a degree in math to figure that one out. Five healthy, happy children would be tempting the gods.

If there was one thing he had learned along the way it was that the gods rarely asked your opinion before they pulled a fast one on you. Every time you thought you were getting a handle on things, leave it to them to throw a banana peel in your path.

The timing was wrong. The situation couldn't be worse. The last thing they needed was for Ellen to be pregnant with his child.

Which, considering the gods and their perverse sense of humor, meant that nine months from now they just might give Shelter Rock Cove a whole lot more to talk about.

Thirteen

By Thursday morning Stanley's interest in their twice-daily walks into town had dimmed considerably. He sat down, quite without warning, in front of the town library, and Deirdre quickly discovered that when a one-hundred-and-fifteen-pound dog decides to make a statement, his human had no choice but to listen. Fortunately Stanley was clever as well as stubborn. The doughnut shop was less than twenty feet away, and Deirdre managed to scare up fifty cents from the depths of her crocheted hobo bag to buy him a raspberry jelly.

"We're splitting this," she said as she broke the doughnut into two pieces. "You're getting away with murder as it is."

Stanley inhaled his half. Deirdre wasn't too far behind. Ellen's fridge was the culinary equivalent of a cloistered monastery: nonfat milk, bottled spring water, containers of yogurt without the sugary fruit preserves at the bottom, which was the whole point of eating yogurt in the first place.

"Okay, Stan," she said in what she hoped was a firm, masterful voice. "Let's go." She knew the dog preferred romps on the beach to these leashed strolls along Shore Road, but what better way to mask her ulterior motive than behind Stanley's cardiovascular health. Her car was still being held hostage in the repair shop, and this gave her a casual, spontaneous reason to pop in and see how they were faring in the search for parts.

Jack, the owner, grinned as she and Stanley approached the bay where he was working on the biggest, reddest truck she had ever seen in her life. That grin had grown progressively wider as the week progressed. He gestured toward the back room. "He's in the office. I promise I'll knock before I barge in."

She assumed that was mechanic's humor and smiled pleasantly. There was a reason girlie calendars hung from the walls in every auto mechanic's shop from Maine to California, some connection between gas fumes and testosterone. Not that she had noticed any pinups visible on the walls of Shore Coast Auto Repair, but that didn't mean they weren't there.

Her Hyundai still occupied the last bay, forlorn and forgotten. It took all of her willpower to keep from scrawling FIX ME in the thick layer of dust that graciously obscured the score of dings and dents that she liked to believe gave the car character.

Scott was hunched over the desk in Jack's office. The phone was wedged between his shoulder and ear while he clicked his way from one Web site page to another. She rapped on the molding and stepped inside.

"I hope you have some good news for me," she said as Stanley led her into the small room. The smell of motor oil hung heavy in the air. It was probably catnip to men, but it made her long for a bubble bath.

He motioned her to wait. "A master cylinder . . . yeah . . . no . . . yeah, that's right . . . a Hyundai . . . you're sure . . . maybe you could . . . yeah, that's the way it goes, alright. Thanks for your help." He hung up the receiver and turned to her. "Another dead end."

"Please tell me you're kidding."

"I told you it was going to be a bitch."

"Yes, but I thought that meant it might take a day or two to locate the part."

"Maybe it would take a day or two to find the part for a ninety-six or ninety-seven. We're talking ten years older than that. I should quit calling parts places and start calling graveyards."

She glanced out the window at his disreputable-looking truck. "And I suppose that's a Caddy you're driving."

"Auto graveyards," he said. "Damn. I probably should have started there. I might have saved a hell of a lot of time."

"I have to be in Bar Harbor tomorrow afternoon or I'll lose my job. And in case I didn't spell it out before, that's not an option I can live with." Especially if he expected to get paid for the work he hadn't done yet.

"You'll get there."

"How? I can't afford to rent a car. My sister needs her Cruiser. Unless you plan on driving me up there, I'd better start walking."

"So I'll drive you."

"Not funny," she said, moving Stanley away from the used coffee cup he was investigating. "Just fix my car."

He settled that unreadable gaze of his on her, and she resisted the urge to look away. Let him be the one to break the connection this time.

"You could always give me a loaner," she said, their gazes still locked.

There it was again, that now you see it now you don't grin that almost made her forget what she was doing there.

"The loaner needs a new tranny. It hasn't been high priority."

She started to laugh. "Annie said this was the best auto repair shop in town."

"We're the only auto repair shop in town. Best, worst, we've got it all covered."

Stanley snuffled his way around the desk and pushed Scott's hand with his nose.

"He's crazy about you," Deirdre said, smiling as Scott awkwardly patted the top of the dog's head. "I told you Stanley was a pussycat."

"The dog's not going to Bar Harbor, too, is he?"

Her smile widened. "Fix my car by tomorrow morning and it won't matter."

Scott heard Jack call out a goodbye to Deirdre and steeled himself for the inevitable.

Five . . . four . . . three . . . two . . . one!

"She's hot for you," Jack said from the doorway. "I'm telling you I know the signs."

"She wants her car fixed," Scott said, turning his attention back to the computer.

"Showing up here twice a day like clockwork isn't going to get it done any faster."

"Time's running out. She's supposed to be up in Bar Harbor tomorrow to start a new job."

"She better have an extra set of wheels hidden someplace because there's no way that heap'll be ready to roll tomorrow."

"You're a real optimist," Scott said over his shoulder. "No wonder Susan—" *Shit. Shut up while you still have a job.* Talk about sports, cars, and politics, but stay the hell away from marriage. Susan's outburst the other night at Cappy's. Jack's bewilderment. Deirdre's curiosity. His own deep embarrassment. Stay away from all of it. He knew how it felt to be on the bad end of a marriage in trouble, and he wouldn't wish it on a dog, much less a good guy like Jack.

"I've been meaning to say something about the other night."

"You don't have to say anything," Scott said. *I'll work free for a month if you promise you won't say anything.*

"She's not usually like that."

"Hey, you don't owe me any explanations."

"She hasn't been herself lately."

Tell me something the entire town doesn't know. He considered launching himself through the monitor, but with his luck Jack would follow him.

"I think it's menopause."

That tore it. He was going headfirst through the monitor.

He felt Jack's eyes boring a hole through the back of his shirt. The guy was waiting for him to say something, and all he could think of was the way Susan had looked when the two doctors headed off to the hospital and left the rest of them to split their lobster between them. She had been staring at Hall Talbot like he had hung the moon, the way Megan used to look at him when they were just beginning to see a future rising from the heat.

Yeah, he knew that look. He had felt its power once, a long time ago. And he knew where it could lead.

The guy had big trouble, bigger even than he probably knew, and there was no way in hell Scott was going to say one damn thing about it. Jack would have to find out for himself.

"There she goes again," Claudia said as Deirdre strolled past the window of Annie's Flowers. "I've never seen anyone spend so much time walking a dog in my entire life." The young woman waved and she waved back reluctantly. "And I can't count how many times a day she pops into Jack's. Doesn't she know how to use a telephone?"

Her former daughter-in-law reached for the wire cutters. "Maybe she's worried about her car. She has that job up in Bar Harbor waiting for her and she needs transportation."

"She's certainly made herself at home around here," Claudia observed. "She was actually waiting on the sidewalk for me to open up yesterday morning."

Ellen Markowitz's sister, who was inexplicably named O'Brien, had made a habit of dropping in for a little chitchat during her rambles. She seemed pleasant enough, if a bit less polished than her older sister, but there was something about the young woman that worried her.

"Did you see that ridiculous outfit she was wearing today?" She nipped an inch off a stem of delphinium, held it up to the arrangement she was working on, then nipped off a little bit more. "You could practically see through her blouse."

"So don't look," Annie said. "I love the way she dresses. I think it suits her."

"She looks like she shops at a thrift shop."

"Kind of funky and feminine. I like it."

"I thought harpists were delicate and refined."

Annie sighed and tossed the wire cutters down on the worktable. "Claudia, we both know you don't care if Deirdre wears a hoopskirt and a thong. What is this really about?"

"I think Jack is having an affair."

Annie's laughter exploded into the room.

"I'm glad you see some humor in the situation, Anne."

"Jack?" Annie said, wiping her eyes with her forearm. "Are we talking about the same Jack Aldrin who worships the ground Susan walks on?"

"That little redhead is throwing herself at him, and he's just the right age to feel flattered."

"Let me put your fears to rest. If Deirdre is flirting with anyone, it's Scott."

"Scott?" Claudia frowned. "That silent young man Jack hired?"

"That *gorgeous* silent young man Jack hired. I saw the sparks fly the second they met."

"So you don't think she's set her cap for Jack?"

Annie's lovely eyes twinkled with amusement. "No, I don't think she's set her cap for Jack. I don't think she knows Jack is on this planet."

"Well, something's wrong just the same." She lowered her voice so that gossipy Sweeney woman from the Artists' Co-op couldn't hear her. "I was told there was some trouble between them the other night at Cappy's."

"Susan and Jack?" Annie's eyes narrowed. "Where did you hear that?"

"Charlie told me," Claudia said. "He said his mother burst into tears at the table when Jack said something to that Deirdre person."

"That's not the way I heard it," Annie said. "Sam bumped into Jack at the bank, and Jack said he was in the doghouse for something he said about Ellen."

"Ellen?" Claudia began plucking blossoms from the delphinium.

"Not really Ellen," Annie amended. "He remarked on how happy Hall has been since Ellen joined his practice, and Susan—"

"Burst into tears."

Annie nodded. The two women locked eyes over the deep blue mass of delphinium piled on the worktable. Neither one said a word. The truth spoke loud enough for both of them. Twenty-five years ago Claudia would have been on her knees in church thanking God that her daughter had finally exhibited the good sense to fall in love with Hall Talbot. Now all she could do was pray he didn't love her back.

*   *   *

"J have good news and better news," Ellen said as she entered Patsy Wheeler's hospital room.

"I'll take the better news first," Patsy said. She was looking much healthier than she had in the emergency room a few days ago. Her color had improved and at least a little of her regular sparkle had returned.

"Where's Doug? He'd like to hear this, too."

"I forced him back to work today. No sense the two of us being trapped in here."

Ellen grinned and sat down on the side of the bed. "He was driving you crazy."

"Big time," Patsy said with the first laugh Ellen had heard from her in days. "His boss said to take all the time he needed, but . . ." She rolled her eyes and let the sentence fade into laughter.

"Hope you can track him down out there in the field, because you're going home today!"

Patsy's whoop of joy had Ellen plugging her fingers in her ears in mock horror. "Tell me it's not the meds making me hear things! Am I really going home?"

Ellen checked her clipboard. "The ambulette will be here to pick you up sometime after two o'clock."

"Oh, God," Patsy said, some of her excitement dimming. "How much will that set me back?"

"I had Janna check and your insurance has preapproved the entire amount."

"You weren't kidding when you said you had good news for me. I'm going home and my insurance will pay for the ambulette." Her eyes glistened with happy tears. "You don't know how much I—"

"Yes, I do," Ellen interrupted, "and now it's up to you to follow instructions to the letter." She handed her a packet of information in a brown envelope. "Instructions, phone numbers, guidelines. I want you to promise to call me no matter how small the problem is. That's part of the deal."

"I'll call you if I think it's serious."

"No." Ellen fixed the woman with a no-nonsense look. "You call and I'll decide if it's serious."

"I don't want to be a pest."

"Be a pest," Ellen said. "I like pests. Pests deliver healthy babies." She stood up. "Trish from Social Services will be in to see you before you leave. She told me the hospital bed arrived yesterday, and Doug had a place cleared for it in the master bedroom."

"He even set up a network so I can use my laptop and connect with the office. I can't afford to lose my job with the baby coming."

"But easy does it," Ellen warned. "Your first priority is bringing that baby as close to term as possible."

Patsy was vice president of Shelter Rock Cove's oldest bank, a position that held a great deal of responsibility and prestige. She was accustomed to making things happen, to bending life to suit her needs. The business of conception was the first time that her considerable drive bumped up against a situation she couldn't influence by the sheer force of her will. The difficult pregnancy had further undermined her self-confidence, which made her tend to overdo anything and everything. Getting Patsy to understand the gravity of the situation and the need to follow instructions to the letter was an ongoing proposition. It was only normal to relax a little once the crisis passed, but Patsy's crisis was one that would be with her every single day until she delivered a healthy baby.

Ellen left Patsy in the capable hands of one of the floor nurses, then checked in on two postop patients who were both making quick recoveries. She had office hours from one until five, which gave her an hour to grab a bite and write up a few notes.

She was halfway across the parking lot when she heard Hall call her name.

"Do you have a few minutes?" he asked. "I need to talk to you."

She started to say what she had said a number of times before over the last few days but caught herself. The look in his eyes brought her up short.

"I was heading over to the diner for a quick lunch."

"I'll come with you."

The protest died in her throat.

Five minutes later they were seated opposite each other at

the Chowder House, a small diner on the outskirts of town. They didn't need to order. It was Thursday and Thursday meant split-pea soup and grilled-cheese sandwiches.

"What's wrong?" she asked after Glenna deposited two glasses of water, then walked away. "You look like hell."

"Karen Blaiser," he said. "Stage IV ovarian cancer."

Ellen felt as if she had been kicked in the midsection by a team of horses. "Oh God, but she—" Her voice caught the words and wouldn't let them go. Karen was a twenty-three-year-old med student who was engaged to marry Jim West-gaard, the hospital's chief pediatric resident. The wedding was set for the Fourth of July weekend, little more than a month away. "Does Jim know?"

Hall shook his head. "Karen's coming in for results this afternoon, and I—" It was his turn to stumble into a wall of emotion. "She shouldn't be alone when she hears this."

"Call Jim," Ellen said. "Make sure he'll be with her."

"That's crossing the line. Legally he isn't—"

"You can't call her parents. She's over twenty-one, and besides, they're down in Florida."

"If I call and tell her to bring someone with her, she'll know."

"That isn't necessarily a bad thing. You'd be giving her time to prepare for what you're going to tell her."

"And she'd still be alone."

"You could call her best friend."

He dragged his hand through his thick silvery-gold hair and met her eyes. "Jim's her best friend."

They fell silent as Glenna deposited their grilled-cheese sandwiches and bowls of soup in front of them.

"They tell you in med school that it stops hurting so much after you're in practice awhile."

"They lie," he said with a rueful smile that tugged at her heart. "It still hurts like hell."

"It's not supposed to. The smart ones learn how to com-partmentalize."

"You didn't."

"Maybe I'm not so smart." She tried to force an answering smile but couldn't quite bring it off. "I'm the one who left the big city to work in some little town in Maine."

"You'd be driving a Mercedes if you'd stayed where you were."

"My dad gave me a Mercedes when I turned twenty-one, but I wasn't terribly impressed. I traded it in for a Jeep."

"I'm glad."

"So am I," she said.

They were, of course, not talking about cars at all.

He reached for the salt as she reached for the pepper. Their fingers touched, then intertwined. A powerful one-two punch of lust and tenderness sent her reeling. She could handle either emotion on its own, but the combination overwhelmed her heart and made it impossible for her to pull her hand away. The diner was crowded. They were far from invisible, sitting there in the third booth from the door. This wasn't how you nipped gossip in the bud. This was how you made more.

Wrong man. Wrong woman. Wrong time. Wrong place.

Wrong everything.

It had no business feeling so right.

Fourteen

Before she became a harper herself, Deirdre had entertained an entire series of fantasies about harps and the women who played them. The women were all beautiful, ethereal beings who floated from venue to venue where their harps, perfectly tuned and magically transported, awaited the golden touch of their talented, perfectly manicured fingers.

Nobody ever mentioned the fact that harps were unwieldy, mercurial, and sensitive to changes in light and temperature, as demanding of time and attention as a first-class diva.

Harps required daily tuning. Depending on the weather, the amount of play, the phases of the moon—or so it sometimes seemed to Deirdre—harpers often found themselves going through the tuning process with greater frequency. You tuned before a performance. You tuned after transporting the harp back home again. You tuned if someone looked cross-eyed at the harp.

She fed Stanley after they returned from the morning's unsuccessful reconnaissance mission, then settled down for some much-needed practice. She plugged in her electronic tuner and set about the task of bringing each string to the perfect pitch and tone. She still cringed when she thought about her impromptu concert the other night. Hall Talbot's little girls had been so excited at the prospect of actually touching a harp that she had paid only the most cursory attention to tuning it.

Still that hadn't seemed to hurt her music any. She had played with an enthusiasm she hadn't felt in a while, and the crowd in Ellen's living room had responded. Those were the times you lived for, when the synergy created between musician and audience lifted both to a higher plane. If only there was some way to bottle the magic for days like today when she needed something to help her push past the insecurities that took over when she wasn't looking.

She had neglected her music the last few days. Nighttime was usually her best time, the time when she was able to let go of her worries and allow the music to seep into her bones. But Ellen's hours were long and unstructured enough as it was. She didn't want to do anything to disturb her sister's sleep. Not that Ellen had complained about anything. She was far too polite for that. She always seemed pleased to see Deirdre, concerned about her welfare, but the sudden burst of sisterly intimacy they had shared the other night had long since disappeared.

And was it any wonder? You didn't drop a bomb like that on a sister you barely knew. She should have kept her big mouth shut about Antonio and the abortion. She had never told anyone about it, not Mary Pat or her mother or any of the acquaintances who passed for friends.

Yet the truth had spewed across Ellen's bed, raw and painful as an open wound. Her emotional radar was acutely tuned to censure, both real and imagined, and there had been nothing but concern in Ellen's voice. Nothing but affection in her eyes. For a second she had found herself wishing she had turned to her sister for help, but then reality stepped in to remind her that Ellen hadn't a clue what it was like out there in the regular world.

Ellen had never had to worry about money a day in her life. She didn't know how it felt to worry about the landlord showing up on your doorstep, demanding last month's rent. She had never watched as the repo man hauled her car back to Auto City or had the phone service and electricity turned off because she couldn't afford to pay the bill. If Ellen was pregnant, she would find a way to handle things, a way that included the best medical care, a private room in the hospital, a baby nurse, day care, Harvard when the kid turned eighteen, and the father of her child.

Deirdre had had nothing to offer a child. She had no medical insurance, no apartment, no steady job, and no prospects. Antonio had disappeared back into the safety of the family she hadn't known he had, leaving her with a baby who deserved better than the load of nothing she had to offer.

So on a sunny May morning so beautiful it made her weep, she made what seemed the only decision possible at the time, and now, almost two years later, she regretted it only every other waking moment.

No, this wasn't something Ellen could ever understand. Ellen's decisions were based on lofty medical and philosophical considerations while Deirdre's decisions were usually based on money. Her lack of it, to be precise.

One of the many reasons she had gravitated toward the lever harp as opposed to the concert pedal harp was a question of economics. Not only couldn't she afford the five-figure cost of the instrument, she couldn't afford a vehicle large enough to carry it from gig to gig. Before she purchased her Hyundai, she had tried loading her harp into the backseat, and it was only when that task had been accomplished that she forked over the money.

She wished somebody had told her early on just how much outlay was involved in establishing yourself as a harper of note. As usual, talent was only a small part of the picture. Harpers required suitably ethereal outfits that were also practical. There was nothing ladylike about wedging a harp between your knees. You needed long flowing skirts, elegant trousers, the right combination of style and functionality. You needed formal but understated costumes for weddings and receptions; tailored outfits for corporate appearances; hippie-chick threads for the folk festivals and coffeehouses. She was surprised to discover that vulgar considerations like finances could figure so prominently in an artist's chosen path, but that was one of the many things Deirdre learned when she turned away from singing the blues and decided to make a go of her new career as a harper. Performing in clubs had required nothing more than her voice, something interesting to wear, and the appropriately love-worn persona common to blues singers. She had all three of those commodities in spades. She even had talent. Too bad the combination had never equaled success.

Early in her career she spent an inordinate amount of time berating God for the record deal that didn't pan out, the concert gig that fell through, the endless stream of disappointments. It took awhile, but she finally realized God either wasn't listening or maybe had other plans for her, plans that apparently didn't include the need for tax shelters or limousines.

She had tried very hard to steer clear of the Celtic harp because of its obvious connection to Ireland. Irish music was her father's territory. Let him keep the toora-looras and the smiling eyes. Let him spend his life singing "Danny Boy." She decided early on that she would quicker embrace the glockenspiel than anything so uniquely identified with the heritage Billy O'Brien had parlayed into something approaching a career. She had a deep affinity for Celtic music, but she buried it beneath layers of rock and cabaret, jazz and blues. Anything that would pay the bills and keep her far away from Billy's venues.

How strange it was now to move in some of the same circles, to meet people who had grown up with her father, people who had known some of her family's secrets before she did. Ellen's mother, Sharon, had been part of his world for a long time. A singer with a classically trained voice, Sharon Cooper had joined up with a group that often traveled with Billy in the late sixties. In Billy's version of the story he had been away from home for a long time. . . . He and her mother had been having troubles and were on the brink of divorce. . . . Sharon was so young and so vulnerable. . . . She had needed his protection. A load of Irish bullshit meant to explain away his sins.

Her mother claimed Sharon had zeroed in on Billy from the first moment she saw him, moving in on the middle-aged singer with the unshakable confidence of a very young and very beautiful girl who knew she wouldn't be turned away.

Sharon had torn the fabric of the O'Brien family asunder, and only God knew if she had paid for her sins.

Deirdre was far beyond viewing music as some sort of therapy for her inner child. As far as she was concerned, her inner child was on her own. She had returned to Celtic music for purely business reasons, because her days as a not-very-successful blues singer happened to come to an end just as interest in all things Celtic came to the fore.

The celestial music the instrument produced was the result of rigorous attention to the care of both harp and harper. Harp strings snapped. Harmonic curves pulled to the side. Pillars twisted and soundboards developed cracks that only sometimes improved the sound. And the harpers themselves didn't get off any easier. Their bodies took a beating few suspected. Only the music was gentle. Harpers were secretly tough as nails. Maybe that was part of its appeal.

She wasn't sentimental by nature. Her family had seen to that a long time ago. You couldn't maintain a belief in the wonders of love and loyalty when you were raised in a household built by a man who screwed around and a woman who let him get away with it. She often wondered how her mother had managed to put up with his philandering for so long. It was one thing to know your husband took lovers. It was something else again when he brought home his child by one of those lovers and expected you to welcome her into the family because he was feeling guilty.

Not that she wasted a lot of time thinking about the past. The past was what it was and all the pissing and moaning in the world wasn't about to change a second of it.

Right now it was the future that was worrying her. If Scott the Mechanic didn't pull a miracle out of his hat before the day was over she was in big trouble. She couldn't ask Ellen for more help. Leaving Stanley there for the summer was probably pushing the generosity envelope as far as it could go. Besides, Ellen knew what was going on with the car and everything, and so far she hadn't made an attempt to bail her out. It was probably hard for her sister to understand that when she said she had no money left, she meant it. The doughnut she'd shared with Stanley had wiped her out.

There was no doubt that Ellen was making the big bucks.

This hotel-sized house had to cost a bundle, especially with the ocean view and dock. She didn't seem to pay a whole lot of attention to petty cash, either. When she paid for the pizzas the other night, she had stuffed a wad of cash in one of the cutlery drawers in the kitchen. There were some fives and tens in the nightstand. Two twenties in the desk drawer. Ellen probably hadn't a clue how much money she had scattered around the house. You had to have a fair amount of the stuff if it was so easy to lose track.

Deirdre doubted if her sister would even notice if she pocketed half of the cash. Not that she would ever do it, of course, but she would be lying if she didn't admit to feeling more than a little bit tempted. If she had some money, she wouldn't have to worry about whether or not Scott the Mechanic would be able to get the job done. All she would have to do was pick up the phone and call a rent-a-car place and reserve a nice roomy air-conditioned sedan to drive up to Bar Harbor.

Then, of course, God would send down a lightning bolt and strike her dead. Probably right at the moment when she was about to sign a seven-figure contract with Virgin Records to become the first multi-platinum harper.

Okay, so she wasn't going to turn to petty crime to bail herself out of her difficulties. If Scott the Mechanic failed her, she would do something much worse: call her sister Mary Pat and beg.

There was nothing in his medical training that had prepared Hall adequately for the task of telling a vibrant, beautiful young woman that she was going to die.

He had ended up taking Ellen's advice and phoned Karen's fiancé, Jim Westgaard, to ask him to accompany her to the office appointment that afternoon.

Jim cut straight through to the heart of the matter. "That bad?" he asked, the quaver in his voice betraying his emotion.

"I think you should be there," Hall said, knowing Jim would understand the subtext without being told.

So did Karen. He saw it the moment she and Jim stepped into his office. It was in her eyes as he outlined possible protocols to attack further spread of the disease. He recommended an oncologist in Camden, and suggested she might want to see a specialist down in Boston who was getting great results on other women dealing with metastasized ovarian cancer. He had learned a long time ago that nobody—no doctor, no medical professional, no well-meaning friend or relative—had the right to strip a human being of hope. Patients came to their own understanding of their disease in their own time. Or not. He had seen women meet the grim reality of their illnesses head-first, no holds barred. He had watched other women of equal sensitivity and intelligence embark on a rigorous course of chemo and radiation and never once admit there was anything wrong with them right up until the end.

Karen and Jim sat there quietly, holding hands, while Hall finished explaining various options available to them. They looked like survivors of a war, shell-shocked and battle-weary.

"Here's my advice," he said, sliding sheets of information into an envelope for them to absorb later on. "I want you to drive out to the Cineplex at the mall. Pick out the funniest, most mindless movie on the marquee and go see it. If it makes you laugh, sit through it twice. Then I want you to head for whatever restaurant you like best and have a good meal. You don't have to talk about any of this today if you don't want to. Give yourselves a little time to absorb the things I've told you before you start making decisions. There's nothing you can do today that you can't do tomorrow with equally effective results."

They thanked him and left, still holding hands, looking much older than they had an hour earlier. Hall whispered a prayer that love would give them both the strength they would need to deal with what lay ahead.

He went back to his office and sat there, staring down at his appointment book. The prospect of death had never become commonplace to him. He had never acquired the proper distance. Not from pain. Not from life.

"Hall?"

He looked up at the sound of Ellen's voice and saw her standing in the doorway. He motioned her inside.

"I saw Karen and Jim on the elevator," she said as she sat down on the edge of his desk.

He removed his glasses and rubbed his eyes. "I took your advice."

"I'm glad," she said, hugging a thick patient folder to her chest. "It was the right thing to do."

"They held hands through the whole visit." He shook his head. "There I am, telling them that Karen is more than likely going to die before this year is over, and I end up envying them."

"I know." Her voice was little more than a whisper. "What they have together is very special."

"They have it all," he said. "Youth, education, superior skills, ambition, commitment, a soul mate—" His voice broke and he had to clear his throat before he continued. "Every fucking thing you need to be happy."

"Except time," she said softly.

"That's right," he said. "Everything but time."

"Life's too short," she said, "no matter how long it is."

Too short and too unbearably sweet to waste a second on anything less than the real thing.

Ellen's eyes hadn't left his since she entered the room. He could almost feel her absorbing some of his pain, quietly easing his burden the way she had every single day since she came to Shelter Rock Cove. She gave so much, to so many. She was there for her patients, ready to listen to their problems, ease their fears, and celebrate their joys. She gave willingly of her free time to run the teen health support group at the hospital and spearhead the breast cancer awareness coalition she had put together in concert with coalitions from five other counties. He wondered who she turned to when the world was too much for her, who lifted the burden from her shoulders if only for a while. She was so self-assured, so competent, but he knew those strengths concealed a dangerously soft heart.

"I owe you, Markowitz," he said with mock gruffness.

"Damn right you do," she said, mirroring his tone. "And I'm keeping score."

Silver, Janna's assistant, appeared in the doorway. "Your four o'clock is in two, Dr. Talbot, and yours is in five, Dr. Markowitz."

They thanked her and she hurried back to the front desk.

Ellen stood up, adjusted her lab coat, and then started for the door.

"Ellen."

She turned and faced him.

"You're doing okay?" he asked.

"Nothing new to report." Her smile didn't falter.

"I meant what I said the other night."

"I never doubted that for a second."

He opened his mouth to say something, but the words wouldn't come. His emotions were too close to the surface to be trusted. The future was in that room. Was he the only one who could see it?

Her smile was gentle. "I'd better go. It's Ginny Lukinowich in five and she doesn't like to be kept waiting."

His world reassembled itself around him. "And I have Moira Cavanagh in two."

Ellen rolled her eyes. "I'll say a prayer." With a wave of her clipboard, she disappeared down the hall.

If this wasn't the real thing, Hall thought, it was closer than he'd ever come before.

The phone rang at two minutes before five and Deirdre pounced on it.

"Tell me it's good news," she said to Scott the Mechanic. "You're either calling to say I won *Star Search* or my car is ready."

"Listen, I'm sorry. I tried, but I struck out."

Tears burned the inside of her eyelids as she tried not to cry. "You don't understand," she said. "If I don't have the car, I don't have the job, and if I don't have the job I—" Oh, hell. Why should she spell it out for him? If he gave a damn, he would have found a way to fix her car.

"An auto graveyard down near Lincolnville Beach said they might have what we need, but they're not willing to do the heavy lifting."

"What does that mean?"

"It means I'd have to go there and take it out of the car myself."

"That sounds expensive."

"The price they quoted was pretty damn good."

They breathed at each other for a few awkward moments.

"Or I could have it sent up from Portsmouth for three times the price, but that's not going to help you get to Bar Harbor tomorrow."

Some more breathing.

"You might as well order the stupid part," she said after her sniffling had subsided. "I'll need it if I'm ever going to get out of here."

"Uh, listen, how about I drive you up to your job tomorrow afternoon."

She ran through her list of Mechanics I Have Known and Loved, some of whom she was related to, and couldn't come up with a single one who would have offered to do such a thing.

"That's a joke, right?" She must have been looking the other way when the punch line flew past.

"No joke. I said I'd drive you and I'll drive you."

"You said it, but that doesn't mean I believed you."

"What time do you have to be there?"

"Around four."

"I'll pick you up at your sister's around one. That'll give us plenty of time."

"What's this going to cost me?" she asked, thinking about her empty wallet and nonexistent bank account. "I won't have any money until after I start work."

"Just be ready at one."

"But I need to know how much this is going to set me back. If I—"

"One o'clock," he said again, and then hung up.

She barely had a chance to put down the cordless when it rang again.

"That was incredibly rude," she said before he had the chance to say hello. "You don't hang up on someone because you don't feel like answering a question. And, by the way, that was a very important question because if you think you're going to rip me off, I'll—"

"Deirdre?" A very female, very familiar voice. "This is Mary Pat returning your call."

"Oops," said Deirdre. "Sorry. I thought you were Scott the Mechanic."

"What are you doing at the Doctor's house? I thought you had a job in Bar Harbor." A normal sister would have said, *So who is Scott the Mechanic?* Not Mary Pat, the human GPS.

Mary Pat should have gone to law school like their mother wanted her to. She had a natural gift for grilling the truth out of a witness like the poor fool was a red snapper.

"It starts tomorrow."

"I would think you'd want to be there a day early so you can prepare."

Deirdre considered beating her head against the wall but she didn't want to ruin Ellen's paint job. "My car dropped dead. I told you that in my message."

"You haven't told me what you're doing at the Doctor's. I didn't know you two were that close."

"We're very close," she lied with the moral authority of your average two-year-old. "In fact, she's going to care for Stanley while I'm working."

The silence went on a beat too long for Deirdre's comfort. It meant Mary Pat was sifting through the evidence and was about to jump to a conclusion.

"Has she *seen* Stanley yet?"

"Of course she's seen Stanley. She loves Stanley and Stanley loves her. He follows her around like a lovestruck suitor."

"He loves me, too. I have the bruises to prove it."

If she wasn't such a masochist, she would have hung up the phone three sentences ago.

"Did the Doctor get the flowers I sent her? I haven't heard from her—"

"Lighten up, will you, Mary Pat? She just moved in. She'll send you a thank-you note as soon as she finishes delivering babies."

"The sarcasm isn't necessary."

"Listen, Mary Pat, about my car—"

"You're not still driving that relic."

"Actually I am," she said, "and it's not a relic. It's a classic." The fact that God didn't strike her dead on the spot for that statement struck her as a miracle of biblical proportion.

"Anyway, I won't bore you with the details, but the parts haven't arrived yet and I need to rent a car."

"Why don't you borrow one from the Doctor?"

"She only has one."

"Why don't you borrow the money from the Doctor?"

"She said yes to Stanley. I don't want her to think I'm greedy."

"But you don't mind if I think you're greedy."

"Mare, you formed your opinion of me the day I was born. I could win the Nobel Peace Prize and you'd think I'd slept my way to Stockholm."

"Oslo," Mary Pat said. "Not Stockholm."

"You're missing the point." Not to mention mangling a perfectly good punch line.

Mary Pat had perfected the maternal sigh over the years. The one she emitted into the phone carried exactly the right blend of weary love and guilt for maximum destructive effect on the intended victim. Fortunately Deirdre had been inoculated against that particular bit of manipulation years ago by their mother.

"You're almost thirty-five years old. When I was your age, I'd been married sixteen years and had five children."

"You also had hemorrhoids," Deirdre said. "What's your point?"

"The Doctor is your age. Look at all she's accomplished."

"Okay. I see where this is going. The semiannual Why Don't You Get a Real Job campaign is underway. You grew up with Billy. Don't you know what a musician's life is like?"

"All too well," Mary Pat said. "No money. No security. No home of your own. You can keep it."

"Thanks," Deirdre said. "I intend to."

Another silence. Conversation between them broke down more often than her Hyundai.

"If that's it, Mary Pat, I'd better get back to work."

"The money," Mary Pat said. "I've decided to give you the loan you asked for. It's not like you aren't trying. You have a job waiting for you and I understand it might take awhile to get that first check. How does three hundred sound?"

Like the answer to my prayers. A few hours ago she would

have jumped all over the offer, but apparently even she had her limits.

"Don't need it," she said, waving a sad goodbye to the easy way out. "I've made other plans."

"What other plans?"

"I'm not one of your kids, Mary Pat. I don't have to answer."

"Speaking of kids, did I tell you that Shawna was named valedictorian of her graduating class?"

"Cool. When does she graduate?"

"Two weeks ago."

"Why didn't you tell me when I dropped by with Stanley?"

"Why didn't you ask?"

Deirdre knew from experience that they were about to enter an endless loop.

"Mary Pat, I'm sorry to cut this short but Stanley's scratching at the door and it looks like an emergency."

"Go ahead," Mary Pat said. "I'll hold on."

"It might take awhile. I don't want to run up your phone bill."

"No problem. I'm on the cell and we have unlimited minutes."

God, her sister could be a real bitch at times. Hadn't she made it crystal clear she wanted to hang up?

Maybe not.

"Is the Doctor there?"

"She's at the hospital."

"When do you expect her?"

"I don't. Mary Pat, I have to go. I'll call you soon."

"Billy's back."

"What was that?" The receiver had been halfway to its base. So close and yet so far.

"I said, Billy's back. He flew in two nights ago."

"I thought he had decided to live in Ireland." Hadn't that been the point of that big farewell party last year, the one where she had played harp behind Billy and his singing had made her cry? Not one of her favorite memories. That kind of vulnerability was dangerous. She had stopped needing her father's approval years ago, right around the time she realized she was never going to get it. "So what are his plans?"

Was that another one of Mary Pat's studied pauses or had her sister's mind wandered?

"Mare, I asked you a question."

"He'll be staying here with us," Mary Pat said. "Perhaps you and the Doctor might like to drive down and see him."

Deirdre burst into laughter. "I'll phone the rest of the Waltons and see if they'll join us for the family reunion."

"It was just a suggestion," Mary Pat said. "You'll make your own decisions. You always do."

Deirdre's eyes unexpectedly filled with tears. "You never could resist the cheap shot, could you?"

"Your paranoia is showing, Deirdre. I made a suggestion, followed by an observation. You're reading way too much into both."

"Listen, I really have to go." There must be something important she had to do, like fill Ellen's ice-cube trays or French-braid Stanley's tail.

"Call Billy," Mary Pat said. "Not for me, but for yourself."

"Whatever that means."

"Just do it," Mary Pat said. "You won't be sorry."

"Funny thing," she said, "but I already am."

Sorry I answered the phone.

Fifteen

Scott waited until they were locking up to ask Jack for the afternoon off.

"You're driving her to Bar Harbor?" Jack's tone told him exactly what he thought of the idea.

"I figure I'll stop at Lincolnville on the way back and pick up the part."

"You're frigging nuts." Jack wasn't shy about sharing his reasons. Some of them Scott even agreed with.

"I did the run for Barney on Memorial Day. You said I could take comp time when I needed it." He waited while Jack pressed in the alarm code. "I need it tomorrow."

"Don't go telling anyone," Jack said as they started toward the parking lot behind the building. "They'll turn us into a goddamn taxi service. We'll end up doing airport runs and prom nights."

"So you want me to cancel the full-page ad in *The Gazette*?"

"Wiseass."

"I've been called worse."

Jack shot him a curious look. "I wouldn't have figured the harp player was your type."

"She isn't."

"I figured you liked them tall and willowy. More like Ellen, come to think of it."

"I do," he said. "That's exactly what I like." His wife had been almost his height, slender as a willow. Beautiful and ambitious and too fucking good for him.

"So why are you doing it?"

"Because she needs a lift."

"Why doesn't she rent a car?"

"Ask her," Scott said. "Why the third degree?"

Jack's grin was part amusement, part relief. "First time I've seen you look at a woman. I was starting to wonder if maybe you played on the other team."

Scott was still laughing when he pulled into Cappy's parking lot and strolled up to the take-out window. Franny didn't bother to ask what he wanted. She had the lobster roll, slaw, and two cans of Coke waiting for him. She also knew he wasn't a talker. He thanked her, added a healthy tip to the bill, then headed back to his truck.

This used to be his favorite time of day. He couldn't get home fast enough after work. The sound of his son playing in the family room. The sight of his wife slicing tomatoes for the salad. The feeling that this was the one place on earth that truly belonged to him. His family. His home. His sanctuary.

Goddamn it. The whole point was not to think about any of it. To push past it. They were dead. He wasn't. Nothing he did, no magic words, no bargain with the devil, could change that. Every day they retreated a little deeper into memory, a little further out of reach. He had to think now to recall the way his son's hair looked in the sunlight or the sound of his wife's voice when she whispered his name. He thought those things were forever, like a fingerprint or DNA.

Nobody told him that you had to hold on tightly to every memory because one by one they would slip through your fingers when you weren't looking.

Deirdre finally slipped her harp back into its travel case and gave up the ghost. Hall Talbot's two little girls played better than she had this evening. Her thoughts were scattered; her concentration nonexistent. Every sound, from the ocean's relentless roar to Stanley's adenoidal breathing, became a barrier between herself and the music.

Ellen phoned a little bit after seven to say she wouldn't be home until midnight. She sounded terribly apologetic and Deirdre supposed she could have been more gracious about it—her sister delivered *babies*, for God's sake, and everyone knew babies didn't appear on schedule. But she couldn't help being disappointed that Ellen hadn't been able to manage to get home so they could spend some time together before she left for Bar Harbor. Not that she had any right to expect Ellen to jump through hoops and rearrange her schedule. It was just—

Oh, hell. What was the point? Ellen had a life that didn't include a freeloading half sister who showed up just so she could find a dog-sitter. She was feeling sorry for herself. That was all. Mary Pat had an uncanny ability to make her feel like an even bigger failure than she really was.

Somebody should invent a detox program for families. A place where you could go and wash away all of those you're-no-good toxins that found their way into your head the second you walked through the front door . . . or answered the phone. Somehow Mary Pat knew all of her weak spots and zeroed in on them with precision. She was almost thirty-five and still alone. She knew her damn biological clock was ticking. God, they could probably hear it in Idaho. She didn't need her big sister reminding her that everything she had ever tried had turned to shit. All she had to do was look in the mirror, at her ring finger, and at her bank account. No mystery there.

Once upon a time she had thrived on chaos. The crazier things got, the more her adrenaline used to kick in and carry her through. She supposed that was some of her father's genes rearing their heads. She had tried her best to keep them at bay over the years, but that wild Irish blood sometimes couldn't be denied and it invariably led her into trouble. The O'Briens followed their hearts. They always had. With the exception of Mary Pat, the conventional worries of everyday life didn't exist for them. Little things like unemployment, overdue bills, and a romantic life in a permanent state of chaos didn't even register on their radar screens. Life was a series of parties and they had invitations to them all.

Not anymore. She wasn't sure if it was age or disappointment that was taking the bigger toll—or maybe a particularly nasty combination of them both—but lately she found herself longing for all the things she used to mock Mary Pat for valuing so highly. A permanent address. A credit card that wasn't maxed out. Somebody who would be there at the end of the day to tell you his stories and then listen to yours.

She tried to imagine herself in a place like Shelter Rock Cove. She could see the street. She could see the house. She could even see Stanley sitting on the doorstep, waiting for her. But no matter how hard she tried, she couldn't put herself in the picture.

There was probably some Freudian explanation for all of it, something to do with Billy and her mother and who the hell knew what else. She wasn't the analytical sister. Both Ellen and Mary Pat could out-logic her with one lobe tied behind their backs. She relied on instinct, on intuition, for want of a better word. She was one of those people who listened to their gut and made life-altering decisions because they felt right at the moment.

She was glad she was leaving tomorrow. Like her father, she had no talent for domesticity, but at least she had figured it out before she destroyed a family.

Midway between the lighthouse and Cappy's was a cliff known as the Widowmaker. Legend had it that Shelter Rock's only murder had taken place on that spot over one hundred years ago when Amos Cardiff discovered his wife Lilah in the arms of a young sailor named Josiah Wilcox. The two men argued, the argument turned violent, and poor Amos ended up crashing to the rocky shore below.

Next to Captain's Landing, it was the place where Scott felt most comfortable. Now that the weather was quickly growing warmer, he had taken to bringing his take-out supper up there where he could watch the gulls and wait for the sky to darken enough for him to head over to the Landing with his telescope. The gulls recognized him and waited impatiently for him to toss scraps of bread to them. One in particular, larger than the others and bolder, circled his head. He half-expected the bird to swoop down and grab the cup of slaw.

Shelter Rock Cove had turned out to be a good fit. He didn't bump into his life around every corner. He didn't see his son skating on the pond near the town square. He didn't see his wife pushing a cart through Yankee Shopper. He didn't see himself, head bowed in grief, at the memorial service where all that was left to bury were memories.

The sun was setting behind him, casting its fiery glow across the flat surface of the ocean. That calmness was deceptive; it hid a vicious undertow at work around Lighthouse Point that had caused the township to outlaw swimming in the immediate vicinity, which in turn made it less popular to tourists and locals alike.

He polished off his lobster roll, ate the rest of his slaw, then was about to slug down the Coke when he saw two figures approaching from the far end of the beach. It only took him a second to identify them as the harp player and that pony she tried to pass off as a dog. Deirdre wore jeans and a floaty top that seemed to catch every breeze. The dog ran ahead, alternately plunging into the surf, then racing back onto the shore where he shook himself into a frenzy of flying droplets. He found himself grinning at the animal's exploits. Funny how much he liked the dog from a distance.

Stanley tore off after a gull and Deirdre's smoky laugh rose up on the wind. The sound hit him the same way her music had, striking the same chord of emotion he fought to suppress. He knew nothing about her beyond the facts that she liked dogs, played the harp, and was Dr. Ellen's sister. He suspected she got her way more often than not with men, but there was an uncertainty about her that got under his skin. She wasn't above displaying some diva temperament, yet that hadn't stopped him from making an uncharacteristically showy gesture when he offered to drive her up to Bar Harbor tomorrow.

He still didn't know where the hell that offer had come from or why he had pushed her into agreement. So what if she had to figure out a way to get to Bar Harbor tomorrow. What difference was it to him if she made it there on time, late, or not at all?

She bent down near the tide line and picked up a shell, shook it, then held it to her ear. He did that, too, when he was a kid, cupped his hand around a shell and listened to the ocean captured within its folds. She walked on with the shell in one hand and Stanley's leash dangling from the other. Her hair caught the dying light of the setting sun. It tumbled down her back like waves of liquid fire.

She stopped again and tilted her head to the right. She glanced behind her, then toward the rocks that led up to the street. Then she looked straight up and saw him.

Deirdre's heart did a quick *thump-thump* when she looked up and saw Scott the Mechanic watching her from the top of one of those rocky cliffs the Maine coast was famous for. She hesitated a second—she really didn't know why—then waved.

She thought he wasn't going to acknowledge her wave, then he finally lifted his hand in her general direction. It reminded her of the Continental bounce, that disorienting time lag she used to experience whenever she called home the year she spent in Europe.

She doubted even Mary Pat would know the etiquette involved in this situation. She barely knew him. He was just the guy who said he'd fix her car, yet they were heading off together tomorrow for Bar Harbor. Was she supposed to scale the cliff like a mountain goat, then make polite conversation between gasps for oxygen, or should she wait down there on the beach for him to join her? Or maybe she was supposed to assume that a wave offered and reciprocated was more than enough.

"The steps are around back," he called down in what she assumed was a halfhearted invitation to join him.

Or maybe not. She didn't know him well enough to be able to read him. Usually she picked up vibes about a person, strong waves of sensation that either drew her closer or pushed her away. But Scott the Mechanic gave her nothing to work with. He was good to look at, she'd grant him that, but whoever he was beneath the surface remained off-limits.

Which, of course, was fine with her. She didn't need to meet his inner child or analyze his dreams. The fact that he had a car and a driver's license was good enough for her.

She whistled for Stanley. The two of them found the wobbly wooden steps that had been attached by some strange wizardry to jagged rock. Stanley looked up at her as if to say, "Are you nuts?" He was probably right. She drew in a few deep breaths, as much to calm her nerves as to increase her lung capacity, and climbed to the top, leaving Stanley on the beach with his leash looped around the railing.

Scott was sitting near the far edge when she reached the top. She instantly noted the empty soda cans, the crumpled paper bag, and that odd feeling inside her chest returned.

"I didn't know Cappy's delivered," she said as he motioned her to sit next to him.

"I would've saved you a Coke if you'd told me you were coming."

"Cheapskate," she said, sitting down next to him on the narrow rock. "I would've hoped for at least some fried clams."

"Lobster roll," he said, turning back to the horizon. "Maine's PBJ."

"Shows how great a Mainer I'd be. Truth is I hate lobster."

"Nobody hates lobster."

"You're looking at her. I'd rather eat liver."

"I know a place on the way to Bar Harbor that might change your mind."

"I doubt it," she said, then, "So you're really driving me up to Bar Harbor tomorrow?"

"That was the plan."

"You really don't have to do this, you know."

"You have another way to get there?"

"No, but—"

"So I'll do it."

"Why?" The harshness of her one-word question startled her. "I mean, we both know most auto repair shops don't moonlight as cab services."

"I'm going up there anyway to look for the part for the Hyundai. Might as well kill two birds with one stone."

Put that way it didn't sound particularly flattering, but at least it made a degree of sense.

"Well, thank you," she said after a bit. "You saved me from

having to throw myself on the mercy of my wicked older sister."

He looked at her. "Dr. Ellen? She doesn't seem so bad."

"Ellen's terrific," she said quickly. "I'm talking about my other sister, the Wicked Witch of Cambridge, Mass."

"She was willing to lend you some money?"

"For a price." She paused for dramatic effect. "My immortal soul!"

He laughed right on cue, and she felt some of her slipping-away self-confidence begin to slip back. "You don't know how much I needed that."

"Your immortal soul?"

"You laughed when you were supposed to. This time tomorrow I'm going to be up there in Bar Harbor, trying to entertain a roomful of aging Preppies who think pink dinner jackets and plaid pants should be featured in Armani's fall collection."

He laughed again and she beamed with delight.

"I've got a million of them," she said. "I've been trying to work out some patter for the Crooked Isle set, but I'm not sure we'll be speaking the same language."

"Be yourself," he said. "That's plenty good enough for them."

She glanced at him for signs of sarcasm or irony, but there weren't any. What was the matter with the man?

"Being myself is how I ended up doing a summer gig at the Crooked Isle Inn. Sometimes you have to know when it's time to compromise." She shadowboxed a right/left combination. "Believe it or not, I used to be a contenduh."

No laugh this time. Maybe he didn't know the reference. Or maybe he knew the reference and didn't think it was funny.

"What are you looking at?" she asked, following his gaze toward the horizon.

"What do you see?"

"Water," she said with a soft, self-deprecating laugh. "Lots of sand, lots of rocks, lots of water." *And the soft blue-gray wash of dusk across everything.* Not that he would notice.

"See how the color's leaching from the landscape? That's the first clue."

A mechanic who recognized *l'heure bleu* when he saw it? No wonder her car wasn't fixed yet.

"First clue to what?" she asked.

"Everything."

"There's a nonanswer for you."

He pointed toward the southeast. Or was it the northeast? Interior geography had always made more sense to her.

"In another hour Cassiopeia will be visible over there." He swiveled his torso and pointed diagonally behind them. "And a little later, you'll see Jupiter near the Moon."

"You're a stargazer!" She glanced around. "No telescope?"

He grabbed the crumpled paper bag and soda cans and stood up. "I'll be right back."

"Where are you going?"

"The truck."

Maybe that was a Maine euphemism for peeing. She wasn't about to ask.

"Would you check on Stanley?" she called out as he started down the makeshift steps. "He doesn't like being alone."

She felt suspended between worlds, as if the past few days had been lifted from her real life and set aside. Last week she was struggling through Pennylsvania with a dog the size of a grown man, wondering what on earth she had gotten herself into. Now here she was on a cliff in Maine, watching the sky darken from rose to indigo to midnight blue waiting for a stargazing auto mechanic to join her.

The evening was soft against her skin and she gathered it around herself like a favorite sweater as she looked out toward the horizon. Every so often a band of light from the Point swept across her line of vision, punctuated once by the bleat of a foghorn. The sound made her shiver. What would it be like to sail away on that dark ocean with only the stars to guide you? She had been weaned on sea chanteys, "Cape Cod Girls" and "Irish Washerwoman" and "Barnacle Bill" with verses far too wise even for the child she had been.

She drew her knees close to her chest and wrapped her arms around her legs. They had spent their first summer to-gether on Cape Cod. Billy had scored a gig at an Irish pub near Hyannis that came with a small cottage overlooking the beach. Mary Pat had been appalled when she realized the three of them would have to share one bedroom. She had gathered up her stuff and hitched a ride into town, where Billy found her waiting for a bus to take her back to Boston. Ellen locked herself in the bathroom, where she sobbed loud enough that the neighbor in the cottage next door called the police.

But, despite the terrible start, it had been a good summer. After supper she and Ellen would clamber down the long wooden staircase to the beach, where they would sit on the huge rock they dubbed the Beached Whale and wait for the stars to come out. Except for the moon, neither one of them could identify a single thing they saw, but the sense of wonder they shared still lingered. She could still hear Ellen's rolling laughter as she stumbled over the lyrics to "Cape Cod Girls."

> *Cape Cod girls they have no combs,*
> *Combs their hair with cod fish bones,*
> *Cape Cod ladies don't have no frills,*
> *Skinny and tight as cod fish gills . . .*

It felt good to remember that it hadn't all been bad. There had been moments of sweetness when she had been glad they were all there together, even if she knew it couldn't last.

The sound of her voice surrounded him as soon as he reached the top step. Smoky, filled with yearning as she sang a chantey, her voice seemed to become part of the darkening sky, the roar of the ocean, the beat of his heart.

> *He said, Ye may drive him out of your mind,*
> *Some other young man you'll surely find;*
> *Love turns aside and soon cold does grow,*
> *Like a winter's morning,*
> *The hills all white with snow.*

Her back was to him. The sea breeze made her shirt billow behind her like a sail. He watched as she gathered up the outrageous tangle of curls and twisted them into a knot that threatened to spring free the second she let go. With her hair pinned up that way, she looked like one of the sirens of legend, waiting on the rocks for an unsuspecting sailor to come along.

She stopped singing and turned around as he walked toward her.

"Don't stop because of me," he said. "I like it."

"How was Stanley?" With her hair up, he could see the long spirals of silver dangling from her ears.

He sat down next to her and unlooped the binoculars from around his neck. "He looked cold, so I put him in the truck."

Her right brow formed a graceful arch. "So you're not as tough as you look."

"Nobody said I was."

"Every time I think I've managed to get a read on you, you throw me a curve."

Like right that moment. She didn't know if he was blowing her off or simply hadn't heard her. He adjusted the binoculars, then handed them to her.

"Ever looked at the moon?"

A couple of snappy one-liners occurred to her, but she ignored them. "Only with the naked eye."

"Give it a try. She won't grab you the way she would through a 'scope, but you'll get the idea."

She prepared herself to be underwhelmed. The moon was the moon. She was a toddler when Armstrong planted the flag on the lunar surface, so there had never been a time in her life when that glowing rock held any mystery. No little green men. No green cheese. By the time she was old enough to care, it was all over.

He handed her the binoculars and told her how to adjust them to her own specifications. She focused on the lighthouse, spun the dial the way he showed her, then laughed out loud.

"I can read the rededication plaque at the base of the lighthouse!"

"Okay," he said. "Now turn to your left and aim for the moon."

"Story of my life," she said as she swiveled to her left. "Aim for the moon, hit Jersey City instead."

No laugh from Scott the Mechanic. Or should she start thinking of him as Scott the Stargazer? Neither one of them seemed to find her particularly amusing. She brought the binoculars up to her eyes again and moved across a blanket of fuzzy stars.

"This isn't very impressive," she said, sliding through the constellations. "Everything looks kind of blurry and—"

Time stopped. So did her breathing. She felt as if she were falling headfirst through the galaxy into the arms of the waning moon.

"My God," she breathed as the roundness of it, the sensuality, filled her head. Now she understood why the moon was female. Her lushness, her ripeness, the play of light and shadow on her undulating surface. The sensations came at her so quickly she marveled that she didn't swoon like an eighteenth-century maiden. She had no words for what she was feeling. The sense of wonder took her breath away.

Moonstruck, that's what she was. Moonstruck.

Dazzled, she lowered the binoculars and turned to him.

"Thank you," she whispered. She barely recognized her own voice. So needy . . . so terribly needy.

His face was partly in shadow. He revealed so little, gave nothing back at all to her. *Come on, Mechanic. Show me you're human.*

She leaned forward and kissed him lightly, playfully, on the mouth, prepared to laugh off both the kiss and his surprise.

Except he wasn't surprised.

He made a sound deep in his throat, a sound of such deep pain and longing that something inside her broke free and the playful mocking kiss turned serious. She melted against his strong body, aware of the places where they fit and the places where they didn't, aware of the binoculars digging into their chests, of his heat. He cupped her face between his hands and asked more of her with a kiss than she had ever given to any man.

This wasn't a game. There was nothing light or playful about it. She felt herself being drawn closer than she wanted to be, feeling more than she wanted to feel, wishing for all the things she pretended not to care about but longed for just the same.

If this kiss went on a second longer, she would end up doing something foolish, something she would regret the same way she regretted so many of the things she'd done along the way. She wanted him. The heat between her legs wouldn't let her lie to herself. But she wasn't a bulletproof twenty-year-old girl anymore. She had learned that, one way or the other, everything—even this delicious heat—had its price, and it was a price she was no longer willing to pay.

Sixteen

Ellen begged off a long-standing dinner date with Sweeney and two other members of the Artists' Co-op that rented space in Annie Butler's flower shop. She hated doing it, both because she liked the women enormously and because they were as committed to encouraging women toward early detection of breast cancer as she was, but time with Deirdre was limited.

"You don't have to explain," Sweeney said when Ellen called to apologize. "She's your sister. Sisters always come first."

Deirdre loved Chinese food, the hotter the better, and she hoped that a spicy feast would smooth things over. Not that they had argued or anything. Neither one of them felt passionate enough about the relationship to argue, but there was no denying she had hurt Deirdre's feelings when she said she wouldn't be home until nearly midnight. They saw each other so infrequently that the least she could do was make an effort to spend some time with Deirdre on her last night in town.

Sweeney's words lingered with her as she drove home from Hunan Garden with her bag of delicious goodies. *Sisters always come first.* Did they? What if sisterhood had come along as an afterthought, a "by the way, we forgot to tell you" kind of surprise you were supposed to embrace without missing a beat? Despite their differences, Mary Pat and Deirdre had that kind of connection. She had no doubt they would both deny it, but their shared background and experiences linked them together in a way that would never include Ellen.

She wasn't a fool. She knew that it wasn't a burning desire to spend quality time with her beloved sister that had brought Deirdre to her doorstep. Deirdre showed up when she needed something: a shoulder to cry on, a source of ready cash, or a place to leave a one-hundred-fifteen-pound dog. She was invariably charming, amusing, exasperating, impossible to pin down, equally impossible to understand, and just at the point when her casual indifference to the rules imposed on the rest of humanity was about to turn infuriating, she waved goodbye and left you wishing she never had to leave at all.

She knew Stanley was the reason for her sister's visit. Deirdre hadn't suddenly been overcome with longing for Ellen's company any more than she had been struck with a sudden yearning for lobster at Cappy's. When Mary Pat refused to take Stanley in, Deirdre aimed her aging Hyundai toward Shelter Rock Cove and the sister who hadn't quite mastered the art of saying no. She couldn't have shown up at a worse time. Hall. The move. Her work. The visit should have been a total disaster, but to Ellen's surprise she realized she would miss Deirdre when she left for Bar Harbor tomorrow. The other night they had let down their guard with each other in a way they hadn't since they were fourteen years old and trying to figure out where they figured in the revised family tree. Deirdre dropped her flaky musician persona while Ellen slipped out of her competent doctor disguise, and for a little while they met in the middle as women and sisters with thorny problems and irrational fears and a common loneliness neither one knew how to cure.

So maybe hot-and-sour soup and a double portion of Kung Pao shrimp wasn't the answer, either, but it couldn't hurt. Most of the women Ellen knew believed in the magical powers of chocolate, but Ellen knew better and so did Deirdre. Chocolate came in a distant second to Chinese food.

Her mouth was watering with anticipation as she pulled into the driveway. Deirdre was going to flip when she saw the assortment of familiar white containers. Unless she missed her guess, Stanley would probably flip, too. She turned off the engine and was about to gather up her stuff when she realized that the house was dark. The porch light was off. So were the lamps in the front rooms. Her heartbeat accelerated just enough for her to notice. She told herself not to read anything into it. Deirdre and Stanley were probably out on the deck, sipping margaritas.

Nothing to worry about.

She grabbed her purse, her satchel, and the bags of food, then hurried up the walk to the front door. She didn't need to fumble around with her keys because the door was partly open.

Now this might be something to worry about.

"Deirdre!" she called as she moved through the darkened hallway toward the kitchen. "Hey, Dee, wait'll you see what I've got!"

No answer.

Her heartbeat took another leap. She set her packages down on the countertop and glanced around the room. There were no signs of trouble. No broken windows. Nothing out of place. The sliding doors that led out to the deck were closed.

It would be just like Deirdre to grab Stanley and leave for Bar Harbor without saying a word to anyone. Maybe she tracked down an old friend who owed her a favor or hitched a ride with a passing stranger. Anything was possible where her sister was concerned.

The phone rang as she stepped out onto the deck. She raced back inside and picked it up midway through the outgoing announcement.

"This is Dr. Markowitz."

"This is your sister." A slight pause. "Mary Pat."

"Mary Pat," she said, forcing her voice into an upbeat register. "It's wonderful to hear from you."

"Surprising, no doubt."

"A little," she admitted. "The flowers were beautiful. Thanks so much for sending them. I'm afraid I'm a little behind on my notes."

"I'm glad you liked them."

"How are you? How is everyone doing?" *Like the husband*

I met a handful of times and all of those nieces and nephews I wish I knew better.

"We're well, thank you. And yourself?"

"Just dandy, thanks." Dandy? Where did that come from. "So what can I do for you, Mary Pat?" There was little point pretending her older sister had called to shoot the breeze.

"I assume Deirdre told you about our conversation."

"Deirdre hasn't told me anything. She's not here."

"Billy's back."

"From Ireland?"

"We picked him up at Logan last week."

"Is he home to stay?" she asked politely. Conversations with Mary Pat often resembled tennis games. There was a very definite pattern of serve and return.

Except this time Mary Pat missed the ball entirely and burst into tears. The sound of her cool, controlled sister in such obvious pain shocked her. Mary Pat kept her deepest feelings hidden away from public view. It was a trait they had in common. She knew exactly what those tears cost her in terms of pride.

"What is it?" she pressed. "Is Billy sick?"

Mary Pat struggled to regain control of her emotions. "I didn't recognize him when he got off the plane. It had only been eight months since we last saw him and—" She coughed to cover up the quaver in her voice. "He's lost a lot of weight. He says he has no appetite." She drew in a deep breath. "The whites of his eyes look a little jaundiced."

A chill worked its way up Ellen's spine as Mary Pat listed the symptoms. "Is he in pain?"

"He says his stomach is a little tender."

"Above the navel or below."

"Above."

"Any digestive problems in addition to the loss of appetite?"

"No, he—wait a second. I think he's having trouble urinating."

"He's almost seventy," she reminded Mary Pat gently. "That comes with the territory."

But there was more, and as Mary Pat listed the symptoms, Ellen's sense of dread intensified.

"Has he seen a doctor?"

"Not yet," Mary Pat said. "I've been trying to get him to see our internist, but he claims he's fine."

"He's not," Ellen said. And it was clear their father knew it or he would still be in Ireland. "He needs to see someone quickly."

"Quickly?"

"Yes," Ellen said, struggling to find a way to bridge the gap between compassion and urgency. "I think he should see someone Monday morning, if possible. He'll probably need blood work, urinalysis, and a CT scan. You need to get him scheduled stat."

Mary Pat's laugh was hollow. "You sound like one of those television doctors."

"I wish I did," Ellen said. "Television doctors always know the right thing to say."

"You're doing pretty good," Mary Pat said, and Ellen's heart twisted the tiniest bit in response to the unexpected words of praise.

"He needs to see a gastroenterologist," she continued, "preferably one who specializes in the upper digestive tract."

"Where do I find a good one?"

"Your internist is a good place to start," Ellen suggested.

"Maybe you could recommend one?"

"In Boston?"

"Or New York. I want the best for—" Mary Pat started to cry again, but, like last time, she quickly brought her emotions under control. "He looks terrible, Ellen. Really terrible."

Ellen called on every skill she had mastered at med school and in private practice as she tried to comfort her distraught sister.

"Let me make a few phone calls," she said after Mary Pat had finally cried herself out. "I'll find the best doctors for Billy. I promise."

"He's in the living room," Mary Pat said. "Would you like to say hello?"

"No," she said, more quickly than she should have. "I mean, I'd love to say hello, but if I'm going to start tracking down some names, I'd better not waste a second."

"Of course," said Mary Pat. "I understand."

The sad thing was they both did.

Scott pulled up behind Ellen's Cruiser and shifted into park. They hadn't said a word to each other since they left the beach.

Deirdre was the first to break the uncomfortable silence. "Thanks for the lift. You really didn't have to. We could've walked back along the beach the way we came."

"High tide," he said, drumming his fingers against the upper curve of the steering wheel. "I had to."

"Sorry if I kept you from anything."

"You didn't."

"Okay then." She debated the wisdom of bringing up the kiss they had shared atop the cliff, then decided against it. She was almost thirty-five years old. If she discussed every kiss that came along, she would be seventy before she knew what hit her. The kiss was a mistake, but one she had managed to stop before it got out of hand. Whatever it was—or wasn't—to Scott the Mechanic was his business.

She climbed out of the truck and opened the back door for Stanley, who bounded out with a wild yip of excitement. She hugged the dog, straightened out his leash, then realized Scott was standing next to her. The world would be a better place if men were required to wear cowbells.

"So what time should I be ready tomorrow?" She made sure to keep Stanley between them. Not because she thought her own allure was so powerful, but because her self-control wasn't.

"Around one," he said, leaning against the truck. "Earlier if I can swing it."

"Great," she said. "I appreciate it."

He looked at her. She looked back at him. They could light Shelter Rock Cove for a year with the electricity crackling between them. She could feel it sizzling along her nerve endings, shooting through her like bolts of lightning in search of ground.

"See you tomorrow," he said.

"I'll be ready."

Neither one of them made a move to leave.

"Are you waiting for something?" she asked.

"For you to go into the house. What are you waiting for?"

"For you to leave so I can go into the house."

"Why?" he asked.

"I have absolutely no idea."

They both burst into laughter, which broke the tension and set Stanley into a barking frenzy that threatened to wake the neighborhood.

"One o'clock," she said.

"One o'clock."

She waved goodbye to Scott the Mechanic, then raced Stanley to the front door before somebody called the cops on them.

He drove from her house to Captain's Landing. He wiped dog slobber off the telescope, slung the binoculars around his neck, then hiked up the rocky slope to his favorite spot.

Only the old guy was there. They nodded at each other. The old guy was somewhere in his seventies, a widower who used to own the dry cleaners in town. He had a state-of-the-art 'scope that looked at first glance like a portable cannon, and if it gave him any pleasure at all, he was keeping it to himself.

He hadn't planned to set up tonight, but he also hadn't planned to kiss Deirdre O'Brien back at the beach. He could still taste her, still feel the softness of her lips, hear her soft sigh when they finally broke apart. He couldn't remember who had initiated the kiss . . . or who had ended it, for that matter. He wasn't entirely sure he'd had control over any part of the process. His brain had shut down completely the moment their lips met, one of those complete meltdowns that reduced grown men to a bubbling cauldron of hormones.

Jesus, it felt good. The rush of heat that went straight to his groin. The gut-level, mind-blowing need that made everything else fall away. Pain, sorrow, loneliness, it all disappeared.

Yeah, it had been a long time. So long that he hadn't been sure he'd ever feel that way again, wasn't sure he wanted to or remembered how, but tonight it had all come rushing back at him with the first wave of desire.

Snippets of songs, images, their wedding day, the day Colin was born, the summer they bought their first house, the year she decided to go back to work, the parties, the christenings, the good times with family and friends ... there had been a lot of good times, so many that he hadn't noticed when it all began to change. Maybe that had been part of the problem. He hadn't noticed a lot of things. She had been growing away from him for a long time before she decided to leave. He had just been too fucking happy, too in love with their life together, to notice.

He struggled to open the tripod and balance it on the rocky ground. He never struggled with the tripod, but tonight his hands were clumsy, as if he were wearing mittens.

She used to tease him about his big mechanic's hands, marvel how those callused fingertips could skim so gently across her skin—

He pushed the memory away. He had spent too many months sleeping with that memory, holding it up to the light, trying to memorize every inch of it before it slipped away forever.

Every day he lost a little more of what they had shared. When you're in the middle of it, you think it will last forever. The old ones tell you to pay attention, to savor every second because life is a mean motherfucker and one sunny September morning you're going to wake up and discover they were right.

She said she couldn't live like that any longer. She was suffocating in their little suburban house on their little suburban street in their little suburban neighborhood. She didn't want the same things he wanted. Not anymore. Words like security *and* stability *sounded like prison sentences to her, and she wanted to break free.*

It wasn't that she didn't love him. She loved him more today than she had the day they got married, but people changed. Why couldn't he understand that? How could you spend your life running in place when the whole world was out there just waiting for you to start exploring? Every book she read, every movie she saw, every class she took or museum she visited changed her, filled her with new dreams and new ideas, and

she wanted to explore every single one of them while there
was still time.

He tried hard to understand. They talked about it, hours
and hours of talk that left her crying and him bereft, and still
they got nowhere. She wanted them to see a family therapist
and he agreed. They talked some more and she still wanted to
leave him, still wanted to say goodbye to their house and their
town and start again somewhere new.

He wasn't good at fighting with her. He never had been.
He loved her too much to see her so unhappy, so he said she
could take their son Colin and go to California to stay with
her sister for a while. Maybe whatever she was looking for
was hiding out there in the sunshine.

That last morning as he drove the two of them to the airport, she had asked if he was really okay with it and he said
he was and meant it. He had Colin in his arms at the time,
trying to memorize his little-boy smell of peanut butter and
crayons, and he was squirming and saying, "Daddy! Lemme
go! Lemme go!" and giggling at the same time. Megan had
looked up at him with a funny expression, then kissed him on
the lips. "Gotta run," she said, then took Colin from his arms
and the two of them disappeared into the terminal.

He wished he had thought something profound at that moment or called out one last "I love you," but he didn't. People
never did except in movies. What he did was run back to his
car before the cop had a chance to slap a ticket on his windshield and head back out to the suburbs, where he planned to
put his auto body shop up for sale.

He drove through that crystal blue morning with his mind
popping with new ideas. Megan didn't know what he was planning. He was going to sell the shop and the house and both
cars, then move out to California, where they could start a
new life. She was right. It was time for something new, something different. They could be anything they wanted to be in
California, whatever would make her happy.

He pulled up in front of the newspaper office a few minutes
before nine. The morning was so beautiful that he stopped for
a second to breathe in the crisp September air and admire the
deep blue sky. Great flying weather. He smiled at the thought
of his son sitting by the window, looking at the cotton-candy

clouds drifting by while his wife clutched the armrest and tried to talk herself out of her fear of flying.

He wished he was up there with them, but they'd be together soon enough.

The second he pushed open the door to the newspaper office he knew something terrible had happened. Forty adults stood huddled around a small color television set on someone's desk. They looked the way the people looked in the old newsreels of JFK's assassination. Shell-shocked. Terrified. Brokenhearted.

He approached the desk.

"What happened?" he asked the woman nearest him.

Her face was wet with tears as she tried to speak. "The World Trade Center," she managed. "A plane crashed into it."

He peered at the screen. Both towers were still standing. Billows of black smoke poured from one of them. A private plane. It had to be. Some little two-engine job that got too close to the buildings and overcorrected. The only surprising thing was that it hadn't happened a long time ago.

"Raise the sound!" somebody called out, and the woman next to him leaned forward and pressed a button.

". . . latest information out of Logan Airport . . ."

Jesus, he thought, no.

". . . American Airlines Flight 11 to Los Angeles . . ."

He must have said or done something because everyone turned to look at him and he shook his head. It's okay. It's okay. They weren't on American . . . they weren't on American . . . something terrible's happening out there, but they're okay. . . . whatever's going on they're okay. . . . He kept repeating it to himself until the words lost all meaning. Hideous images of smoke and flames filled the television screen, obscene against that deep blue September sky.

"Terrible," the woman next to him murmured. "Such a terrible accident . . ."

So random. So tragic.

He was trying to wrap his mind around the senselessness of it when a tiny plane appeared at the right side of the screen. So small against the sky, against the backdrop of the Towers, that it looked like a toy. Nobody reacted. He assumed it was

*a police plane trying to get a closer look at the damage so
they could direct firefighters. The idea was just forming itself
into words when it happened.*

*The world slowed to a crawl as the plane crossed the mid-
point of the screen. He saw his son's face in his heart's eye,
heard his wife's laughter. The plane tilted slightly, then drove
straight into the second Tower before he had a chance to say
goodbye.*

"Are you okay, son?"

The elderly man placed his hand on Scott's shoulder. His
voice was deep with concern.

Scott nodded his head. He couldn't speak, not with the
goddamn tears pouring down his face.

"I'm here if you need anything," the man said, then with-
drew to his telescope.

He had believed himself long past crying. At first he had
been torn apart by physical grief. The racking sobs and sleep-
less nights. The endless loop of memories meant to destroy
what was left of his heart. His son's toys still scattered
throughout the house. His wife's clothes hanging expectantly
in the closet, smelling faintly of perfume.

Two months after 9/11 he sold the business and the house
to a family from Barnstable. He fished out a few necessities,
then sold what he didn't need. Anything left over went into a
Dumpster. He bought an old Jeep Cherokee, tossed his be-
longings in the back, then drove away for the very last time.

Grief should be a private thing, but his was shared with
millions of strangers. Everyone had a piece of his sorrow. He
saw that plane slam through the Tower every night in his
dreams. He saw it every day on CNN. Somebody sent a photo
of his wife and son to a Boston television station to be used
as part of a tribute to the victims, and that photo somehow
made its way into the national press. His private tragedy was
a public spectacle and the entire country was his audience. He
didn't need a lawyer to calculate the price of his loss. There
wasn't enough gold on earth to bring back his wife and son.
He didn't want to write a book about it or talk to journalists
or grant television interviews so commentators could gaze into

the cameras with sad-eyed concern designed to garner ratings.

He rented a cabin in the woods near the Canadian border, where he grieved hard and long and privately for his family. There were nights he prayed he wouldn't wake up the next morning, but death refused to make it easy for him.

And then one night not long after the string of memorial services that marked the first anniversary, he looked up and saw the moon and stars. They had been there all along, but he hadn't been able to see them through his sorrow. Beautiful and constant, they had waited patiently for him to open his eyes, if not his heart, to life. It wasn't the same life he had known before he lost his family. It sure as hell wasn't the life he had dreamed about. But it was his and tonight, to his surprise, he almost liked it.

Seventeen

Ellen noticed there was something different about Deirdre as soon as her sister walked into the kitchen. She seemed both excited and pensive, as if she were holding a secret close. Very unlike her spill-it-all sister.

"I was worried about you," she said, bending down to add some scraps to Stanley's food dish.

"Sorry." Deirdre cadged a crispy noodle from the bowl on the center counter. "I took Stanley out for a quick run on the beach and bumped into the Mechanic."

"He drove you home from the beach?" The same beach that was fifty feet from the back door.

"High tide," Deirdre said with a grin. "It was that or swim."

"So where did you bump into Scott?"

Deirdre peered into white cartons and let out a sigh of sheer delight. "Oh, God, you remembered! Kung Pao!" She grabbed another noodle. "He was up on the cliff near the lighthouse."

"Doing what?"

"Would you believe looking at the moon?"

"You're kidding."

"Nope. He's a stargazer. He had a pair of high-powered binocs with him, and he let me take a look." She feigned a knee-trembling swoon against the counter. "It was the most beautiful thing I've ever seen."

Ellen pulled two plates from the box marked DISHES. "Really?"

"Really. You should get a telescope and set it up on the deck."

"I'll put that on my list," she said. "Right before window shades and after a new kitchen table."

"Okay," Deirdre said as she popped the lid off the container of hot-and-sour soup. "What's wrong?"

"Who said something's wrong?"

"You look pissed off."

She started to deny it, then caught herself. "You're right. I am pissed off. I managed to get away early so we could spend a little time together, and I come home and find the house dark and the door unlocked."

"Oops," said Deirdre. "Sorry 'bout that. I didn't know you had a big crime problem here in Mayberry."

"You could have left a note."

"Why?" Deirdre asked. "You weren't home and I wasn't going to be gone long."

"Because things happen."

Deirdre started to laugh. "Do you hear yourself? You sound like Mary Pat."

Ellen winced and pulled two spoons from the cutlery drawer. Doing anything like Mary Pat had always been the ultimate insult. Right now, with the sound of her older sister's distress still fresh in her mind, she felt protective.

"Dive in," she said, positioning the container of hot-and-sour soup between them. They couldn't disagree if they both had their mouths full.

"Dive in? Now, *that* doesn't sound at all like Mary Pat."

They both spooned up some of the spicy broth.

"She called while you were out."

Deirdre rolled her eyes. "I spoke to her earlier. She probably forgot to criticize me about something."

"She's worried about Billy."

Deirdre took another sip of soup. "She's always worried about Billy. She was trying to make me feel guilty because she forgot to tell me about Shawna's graduation."

"Shawna graduated?"

"She didn't tell you, either?"

"Not a word."

"That makes me feel better," Deirdre said.

It didn't do much for Ellen, but she had more serious concerns on her mind. "She described Billy's symptoms to me, Dee, and I think he might be in trouble."

Deirdre dipped her spoon into the soup container again and didn't meet her eyes. "What kind of trouble?"

"I don't want to speculate."

"Don't pull the good-doctor routine now," Deirdre snapped. "He's our father. Tell me what you're thinking."

Their eyes met. "I think he has cancer."

Deirdre's expression never changed. "What kind?"

"I suspect either a primary liver or secondary liver with undetermined primary."

"Which is—?"

"Bad," she said. "Very bad."

"Did you say that to Mary Pat?"

"I didn't have to. She knows something's terribly wrong. That's why she called."

Deirdre busied herself dividing Kung Pao shrimp and rice onto two plates. "They don't skimp on the peanuts, do they?"

It took her a moment to shift gears. "It's a great restaurant."

"I don't suppose we have any beer in the fridge."

"Dee, forget about the beer. It's okay if you're worried about Billy."

Deirdre shot her a look. "Is it okay if I'm not?"

Bull's-eye. The one truth Ellen would give anything to avoid having to deal with.

"Listen, I'm not about to give anyone lessons in how to be a good daughter. All I'm saying is that this doesn't look good. I think you should know that."

"Okay. You told me. Now let me tell you something: We've been through a thousand crises with Billy, and we'll probably go through a thousand more before it's over. He probably ran up some gambling debts in Ireland and decided to come home until things cooled off."

Ellen picked up her fork. "Anything's possible."

But not that. She had the feeling that this time Billy's luck was gone for good.

Eighteen

"Good meeting, Hall." Lucinda Davenport, head of the Chamber of Commerce, corralled him outside the boardroom. "I very much like your idea for the Gala Fund-raiser to coincide with the opening of Warren Bancroft's museum."

"I can't take credit," he said, inching toward the exit. The meeting had extended two hours past its usual time and if Lucinda got started, he would be stuck another two hours. "It's an old idea whose time has finally arrived."

"You're too modest," Lucinda said, inching toward the exit along with him. "We all know you're the one who broached the idea two years ago."

The woman had an elephantine memory. He wondered what she would do if he broke into a run. The idea made him smile.

Another woman might ask a few questions about the genesis of that smile, but not Lucinda.

Lucinda, however, was still talking. He tuned back in just in time to field an invitation to stop by her condo for a cup of Kona and a little brainstorming.

Was it possible to decline an invitation while it was still being tendered?

"It's been a long day," he said with just enough regret to salve hurt feelings, "but thanks anyway, Lucy."

"You can't work all the time."

He laughed. "Obviously you're not an OB."

They walked out together to the parking lot and he waited a second while Lucinda slid behind the wheel of her Lexus, then he retreated to the welcome silence of his Rover. Four hours of debate on mainly inconsequential issues were three hours too many for him. His tolerance level for ego-driven battles had decreased in proportion to the increasing number of said battles erupting at township meetings.

Lucinda's headlights cut across his line of vision and he lifted his hand in salute. Lucinda was Shelter Rock Cove born-and-bred. They had played together as children, danced at each other's many weddings, but somehow they had missed each other when it came to romance. Apparently Lucinda was looking to make up for lost opportunities.

He knew how she felt. He had spent most of his adult life feeling the same way. She wanted someone who understood her shorthand, who shared her frame of reference, who was tired of being alone. Loneliness always got him into trouble. How many wrong decisions had he made because he had had his fill of going home to an empty house? It had taken him years to appreciate solitude, to understand the difference between being alone and being lonely. For a man with an Ivy League education, he'd been one hell of a slow study.

His cell had stayed remarkably quiet all evening, which meant his voice mail was probably overflowing with minor emergencies. He might as well check now in case anything required a swing by the hospital. He punched in the code. Seventeen messages. He punched in his access number, then pulled a notepad and pen from his pocket while he waited for the messages to start playing.

Three were from his daughter Elizabeth, two were from his daughter Katharine. Same message: send money. Nothing new there. A handful of scheduling changes. His ex-wife Yvonne needed him to watch Willa and Mariah on Saturday while she attended another out-of-town event. He wondered if these out-of-town events had any connection to the businessman she'd met in Boston last Christmas, the one his daughters had raved about for three weeks after he took them skating.

One call from the cable company, offering new services he didn't need. A wrong number.

Ellen.

Next time one of his kids said that her heart skipped a beat when a guy called, he wouldn't correct her. Your heart could skip a beat at the sound of someone's voice. The right voice.

"Sorry to call so late. . . . It's me . . . Are you home yet? Okay, guess you're not. . . . Hall, I need a referral to a GI specialist for my father. . . . My sister called. . . . He seems to be presenting symptoms consistent with liver disease . . . maybe cancer. . . . If you can, give me a call when you get in."

He could do better than that.

"**J** can't eat another bite," Deirdre said as she pushed her plate away. "The food is way too good in this town. I'd be the size of the Michelin Man if I lived here."

"Another two weeks and Fay's Creamery opens for the season. Her Rocky Road puts Ben & Jerry's to shame."

"Good thing I'm leaving tomorrow. I've been known to eat a pint of Chunky Monkey without stopping for breath."

She leaned across the counter and gave her sister's hand a quick squeeze. "I'm going to miss you."

"Bet you say that to all the girls."

"Of course," she said. "Kung Pao always makes me sentimental."

"You always did have a soft spot for hard-luck cases."

"I wouldn't call you a hard-luck case."

"Which proves my point," Deirdre said. "Mary Pat didn't have any trouble turning me away."

"Mary Pat turned Stanley away," she pointed out. "Not you."

Deirdre shrugged. "Love me, love my dog."

"You have to admit Stanley is a pretty big surprise to spring on someone."

"You let him stay."

"We've already established that I'm a sucker for hard-luck cases."

"No," said Deirdre, "it's more than that. You're a better

person than I am. I'm not sure what I would have done if you and Stanley had shown up at my place one morning."

"That's something we'll never know," she said, "since you don't have a place."

"Trust me," Deirdre said. "I'm not that nice. I probably would have made up some excuse and turned you away."

"I think you would have done the right thing."

"The right thing for me," she said. "I always have. It's the O'Brien way."

Ellen began to gather up the dirty dishes. "You make being an O'Brien sound terrible."

"Isn't it?" Deirdre shot back. "You're one, too, and I don't see you embroidering the name on your bed linens."

"I don't think you can compare our situations. You grew up knowing Billy was your father. I was handed over to him like"—she glanced down at the half-empty cartons in front of her—"leftover Chinese take-out."

"But you worked it out with Cy. He's still your family. I mean, he put you through med school."

"That's ancient history." She carried the dirty dishes over to the sink. Some wounds never really healed; you simply learned how to live around them. "Let's talk about something interesting, like your gig in Bar Harbor."

"You should drive up for a weekend," Deirdre said as she closed the tops of the take-out containers and put them in the fridge. If the change of topic surprised her, she didn't let on. "The Crooked Isle is gorgeous, lots of atmosphere. You could even bring Hall with you."

Ellen's cell phone rang and she glanced around the kitchen to see where she had hidden it this time.

"On the windowsill," Deirdre said. "And don't think I'm going to let you change the subject again this easily."

"Speak of the devil," she said after Hall's hello. "We were just talking about you."

Deirdre threw back her head and laughed. She couldn't hold back a grin of her own.

"I got your message. Hope I'm not calling too late."

"We just finished some Kung Pao shrimp," she said. "If you'd called earlier, you could have joined us."

"Any leftovers?"

"Lots. Want me to save some for you?"

"Not a bad idea."

Deirdre tapped her on the shoulder. "I think there's some-one at the door."

"At this hour?"

"Go answer it," Hall said. "I'll wait."

She whistled for Stanley, who came bounding down the stairs. "Time to earn your kibble," she told him as they approached the door. "I want you to pretend you're a vicious guard dog."

"He doesn't need to growl," Hall said. "All he has to do is stand there."

"If you hear me scream, hang up and call 911," she said into the phone as she opened the door, then yelped.

Hall was standing on the other side of the screen, cell phone to his ear, big smile on his handsome face. Her heart did another one of those strange flip-flops inside her chest. If it kept doing things like that, she was going to need a good cardiologist.

"Very funny," she said, unlatching the screen. "Come on in."

He brought the night air in with him, the scent of pine mingled with the wet salty smell of the beach.

Stanley, the world's worst guard dog, did the canine equivalent of a cartwheel when Hall scratched him behind the ears. *I know exactly how you feel, Stan. I did a few cartwheels myself the other night.*

"I should've called first," he said.

"You did call."

"I'm not sure from the driveway counts." He reached out and touched her cheek with the tip of his finger. "I felt like a stalker."

Oh, God, what was the matter with her? Was she so starved for affection that a gentle touch could turn her inside out?

"Tell me what's wrong," he said, bringing all of his considerable powers of persuasion to bear. "We'll make sure Cy gets the best help available."

"Not Cy," she said. "Billy."

He looked blank for a second, then nodded. "Sorry. I'm still adjusting to the sister."

"Sisters," she corrected him again. "There's another one down in Cambridge."

"This is all going to make sense to me one day, isn't it?"

She laughed softly. "I'm not sure it makes sense to me."

He draped a companionable arm across her shoulders. "First the food, then the story."

"You haven't had dinner yet?"

"The meeting ran long."

"Very long," she said, noting the time. "Problems with the gala?"

"Problems with the gala, the museum, the banquet menu, the size of the typeface on the invitations, overweening egos—"

"You must be talking about Lucinda."

"I was being a gentleman."

"Don't bother on my account. I served on the Memorial Day Parade committee with Lucinda last year, and I still haven't recovered."

"She can be formidable."

"You really are a gentleman," she said, starting to laugh as they entered the kitchen.

"Hey, Doc!" Deirdre bent down to pour fresh water into Stanley's bowl. "We have plenty of leftovers if you feel like a midnight snack."

He grinned. "Why do you think I'm here?"

Ellen pulled a microwave-safe plate from the carton on the floor and ran it quickly under the faucet while Hall and Deirdre exchanged minor pleasantries about the wonders of Shelter Rock Cove cuisine.

"Do we have any soup left?" she asked Deirdre during a lull in the conversation.

"No soup but we have some shrimp and a fair amount of string beans in garlic sauce."

She turned to Hall. "How does that sound?"

"Like I picked the right night to drop by."

Deirdre's throaty laugh filled the room. "I have the feeling every night is the right night for you."

Ellen wanted to crawl under the counter and stay there, but Hall, bless his easygoing heart, threw back his head and laughed along with her big-mouthed sister.

"There's beer in the fridge," she said to Hall, shooting a look Deirdre's way. "I'll zap the food and we can take it out onto the deck."

"Why didn't we take ours onto the deck?" Deirdre asked.

"Because we ate so fast we never made it out of the kitchen."

"Good point." Deirdre grabbed a bottle of springwater from the case near the fridge. "It was good seeing you," she said to Hall as she made for the doorway.

"Stay," Ellen said. "We have lots to talk about."

"And I have lots to do before I leave tomorrow."

"Hall's going to help us find a good doctor for Billy."

"Terrific," Deirdre said with a big smile. "He couldn't be in better hands."

"We could use your input."

"I trust you." Deirdre waggled her fingers at them, then left the room.

Hall pulled a bottle of beer from the fridge and leaned against the counter while Ellen arranged the leftovers on a plate, then nuked them.

"The deck," she said when the timer sounded.

He nodded and followed her outside.

"Are you going to tell me," he said once they had settled down in their lawn chairs, "or do I have to ask?"

She leaned back in her chair and closed her eyes. She heard the sounds of the ocean, crickets, and Hall's fork scooping up string beans in garlic sauce. "What do you want: full family history, family history with the extraneous matter edited out, or my guess on why Deirdre didn't hang around?"

"Family history, edited version."

"Good choice," she said, "because I don't know enough about my family's history to give you the full version, and I sure as hell don't know enough about my sister to explain why she does anything."

"You could start by telling me about your father."

"Which one?" she asked with maybe a bit more of an edge than she had intended. "Up until I was fourteen, I thought Cy Markowitz was my father. I thought his parents were my grandparents. I thought his sisters were my aunts. I thought I had his smile and his ambition and when I grew up I was going to be a doctor just like him so I could make him proud of me."

"And you did."

She opened her eyes and glanced in his direction. "I became a doctor. I'm not sure about the rest of it."

"What happened when you were fourteen?"

"That was the year my mother died," she said. "She was pregnant with Cy's first child, although I didn't know it at the time." After almost fourteen barren years of marriage Cy and Sharon were finally going to have a baby. Sharon had just started her second trimester when the taxi she was riding in was hit by a bus near the Park. Both she and the baby she was carrying died on the way to the hospital.

"It was like our world went crazy. Cy completely fell apart. He wouldn't come out of his study for three days, and when he did he couldn't stand to be in the same room with me. He was my father—my daddy, for God's sake—and he wouldn't let me near him." Her mother was dead, her unborn brother was dead, and her father was treating her as if he wished he could trade her for the ones he'd lost. "His sisters were sitting shiva at the apartment, and I was crying for my mother and, to be honest, for myself when I heard my aunts in the kitchen, speculating about what was going to happen to me."

The sound of Deirdre's harp floated through the open door and mingled with the hushed roar of the ocean. He put his plate of food down on the deck and focused his full attention on her. From the day they met he'd had the unnerving ability to listen to her words and somehow hear her heart.

"I asked them what they were talking about and they got angry and defensive. Cy came into the kitchen—I can still see him in a sweatshirt and robe. He hadn't shaved for days and his beard was coming in gray. I couldn't stop staring at the thick gray stubble on his cheeks and along his jawline. He wanted to know what was going on, and they started arguing. I think they forgot I was there, because the next thing I knew one of his sisters called me 'that Irishman's bastard' and everything kind of went dark."

She hadn't eaten for days and she passed out on the kitchen floor. When she came to on the living room sofa, they were all fussing around her, but the stench of guilt hung heavy in the air, and she knew she hadn't been dreaming.

"It was like it all started to make sense at that moment. I think I had spent my entire life knowing but not knowing that something was wrong."

"Is that hindsight speaking?" he asked.

"I don't think so. Kids usually have an intuitive sense of their place in the family structure, and I could never figure out where mine was."

"You grew up as an only child. Your place should have been secure."

"But it wasn't. That's what was so odd. Cy was friendly and kind, but we never really connected. My mother always blamed it on the demands of his practice, but I wasn't buying it. I saw the way he came to life every time she walked into the room. He knew how to love. He just didn't happen to love me."

Cy remarried the year she turned twenty-one, and his young wife Nancy gave birth to their only child, a boy named David, eight months later. He was her father by virtue of shared history and sense of responsibility, but the deep bonds of emotion were no longer there. She now understood that they had never really been there at all, at least not for him. He had loved her mother deeply and had never managed to capture her heart the way she had captured his. Ellen's existence was daily proof of that fact.

"He never formally adopted me," she went on, "but I didn't know that until I was putting the paperwork together to join that practice in Manhattan. You should have heard the uproar when I tried to explain the story to some bureaucrat behind a big desk." She had ended up changing her name legally to the name she had grown up believing was hers.

"That must have hurt like hell," Hall said.

She didn't deny it, even though for years she had done exactly that.

Her mother had believed a child would finally pry Billy away from his wife. His wife had believed a new baby would keep her wandering minstrel husband home where he belonged. Ellen and Deirdre were born six months and three hundred miles apart, and when all was said and done, Billy said goodbye to the woman he loved and stayed with the woman he had married.

But nothing in life was ever that simple. Sharon married Cy Markowitz six weeks after Ellen's birth and cut Billy from her life as if he had never existed. No photos of the baby. No updates on her progress. For the first two years he showered her with impassioned love letters that she hid away in a box at the back of her closet. The letters finally stopped, but Billy could never manage to break the connection between them. Every year on her birthday he sent her a card, a silly sentimental Hallmark with roses and kittens on the outside. He never signed the card. He didn't have to. At the bottom, beneath the hearts-and-flowers sentiments, each year he scrawled the same two lines from Yeats:

> *But one man loved the pilgrim soul in you,*
> *And loved the sorrows of your changing face.*

She stood up and walked over to the railing. The wood was slick with mist beneath her elbows as she looked out into the darkness. She heard Hall's chair scrape against the deck, and moments later he joined her at the railing.

"I'll bet this sounds like a bad soap opera to you," she said, trying hard not to lean into his warmth. "Families behaving badly."

"My parents weren't Ozzie and Harriet," he said. "Some day I'll tell you about it."

She glanced over at him. "Now's a good time."

"Nice try," he said, "but this is your story."

They were quiet for a few moments, listening to the sweetly evocative music drifting toward them from the house.

"Cy found the cards about six months after my mother died. We had all been pretending that everything was normal, that I didn't know the truth, and we were still one big happy family, but the cards changed everything. The next thing I knew Cy was telling me that it was time I met my birth father and learned something about my heritage and that I'd be spending the summer with Billy and my two half sisters getting to know one another."

She told him about the day Cy put her on a plane to Boston, where she met Billy O'Brien, the love of her mother's life. He introduced her to Mary Pat and Deirdre, who seemed every bit as unhappy as she was.

Billy tried. She had to give him that. He brought Ellen into his life over his wife's objections and took his three daughters to East Hampton with him for the summer.

"It was a disaster," she said. "We hated one another. We hated being there. We hated Billy for ruining our lives."

Yet despite it all Deirdre and Ellen were drawn to each other. Anyone who saw them together would know instantly that they were sisters. They both had blue eyes, curly auburn hair, and a quick sense of humor that invariably drove Mary Pat screaming from the room.

She began to look forward to those summers with her sisters, even after Mary Pat married and settled down. Deirdre was wild and spontaneous while Ellen was cautious and deliberate. Every decision Ellen made she made with her future in mind.

"My goal was to graduate at the top of my class, get into a great school with a great premed curriculum, and make Cy proud of me."

"And Deirdre's goal?"

"To snag a fake ID so she could go out drinking on prom night."

His laughter rang out and she smiled with him.

"I adored her," she said, remembering early mornings on the Cape as they raced each other down to the beach. "She was everything I wasn't and wished I could be."

"Past tense," he noted. "What happened?"

"Who knows? Everything, I guess. Billy seemed to lose interest in these summer reunions. Mary Pat was busy with her own family. Deirdre was thinking about hiking across Europe, and I resented anything that took me away from my studies."

"Sounds like a normal American family to me."

"As long as you didn't look too closely."

"You stayed connected."

"Maybe we didn't know how to let go."

"Maybe you didn't want to."

"If you'd said that to me this time last week I would have laughed, but now—" She shrugged her shoulders. "I'd forgotten how much I love her. I know she only came to see me because she needed a place to board Stanley, but I'm going to miss her when she leaves tomorrow. Talk about being a soft touch . . ."

"You have a soft heart," he corrected her. "Why do you think I brought you into the practice?"

She poked him softly in the bicep. "For my skills as a doctor."

"I spoke to a lot of highly skilled doctors before you came along, Markowitz. If that was all I was looking for, I could have taken any one of them on board."

"So why me?" she asked, praying he wasn't about to blow their three-year association with an appallingly sexist remark.

"Because you had the skills and the heart to go with them. It's a rare combination."

A burst of pleasure flooded her chest. "It shouldn't be."

"Remember when that medical practice efficiency analyst crunched our numbers last year?"

She made a face. "That horror show of a man who expected us to keep a running total of the minutes we spent with each patient so we could find ways to 'trim the fat.' "

"Fourteen minutes of face time. That was his recommendation."

"No, no," she said. "Eight minutes! That was his recommendation. Eleven, but only if the patient had a life-threatening condition."

"I remember what you told him."

She felt her cheeks redden with heat. "Not my most shining hour."

"Your best hour," he said. "The hour I—"

"Don't," she whispered. "Don't say it." It was too soon. Too impossible. Too scary.

"There's something happening between us. It's been growing for a long time. I think it's time to see where it leads us."

"My period's due next week. I guess we'll know where it's leading us then."

"This isn't about a baby," he said, refusing to back down. "This is about us. Who we are when we're together."

She made a show of peering up at the sky. "Not even a full moon up there tonight. You're crazy all on your own."

"Not crazy enough," he said. "If I really was crazy, we wouldn't be standing here talking. You'd be in my arms."

Her sister's music, painfully sweet, dangerously powerful, encircled them like a shimmering mist. Ripples of sensation washed over her. An awareness of change, of doors opening in rooms she had yet to discover, a glimpse of something she could only imagine.

"Deirdre said people used to believe harpers used their music to cast spells."

"Maybe it isn't the music," he said quietly, taking her hand in his.

And because she didn't know what to say, she held on tight and said nothing at all.

Nineteen

Every Friday morning a group of local women gathered at Annie's Flowers for coffee and jelly doughnuts. If you asked Claudia, none of them needed either the caffeine or the carbohydrates, but the younger generations lacked the well-honed sense of discipline of her own peer group.

Of course, they liked to pretend they were gathering to work on the enormous quilt they planned to donate to Warren Bancroft's museum to commemorate the lives of local fishermen who had been lost at sea. Claudia knew better. More gossiping than quilting went on during these Friday morning get-togethers.

Her dear friend Roberta could barely thread a needle—she blamed her arthritis, but Claudia suspected it was sheer willfulness—but that didn't keep her from joining the group each Friday and partaking liberally of raspberry doughnuts.

"You have powdered sugar on your upper lip," Claudia informed her during a lull in the conversation.

Roberta reached for a paper napkin and laughed. "I suppose that's God's way of telling me I've had enough."

"I would think your waistline would be telling you something, too," Claudia said, then instantly regretted it when she saw the stricken look on her friend's face.

Roberta dabbed at her mouth, then crumpled the napkin in her hand. "And you were wondering where your Susan got her sharp tongue."

Claudia let out a long sigh and patted her dear friend's arm. "I'm sorry, Roberta. I'm a tad on edge today."

"Oh?" Roberta still sounded aggrieved.

She leaned closer to her friend and lowered her voice. "Does Susan seem different to you?"

Roberta glanced toward Susan and Annie, who were doing hand piecing at the other end of the table. "Well, she does need a touch-up."

"Her mood," Claudia persisted. "Does she seem crabbier than normal?"

"She's that age," Roberta said with a shrug. "The moods come and go."

"It's more than moodiness," she said. "I think—"

"Morning, everyone!"

Eight pairs of eyes looked toward the doorway to the workroom, where Dr. Ellen's sister stood with that gigantic horse of a dog.

"Deirdre!" Annie leaped to her feet and hurried over to hug the young woman. "I thought you were leaving for Bar Harbor today."

"Around lunchtime," she said, waving a greeting at everyone. "I wanted to pick up something for Ellen before I left."

"How sweet!" Roberta practically cooed. Sometimes the woman didn't have the sense of a goose.

"Take a look at some of the stained-glass items," Sweeney called out. "They're pricey, but they last longer than flowers!"

The woman had no shame.

Annie rolled her eyes and linked arms with Deirdre. "And to think I was dumb enough to open my doors to my competition!" She winked over her shoulder at Sweeney, who threw back her head and laughed one of those bawdy laughs that made Claudia's bones rattle.

She pushed back her chair.

Susan looked up from the piece of cloth she was mangling.

"Where are you going, Ma?" Her daughter never had been very good at detail work.

"I'm going to see if I can offer any assistance."

"Don't forget to take notes," Susan said.

They all burst into good-natured laughter, a fact she chose to rise above.

Deirdre was standing in front of the refrigerated display case they used to store the blooms.

"What do you think, Mrs. Galloway?" Deirdre gestured broadly toward the profusion of flowers. "Annie thinks Ellen is a larkspur type, but I think of her more as a daisy kind of girl."

"She sometimes wears a crisp, lovely carnation scent. Perhaps a mass of pure white carnations with some glossy foliage would be just right."

Deirdre beamed a smile at Claudia, who couldn't help but be charmed, even if she could see the young woman's bra through her gauzy shirt. "That's perfect!" She kissed Claudia first on the right cheek, then on the left. "Thank you so much, Mrs. Galloway!"

"Call me Claudia."

The smile grew even wider. "Claudia."

Annie pulled a twenty-gallon bucket of paper-white carnations from the cooler and plopped it down on the workbench. "Modest, showy, or holy cow?"

Deirdre laughed and Claudia heard more than a touch of Dr. Ellen.

"Modest," Deirdre said. "I'd like to go for holy cow, but since I'm charging it to her account, I figure I'd better settle for just show."

It took every ounce of Claudia's self-control to keep from locking eyes with Annie across the mountain of flowers.

Stanley the giant dog ambled over to Claudia and nudged her hand with his head. She had grown quite fond of the dog over the last few days and caressed him behind his left ear.

"You're just a big baby," she said, bending down as far as her creaky bones would allow. "Just a big sponge for love."

"I think you're one of his favorites," Deirdre said. "He looks downright goofy when he sees you, Claudia."

"He reminds me of Bear," Annie said as she clipped a stack of flower stems.

Claudia's eyes misted over with tears. "Dear Bear! I haven't thought of him in years." She smiled at Deirdre. "Bear was a mixed breed much like Stanley. He helped me raise my brood."

"Bear was part shepherd," Annie said. "He could corral a group of kids faster than their parents could."

"Ellen bought your house, didn't she?" Deirdre asked.

Claudia nodded. "There are many happy memories there."

They chatted amiably about dogs and houses while Annie arranged the carnations in a beautiful white basket then added some dark and glossy greenery.

"You must be glad to have your automobile back again," Claudia observed as she straightened out one of the stems in Annie's arrangement.

"Oh, my car is nowhere near ready," Deirdre said.

"So how are you planning to get to Bar Harbor? A rental?"

"Actually Scott, the mechanic, is driving me up. He has to stop at Lincolnville for a part, and he said Bar Harbor is on the way."

Claudia and Annie locked eyes.

"It's not on the way?" Deirdre asked, looking from one to the other.

"Not exactly," Annie said with a grin. "Let's just say he must like your company."

"A great deal," Claudia added.

Deirdre had the grace to blush. It really was quite becoming.

"There you go," Annie said, handing the basket to the red-haired young woman. "Twenty-two dollars, including tax."

"Put it on my sister's tab," Deirdre said breezily. "I'll write her a check."

Annie didn't bat an eye. She wrote out a receipt for Deirdre, who folded it and stuffed it in the pocket of her flowing skirt.

"Can you send flowers to Cambridge from here?"

"We can send flowers to Timbuktu, if you'd like."

"I'll settle for Cambridge," Deirdre said with that Ellen-like smile. "I want to send some tulips to my father."

Claudia could almost see her daughter's ears wagging behind the workroom curtain.

Deirdre and Annie quickly settled on a style and a dollar amount. Deirdre dictated a five-word message—Feel better soon. Love, Dee—and Annie phoned in the order.

"Put it on Ellen's account, too?" she asked blandly.

"Why not?" Deirdre laughed gaily. "He's her father, too."

If Susan's ears were twitching before, they must have separated themselves from her head by now.

Her daughter exploded from the back room the second the door jingled closed behind Deirdre and the dog.

"I couldn't believe my ears!" her daughter crowed. "She buys a present for Ellen, then charges it to her sister's account!"

It seemed to Claudia that mention of Billy O'Brien of Cambridge was a more interesting discovery, but to each her own.

Annie shot her best friend the quelling look that she had mastered since becoming a mother. "None of our business, Susan. They have their own arrangements."

"What if Ellen doesn't want to pay you? What then?"

"Then I'll worry about it." Annie turned to Claudia. "Was she this nosy as a kid? I don't remember her being quite this bad."

Claudia chuckled. "Unfortunately it's a family trait."

The three women rejoined the quilters in the workroom.

Susan picked up her mangled piecework. "If you ask me, she could stand to lose a few pounds."

Sweeney poked her with the tip of her motorcycle boot. "Except for Claudia, everyone at this table could stand to lose a few. So the hell what."

"That gauzy stuff isn't very flattering."

"It isn't to my taste," Claudia said to her daughter, "but it actually looks very good on her."

Next to her, Annie pretended to faint while the other women burst into laughter.

"I can admit when I'm wrong," Claudia said. "She's very soft and feminine. The style suits her."

Annie looked toward Susan. "Scott certainly must think so. How did he ever convince Jack to give him the afternoon off?"

Susan had the poor piece of fabric in a death grip. "Jack gave him the afternoon off?"

"Scott's driving Deirdre up to Bar Harbor," Annie said. "You didn't know?"

"Why should I?" Susan snapped. "I don't work there. How come you know?"

Poor Annie looked very uncomfortable pinned beneath Susan's fierce Galloway scowl. "Deirdre mentioned it."

"Just now," Claudia said. "I'm surprised you didn't hear it when you were listening at the door."

Her daughter threw the square of fabric onto the table and leaped to her feet. "I absolutely do not need this shit today."

"Susan!" Claudia snapped.

"I'm not fifteen anymore, Ma," she said, slinging her purse over her shoulder.

"That's right. You're old enough to behave in a civilized fashion."

Susan stormed from the store without so much as a goodbye.

Roberta turned to Sweeney. "You know all the new expressions," she said. "What does 'bite me' mean?"

Then again, maybe she did say goodbye.

ЯS if the morning didn't suck enough, Susan practically fell into Hall's arms as she left Annie's Flowers.

"Damn," he said, steadying her by the elbows. "Hope you have collision insurance, Susie."

"Why don't you watch where you're going?" She pushed herself away from him.

He raised his hands in surrender and took a giant step back. "Was it something I said or did you wake up this way?"

"Not funny. And if anyone suggests an HRT patch, I won't be held responsible for my actions."

"I'll warn Ellen."

It was worse than she thought. Now Ellen Markowitz was the first person he thought of.

"I suppose you're buying up some more roses for the housewarming."

"Wrong," he said. "I'm on my way to the bank."

She didn't look as if she believed him as she made to move past him.

"Sorry I didn't get back to you again last night," he said, blocking her escape. "I didn't get in until late."

"Since when has that ever stopped you?" Jack had been bitching about their late-night gab fests for the length of their twenty-year marriage.

"What did you want to talk about?"

"I don't remember."

"Quit pouting, Galloway. You're too old and I'm too tired."

"I have to get to work. I have a closing at eleven and a lot of paperwork to put in order."

"How about I call you tonight," he said. "Around ten."

"I won't be home."

"Bullshit."

"Fine," she said. "Don't believe me. You're the one who didn't return my call. You can work around my schedule this time."

"I said I got home too late."

"You could have e-mailed me."

"Was it an emergency?"

"Damn it. Why don't you just come out with it? I saw your car turning down Laidlaw Road last night. Quit pretending you were too tired to call me. You were busy with Ellen."

"And Deirdre." He grinned. "Stanley was there, too, in case you're taking a census."

She felt wild with emotion. She wanted to slap him hard across the face. She wanted to fling herself at him. She wanted to crawl under her mother's Lincoln and stay there until the feelings passed. What in hell was happening to her? She felt as if she had gone to bed one night a normal, happily married woman and awakened a love-starved menopausal stalker with her sights trained on her best friend. The guy she had buddied around with since kindergarten. He was godfather to two of her children, for heaven's sake! He had delivered all of her babies, which meant he already knew everything he needed to know about the state of her thighs and liked her anyway.

At least he used to.

He was watching her with those compassionate eyes of his. The man could look at a glass of milk and make it think it was champagne. Was it any wonder he had such a thriving practice? What woman wouldn't love telling her problems to a man who looked as if he not only cared about her problems but could make them go away with one dazzling smile? Not that he wasn't a good doctor. He was terrific. It was just that there were lots of good doctors out there, but not many who made you feel that they actually cared when you were hurting or scared or confused.

He was that kind of friend, too. He would have stood up for her at her wedding, but her mother had threatened to disown her if she didn't ask her sister Eileen to be maid-of-honor.

And it wasn't a one-sided friendship. She had been there for him, too, over the years. She had held his hand, listened to his problems, tried very hard not to say "I told you so" when his marriages ran out of steam. She was the one who had pushed him to let Annie know how he felt about her. She was the one he had trusted, the one he had confided in, the one he called late at night after a difficult delivery.

At least that was the way it used to be before Ellen joined his practice. Oh, their friendship was still important to him—he was nothing if not loyal—but Ellen was the first person he thought of now after a tough day, the one whose advice he sought out.

"Suz, what's going on?" He draped his arm around her shoulder, and this time she didn't pull away. "You're not acting like yourself."

"I don't feel like myself," she said, resisting the urge to rest her head on his shoulder. "Everything's changing and I hate it like hell."

He understood exactly what she was saying, text and subtext.

"Not everything," he said. "It just feels that way."

"Don't patronize me, Talbot."

"Like I'd ever try, Galloway."

"It's Aldrin." A small smile broke through her fierce anger. "Remember?"

"You'll always be a Galloway to me."

She feigned a punch to his rib cage. "That's a hell of a thing to say."

"You still owe me a lobster special at Cappy's."

"Okay," she said, "but this time let's leave the families at home." All of them, including the O'Brien-Markowitz sisters.

He kissed the top of her head the way he always used to do when they were teenagers. "You've got yourself a deal."

He hadn't planned to stop in at the flower shop, but Annie waved him inside.

"She's in some mood, isn't she?"

"No comment," he said, "but I've seen her worse."

"She told Claudia, 'Bite me.' "

He cracked up despite his best intentions. "You lie."

"I never lie," she said as she swept a pile of clippings off the workbench and into the trash. "It's my only character flaw."

"What did Claudia do?"

"We stopped short of calling 911, but it was close. I think Roberta is still in shock."

He couldn't wipe the impolitic grin off his face. "Who translated for them?"

Annie's own grin was wide and wicked. "Sweeney. It was her finest hour."

"Any particular reason for the 'bite me'?"

"Good question." She leaned her elbows on the workbench and considered it. "She seemed a little off-bubble when she came in this morning but nothing noteworthy until Deirdre and Stanley showed up." She mimed an explosion. "It wasn't pretty."

"She's got a problem with Ellen's sister?"

"Beats me," said Annie. "Maybe she has a problem with Ellen's sister's dog. Our Susan has been a little tough to read lately."

He took a good look at her. "You know more than you're telling me."

"I would hope so."

"If I remember right, didn't she get a little bent out of shape when you first met Sam?"

Annie nodded. "One thing about our Susan: She doesn't like change."

"What's changed?" Sure, the town was growing by leaps

and bounds, but that had been going on for a few years now and they had all managed to reach an accommodation with the rising tide of tourism in sleepy Shelter Rock Cove. "She has the same job, the same husband, the same family, the same friends, the same house." If anything it sounded to him like she was in a rut.

"You've changed," Annie said, "and she doesn't like it."

"You're talking about—" He stopped midstream. He wasn't going to compromise Ellen any further than he already had.

Annie, however, was a half-dozen steps ahead of him. "Yep," she said with a gentle smile, "that's exactly who I'm talking about."

"Susan saw me through three failed marriages. Why should this seem any different to her?"

"Because it's different to you."

She was right. It was different in every way he could name and some he could only imagine.

Their eyes met and their shared history of friendship filled the room. He had loved her once, carried her image in his heart like a talisman, the woman against whom all other women had been judged and found wanting. It no longer hurt to remember the missed chances, the failed opportunities, the hundred times when the Good Doctor, the Family Friend, couldn't find the way to tell her he loved her. Sam Butler hadn't had that problem, and now they were the proud parents of two beautiful children and had the kind of life Annie had always wanted.

And it was okay. No more pain. No regrets. He had loved her for most of his adult life, and there was a part of his heart that would always belong to her. But he wasn't in love with her any longer. The last doubts he might have had were gone.

When he looked at her beautiful face, he saw Sam's wife, he saw Sara's and Kerry's mother, and he saw a dear friend, but he no longer saw his future.

Now all he had to do was figure out a way to make Ellen understand.

Twenty

Patsy Wheeler's house was located only a few minutes away from the hospital, an easy stop on Ellen's way to work.

"She's still asleep," Doug said as he poured her a cup of coffee, "but I could wake her up."

"No, no!" Ellen thanked him for the deliciously dark brew. "Sleep is exactly what she needs. I just wanted to make sure things were going well."

"So far, so good," Doug said, stifling a yawn. "She was pretty cranky yesterday. I suppose this bed rest takes a lot of getting used to."

"Especially for someone as active as Patsy." She took another long sip of coffee. "Has the bank worked out a way for her to telecommute?"

"I have the high-speed cable line ready to go. Now all we need is the okay from corporate headquarters and she's back in business."

"Tell Patsy I stopped by," she said, placing her empty cup in the sink. "I'll phone midafternoon to see how she's doing."

"You don't have to do that," he protested. "We're doing fine. Patsy's mother said she'll start coming over next week when I go back to work."

"Humor me," she said. "I'm a worrier. If I don't check up on her, I can't sleep, and you wouldn't want a sleepy OB, would you?"

Doug grinned. "Nope, we wouldn't want that at all. You're always welcome here, Dr. Ellen."

Sometimes she walked a fine line between being careful and being a flat-out pain in the ass, but that was a risk she was willing to take. So far nobody had complained.

She drove back to the hospital and completed her morning rounds by ten o'clock. She left messages for Grady, chief of internal medicine, and Sabatino, head of hematology/oncology, and one for a colleague back in New York who specialized in diseases of the digestive tract, then she dialed Cy's number down in Boca Raton.

"Honey!" Nancy, her stepmother-once-removed, always sounded delighted to hear from her. "How long has it been? Don't answer. I know how long it's been: too long."

"Good to hear your voice, too, Nancy. How's everyone?"

"We are up to our ears with David's bar mitzvah. Planning a wedding would be easier."

She did some quick math. "David's bar mitzvah? He won't be thirteen for another four months."

"And we'll need every single one of them. I've had the restaurant booked since Thanksgiving. Cy has been beside himself over this. If he had his way, he'd invite everyone in the Boca phone book." Nancy's laugh was as sunny and good-natured as she was. "The way he loves that boy!"

Who didn't know how much Cy Markowitz loved his son? The pharmacist knew. The cabana boy at the club. His cardiologist, his barber, and his dry cleaner could probably recite David's vital statistics from memory. Ellen was almost thirty-five, which was far too old to feel jealous over the existence of a skinny twelve-year-old kid with spotty skin and braces, but the ugly traces of not-quite-sibling rivalry were still there.

Actually she loved the kid. He was bright and funny and not half as spoiled as he should have been, considering the way his parents doted on him. It wasn't often you met a twelve-year-old with a highly developed sense of irony. But David saw life through interesting eyes, and Ellen always enjoyed their encounters immensely. It would be nice to be there for his big day, but she felt more like an outsider than family.

She and Nancy chatted a few minutes about menus and guest lists. Ellen heard herself promising to clear a spot on her calendar so she could join the family in October.

"What's wrong with me?" Nancy said with one of her bubbly laughs. "Here I am bending your ear on your dime when you called to talk to Cy. Hold on, honey. I'll go get him."

She heard the sound of Nancy's heels on the tiled floor, bits and pieces of conversation, then the squeak of rubber-soled shoes approaching.

"So how's the new house?" Cy asked after they had exchanged hellos.

"Big," she said with a laugh.

"The mortgage or the house itself?"

"Both."

"Looks like you're up there to stay, Elly. I hope you're doing the right thing."

"It's a great town, Cy. I love being right on the ocean and I love the people."

"But it's not New York."

"Neither is Boca," she pointed out.

He had the grace to laugh. "There are more native New Yorkers down here than in the five boroughs."

He asked about her practice, and she told him a little about Patsy Wheeler's situation. Cy was a skilled OB-GYN and his insights were always welcome. He mentioned the name of a hospital Web site that had links to a physician's online forum she might find useful. She typed the URL into her browser window, then bookmarked it while they were talking.

"I appreciate the help, Cy."

"You never were one to ask for anything," he said. "Good to know experience is still good for something."

She wasn't exactly sure how to take that comment, but this wasn't the time to start parsing it for hidden meanings.

"Sorry to have to cut this short, Elly, but I'm due for my annual stress test in an hour."

There was no nice way to ease into it, so she jumped in feet first. "I need a referral, Cy. The person in question is presenting signs of liver cancer, most likely secondary. I sus-

pect a primary pancreatic tumor, but I haven't done an ex-
amination."

"Male? Female? Age?"

"Male," she said, keeping her tone even. "Sixty-five."

A silence. "Heavy drinker?"

"Moderate."

"Smokes?"

"Used to." Maybe still did. She really couldn't say.

"I can think of three top-drawer choices. One is up in Palm
Springs. The other two are in the New York City area."

She copied down the names then took a deep breath. "Anyone in the Boston area?"

He gave her a name. "He's good but nowhere near as gifted
as the others I've mentioned." Another one of those uncomfortable pauses. "Are we talking about Billy O'Brien?"

She bristled slightly at his tone of voice, even though he
had every right to resent the man his wife had loved. "I spoke
with my sister in Cambridge and she says he looks pretty bad."

"Then he should definitely see one of the men in New
York. We both know the odds are against him if it's pancreatic, but if there's anything to work with, they'll bring their
entire arsenal to bear."

"Thank you," she said. "This information will mean a lot
to Mary Pat."

"And to you?"

"I'm pleased to be able to help."

"That isn't the same thing."

"I'm calling from the office, Cy. I can't really get into this."

"Findlay is the man you want to speak with," Cy said. "Tell
your sister to make sure they don't try to hand her over to one
of his partners. They don't have the depth of experience James
has."

It cost him as much to share that information as it had cost
her to ask for it. Just the mention of Billy's name had changed
the atmosphere between them from warmly cordial to wary
and uncomfortable. Two decades had passed since the day she
found out she wasn't Cy's daughter and they were still frozen
in place, held together by history and habit, each one unwilling
to be the first to let go.

Cy promised to e-mail her if he came up with any more

names. She promised to keep him posted on Billy's illness. They both said how sorry they were that they couldn't speak longer, but 1) she was at work and 2) he had a stress test scheduled. They couldn't have planned it any better if they'd tried.

She hung up the phone, then slumped back in her leather chair. She felt drained, as if all of her emotional energy had seeped out through her shoes when she wasn't looking. Despite everything Cy Markowitz was still her father in all the ways that counted, and his approval continued to carry a great deal of weight. Probably more than it should, she supposed, but whoever said family dynamics made sense? She used to laugh when Susan launched into a rant about the complex dynamics at work within the Galloway clan. Some of the goings-on sounded downright Machiavellian to her—who would have thought planning Thanksgiving dinner required diplomatic maneuvers that rivaled the SALT talks?—but still she envied Susan every second of aggravation. She had always longed for family, to be surrounded by all of that shared history and love and support.

When Cy married Nancy, her new stepmother had opened both her heart and her home to her, but Ellen had been too young and still too angry to be able to accept kindness when it came her way. She had hated Cy for not being her father, hated him for bringing Billy O'Brien into her life, for taking away the family she knew and loved and replacing it with a group of strangers. She had cultivated her anger the way Nancy cultivated her roses until it became a habit she couldn't break even if she wanted to.

When David was born she thought her heart would split apart. Cy's joy had spilled over onto everyone; it was wide enough to cover the world. If only she had been old enough, mature enough to understand the things that seemed all too clear to her now. At the point when Cy had stopped believing in miracles, the greatest miracle of all was handed to him. He was fifty-six when love found him for the second time; fifty-seven when their first child was born. Sometimes it hurt to look at him; his joy was that blinding.

There was nothing she could ever do that would surpass the simple fact of David's existence. No award she could win, no mountain she could conquer. Once again the illusion of being part of a family didn't hold up to the light of day.

But she couldn't change the past and she refused to spend the rest of her life with her nose pressed up against the meta-phorical window, always on the outside looking in. She threw herself into her studies, falling more in love with the practice of medicine with each day that passed. She had a natural gift when it came to dealing with patients. Her diagnostic skills were razor sharp. She heard both text and subtext. She was able to read subtle changes in body language and interpret them correctly and when the result was the birth of a healthy baby to a healthy mother—well, nothing on earth came close.

One way or another, it always came down to family. Every-thing you did (and the way you did it) could all be traced back to someone very much like you. You woke up one morning and looked in the mirror and saw your mother looking back at you just when you thought you had forgotten . . . or you laughed and heard your aunt, the one with the overplucked eyebrows and bad taste in men. Grandma Bess used to do the *Times* crossword puzzle in ink same as you do. And what about that auburn hair and the skin that freckled in the shade— everyone knew that was pure O'Brien.

She wasn't part of Cy's family, not the way David was, but she had inherited his love of medicine the same way Deirdre had inherited Billy's love of music. There were no med school classes to explain this, no asterisk attached to the DNA. Family ties required no explanation. They just were, and that was usu-ally more than enough.

This past week with Deirdre had been trying but wonderful. That big empty house felt like a home to her now with her sister's harps in the front room, Stanley's water bowl near the back door and his food dish anywhere he felt like carrying it. And although she wouldn't admit it to Deirdre for fear of encouraging her, she was glad Stanley the One Dog Wrecking Crew would be staying behind while her sister was up in Bar Harbor.

She glanced at her watch. It was almost eleven. The odds were that she wouldn't hear from any of the doctors she had called until after office hours. She debated e-mailing Mary Pat with the names of the doctors Cy had suggested, then decided against it. She pulled out her address book, flipped pages until she found Mary Pat's number, then dialed.

The machine answered and she was ashamed of the sigh of relief that escaped her lips. What did it say about a relationship when you would rather speak to a machine than your own sister?

"You have reached the Galvin residence. We're all busy right now, but we hope you'll leave a message. To leave a message for James, press 1. For Mary Patricia, press 2. For Shawna, press 3. For Sean, press 4. For Caitlin and Duffy, press 5. And if you're calling for Declan, call back in another two years when he's old enough to talk."

Mary Pat's outgoing messages tended to sound like the begats in the Bible. She and Deirdre used to mock Mary Pat's outgoing messages mercilessly when they were younger. Once, when Ellen was interning at Mount Sinai, Deirdre taped a devastating parody on Ellen's answering machine without her knowledge and only the actions of a very benevolent God saved them all from terminal embarrassment. She had never been so grateful for a power outage in her life. And if that wasn't a metaphor, she didn't know what was.

She pressed 2, then waited for the tone.

"Mary Pat, this is Ellen. I have some information for you." She read off the names and phone numbers Cy had given to her, along with his recommendation. "My partner is looking into it and I have calls in with some other sources as well. I'll call you tonight with some more names." She hesitated a moment. "Say hi to Billy for me, okay?"

Years of training, years of practice at dealing with patients and their families, years of knowing exactly what to say and when to say it, and when it came to her own family, this was the best she could do.

Pathetic didn't begin to cover it.

"Look," Scott the Mechanic said as they merged onto the Maine Turnpike a little before one in the afternoon, "we still have a long way to go until we get to Bar Harbor. You're not going to talk about that dog the whole way, are you?"

Deirdre glared at him through her sunglasses. "I'm worried

about him," she said. "Stanley doesn't like being left alone."

"Maybe you should've thought of that when you adopted him."

"Not that it's any of your business, but I didn't know it when I adopted him. He didn't start acting out until the other night."

His snort of laughter wasn't the most attractive sound she had heard lately. "Acting out? He was being a dog."

"I did some research while I was at Ellen's house, and dogs suffer terribly from separation anxiety."

"Don't tell me you're one of those lunatics who take their dogs to pet shrinks."

"I can't afford to take my dog to a pet shrink, but if I could—"

His groan rattled the windows.

"Okay, we won't talk about Stanley anymore," she said, glancing down at the nifty little red convertible whizzing past them in the right-hand lane. "So what do you want to talk about?"

"You much of a sports fan?"

"I love figure skating."

"That's not a sport. That's a popularity contest."

"And I suppose you're going to tell me they're not athletes."

"So forget sports," he said. "How about politics?"

"I don't have any."

"You don't vote?"

"I vote but my candidates are never on the ballot, so I write them in."

So much for politics.

The frequent silences that fell between them had started to feel as comfortable as a pair of old Birks to her. She was happy to hum along with some early Bonnie Raitt on the radio and watch the pine trees roll by. Being celibate had its advantages. A few years ago, back when she still believed in the concept of Mr. Right and all that came with him, she would have been compelled to look at Scott the Mechanic as a candidate for the job. These conversation-free stretches would have sent her self-confidence into a major decline. Why wasn't he talking? What had she done wrong? What could she do to make it right? The posing and posturing with one goal in mind.

The nuns were right. Celibacy was definitely the way to go.

If Scott the Mechanic didn't want to talk, he didn't have to talk, and she didn't have to fill up the silence with chatter. Her entire future wasn't wrapped up in whether or not she was pretty enough, sexy enough, entertaining enough, everything enough for whoever the date *du jour* happened to be.

"O'Brien and Markowitz," he said as they passed the exit to Bath. "How'd that happen?"

"We're half sisters." She had nothing against telling him the story, but this was Ellen's world. She was only visiting.

"Same mother?"

"Same father."

"Markowitz or O'Brien?"

"O'Brien."

"So how did Dr. Ellen end up a Markowitz?"

"Her mother married a Markowitz?"

"Did you grow up together?"

She shook her head. "We didn't even know about each other until we were fourteen."

He glanced over at her. "That must have been one hell of a surprise."

"Sometimes it still is." She curled her legs under her and smoothed her long gauzy skirt. "So what's your story. How did a Southie stargazer end up fixing cars in Maine?"

His expression didn't change, but she noticed the tiniest twitch beneath his right eye. "It seemed like the thing to do at the time."

"C'mon," she said, her tone light and teasing. "You can do better than that. I want to know all about your ex-wives, your kids, the broken hearts you left behind in Boston."

"There's nobody."

"There has to be somebody."

"Not anymore."

"Divorce?" The word no sooner left her lips than she knew how wrong she was. His expression still hadn't changed, but sorrow was in that truck with them, taking up space, breathing the air.

"I'm sorry," she said, placing a hand on his forearm. "I shouldn't have pushed."

"No problem."

She waited, but that was all he had to say on the topic. She was filled with questions she knew she couldn't ask. She pictured him as a newlywed, still high on discovery, one of those guys who married in his early thirties and got it right the first time. Or maybe he had married his high-school sweetheart right after graduation and lived a white-picket-fence kind of life until fate tore them apart, leaving him alone and brokenhearted and in need of the kind of comfort only a woman could provide.

Not her, of course, since she was celibate, but her imagination was still having trouble processing that fact. It persisted in conjuring up images of herself as a modern Florence Nightingale tending to the wounded on love's battlefield, mending brokenhearted men, then sending them on their way to a lifetime of happy fidelity with somebody else while she waved goodbye and blinked back one perfect tear.

That was the O'Brien in her, proof positive that she was very much her father's daughter. She was always looking for the romance behind the story, the pink satin bow on top of the pile of shit. Give her enough time and she could find the happy ending in *Romeo and Juliet*. You wouldn't think Scott the Mechanic would be one of her bigger challenges, but he was. She studied his face for clues, but he might as well have been carved from granite. He said he had no one, but lots of men said that while their voice mail was busy logging *you're late for dinner* messages from the wife and children. For all she knew he had a few kids out there somewhere who were being raised by a friend or distant relative, with only the occasional e-mail or phone call from daddy dearest to remind them that their father was still alive.

With the possible exception of her sister Mary Pat, everyone had secrets. Big ones. Small ones. Life-changing ones. Secrets that could break your heart or break your spirit if you let them. Billy's secret had wrecked their family. That was a fact even she couldn't find a way to romance. Her mother was forced to face her husband's flagrant infidelities. Mary Pat ditched college for marriage and escape, while she and Ellen struggled to figure out their respective places in the revised family tree.

Sometimes she had the feeling the struggle would outlive both of them.

In the background Bonnie Raitt sang about heartbreak, one of those bluesy songs about bad men and good women and the mess they made with their lives.

With all due respect, Bonnie didn't know the half of it.

Twenty-one

"Do you have the girls this weekend?" Ellen asked Hall as they walked across the parking lot to their cars.

"All four of them."

"Kate and Elizabeth are coming up from New York?"

"Tomorrow morning. They'll pick up Willa and Mariah and be here by ten."

"Special occasion?" She still didn't have all of the birthdays straight.

"Job interviews. The friend of one of their friend's father owns a resort near Ogunquit, and he needs more wait staff for the outdoor dining area."

"I waited tables one summer," she said as they stopped next to her Cruiser. "I was probably the worst waitress the Hamptons ever saw."

He laughed and leaned against the door of her car. "I'm surprised. You have a great memory, good personality, and superior upper-body strength."

"I'll admit my triceps are second to none," she said, grinning at him, "but kitchen politics were my downfall."

"Kitchen politics?"

"Let's just say the cook had his favorites and I wasn't one

of them. His favorites waited the big tables with the heavy tippers. I ended up bussing."

"You're saying he hit on the girls."

"Big time. I could take a stand because I didn't need great tips to survive, but some of the others—" She stopped, remembering Hall's daughters were going to spend the summer waiting tables.

"God damn." He dragged a hand through his silvery blond hair. "If anyone tries anything with my kids, I'll—"

"Kate and Elizabeth wouldn't put up with that garbage for a second. They know you're behind them emotionally and financially." And, thank God, the world was changing. It wasn't there yet, but it was better than it had been when she was in college.

From the look on Hall's face, he wasn't interested in her historical overview. Not when it came to his daughters.

"I'm going to drive down there and talk to the owners before they sign anything."

Her eyes widened. "Your daughters will be furious with you."

"They've been furious with me before and I've survived. It comes with the territory. They'll be on their own in a handful of years, and I won't be able to protect them. I'm going to do what I can while I still have the authority." He bent down and peered into her face. "Are you crying, Markowitz?"

She didn't bother to try to hide her emotions. They were too big to contain. "You really are a terrific father."

"I've been at it awhile. Sooner or later I'm bound to get a few things right."

"Sorry." She swiped her eyes with the back of her hand. "It's been one of those days. Fatherhood's been on my mind." Cy. Billy. All the twisted limbs of her family tree.

"Did you get the callbacks you were waiting for?"

"Two of them so far. The doctor you came up with seems to be on everyone's short list."

"He's a good man and right there in Boston."

"I was thinking about suggesting a trip to Rochester."

"The Mayo's always a good choice."

"But?"

"Just a hunch." He took her hand in his. "I don't think

there's a lot of good news up ahead. He might be just as well off sticking close to home."

"Assuming he has one. He's never been the kind of guy who sticks around for long." Her eyes welled again with tears. "Isn't this ridiculous?" She swiped her eyes again. "I haven't seen the man in almost four years. He never calls, he never writes—" She tried to force a laugh but the sound wouldn't fool anyone. "Mary Pat is a daddy's girl. I'm trying to find a way to prepare her for bad news, but I'm not sure she really hears what I'm saying."

They both knew that very often a patient or her family heard only as much as they were capable of handling at any given moment. She had once had a patient who endured eight months of grueling chemotherapy before she was able to acknowledge that she was fighting cancer. No one could predict who would handle bad news with grace and courage and who would fall apart. It was a gamble not even Las Vegas would touch.

"Did Deirdre get off okay?"

She was grateful for the change of topic. "Scott came by for her around one o'clock." She glanced at her watch. "They should be there by now."

"So that means Stanley's alone."

"Scary thought, isn't it? For once I'm glad I don't have much furniture. I promised him a long run on the beach tonight if he was a good dog."

"Feel like company?"

"Hall, I don't think—"

"Do you feel like company?"

"Yes," she said, "but—"

"I have a pair of jeans in the back of my truck. I'll change at your place."

"People are going to talk."

"People are always talking around here. Another ten years and you won't even notice."

"Wanna bet?" she asked in her best New York accent.

"Ten bucks," he said and she agreed.

She would trade ten bucks for another ten years in Shelter Rock Cove any day of the week.

*   *   *

ЄΙΙℓℿ ran upstairs to change out of her work clothes. "There's some beer in the fridge," she called down over her shoulder as she reached the landing. "Maybe some tuna salad. Grab whatever you want. And let Stanley out the back, would you?"

Stanley obviously understood English, because he threw himself at Hall like a guided missile.

"I get the message," he said, tossing his jeans over his shoulder. He followed the dog down the hallway, through the kitchen, straight to the back door. "There you go, Stan. Knock yourself out!"

Stanley launched himself into the yard, then started tearing around like an escapee from canine prison. Hall left the door open, then ducked into the bathroom to change into jeans. Willa and Mariah still hadn't stopped talking about Stanley. Their odes to the dog's big brown eyes were meant to inspire him to buy them a puppy, but Yvonne had given him strict orders. "No dogs, no cats," she had told him when he broached the subject. She was severely allergic and just the thought of living with a quadruped made her break out in hives. But what was stopping him from driving over to the shelter and finding a Stanley of his own?

He had a big empty house just like Ellen's. He had a yard and no problem with slobber or chew toys.

The more he thought about it, the more he liked the idea. Maybe Ellen would go with him tomorrow. They could take the long way to Idle Point, weaving in and out of the scores of shore towns that dotted the Maine coast, maybe stop at one of the steak houses that provided occasional relief from the basic seafood diet of the native Mainer.

He zipped up his jeans, then grabbed his dress shirt and trousers. Ellen was still upstairs. He could hear the water running as he walked back through the hallway toward the front door. There had to be a T-shirt stowed somewhere in the truck. Every time the hospital held a fund-raiser, he seemed to walk away with a couple more of them. He usually gave them to his girls to wear as nightshirts, but now and then he tossed one in the back of the truck for times like this. It was still too cold to go shirtless, and, face it, he wasn't exactly eighteen any longer. At eighteen he could have gone shirtless in January and never noticed. Hot blood had its benefits.

He swung open the front door and found himself face-to-face with Susan and Claudia. Claudia toted a cake wrapped in some kind of fancy hot-pink cellophane tied with ribbons and streamers while Susan had a lock on a stack of casseroles in foil pans.

"Surprise!" Only Susan could make an innocent word sound like an indictment. She gave him one of those Mr. Spock eyebrow lifts that she used to practice in front of the mirror when they were kids. "Hope we're not interrupting."

Claudia's eyes never glanced lower than his nose, even though she had probably seen his bare torso ten thousand times over the years, beginning when he was five years old. It seemed as if he had spent entire summers camped out on the beach behind her house—this house that now belonged to Ellen—girl-watching, catching rays, wishing he had been born a Galloway.

"I brought Ellen some housewarming gifts," Claudia said, trying not to appear obvious as she peered over his shoulder into the shadowy front hall. "I probably should have phoned first."

"Why?" asked Susan with the kind of snarky smile that would consign a kid to permanent detention. "This is much more fun."

He blasted her with a look. "Ellen's upstairs," he said casually. "I'm going to the truck to look for a T-shirt."

"And Stanley?" Susan asked.

He ignored her and headed for his truck. He had known the woman his entire life and never seen her like this before. Susan was known for her cutting humor. Her acerbic one-liners were legendary among her friends and family. But this was something different. These remarks were pointed, emotional, and aimed directly at him. If he didn't know better, he would think she was jealous, but the thought was too ridiculous to pursue. They were friends. Wasn't it Susan who had championed his feelings for Annie? She was the one who had encouraged him to state his case, to quit treating her like the Widow Galloway and start treating her like the woman he had loved for more years than he cared to remember. Susan had been behind him every step of the way, and when it became clear Annie's heart belonged to Sam Butler, it was Susan who played matchmaker for him with every single woman who stumbled into her path.

But he couldn't deny the fact that she was acting weird as hell and that it had all started the morning after his night with Ellen.

"Still think nothing's going on, Ma?"

Claudia had to admit that catching Hall, shirtless, in Ellen's house seemed highly suspicious, but she would rather cut out her tongue than admit it to her daughter. Susan had been acting very strange the last few days and she wasn't about to fuel this particular fire if she could help it. She liked gossip as well as the next person, but there was something about the situation that made her feel quite protective of Hall and, in some ways, of Ellen as well.

They stood together on the front porch and watched as Hall dropped the rear gate on his Rover and rummaged through a pile of sporting equipment in search of a shirt.

"Don't you have one of Jack's T-shirts in the trunk?" she asked.

"They're covered in axle grease," Susan said.

"I saw a clean one under Charlie's soccer gear."

"Ma, will you mind your own business. I'm enjoying the show."

"You sound like Sweeney. It's unseemly for a woman of your age to ogle men."

"First of all, I'm only forty-six. Second of all, I'm not dead."

"And you're married."

"I know I'm married."

"I'm not so sure you do," she said. "You've been acting very strangely all week. Everyone's noticed."

"I'm menopausal," Susan said. "Isn't that what you've been telling everyone?"

"Would you rather I tell them that you're throwing yourself at Hall?"

Susan plopped the casserole tins down on the top step, then

stormed off in Hall's direction, leaving her feeling much as she had during those long years when it seemed as if all of her children would be teenagers forever. She and her oldest daughter were too much alike for comfort. They were both strong-willed and pragmatic, a combination that led to constant skirmishes that had evolved over the years into a form of entertainment. And like her mother, Susan was a one-man woman. Jack Aldrin might not be the kind of man you would find on the cover of a magazine, but he was a hardworking man who was devoted to his family, and the thought that her daughter might jeopardize her marriage for the possibility of a fling with an old friend made Claudia's blood run cold.

"Hi, Claudia!" Ellen appeared in the doorway. She wore a pair of cutoff shorts that left her long slim legs bare to the evening breezes, a snowy white T-shirt with a bright red sweater tied loosely around her narrow waist. "Come on in."

Claudia couldn't help but smile. "You look like one of my grandchildren, dear. I forget sometimes how young you are."

"Thirty-five next month," she said with a fake shudder. "One step away from middle age."

Ellen's glance drifted toward the driveway, where Hall and Susan were engaged in animated conversation. Her expression softened, grew almost dreamy. Claudia's heart seemed to expand inside her chest as she remembered the last time she saw a young woman look at a man that way. It was the first time Sam Butler walked into the flower shop. She had turned to ask Annie who he was, and the look of wonder and longing in her eyes had stopped her in her tracks.

Oh, Lord, what had they walked into?

"My special carrot cake," she said, extending the gaily wrapped platter to the young woman. "We should have called first. I'm sorry."

"No apology necessary," Ellen said. She possessed the fair, translucent skin found on most natural redheads, the kind that blushed at the drop of a secret. She took the carrot cake from her. "My favorite! Why don't you join me in the kitchen for a slice?"

Claudia retrieved Susan's casseroles from the top step, then followed Ellen to the kitchen in the rear of the house.

"I don't have much furniture yet," Ellen said as she gestured toward two high stools near the work island in the center of the room. "I'm using the counter as a table for the interim." She told Claudia about the beautiful light oak table and chairs she had found at an online furniture gallery.

Claudia deposited the trio of casseroles on the counter, then eased herself up onto the stool. It wobbled. She tried very hard not to notice how much. The older she got, the more vulnerable she felt. Things she wouldn't have noticed ten years ago filled her with terror today. Her independence seemed sometimes to be a day-to-day proposition.

"You bought furniture online?"

"I would buy groceries online if I could." She pulled two small plates from a box near the refrigerator and silverware from the dishwasher.

"Roberta has been trying to convince me to go online."

"You should," Ellen said, cutting two generous pieces of cake. "I don't know how I survived without it."

Ellen described the table she had ordered, right down to the depth of the chair seats. "They deliver on Monday."

"I'm impressed," Claudia admitted, "but I'm still not ready to give up going to a real store."

Ellen complimented her on the carrot cake. She ate with an appetite that belied her slender form. The Galloway women had only to look at dessert and it miraculously appeared on their hips. Stanley bounded through the back door. He nuzzled against Ellen's bare leg, paid his respects to Claudia, then barreled down the hallway and out the front door.

"I've been meaning to call and ask you about that secret panel in the pantry," Ellen said as she sliced herself a second piece of cake.

"Oh, what a wonderful story that is! You see, the original owner was a man named Laidlaw who—"

The phone broke in with its shrill demand.

"I won't be a second," Ellen said as she went to answer it in the other room.

Normally Claudia would feel a trifle piqued if Susan interrupted her mid-sentence to answer the phone, but Ellen was a doctor, after all, and it came with the territory.

And would it be so terrible if she managed to catch a few words of the conversation while she waited?

*   *   *

"Thanks a lot, Suz," Hall muttered as his old pal screeched down the street in her mother's Chrysler. She picked a fight with him over who was carpooling to soccer practice three weeks from next Sunday, then took off, leaving her mother behind. She had made it look spontaneous, but he wouldn't be surprised if she had planned the whole damn thing.

Okay, so maybe that was over the top even for his old friend, but she had been so volatile the past few days that she should be wearing caution signs on her back.

He loved Claudia Galloway, who had her own streak of volatility, but she wasn't the woman he had been hoping to spend the evening with, and Susan was probably having a good laugh over it right now.

He whistled for Stanley, and the two of them strolled back into the house.

"Was that my car I heard?" Claudia asked as he entered the kitchen.

"Afraid so," he said, snagging a piece of carrot cake from her plate.

"Did she forget something?"

"We had a fight about the soccer carpool, and she decided to make a grand exit."

"I love my daughter, but she has been behaving like a horse's hindquarters all week."

"You noticed, too?"

Claudia's lightly powdered cheeks reddened. "I won't tell you what she said to us at the flower shop."

"Annie told me." He couldn't hold back his grin. "She said Sweeney had to translate."

"Anne usually displays more discretion."

"You have to admit it was quote-worthy."

Claudia made one of those ladylike Yankee sniffs that signified great disapproval.

"Chili mac!" he said, lifting the lid on one of the foil casserole pans.

She slapped at his hand. "Those are for Ellen."

He glanced around. "Where is she?"

"Taking a phone call," Claudia said. "There seems to be

some health problem with her father." She cleared her throat. "Not that I was eavesdropping, you understand. I couldn't help but overhear—"

"I know all about it," he said, making sure he held back this grin. Claudia's eavesdropping skills were as well-honed as her daughter's sharp tongue.

"Poor Dr. Markowitz," Claudia said. "And if I recall, he has a young son."

"Actually it's not Cy who has the problem. It's her biological father. Deirdre's father."

"It sounded very serious."

"I think it has that potential."

Claudia's reaction wasn't at all what he expected. Her eyes filled with tears, and she looked down at her hands.

"Claudia?"

"Don't mind me. When you get to be my age, you'll understand."

"You were thinking about John." Claudia had never gotten over the sudden death of her husband. For years this big house had been a shrine to his memory, the place where she felt closest to him.

"Actually I was thinking about you, dear."

His look must have conveyed his surprise because she leaned over and patted his hand the same way she used to when he was ten years old and his world was coming apart at the seams.

"Oh, don't look at me that way," she said gently. "I've been around long enough to know men and women sleep with each other now and then. What would we talk about at the flower shop if they didn't?"

He was over forty-five and a three-time loser in the marriage stakes. You would think embarrassment would no longer be an option, but it was. At least around Claudia Galloway.

"Any fool with eyes could see there's more than just sex between the two of you. This has been growing for a very long time."

"We've lost a dozen patients since Sunday night."

"And they'll come back before too long."

"There's no guarantee."

"So you'll find new ones." Her tone shifted from gentle to

fierce. "I wasted so much time worrying about what John's family would think of him marrying a poor girl from the docks that we almost didn't get married at all. I wish I could go back and gather up those lost hours and minutes and spend them all with him."

"It still takes two and I'm not sure the lady in question wants to take a chance on a man with a track record like mine."

"You'll never know unless you try, will you?"

"Take a look around, Claudia. It's Friday night. We were alone and you know I don't make house calls."

She looked at him and they both started to laugh.

"There's no fool like an old fool, is there?" she asked, wiping away tears of mirth.

He could think of at least one middle-aged fool who might give her a run for her money.

Mary Pat might not have inherited their father's musical ability, but she definitely had inherited his theatrical flair. She knew how to drop a bombshell better than the U.S. Army.

Her first words were "Deirdre's gone missing," followed by a word-by-word transcript of her entire conversation with someone at the Crooked Isle Inn who claimed she had never heard of a harpist named Deirdre O'Brien.

"I need to talk to her about Billy." Mary Pat sounded annoyed, frazzled, like a woman who was rapidly approaching something too terrible to contemplate. "She's been doing her best to avoid me, but she's his daughter, too. She needs to be involved in the decision making." Her voice broke and Ellen felt a surge of sympathy for the sister she barely knew. "Would you call Crooked Isle and see what you can find out? Tell them you're a doctor. They might pay more attention."

She wasn't convinced flashing her credentials would make much of a difference, but it was worth a shot. Mary Pat gave her the number for the Crooked Isle.

"You'll call me right back?" Mary Pat asked.

"I promise."

It took a few tries, but she was finally put through to the right person. She repeated her question, and the woman's words were lost in a gale of laughter floating toward her from the kitchen. She cupped her hand around the earpiece and strained to catch the woman's words.

"I'm sorry," she said. "Would you mind repeating that?"

Funny how the woman's huff of annoyance came through loud and clear. "I said there is no one by that name on our staff. You must have the wrong establishment."

"Is this the Crooked Isle Inn?"

"It is."

"And you're in Bar Harbor."

"We are."

"Then I have the right establishment."

"I'm sorry, miss—"

"Doctor."

"I'm sorry, Doctor, but for the last time there is no Deirdre O'Brien on staff here."

"She's the new harpist." Or harper. Or whatever they called people who played harps.

"As I already told you, we don't have a new harpist."

She hung up and dialed Mary Pat back.

"The same thing happened to me," she told her older sister. "The woman said she had no record of a Deirdre O'Brien."

"And she said they didn't have a new harpist, right?"

"Right."

"I knew she was up to something when she showed up with that monster of a dog last week, but I never suspected this."

That monster of a dog was currently sprawled on his back across Ellen's feet having his furry belly rubbed. "You don't really think she had this all planned out."

"Rescuing Stanley was probably spontaneous. Dumping Stanley on one of us took a little planning."

"Her car is still here."

"A fifteen-year-old Hyundai that's laid up in the shop. She'll never miss it."

"She had Scott, the mechanic, drive her up to Bar Harbor. Why would she do that if she was looking to disappear?"

"I don't have all the answers," Mary Pat said, "but the fact remains that nobody at Crooked Isle Inn ever heard of her and you're left holding the dog."

"Well, I'm sure Scott didn't run off with her. He has to come home sometime and then I'll ask him." Okay, so she wasn't absolutely positive he hadn't run off with Deirdre, just reasonably sure. Mary Pat didn't have to know everything.

Ellen promised to call her sister tomorrow with an update, then hung up the phone feeling even more drained than she had that morning. Mary Pat had done a remarkable job of getting her emotions back under control. Some women ate chocolate, some women shopped to conquer stress. Mary Pat made lists. She read columns of To Do items to Ellen until she thought her ears would fall off and drop into her lap. Compassion had never been her first response to a conversation with her older sister, but this time it was. There was no way either one of them could deny Billy was in trouble. He refused to eat. He sat in the lounge chair in the family room and nodded off to *Buffy the Vampire Slayer* reruns when he wasn't sound asleep in the guest room.

His doctor's appointment couldn't come fast enough for any of them.

"I'm so sorry," she said as she rejoined Claudia and Hall in the kitchen. "Family difficulties." She glanced around. "Where's Susan?"

"We had words," Claudia said.

"Then we had a fight," Hall said, "and she drove off in Claudia's car."

"I have a good mind to call Barney and have him arrest her." Claudia looked as if she meant every word.

"I can top both of you," Ellen said as she filched a piece of carrot cake and popped it in her mouth. "Deirdre's disappeared."

Twenty-two

Deirdre didn't mean to melt down right there in the lobby of the Crooked Isle Inn, but there was a first time for everything.

"We did everything possible to contact you, Ms. O'Brien," Stephen Logan, owner of the Inn, backed away ever so slightly. "We phoned your manager, sent a telegram to you at your last address. We even tried to contact your last employer in case he knew where to find you. I can say with utmost sincerity that we exhausted every means at our disposal to let you know we didn't require your services."

"Are you telling me I've been fired?"

"No, no!" Stephen Logan looked appalled. "I'm afraid you were never hired."

"But I signed the paperwork."

"Yes, but we didn't countersign." He took her by the elbow and gently led her to the far corner of the room, where her sobbing wouldn't upset the paying guests. "That's what I'm trying to tell you, Ms. O'Brien. By that time our regular harpist had come back to us permanently."

"But I'm here," she said through her gulping tears. "I gave up a gig in New York to take this job." Every time she went out looking for security, she ended up with a kick in the head. When was she going to learn?

"I understand your distress. We're every bit as distressed as you are."

She shot him a fierce look. "I doubt that." The guy owned two hundred acres of prime property on Frenchman's Bay. He hadn't a clue what she was feeling.

"While we can't offer you the job, we would very much like to offer you some small reparation for your inconvenience."

She perked up just the slightest bit. "A month's salary would be nice."

"We were thinking of two weeks' salary and a three-night stay in one of our best suites. All meals included, of course."

She noticed Scott the Mechanic lugging her harps in from the truck. "A friend drove me up."

She had to hand it to Logan. He didn't even flinch. "He's welcome to join you."

At least she could see to it that Scott the Mechanic got a decent meal for his trouble. It wasn't much, but it was better than nothing. She agreed to it.

"We'll check you in at the front desk," Logan said, "and we'll see to it that a bottle of champagne is delivered to your room."

Scott waited off to the side while she checked in. A member of the bell staff approached with a rolling cart, and she directed him to the harps and to her two battered garment bags.

"Suite 6B," the desk clerk told the bellman, who headed toward the service elevator.

She walked over to Scott, who had been watching her with a look of concern and free-form irritation.

"What the hell happened?" he asked, looking at her tear-streaked face. "What did he say to you?"

"I've been fired."

His jaw actually dropped. "Fired? You never had a chance to play."

"Tell me about it." She explained the situation as well as she understood it, garbling some of the words through a fresh onslaught of tears. "He's giving me a three-night stay and two weeks' salary as compensation."

"He's afraid you'll turn around and sue his ass off."

She started to laugh despite herself. "I couldn't afford the lawyer."

"Come on," he said. "I'll drive you back down to your sister's."

"I'm not going."

"You're not going to stay here, are you? The place screwed you over."

"A free weekend is a free weekend. It's not like I have any place else to go, is it?"

"You can stay with Ellen."

The thought of crawling back into town with her tail between her legs was more than she could bear. It was one thing to know you were a loser. It was something else again for everyone else to know it. Especially when one of them was your sister the doctor.

"I'm staying here," she said, "and unless you're a fool, you'll stick around for a free meal before you head back."

He hesitated a few moments. She could almost see the wheels spinning inside his gorgeous head. Stay. Don't stay. Stick around. Dump her now.

"Okay," he said. "Thanks."

She had never seen that expression in his eyes before. There was a softness there as he looked at her. She hoped it wasn't pity. She wasn't even thirty-five yet. He should be looking at her with unbridled lust, not pity.

"Stop looking at me that way," she said as they walked toward the curved staircase to the left of the check-in desk. "I like you better when you're pissed off."

He laughed. Thank God. There was nothing like a blast of pity from a guy like Scott the Mechanic to pull a girl up by her bra straps.

"Don't worry," she said. "I promise I won't sob through dinner."

"I was worried about that."

The door to Suite 6B was ajar. The bellman was bustling around inside opening curtains, adjusting the air, generally keeping himself busy until she had a chance to reach into her pocket and pull out a tip.

He thanked her, glanced over at Scott, then left the room.

"Not bad," Scott said as he bent to check out the Jacuzzi in the corner of the room.

She peeked into the larger of the two bathrooms. "My last apartment was smaller than this!" Gleaming white tiles, sparkling fixtures, a tub the size of her Hyundai.

He gestured toward the smaller bathroom. "Okay if I—?"

"Feel free," she said, then disappeared into the porcelain palace where she made the mistake of looking into the mirror.

Wouldn't you think whoever had decorated the place might have dropped a few dollars into good lighting? The harsh white glare from the overhead light made her look like something that just crawled out from under a particularly nasty rock. Her skin was pale and pasty. Her eyes were red and puffy from crying. Her hair looked as if she styled it by sticking her finger into the nearest electrical outlet. And what was with that hideous top she had settled on? It made her look as if she'd eaten her way through the Ben & Jerry's case at Yankee Shopper. No wonder Scott the Mechanic had looked at her with pity. She was pitiable. She wouldn't be at all surprised if maybe Stephen Logan had taken one look at her, then fabricated that story about the return of the prodigal harpist. Who could blame him?

She could just picture Mary Pat with this news. No warm milk and cookies from her sister. Mary Pat would be tapping her foot like the velociraptor in *Jurassic Park,* waiting for her to get over it. It didn't matter if the wound was still bleeding. Mary Pat slapped a bandage on it and sent you back outside. Her sister had no patience with underachievers. She hadn't a clue how it felt to fail at something, because she had never failed at anything in her entire life. Neither had her husband. Or her kids. They were all just one big fat freaking success story after another. Good thing it hadn't worked out for Stanley down there. The poor dog would have ended up shampooed, permed, and winning Best in Show at Westminster.

Ellen might be a tad anal, but at least she allowed you to live your own life. Not Mary Pat the control freak. Her older sister was the type of person who slept with her Day Runner under her pillow. She had seen Mary Pat photocopy her address book "just in case."

In a twisted kind of way it would be fun to pick up the

phone and dial her sister. *Guess what, Mary Pat? I managed to get fired from a job I never had in the first place.*

Not even Mary Pat could top that one.

Megan had loved fancy restaurants. They used to save spare change, then bring it to the coin machine at Stop and Shop, where they dumped all the pennies and nickels and dimes and quarters onto the tray and waited while the machine counted it all up for them. She would pore over Zagat's, circling possibilities, comparing menus and price lists, calling for reservations. He had always wondered if she liked anticipating the dinner more than the food itself.

He used to hate those dinners even though he never let his wife know how he felt. Rich sauces and sky-high architectural desserts didn't do it for him. Terrine of this and mélange of that just weren't his speed. Give him a broiled steak with a baked potato, some creamed spinach on the side, and a bottle of Sam and you had him for life.

Deirdre said they had reservations out on the patio and the maître d' nodded politely, then showed them through the dining room and out onto the biggest, greenest lawn he had ever seen. It made a country-club golf course look neglected. He had heard the term "rolling lawns," but he had never been able to conjure up an image to explain it until now. The lawns at Crooked Isle Inn actually didn't just roll, they undulated all the way down to the harbor. Round white tables with furled yellow umbrellas dotted the lawns. They reminded him of the dandelion flowers in his front yard and he grinned.

"What's so funny?" Deirdre asked after they settled down at their table.

He told her and to his surprise she laughed, too.

"You're right," she said. "Do you think it was deliberate?"

He glanced around at the obviously wealthy clientele at the surrounding tables. "I don't think anyone here even knows what a dandelion is."

Lisa, their waitress, introduced herself and supplied menus. "We have a few specials tonight you might be interested in: grilled salmon in a lemon dill sauce; breast of free-range chicken sautéed with leeks and served with a balsamic reduction; and—my personal recommendation—shrimp with garlic and fresh tomatoes served on a bed of angel hair pasta."

Deirdre put down the menu and smiled up at the waitress. "I'll have a bacon cheeseburger with fries and a margarita."

He put his menu on top of hers. "And I'll have a New York steak, medium rare, with a baked potato and a bottle of Sam Adams."

"Can I interest either of you in the house salad?"

They both shook their heads.

"But if you have any fresh bread and butter, you won't hear us complain," Deirdre said.

"And a bucket of creamed spinach."

"Be right back," Lisa said and she was barely out of earshot when they burst into laughter.

"A fellow carnivore!" Deirdre reached across the table to shake his hand.

The handshake was brief, but he liked the way her hand felt in his. Her fingers were long and delicate with calluses on the tips. Strong and capable and lovely. He remembered how much he had liked the feel of her body against his last night on the beach.

"Our numbers are declining," he said, leaning back in his chair as Lisa deposited a basket of bread and a crock of butter on the table between them.

"Probably the cholesterol," Deirdre said as she helped herself to a muffin bursting with blueberries.

He grabbed a warm dinner roll and slathered it with butter. "Could be."

"In my own defense, I have to admit I don't always eat this way."

"You don't owe me any explanations. I'm not the Food Police."

She bit into her muffin and sighed with delight. "My sister Mary Pat polices the kitchen like it's a demilitarized zone. Dining out with her is like picking your way through a minefield."

"And I'll bet you make sure you detonate every single one you can find."

"One night I ordered a porterhouse steak with herb butter

and followed it up with cheesecake and a visit to the friendly neighborhood cardiologist."

She made him laugh. Laughter felt almost as good as her soft warm body against his.

"You're not really going to stay here all weekend, are you?"

She shrugged. "It's not like anyone's expecting me some place. I might as well."

"Then where will you go?"

Suddenly he understood. She relied on her quick wit to keep the world at bay, but the expression in her eyes gave her away every time.

"Maybe I'll drive down to Savannah. Lots of inns around there. Somebody's bound to be looking for a harper to play the dining room."

"Can't your manager find that out for you?"

"Screw him," she said. "He didn't exactly score a home run this time around, did he?"

Oh, yeah, she was hurting big time. Behind the flip comments and the big sunny smile was exactly what you would expect. She was hurt. She was embarrassed. She was scared shitless.

Lisa sailed up to them with the margarita and the bottle of Sam and a glass.

"To whatever lies beneath," Deirdre said as she raised her glass.

"To whatever the hell that means," he said as he lifted his bottle. *"Slainte."*

She paused, glass halfway to her lips. *"Slainte?"*

"It means 'cheers.' "

"I'm an O'Brien. I know what it means. I'm surprised that you do."

"My mother was a Dougherty."

"Irish and Italian," she said. "Now, there's a combination for you."

"I've heard all the jokes."

"I'll bet you have. You should hear some of the ones Ellen's heard."

"Did you hear the one about the rabbi and the priest who—"

She burst into laughter, which he suspected was really the flip side of her earlier tears. She radiated pure emotion. Joy. Despair. Longing. She couldn't hold back if she tried. No wonder her music had moved him to tears. She put her heart and soul into it because she didn't know any other way.

Same with that big dog of hers. So what if she had no money and no place to live. The mutt needed her and she stepped up to the plate. It screwed up her plans big time, but she did it anyway because it was the right thing to do.

He took a long pull on the bottle of Sam. Of course, she wasn't exactly Mother Teresa. She had badgered the hell out of him about her Hyundai and wasn't exactly shy about letting him know that her plans were much more important than his, which made his offer to drive her up to Bar Harbor even tougher to understand. She had landed on her sister's doorstep strictly as a matter of convenience. She had the slightly off-kilter sense of right and wrong that kept you wondering what she was really after, but before you could put up your defenses, she knocked them back down again with those eyes and that bawdy laugh.

The more she badgered him at the garage, the more Jack rode his ass about her, the more he started to look forward to those visits. He had found himself listening for the swish of her skirts in the doorway, the *click-click* of Stanley's toenails against the cement floor, the faint whisper of her perfume wafting above the heavy smells of axle grease and old tires.

"Wouldn't you love to sneak down to the docks and grab one of those?" She gestured toward the brightly colored boats thumping gently against the docks.

"Nope. I'm not the sailing type."

"An Irishman who doesn't love the sea? Impossible!"

"You ever see *Jaws*?"

"Maybe a million times."

"They don't make a boat big enough to get me out there."

"I'll take you sailing one day. I promise you'll love it."

"So you're coming back to Shelter Rock after all."

She took a sip of her margarita. "My car's there. Stanley's there. Of course I'm coming back."

"But not tonight."

"I love my sister, but she doesn't have a Jacuzzi."

He opened his mouth to press his point, then stopped. *Let it go, asshole. What's it your business if she stays here all summer?*

"And here we go!" Lisa popped up next to their table with a tray of food. "New York strip for you with baked and a side of spinach, and bacon cheese with fries for you."

"Listen!" Deirdre tilted her head to the right. "I'll bet we can hear our arteries shutting down."

"Right now I don't give a damn," he said. "This is about as good as it gets."

"Oh, I agree!" She popped a fry in her mouth, then handed him one. "I'll bet this is the last place you thought you'd be tonight."

"You're right. I—" He looked down at his watch. "Shit. I was supposed to pick up the parts for your car in Lincolnville."

"So pick them up tomorrow."

"Tomorrow I'll be back in Shelter Rock."

"Where is this Lincolnville anyway?"

"Closer to here than it is to there."

"That tells me a lot."

"This is going to screw things up for you. I probably won't be able to get your car fixed before Tuesday now."

"Great. I'll stay here until it's ready."

He gestured to Lisa for another bottle of Sam. Deirdre asked for another margarita.

They ate and drank in silence for a while. He had figured her for the type who talked nonstop, but she continued to surprise him. There was a mellow side to her he hadn't suspected, and he discovered he liked it a lot.

"So enough about me," she said as Lisa cleared away their empty platters. "Tell me how a mechanic from Boston ends up stargazing in Maine."

"Same way a harper from Boston ends up in Bar Harbor."

"Your manager called you with a job offer, too?"

"I sold off my old man's garage and was trying to figure out what to do next when I heard about the opening and jumped on it." All true, just not the whole story.

"Just like that?"

"There's more."

"I kind of thought so." She popped another fry into her

mouth. "How does the stargazing figure into it?"

"Long story," he said. "I was halfway to a degree in astronomy when my old man got sick and I had to step in and help him out."

"So you dropped out of school?"

"Things happen," he said. "I met someone. We got married. We bought a house. Next time I looked we were up to our eyes in debt and there was a baby on the way."

And then he blinked and they were gone.

"You miss them."

"Yeah," he said, reaching for the bottle of Sam. "I miss them."

"What happened? You don't have to answer if you don't want to, but I'd like to know."

Megan's unhappiness. Colin's tears. Her big plans for California. His big plans to sell the garage and surprise her there. A second chance. That was what they needed. A second chance to get it right. They still loved each other. All they had needed was a little luck, a change of scene. He would have done anything to make it work, but in the end he didn't have the time.

He wanted to tell her the whole fucking story, but the words wouldn't come.

"I'm sorry." She reached across the table and touched his hand. "I shouldn't have pushed."

"You didn't push."

"Sure I did." She gave him a quick smile. "I'm known for it."

They waved away dessert and he waited while she signed the check. She reached into her bag for her wallet, but he stopped her and left Lisa a tip that opened Deirdre's eyes wide.

"Are you always that generous?"

"Did you ever work for tips?"

She groaned. "More times than I can count."

"So did I."

They stood up to leave. "It's such a gorgeous night. Let's walk down to the dock and sit for a while."

"I should get moving," he said. "It's a long drive back."

"You're not going anywhere yet," she said. "You had three beers and half a margarita. You'd better walk it off."

"Two beers and I didn't touch your margarita."

"Can't blame me for trying." She lightly punched him in the forearm. "Come on. Be a sport. We'll sit out on the docks for a while and watch the moon rise over the water. Whaddya say?"

No would have been a good place to start. *No* would have been the smart thing, the wise thing. She was too vulnerable. He was too raw with need.

And the night was too damn beautiful to trust.

They sat on the dock while the sky went from pink to red to blue to midnight black. One by one the stars blinked on until it seemed the entire sky was ablaze with light. Deirdre was almost thirty-five years old and had seen more night skies than she could count, but Scott the Mechanic made it all seem brand-new.

"Hold your arm straight out," he told her, "and make a fist."

She took a sip from the champagne bottle they had found back at her suite. "Anything you say, Peretti." She curled her right hand into a fist and extended her arm. "I feel like I'm in a bad World War II movie."

"We're going to use the width of your fist as a tool of measurement and locate a few stars."

"I think I'm a lost cause," she said. "I've never been able to find the Big Dipper."

"Line up your fist against the right side of the moon."

"Okay."

"Now move three widths to your left."

"Got it."

"Now move down four."

"One . . . two . . . three . . . four."

"See the angle?"

"What angle? I can't see past the stars."

He didn't laugh. The man was very serious about his stars.

"Look closely. Forget individual stars and look for patterns."

"I don't—wait! I think I see what you mean."

"Eight stars of the same intensity—"

"In a kind of boxy shape."

"That's the Cradle."

She could barely hear him. His voice had dropped to little more than a whisper. "The Cradle?"

"Where the children of the gods sleep."

Maybe it was her mood or the sadness that seemed to pour off him in waves. Or maybe it was the fact that she had been wearing her emotions on her sleeve since they pulled into the parking lot at the Crooked Isle Inn, but that cradle of stars was her undoing and she started to cry.

"Pay no attention," she said, trying to pull herself back together. "This just hasn't been my best day."

"It's the champagne," he said. "It depresses the hell out of me, too."

"Stinking champagne. What the heck were we thinking anyway?" She emptied the rest of the bottle into the harbor. "I hope that doesn't kill the fish."

He peered down into the darkness. "Doubt if they'll even notice, since the bottle was empty."

"We drank the whole thing?"

"And I don't even like the stuff."

She swayed forward and would have tumbled into the harbor if he hadn't reached out and grabbed her.

"We'd better get you back to your room."

"I don't want to go . . . it's so beautiful out here." She leaned against his chest and closed her eyes. "I want you to show me more stars."

He helped her to her feet and she giggled as her legs seemed to fold beneath her like tired chair springs.

"Put your arms around my neck," he said. "I don't think you'll make it up the slope on your own."

She did as told and melted against him. She hadn't meant to, but her body seemed to have a mind of its own. Damn champagne. The world was spinning. The lawn rolled under her feet. If she didn't hold on to Scott the Mechanic, she just might fly away.

Finally he scooped her up into his arms and carried her back to the suite. Good thing they had already fired her. Things like this simply didn't happen at the Crooked Isle Inn.

"The bed is moving," she said as he set her down. "Make it stop."

"Lie down," he said as he slid her flimsy sandals off her feet. "It will stop soon."

"I need some water."

"Not a good idea. Just lie down and close your eyes."

That was the last thing she heard.

He couldn't leave her. Not like this. She looked so young, so vulnerable, so miserably unhappy as she lay there on the bed. The combination of disappointment and too much champagne was going to make her feel a hell of a lot worse before she felt better. The thought of her waking up alone in the middle of the night, in a strange place, the place where she had already suffered a major embarrassment, didn't sit right with him.

And what if she woke up in the middle of the night, stumbled to the bathroom, then fell and cracked her head on the sink? She would lie there on the cold tile floor for hours until housekeeping showed up to change the sheets.

Besides, he had sucked down enough champagne to give himself a buzz. Getting behind the wheel wouldn't be the brightest idea.

There were two beds. Two bathrooms. He could sleep in his clothes, then head out at dawn.

It sounded like a plan to him.

Twenty-three

"Stanley!" Mariah and Willa burst from Hall's Rover and raced up the driveway toward the backyard where Stanley was barking a greeting.

"Be careful, girls," Ellen called out as they dashed by. "Stanley's been playing down on the beach again. He smells like a giant haddock."

"Hi, Dr. Ellen." Elizabeth, Hall's eldest daughter, exited the car, followed by her sister Kate.

She hugged them both. "It's been ages since I saw you two."

"Last Thanksgiving," Kate said. "Your hair was longer and straighter."

She winced and tugged at an auburn curl. "I was spending more time with the blow-dryer than I was with my patients. I finally gave up the fight."

"I like it curly," Elizabeth said as her sister nodded her head. "It suits you."

"It better since I'm stuck with it."

"The munchkins can't stop talking about Stanley," Kate said. "I think they're in love with him."

"He is pretty lovable," she admitted. "Go on back and meet him if you want."

Laughing, they went off to join the little girls.

"They get more beautiful each time I see them," she told Hall as he joined her.

"Too beautiful, if you ask me. The phone started ringing before they pulled into the driveway. I swear every damn guy in town knows the number."

"You can't put them in a convent," she said.

"Wanna bet? I've been looking into a nice cloistered convent near Calais. Maybe I can get group rates."

They went around back and sat down on the deck. Stanley was putting Hall's girls through their paces as he ran rings around them, occasionally stopping to shake his sopping wet fur and make them shriek with pretend horror.

"Did I hear you say he smells like a giant haddock?"

"Afraid so. I took him down to the beach for a run, and he decided to swim instead."

"So we're going to ride around all day with a giant slobbering haddock in the back of my Rover."

"This was your idea," she reminded him. "But now that I've told Stanley, you can't uninvite him. His feelings will be hurt."

"You're starting to sound like your sister." He took off his sunglasses and wiped the right lens with the hem of his Shelter Rock Cove High School T-shirt. "Any news?"

"Nothing. Mary Pat is thinking about calling the police."

"On a thirty-five-year-old woman with a history of being unavailable?" He laughed so loud that all four of his daughters looked up at him with identical expressions of embarrassment.

"Mary Pat's a control freak."

"I figured that out."

"And get this: Scott's not back, either," she said. "Jack said he usually works Saturdays, but he didn't show up this morning."

"I guess Mary Pat doesn't need to call in the cops."

"I'm not sure. Deirdre told me she was celibate."

"*Was* being the operative word here."

"She's not the type to run off with an auto mechanic. My sister has her sights set a little higher."

"Things happen." What a lot of history you could pack into three syllables.

"I know," she said softly, "but it isn't like that with them. She's only known him a few days."

"C'mon, Markowitz. You never heard of a one-night stand?"

"She's made some mistakes. She really doesn't want to make any more. Believe me, she's not looking to sleep with Scott Peretti or anyone else."

"Have it your way."

"I'm not looking to have it my way. I'm simply telling the truth."

"As you see it."

"As I know it."

"You're the one who told me the two of you are practically strangers. She's lived an entire life you know nothing about."

"That's true," she acknowledged, "but I feel like I've gotten to know a lot more about her this past week."

"In some ways she reminds me of you."

She dragged her fingers through her tangle of curls. "It's the hair."

"I like her a lot."

"So do I, and I'm worried." Not that there was anything she could do about it. She and Deirdre didn't have the kind of rich sisterly history that would give her the right to tell her what to do. And they sure didn't have the kind of history that would make Deirdre listen.

"She's a big girl, Elly. She can take care of herself."

"If she could, she would have a cell phone or a forwarding address. Normal people usually have a way for other people to reach them."

"Maybe she doesn't want to be reached right now."

"So you think she took off, too."

"I didn't say that." He looked toward the path that led down to the beach just as Kate, Mariah, and Stanley disappeared. He cupped his hands around his mouth. "Hey! If that dog goes swimming again this morning, we're not going for that drive I promised you."

Ellen dissolved into laughter. "That'll put the fear of God into Kate and Lizzy. What teenage girl wouldn't want to be locked in a Land Rover with their kid sisters, two gynecologists, and a dog who smells like a giant haddock."

He sat back down, looking borderline sheepish. "Sometimes I forget they're not all still six years old."

"Better have those eyes checked, Dr. Talbot, because Kate and Lizzy are all grown-up."

"The day before yesterday they were crawling through my office in their foot pajamas."

"The day before yesterday was a long time ago."

They applauded as Willa, under Lizzy's tutelage, cartwheeled across the yard. "At least I got that part of the equation right."

"More than right. Fatherhood suits you."

He turned from his children and met her eyes. "Believe it or not, so does being a husband."

"Your track record might suggest otherwise."

"That's one of the things I love about you, Markowitz. You never pull your punches."

She touched his hand. "You know I didn't mean to hurt you. I'm probably not the best bet in the marital sweepstakes, either. I formed my idea of the perfect family from watching *Brady Bunch* reruns."

"You should give it a try," he said. "You might surprise yourself."

"I came close once, but the gentleman ended up making other plans."

"You picked the wrong man."

"Actually he picked me."

"Did you love him?"

"I loved the idea of him more than the flesh-and-blood reality." She let her gaze drift across the yard, his daughters, the sun-dappled grass, the years of longing. "What I really loved was the idea of being a family."

"I've made that mistake a few times myself."

Her mouth curved in a smile. "So I've heard."

"Lizzy! Willa!" Kate's voice lifted toward them from the beach. "Come down here and see what Stanley found!"

"Uh-oh," said Ellen, laughing as the girls ran for the path that led down to the shore. "Your poor Rover will never be the same."

"I'll deduct the cleaning bills from their inheritance."

He laced his fingers with hers and she stopped laughing. She almost stopped breathing.

"This is perfect," she said, meaning the morning sun and his girls' laughter and sitting there together. "I don't want anything to change."

"Too late," he said. "It already has."

She let the silence drag on for maybe a year or two. "The sun's almost straight up. Maybe we should get the girls and—"

"It didn't just happen Sunday night, Ellen, in case you're wondering. I've been falling in love with you for a long time."

"You fall in love too easily."

"Only once before," he said, "and I was never in the running."

"Did you ever think that might be the way you like it?"

"I loved someone who didn't love me. It was bad luck, not bad psychology. We don't always have a choice when it comes to who we love."

Her heart ached so much it hurt to draw in a breath. "I was there with you Sunday, Hall, and I know who else was there with us."

"You're wrong."

"I know what I heard."

"I don't know why it happened, but it did." He stared out across the yard toward the beach path. "I would trade away that night with you if it would erase the doubt from your mind."

"It's more than Annie," she said after a moment. "I'm not sure either one of us knows how to make a marriage work."

"Life doesn't come with guarantees, Elly. Sometimes you have to jump into the deep end and swim like hell."

"What if you can't swim?"

"I'm out of metaphors," he said, releasing her hand. "I spent most of my life waiting for the right moment to tell a woman what was in my heart, and while I was busy waiting, some other guy came along and told her 'I love you' and it was all over."

A gull swooped overhead, his cry loud and raucous and full of life.

"I won't make that mistake again." He met her eyes. "When

I read a good book or see a great movie, you're the one I want to share it with. You're in my dreams at night and in my heart when I wake up in the morning, and when you go away it's like you took the sun along with you."

"You're thinking I might be pregnant."

"I'm aware it's a possibility," he said, "but that's not what I'm talking about."

"I know you. I know the kind of man you are. You've probably already calculated a due date."

"I'm an OB. It comes with the territory."

"I know," she said, starting to soften just a little bit. "I calculate due dates in my sleep."

"You've delivered hundreds of babies, but I've never heard you say you wanted a baby of your own."

"I want the whole enchilada," she said. "Husband, babies, in-laws, PTA meetings. I already have the house and the dog."

He took her hand in his again and kissed her palm. Such a simple gesture, but what powerful emotions it unleashed inside her.

"I don't know how to tell you this, Markowitz, but your dog's a loaner."

She rested her forehead against his shoulder and laughed until she cried.

$\mathcal{J}t$ was after ten by the time they crossed Mount Desert Island and began driving south on Route 1A to Lincolnville. They hadn't said a word since they left the Crooked Isle Inn, which was fine with Deirdre. His reaction when he woke up to find her in bed with him didn't rank high up on her list of memorable moments. For a man who had held her like she was all that stood between him and grim death, his retreat into monosyllables was downright insulting.

"You were having a nightmare," she told him when he leaped from bed like his feet were on fire. "I tried to wake you up, but you weren't having any of it."

He had been crying, too, although she didn't tell him that. Ugly silent sobs that racked his body and made the bed shake beneath him. She had stroked his shoulder, whispered soothing words, nonsense sounds you would whisper to a small child who was afraid of the dark, and somehow she ended up on top of his bed with her arms around him, holding him while he slept.

She could have stayed behind at the Crooked Isle, enjoying the Jacuzzi and room service until they finally tossed her out, but what was the point to hanging around where you weren't wanted? She had done that too many times in her life. Sooner or later she would have to figure out how to get herself back down to Shelter Rock Cove without a car, and it was crystal clear that Scott the Mechanic's taxi service ended today.

"There's a McDonald's up ahead," he said as they neared the sign for Lincolnville Beach.

"Great," she said.

He barely slowed down long enough to place the order and grab the bag of Egg McMuffins. The plan was to stop at an auto wrecker so he could pick up the parts for her Hyundai. The sooner the better as far as she was concerned. She had been geared up for summer in Bar Harbor. Free room, free food, the chance to earn some real money and maybe begin to figure out what she wanted to be when she grew up.

Now it was all shot to hell and that old itchy feeling of having stayed too long at the fair was all over her. The Mechanic said he could have the car up and running by Tuesday or Wednesday. It couldn't happen soon enough for her. Ellen had her own life, and if she spent any more time mooching coffee at Annie's Flowers, she might as well join the payroll. Unless she pitched a tent on the beach behind her sister's house and spent the summer working on her tan, it was time she figured out her next step.

She closed her eyes as the car rocketed down the highway. She had worn out her welcome in Maine. Monday morning she would be on the phone with her agent. It was probably too late to snag another cushy summer gig at a resort, but there had to be a place out there somewhere for a girl, her harp, and her dog.

Saturday afternoon was their time. Susan usually farmed the kids out with her mother or one of her sisters so she and Jack could have some quality time together. Quality time used to be a euphemism for loud dirty sex, but over the years it had devolved into a PG-13 rental from Blockbuster and a nap. She had no business being angry with Jack for sacking out during *Unfaithful*. It wasn't like she wanted him getting an eyeful of Diane Lane in the bathtub. He had a right to take a nap. The guy worked hard. If he wanted to catch a few winks, she would be a major bitch on wheels if she tried to deprive him.

She felt like an oyster with a piece of grit except she wasn't about to produce a pearl for her troubles. Everything about poor Jack bugged her lately. Truth was, everything about her entire life seemed a size too small, a shade too loud, a bit too familiar. She hated being home. She hated going to work. Her children got on her nerves. She was a handful of years away from turning fifty and she couldn't remember the last time she looked forward to anything more exciting than a house closing. She had never been to Europe. She had never taken a cruise to the Caribbean. The last time she went skinny-dipping, Nixon was still in office. The last spontaneous thing she could remember doing was changing toothpaste brands.

She was short-tempered with the people she loved most and indifferent to everyone else. Small work crises that might have bounced off her radar screen last month turned her into a screeching harridan now. If she closed her eyes she could see her life slipping away faster than she could pull the days back. One morning she would wake up and see her mother in the mirror and her brains would fall into the sink and it would be all over.

Her mother thought it was menopause and maybe some of it was. She had been feeling restless and irritable since Christmas, but that was nothing compared with the onslaught of tangled feelings she had been experiencing since Kerry Amanda's christening on Sunday. Seeing Hall and Ellen laughing together had awakened a longing in her so fierce that it almost brought her to her knees. She felt as if she were seeing him for the first time. The gold hair streaked with silver. The clear blue eyes. The way he always looked as if he'd stepped fresh out of the shower and straight into clothes tailor-made for his tall, muscular form.

She knew him as well as she knew her own siblings. He was part of the family in every way except DNA. She had watched him fall in love with Annie, then marry women he liked but couldn't love. She was godmother to his children, occasional baby-sitter, repository of many of his juiciest secrets.

She loved Jack, but she wasn't in love with him anymore. Her knees didn't knock when he walked into a room. Birds didn't start singing love songs.

She wanted love songs. She wanted hearts and flowers. She wanted to wake up in the morning and not know where the day would take her. She wanted it to be new again, the way it used to be, the way it never was. New smells. New sounds. New touches.

But most of all, she wanted Hall. He was gorgeous, he was familiar, and best of all he would never tell.

All in all, it wasn't Stanley's finest hour.

Halfway to Idle Point and the animal shelter, he decided he needed to go out now, as in five minutes ago, and they had to pull over to the side of the highway so Ellen could walk him into the woods.

That took forty minutes.

Once back in the car he panted faster and faster until they pulled over again, barely in time for him to make a beeline for a secluded area where he could take care of business.

"He was fine all morning," Ellen said, puzzled by his predicament. "This seems to have come from nowhere."

They settled back into the Rover and headed once again for the highway.

"Stanley smells funny," Willa announced ten minutes later.

"I think he's going to be sick," Mariah said, inching away from the dog.

Hall, jaw set, kept his eyes on the road.

"Something stinks!" Lizzy took off her headphones and glanced around.

A second later Kate let out a groan. "Stanley's about to blow."

Ellen sniffed the air. "Hall, I think we'd better stop. He really doesn't smell too great."

"We stopped six times already and we're still not halfway

to Idle Point." He looked at his daughters through the rearview mirror. "Have you been feeding him back there?"

Lizzy and Kate shook their heads in unison while Willa and Mariah feigned a sudden hearing problem.

"You didn't give him that box of beef jerky we had left over from your camp-out, did you?"

"We didn't really give it to him, Daddy," Mariah said in a tone of utter innocence. "He found it."

"We just opened it for him," Willa said, then yelped when her sister whacked her in the arm.

"Great," Hall muttered. "He ate a two-pound package of beef jerky."

"You'd better do something, Pop." Kate was starting to sound desperate.

Finally Hall clicked on his right turn signal and was just about to ease onto the shoulder when Stanley redecorated the backseat.

"Just drop us off at the corner," Ellen said an hour later as they entered the Shelter Rock Cove town limits. "I think you need to get the girls home stat."

"I think you can't wait to get out of this car."

"You always were able to read my mind, Talbot."

"Not the afternoon I had planned for us." He turned to her as he stopped for the town's only traffic light. "Welcome to life with kids."

"The kid part was great," she said. "The dog part needs a little work."

"I should put them to work hosing this thing out."

She grinned. "Their inheritance?"

"Shot to hell."

"Daddy's laughing." Mariah's stage whisper could have carried all the way to Canada.

"Maybe he's not mad anymore," Willa stage-whispered back.

"Maybe you two should think about what you did to that poor dog," Hall said, looking at them through the rearview mirror. "You show him two pounds of beef, and he'll eat two pounds of beef. He doesn't know it's going to make him sick. You're supposed to know that."

"We thought he'd stop when he had enough," Willa said. "We didn't know he was a pig."

"You only made him sick this time, but it could've been a lot worse. Dogs don't know how to look out for themselves. They depend on us to do it for them."

Willa burst into tears. Mariah wasn't far behind. His older daughters rolled their eyes.

"You're good," Ellen said to Hall as she and Stanley climbed out of the Land Rover. "You could give lessons."

"You can manage Stanley?"

"I'll let him run through the sprinklers, then take him down to the beach. We'll be fine."

He touched her hand just long enough to register his warmth but not long enough for the girls to notice.

"I'll call you later."

She waved goodbye, then started up the road with Stanley by her side. "We'll get you all cleaned up, Stan, I promise."

He wagged his tail, then started tugging her to walk faster.

"I know, I know. You can't wait to run through the sprinklers. I don't blame you one bit."

She hadn't been kidding when she told Hall she'd considered running alongside the Land Rover. Clearly parenthood required a strong stomach along with nerves of steel.

Late afternoon sun spilled across her shoulders, hinting at the approaching summer. The wonderful scent of beach roses wafted toward her as they rounded the bend toward her house. Even Stanley seemed to appreciate it. He greedily sniffed the air, tail wagging madly.

The day hadn't been at all what she had expected. There was no denying that she could have done without poor Stanley's discomfort. Still, there had been something wonderful about being part of a Saturday with Hall and his daughters. She had enjoyed watching the way they laughed and joked together, the obvious devotion he felt for them, and the equally obvious love they offered in return.

He might not have mastered Marriage 101, but he was Phi Beta Kappa when it came to fatherhood.

A child couldn't ask for a better father. What would it be

like, raising a child with a man like Hall to share the burden and pleasures? Someone who understood the importance of it all and embraced it. What a wonderful gift to give a child.

Not that she was thinking about children. The odds were against a pregnancy. She had had no reason to be charting her periods or keeping tabs on her BBT, but simple arithmetic told her that fertilization was unlikely. Still, she had enough experience trying to convince astonished expectant mothers that yes they really were going to have a baby to know that in this world just about anything was possible.

"Okay, Stan," she said as they started up the driveway. "First we wash you off, then I'll take you down to the beach and—I don't believe it!"

The front porch was littered with battered luggage, an empty McDonald's sack, a bottle of Poland Spring, two harps, and there, sprawled on the glider in the corner was her missing sister Deirdre.

Twenty-four

"I'm not really asleep," Deirdre said as she heard her sister's approaching footsteps.

"I didn't think so," Ellen said as Stanley galloped onto the porch.

Deirdre sat up and rearranged her floaty shirt. "Stanley!" She wrinkled her nose and ducked the dog's enthusiastic hello. "He stinks! What happened?"

"Hall's kids plied him with beef jerky. Our boy turned the back of Hall's Rover into a biohazard."

"He needs a bath."

"I was going to rinse him off, then take him down to the beach before it gets any later."

"Sounds like a plan." She stifled a yawn.

"You're going to help, right?"

"Oh." She smiled widely. "Sure . . . of course I am. He's my dog, isn't he?"

Ellen and Mary Pat had more in common than either one of them might realize. Both sisters had the uncanny ability to make her do something she really didn't want to do. Mary Pat did it by intimidation. Ellen did it with a smile and a wink.

She stood up, stretched, then followed Ellen and Stanley

around the side of the house and into the backyard.

"The hose is hanging on a hook beneath the kitchen window, and there's dog shampoo on the shelf in the garage," Ellen said, pointing somewhere to the right of the deck. A familiar beep-beep-beep sounded from her waistband. "I need to make a phone call. You get started. I'll be right back."

"Suspiciously good timing," Deirdre called out as Ellen unlocked the sliding doors. "How much did you pay someone to call you?"

"A bargain at half the price," her sister said and disappeared inside the house.

Stanley was a lot of dog and he required a lot of dog shampoo and water. By the time she finished they were both drenched and exhausted. Each time he shook out his fur, it looked like a nor'easter had blown in.

Ellen finally popped out of the house. It occurred to her that you could deliver twins in less time than her sister had taken on the phone, but she was probably on shaky enough ground as it was. She kept the observation to herself.

"So how's it going?" Ellen asked.

"All done. He smells like a lavender dandy."

Ellen's smile widened. "Great timing, huh?"

"I hadn't noticed." She shivered in the evening breeze. "I think it's too cold to take him down to the beach."

Poor Stanley looked up at them with beseeching eyes.

"Maybe we should go inside and dry him off. I have an enormous stack of beach towels Claudia left behind."

"I have a blow-dryer we can use."

They trooped inside. Ellen started a pot of water for tea while she dug her blow-dryer from one of the overstuffed bags she dragged in from the front porch. The night air was damp and chill, not the best of conditions for her temperamental harps. She brought them into the living room, took them out of their cases, and hoped for the best. Not that it really mattered, come to think of it. It wasn't as if she had a gig on the horizon or anything.

Two steaming mugs of tea rested on the counter when she returned to the kitchen. Ellen was crouched down near the open back door, chatting away while she toweled Stanley off with an enormous hot-pink beach towel.

Stanley adored Ellen. All you had to do was look at him and you could see waves of love radiating from him. And why not? It was clear she adored him right back.

The more things change. She had read all of the books on birth order. The youngest child was supposed to be cosseted and spoiled, the one everyone couldn't help but love best of all. Too bad nobody in her family had ever bothered to thumb through any of those books. They might have learned a thing or two.

She grabbed a towel from the stack near the stove and started drying Stanley's fluffy tail.

"So what happened? Mary Pat's been trying to find you since yesterday afternoon. She's a half-step away from calling in the FBI."

"I was fired." She laughed as Stanley shook himself again. "Actually I wasn't really fired. Turns out I never had the job in the first place." She managed to fill in the blanks of the story in less than one hundred words.

"Those bastards."

No lecture. No probing questions. No critical comments. Welcome to Bizarro World.

"I didn't handle it too well," she said, burying her face in Stanley's sweet-smelling fur for a second. "I melted down right there in the lobby when the owner told me."

"Who wouldn't," Ellen said. "He just screwed up three months of your life." She reached for a dry towel. "Did he at least give you compensation of some kind?"

"Two weeks' salary and a stay at the inn with all the amenities."

"And you only stayed one night?"

"One night was okay. Two smelled of desperation."

Ellen drew a flat brush through Stanley's thick fur. "So how did you get home?"

"Scott."

Ellen stopped mid-stroke. "They gave him a room, too?"

"We shared the suite, and believe me, it isn't what you were thinking."

"He's pretty easy on the eyes."

"Is he?" She busied herself detangling Stanley's tail. "I hadn't noticed."

"Neither have I."

"My sister, the stand-up comic." She couldn't wipe the smile off her face. "Maybe we should go on the road together. O'Brien and Markowitz: music and mirth for your listening pleasure."

"Markowitz and O'Brien, thank you very much. I'm six months older than you are. It has to count for something."

"Ask my agent," she said, laughing. "He'll tell you he always gets me top billing." She paused for emphasis. "No jobs, you understand, just top billing."

"Back to Scott," Ellen said. "Does he talk? I swear he's the most silent man in town."

He cried, Elly, that big strong guy cried in my arms last night, and now he can't even look at me.

"We had a great time," she said. "Thanks to him, I can finally locate the Big Dipper."

"Way to go," Ellen said. "I wish you'd show me, because when I look up, all I see are stars."

"That's what I said to Scott."

"Must be a family thing," Ellen said, "like the red hair."

They finished grooming Stanley, who, by that time, wanted nothing more than to curl up in the corner of the sofa and go to sleep.

Ellen warmed up their mugs of tea in the microwave, and the two of them wandered out onto the deck. The scent of beach roses and sea air was more intoxicating in many ways than last night's champagne. Ellen pulled her chair closer to the railing and propped her feet up while she curled her legs beneath her.

"You should call Mary Pat and let her know you're okay."

Deirdre took a sip of tea. "I was hoping you had already done it."

"I did but that doesn't mean you shouldn't call her yourself. She really was very worried about you."

"She's a control freak."

"Cut her a little slack, Dee. She has a lot on her plate right now. Things aren't going too well for Billy. He has an appointment with a specialist on Monday."

"And she was calling me in Bar Harbor to let me know?" She wasn't the one with the medical degree. There wasn't anything she could do to make things right. There never had been.

"You'll have to ask her."

"I will," she said.

"Tonight?"

"Tomorrow sounds better."

They fell quiet for a while, sipping tea, listening to the ocean, thinking their own thoughts about Billy and Mary Pat and the strange set of circumstances that had turned them into family.

"You're welcome to stay with me as long as you'd like," Ellen said, breaking the silence. "You and Stanley both."

"I'm sure a new gig will turn up any day," she said, "but thanks. It helps to have a place to field offers and pick up my mail."

"Glad I can help," Ellen said. She sounded a little amused, maybe a little bit hurt.

Deirdre knew she should thank her again, let her know how much she really appreciated the offer, but there was a stubborn, ugly little part of her heart that wouldn't let her. How had her life gone so wrong that she was reduced to begging for shelter from the sister she barely knew when the sister she grew up with had room to spare?

And while she was asking questions nobody could answer, how could silence sound so loud?

"Victoria Abigail Thornton," Ellen said to Hall as they waited for the elevator on the maternity floor a week later. "Six pounds, three ounces; twenty inches long."

"I heard her all the way down in Four," he said.

"That was you in Four?"

"Adam and Jason Harris. They each weighed in at a little over five and a half pounds, eighteen inches long."

Tears sprang to her eyes and she quickly brushed them away. "How are Ginger and David?"

"Over the moon," he said. "Her mother was there with the videocam."

"What about her father?"

Hall laughed. "Every time he came within five feet of the

delivery room door, he felt faint. The poor guy spent most of Ginger's labor with his head between his knees."

The elevator doors slid open and they nodded to the two nurses who exited as they waited to enter.

"I never asked you how you held up when your girls were born," she said as the doors slid closed. "Did—"

He turned to her and she was in his arms so quickly it felt like a dream. The smell of his skin, the hard warmth of his body, the wet heat of his mouth, the low moan she couldn't suppress as he cupped her bottom and pulled her up against him.

They broke apart as the elevator shuddered and clanked into position at the ground floor.

"Talbot. Markowitz." Joe Wiley, the hospital's chief of staff, moved aside so they could exit. "When are we going to set up a golf date? I made Maria promise she'd join us so we could have ourselves a wicked good foursome."

"I still need practice, Joe." Ellen was positive he knew exactly what they had been doing before the elevator stopped. "If you don't mind a rank amateur in your midst, I'd love to."

"Same here," said Hall. "Ellen can putt. I can hit for distance. Put us together and we're Tiger Woods."

Joe threw back his head and laughed heartily. "Then let's check our schedules and do it before I leave for Wyoming."

"He knows," Ellen said as they walked through the lobby toward the main entrance.

"You said that the last time, too."

"Did you see the way he looked at us? I swear it was like he had X-ray vision." She stopped dead in her tracks a few feet away from the information desk. "Do they have cameras in the elevators?"

Hall shrugged. "Probably."

"You don't mean they filmed us kissing, do you?"

"You should see the tape they had of Doug Flax and Connie Della Cruz a few years ago. You could have sold tickets."

"Please tell me you're kidding."

"It didn't slow down their careers any."

They pushed through the heavy glass doors and stepped out into the soft and fragrant early June air. "You're not funny, Hall."

"Okay. Doug and Connie had a fling, but it's not on tape. At least not as far as I know. And yes there's a security camera in the elevator."

"Don't tease me that way! I'm furious with you."

"No, you're not. You're wishing we could find a place where we could kiss again."

He was right. Damn him. Ever since that crazy drive to Idle Point last Saturday, she had the feeling she was standing at the center of one of those nor'easters that make even the old-timers sit up and take notice. She could feel destiny swirling around her, faster and faster, until there was nothing she could do but give in. The truth was, they couldn't keep their hands off each other. The elevator. The back stairs. The parking lot under cover of darkness. The movie theater three towns over where they made out like teenagers during a Jackie Chan double feature.

Deirdre, who usually wasn't known for either her discretion or her sensitivity, gave them lots of space when Hall came over. Sometimes she grabbed her car keys and went for a drive in the repaired Hyundai. Other times she carried her lap harp up to the bedroom and practiced while the heartbreaking sound of her music spilled from the window like a blessing.

And, thinking of blessings, it seemed they had Claudia's as well. She had met Claudia for lunch at Cappy's the other day as a way of thanking her for the delicious carrot cake and casseroles she had brought over the night of Deirdre's adventure in Bar Harbor. Some invisible barrier between them had disappeared that night in her kitchen, and they spent a long, agreeable interlude together over a bowl of creamy clam chowder. Her house had a rich and wonderful history, and she had listened with rapt attention as the older woman spun out the stories. She found herself telling Claudia about Deirdre's return, about her surprise at the relief she felt when she saw her sister asleep on the front porch. She even touched briefly on Deirdre's brusque response to her open-ended invitation to stay with her. Claudia had been very maternal, if occasionally acerbic, and she began to see why Hall loved her in a way he didn't seem to love his own mother.

She and Hall wandered out into the sensory garden behind the hospital where ambulatory patients and their families liked to drink up the sun on nice days like this. A young man in a wheelchair sunned himself near the fountain. His eyes were closed, his face tilted toward the sun. They claimed a bench on the side nearest the herb garden. The smells of lemon verbena, sweet basil, and mint almost made you forget you were on hospital property.

"Do you know what I would do if I were a chemist?" she said. "I'd find a way to bottle the smell of fresh basil on a summer's day and use it as a perfume."

"Chocolate might be even more effective."

"Men should wear chocolate after-shave. You wouldn't be able to keep the women away from you." She laughed at the thought. "Of course, they would all be premenstrual."

He looked as if he wanted to say something but censored himself.

"Not yet," she said in answer to his unasked question, "but I think it's any minute now. All the signs are there." She tried to read his expression. "Are you disappointed?"

He again looked as if he was censoring his response.

"We've always been honest with each other," she said. "Don't stop now."

"Yes," he said. "I'm disappointed."

God help me, she thought as they touched hands for an instant, *so am I.*

As the days passed, Deirdre was reminded more and more of the old joke about the musician who went away for the weekend only to return and find that his house had burned down.

"It was terrible," his neighbor said. "There was a forty-foot wall of flames! Everything you owned is gone, but your agent managed to save your wife and children!"

And the musician said, "My agent came to my *house*?!"

So far her agent had managed to duck all of her calls since she returned from her brief stay at the Crooked Isle Inn. He was in conference, out of the office, on the other line, working from home, on a business trip, everywhere but on the other end of the telephone.

Kind of like her and Scott the Mechanic, come to think of it.

For a while there he had been her best friend in town, the object of her morning walks, the focus of her days. And unless she missed her guess, he had kind of enjoyed it. At least up until their misbegotten trip to Crooked Isle Inn.

Two days after they returned from Bar Harbor, he called to say her Hyundai was ready. She and Stanley walked down to pay the bill, and Scott had been what she called business-friendly. You would never know to look at him that they had spent a night in each other's arms.

The truth had come to her in a flash as she waited for him to fill out a receipt. He hadn't been sleeping that night when he sobbed in her arms. It wasn't a nightmare that caused him so much sorrow. He had been painfully awake and aware, and he hated her for being there to see it. Now the only thing he could do was push her away.

Men were so strange when it came to expressing their emotions. They would think nothing of painting their faces in team colors, stripping off their shirts, and yelling themselves senseless at some ridiculous sporting event, but ask them to admit to one single drop of sorrow for anything other than a lost playoff spot, and they turned to stone.

She had cried on his shoulder when the Inn dumped her, but that didn't mean she had to hide herself away from him for the rest of her life. So what if he had cried on her shoulder a few hours later. It was nothing to be ashamed about. Twice she had phoned him at the garage, but both times Jack said he was out test-driving a car.

Sure he was. She had too much experience ducking Mary Pat's phone calls to believe that one.

Mary Pat had taken to calling Ellen's house at all hours to deliver updates on their father's rapidly worsening condition. She managed to duck most of her sister's calls, but every now and again Mary Pat timed it just right and snagged her.

"I need to speak with Ellen," Mary Pat had said last night when Deirdre answered the phone without thinking. "Is she there?"

"Ellen?" She gave the phone her most theatrical double-take. "Since when do you call her Ellen? I thought she was the Doctor."

If she didn't know better, she would think they were actually starting to like each other.

This morning she'd sat right there at the kitchen counter and listened to Ellen patiently explain the possible meaning of Billy's symptoms and urge once again that he see the doctor they had agreed was their best hope.

So far Billy had blown off three appointments with the specialist, and he threatened to blow off a fourth if Mary Pat was stupid enough to schedule one. Which, of course, she would. Once Mary Pat got the bit between her teeth, it would take a stick of dynamite to shake it loose.

They just didn't get it. Neither one of her sisters seemed able to get it through her skull that this was all nothing more than Billy being Billy. She had said it right from the start: He fled to Ireland because things got a little too real at home, and he came back because things got a little too hot over there. That had always been his pattern, and there was no reason to think he was going to change now.

She had to hand it to him though. He really had them believing he was sick. Talk about a great scam. Free room and board with his devoted oldest daughter. Cable TV. An open bar. Someone to take his calls and keep the wolf from the door. What more could he possibly ask for? Maybe he had to work a little to keep up the charade, but that was a small price to pay for a place to camp out until he could return to Ireland and whatever the hell he had been doing over there.

Mary Pat had been leaning on her to talk to Billy, which only gave her more reason to duck her sister's phone calls. Turnabout was fair play, right? Billy had ducked her calls more times than she could count when she was trying to get her singing career off the ground. He had been flying high at the time. For a little while there it had looked as if he might become one of those twenty-year overnight successes you read about in *People*. He knew the people he needed to know, the same people who just might have seen fit to give Deirdre a hand up the ladder. Let him see how it felt to be on the receiving end of that big sucking sound of silence.

A taste of his own medicine might be exactly what the doctor ordered.

Twenty-five

"Dr. Markowitz?" The woman's voice was familiar. "I thought that was you! What brings you to Westcliff Harbor?"

Ellen quickly hid the home pregnancy test kit behind her back and turned to find Sarah Cummings from Admissions smiling at her with open curiosity.

"I was on my way home from a lecture," she said, appalled by the ease with which the lie spilled out. "I had a headache and thought I would stop for some Advil."

"Advil's over there." Sarah gestured farther down the other side of the aisle.

"No wonder I couldn't find it," she said with a nervous laugh.

"Are you okay?" Sarah asked, stepping a little bit closer. "You look a little pale."

"Just tired," Ellen said.

"And the headache," Sarah reminded her.

The two women smiled at each other, but neither one moved. She couldn't back away from Sarah or scuttle across the aisle like a turtle. Sarah was suspicious enough already. If she tried to hide the box under the hem of her silk blazer she would probably end up being arrested for shoplifting. She considered dropping it, then pretending it fell off the shelf on its own, but that wouldn't fool even Stanley. She was at the point of feigning a swoon when two little boys ran up to Sarah and started shrieking that their other brother was getting into trouble in the dairy department.

Bless you, she thought as Sarah hurried away to see what her third son was up to. She considered starting a scholarship fund for the three of them. The experience gave the phrase *too close for comfort* a whole new meaning.

If she wasn't so paranoid about being discovered, she would have taken a test right in the office. Unfortunately Janna was a highly organized manager who kept track of every supply right down to the number of swabs in the jar. She also was the one who ran the tests and notated the results.

The irony of an OB-GYN having to sneak out of town in order to snag an over-the-counter pregnancy test kit wasn't lost on her. It was yet another part of small-town life that required some adjustment. It didn't matter if you were purchasing aspirin, Preparation H, or a lifetime supply of condoms. Every purchase was noticed by someone in town and usually mentioned at that night's dinner table to someone else. Claudia, who was no slouch in the gossip department, liked to say that if the U.S. Army had had access to Shelter Rock Cove's communications during World War II, the war would have ended two years earlier.

Deirdre's Hyundai wasn't in the driveway when she pulled in. She and Stanley were over at Annie's Flowers, where Deirdre was playing her harp at a reception the Artists' Co-Op was giving for Sweeney. She planned to drop in later and show support, but first things first.

It wasn't that she suspected anything, because she didn't. No morning sickness. No breast tenderness. Just the absence of her period and the nagging sense that something wasn't quite right. Two weeks had elapsed since that night with Hall. If she was pregnant the test should be able to pick it up. If not—well, it was probably just stress. Moving into your first house was a big enough source of stress, but if you added to it a new love affair, the arrival of your eccentric younger sister, a one-hundred-fifteen-pound dog, and a thriving medical practice, it was a wonder she wasn't hiding under the covers and waiting for some of the excitement to die down. Four days late wasn't anything to worry about.

Her imagination was beginning to run away with her. Twice she had found herself daydreaming about a blond-haired daughter who would be taken under the collective wing of her four beautiful older sisters. On more than one occasion she had found herself scribbling the name "Emilie" on a prescription pad or on the back of an envelope. She already had a room on the second floor picked out for the nursery. She would paint the walls sunny yellow with pure white trim and decorate the room with handmade quilts and soft sculptures from the Co-op. Big whitewashed shutters at the windows. A crib.

She put her medical bag down on the floor near the hall closet, then slipped out of her blazer. Her shoes were already off. She couldn't endure heels, not even low ones, for a moment longer than absolutely necessary. The test kit practically screamed "Open me!" so she did. The instructions were simple enough and it wasn't as if she had anything else to do at the moment. Besides, no matter the situation, knowing was always better than not knowing, and that was never more true than when it came to pregnancy.

Okay. No more procrastination. She and the test kit would march into the bathroom, and in a few minutes she would know her fate.

Of course, that was the exact second her cell phone rang. Only one person on earth had timing like that.

"Why are you laughing?" Mary Pat demanded the second she picked up the phone. "Do you have caller ID?"

"No, I swear I'm not laughing at you, Mary Pat," she said, trying to rein in her amusement. "Did Billy keep his appointment today?" Not that there was a chance in hell that he had, but still she had to ask.

On the other end of the line Mary Pat erupted into sobs that she could feel inside her own bones. She felt like a louse for laughing when she answered the phone, but how could she possibly have known her sister was about to fall apart on her? Mary Pat was the human Rock of Gibraltar. She never lost control of anything: not her family or a situation, and definitely not herself. This display of vulnerability would exact a price from her, no doubt about it, and Ellen's heart went out to her.

There was more than a touch of Mary Pat at work inside her own personality. Neither one of them had been able to hold their families together, no matter how hard they tried, and that failure had shaped their futures.

Funny how she had never thought of it that way before. She and Deirdre were the same age, they shared auburn hair, a tendency to freckle in the sun, and a mutual disdain for their older sister. Beyond that she thought she had little in common with either one of them. But that wasn't true. Not even close.

Mary Pat's sobs were beginning to subside. She murmured something into the phone, but Ellen knew the only thing she could do was wait quietly until her sister gathered herself together again. All of her medical training, the endless courses on the psychology of dealing with patients, her reputation as a physician who actually listened and understood her patients' emotional needs, and this was the best she could do. Face-to-face you could offer so much more to someone in pain. A sympathetic look. A touch. The simple act of sharing space and breathing the same air could be as therapeutic as anything modern science had created, but as of yet no one had devised a way to transmit touch through wires.

She began to quickly piece together the clues. Clearly this had to do with Billy's health. Gut instinct told her that Mary Pat had finally managed to get him to the doctor and the news hadn't been good.

Unfortunately she was right.

". . . you should have seen the way they acted when Daddy walked into the office . . . like they were ready to diagnose him on the spot."

"He was presenting some pretty telling symptoms, Mary Pat. You don't see pronounced jaundice every day of the week."

"They had no business staring at him that way. They're supposed to make patients feel comfortable, aren't they?"

"Of course," she agreed, but there were times when even the most jaded medical professional was taken aback by a patient's symptoms. "Now tell me exactly what they said when they examined Billy."

"They were all over the jaundice. I mean, that's hardly the end of the world, is it, Ellen?" She didn't wait for a response.

"We sat in the examining room forever—like they think this doesn't count as waiting?—and then when the doctor came in, his first words were, 'I want you to know this has the potential to be very serious.' " She paused to pull in some oxygen. "Daddy got up and started to put his shirt back on. He was going to walk out the door and I don't blame him. What kind of way is that to treat someone?"

"A lousy way," Ellen said, "but right now let's stay focused on the diagnosis. Did they run blood tests?"

"Yes."

"Urinalysis?"

"Twice."

She could hear Mary Pat struggling to retain her composure. "He said, and I'm quoting here, I took notes, 'There is a marked prominence to the liver.' Is that bad?"

It was the worst news possible. This time it was Ellen who struggled to retain her composure. "It's bad, Mary Pat."

No gut-wrenching sobs this time from her older sister. Just the soft sound of muffled tears.

"Are you still there?" she asked after a few minutes had passed.

"I'm here," Mary Pat managed. "I knew it was bad. I'm on the Net all the time, looking up his symptoms, but I just couldn't face it."

"Has the doctor set up appointments for tests?"

"He wants to do a CT scan, maybe an MRI, and something called ERCP."

"I'm sure the doctor told you Billy will require sedation for the ERCP."

"They want to check him into the hospital on Wednesday for a few days and do all of the tests while he's there."

Not a good sign at all. "That's probably a wise decision."

"Maybe you and Deirdre would like to drive down and see him."

"That's a wonderful idea," she said quickly, "but I have ten prima gravidas about to go into labor. I'm afraid I just can't get away."

"Deirdre's not working. She told me her car is out of the shop. There's no reason she can't drive down. Billy's been asking about you. Both of you."

Oh, no, you don't, Mary Pat. No Guilt Trip Express for me.

They talked for a few minutes about their father's insurance coverage. It was easier to discuss co-payments and per diem hospital charges than the fact that he was dying.

"If you need me to, I'd be glad to speak with hospital administration," she said as the conversation began to wind down. "Insurance jargon can be off-putting to say the least."

"I have no trouble with it." A glimmer of the old Mary Pat she knew and couldn't quite bring herself to love.

"That's great." Ellen maintained an even tone. "Not everyone is comfortable with it."

"Maybe you wouldn't mind speaking to the doctor. Every time he spoke, all I could hear was this whooshing sound inside my head. I took notes, but I'd feel better if he knew we had a doctor in the family."

"Glad to be of help." For a moment there she had actually felt something approaching sisterly affection.

"Did I say something wrong?"

"Not at all. I'll phone the doctor tomorrow and touch base with you in the evening."

"Really, I can't imagine what I might have said to upset you, Ellen."

"Because I'm not upset, Mary Pat. We'll talk tomorrow."

What was wrong with her? She never let Mary Pat get under her skin this way, not even when her sister was at her most obnoxious.

It was her own fault for letting down her guard when Mary Pat started to cry. She had always been a sucker for tears, anyone's tears, and for a second she had actually believed she and Mary Patricia Anne O'Brien Galvin were actually starting to like each other the slightest bit. Obviously Mary Pat was deeply distressed over the state of their father's health, and while she didn't share the same depth of feeling for Billy, she understood.

Mary Pat called when she needed something. She sent birthday cards and Christmas cards. She marked important nonannual events with flowers. Deirdre told her that their sister kept a database on her computer with the names of friends and family neatly entered, along with pertinent information. Every morning when she logged on, the database popped up and red-flagged items that needed her attention.

Tonight Mary Pat needed a doctor in the family and she got one. What she didn't need was a sister.

No problem there, either.

$\mathcal{F}$or the first two hours of the celebration, Deirdre played the kind of watery, dreamy music most people associated with the harp. Guests had drifted off into small groups—she saw Ellen talking to Claudia Galloway near the punch bowl—and the general vibe was getting kind of sleepy.

Time to show them what a Celtic harp could do when the harper put her mind to it.

She slid from a sleepy "Greensleeves" into a Chieftains-esque jig that caught their attention in record time. One of the co-op's artists knew a little about percussion, and she began tapping out a rhythm on the workbench. Sweeney, the guest of honor, had played folk guitar back in the late sixties, and she borrowed an old acoustic from one of the other women and began to improvise alongside her.

Next thing she knew Annie and Susan cleared a spot in the middle of the store and began to stage a *Riverdance* revival right there. Claudia and Roberta claimed their old bones couldn't take the pounding, but before long they joined the chorus line next to Ellen, who was laughing too hard to do anything but stomp her feet when they pointed to her. Her hair was wild and curly. Her cheeks were flushed. Her eyes glittered with an almost manic light she had only noticed once before. She hadn't seen this side of her sister since the summer they were sixteen and sneaked out to the Cape for what Billy had called a weekend of "debauchery."

When they were sixteen they would have sold their souls to be even within shouting distance of debauchery. The fact that their father used the word to describe what had turned out to be a weekend of drinking beer and watching while other girls went off with the cute guys had delighted them. It had almost made up for the fact that they had returned home as virginal as they had been when they left.

She could see Ellen dancing alone, moving in and out of

the dying light from the fire they had built on the beach. Her fierce, beautiful, ambitious sister looked like a warrior preparing for battle. Ellen was so self-sufficient, so unlike Deirdre, whose need was almost a second self. Ellen didn't care what any of them thought about her. She enjoyed the campfire, the surf, the sand, the music, and if none of the guys fell over dead at her feet, it was their loss.

Deirdre had always needed validation. A boy's approval meant more to her than a scholarship to Juilliard. Not that Juilliard had come calling, but if they had, she probably would have said no thanks if it meant being separated from her love of the moment. That was the way it was supposed to be, wasn't it? Love came first even if you couldn't remember his name.

"C'mon, Deirdre!" Ellen called out. "Put down that harp and dance with us!"

She rested the harp on its stand, kicked off her shoes, and joined them as they started improvising one of those country-western line dances that had been popular a few years back.

Stanley, who had been amusing himself in the yard behind the store, decided he couldn't stand being left out another second and he burst through the back door and galloped toward them, all one hundred fifteen pounds ready to boogie.

"You don't know how much I wish I'd had my camera with me," Ellen said for easily the tenth time as they were getting ready for bed. "If you could have seen yourself riding poor Stanley down Shore Drive—" She started laughing again; that slightly out-of-control note Deirdre had noticed earlier was even more noticeable. "You and Stanley have achieved legendary status."

Deirdre twisted her long hair into a knot and pinned it to the top of her head with a chopstick. "Back in Boston it takes at least three sailors, a runaway fire truck, and a quart of Scotch to even begin to qualify for legendary status."

Ellen sat cross-legged on the bed. Her long slender legs were bare beneath an old Hard Rock Café T-shirt.

"Just tell me why I couldn't inherit your thighs," Deirdre said as she sprawled across the bed next to her sister.

Ellen laughed and swatted her with a pillow. "I have my mother's thighs."

"So do I," Deirdre said. "My lucky streak remains unbroken."

"Mary Pat called this evening."

She picked a fuzzball off the coverlet. "Glad I wasn't here. I'm over my limit on sanctimonious bad advice."

"They're checking Billy into the hospital on Wednesday."

Deirdre felt as if she had been sucker-punched as she doubled over. An implosion of pain that pulled her into it and wouldn't let go. The simple act of drawing in her next breath seemed impossible for a long time. "He's really carrying this act of his all the way, isn't he?" she said at last.

"It's not an act this time, Dee."

"You don't know him the way I know him."

"Mary Pat said he's been asking about us."

This pain was different, all too familiar. "You, maybe."

"She specifically said he mentioned you."

"Are you going?"

Ellen's cheeks reddened. "My workload is intense right now. I can't get away."

"Same here," she said, closing her eyes. "I'm afraid I just don't have the time."

"I think I'm going to write one of those mystery series and set it in Shelter Rock," Ellen said to Hall over lunch at Cappy's the next afternoon.

"We don't have any crime."

"That's only because nobody has enough privacy to commit one. All a P.I. would have to do is grab one of these tables first thing in the morning and wait for information to come streaming through the doors."

He glanced around and started to laugh. "You're right. Sooner or later everyone in town shows up here."

The crew from Admissions was sitting over there near the patio. Susan and two of her real estate colleagues were holding court near the door. The head of oncology was tearing into a lobster roll while two of their patients sipped glasses of lemonade and pretended to read the menu.

"I don't know why they bother to hand these things out," Ellen said, tossing her menu down on the tabletop. "We all have it memorized."

"You're beginning to sound like a native Mainer."

"I don't think the other native Mainers would agree, but thanks."

Penny, their waitress, who was also one of Ellen's patients, hurried up to them with steaming bowls of creamy clam chowder.

"Here you go." She deposited the bowls on the table, then fished four packets of oyster crackers from the pocket of her apron. "You want anything else?"

"We're okay for now, Penny. Thanks."

"I think you should go," Hall said as Penny raced back to the kitchen.

She took a sip of chowder. There was no point pretending she didn't know exactly what he was talking about. "Thank you for the advice. I'm not going."

"You're making a mistake."

She let her spoon fall with a clatter into her bowl. "I didn't ask for your opinion."

"You're getting it anyway, Markowitz. He's your father and he's dying. The decisions you make now will haunt you for the rest of your life."

"You sound like one of those radio psychologists who think they have all the answers."

"I have this answer," he said. "Go down to Boston and see your father one more time."

She shook her head. "I don't think so."

"Did he beat you?"

She looked up at him. "No."

"Abuse you?"

"Don't be absurd."

"Do you hate him?"

"Of course not. I don't feel much of anything."

"So drive down there and see him. He can't hurt you and you might help him."

He had angered her many times, but never like this. It had never been personal before.

"I don't see you flying out to Scottsdale to spend quality time with your parents."

His face shut down. That was the only way she could describe it. Like he had flipped a switch and turned out the lights.

"If they ever ask, I'll be on the first fucking plane out of here."

All of the pretty fantasies she had constructed about his perfect privileged life came tumbling down.

"And here I thought you were one of the lucky ones." Tall, gorgeous, kind, accomplished—any more gifts and you would accuse nature of playing favorites.

"I am," he said. "I had the Galloways on my side."

The Galloways, Sweeney, Annie, an entire townful of friends who had become family while his parents went about the business of living. He had no idea how lucky he was or how deeply she envied him.

"Why didn't you ever tell me?"

"Why didn't you tell me about your sisters or Billy?"

"I never gave it a thought. Before Deirdre and Stanley showed up, they hadn't been a big part of my daily life."

"My parents haven't been part of my daily life since I started grade school."

She pushed her bowl of soup away from her. "I wanted you to think my family was as perfect as yours."

"Maybe I wanted you to go on thinking that."

"We have more in common than I figured, Talbot." She linked fingers with him beneath the table.

"When Kate and Lizzy were born, I made a promise that I would be there for them. Not just for the big things, the school plays and birthday parties and graduations, but the small things as well, like waiting for the school bus and driving them to soccer practice and really listening to them when they wanted to talk, and especially when they didn't. I wasn't going to make my parents' mistakes."

"You couldn't make those mistakes, Hall. Those girls are part of your heart."

"It'll be the same with our children. They'll know their parents love them."

They'll know their father.

"I bought a test kit," she said.

"We have an entire lab in the office."

"I stopped in Westcliff Harbor so I wouldn't bump into anyone I knew, and who was standing there but Sarah from Admissions."

"Which proves my thesis that you can run from Shelter Rock Cove, but you can't hide."

"Do you think anyone knows we're holding hands under the table?"

"Everyone knows," he said. "Penny made a notation on the—"

Right on cue, Penny skidded to a stop next to their table.

"You haven't touched your soup, Dr. M.! Eat up. I have a blueberry cobbler in the kitchen with your name on it."

"You're always trying to fatten me up, Penny."

"Just think of it as eating for two."

She pulled her hand away from Hall's so quickly that the table rocked, sloshing clam chowder across her paper placemat.

"You really do think like an OB," Penny said, laughing at what Ellen could only assume was a look of total shock on her face. "I meant, you can eat the blueberry cobbler for me since all I have to do is look at the stuff and my butt starts to grow like a cellulite soufflé."

"I thought I handled that quite well," she said as Penny moved out of earshot. "I only spilled half of my soup, not the entire bowl."

He handed her some more paper napkins. "Screw medicine," he said, grinning. "With that poker face, you should head for Vegas."

She polished off the remainder of her soup, then leaned back in her rickety wooden chair. "Would you be able to take over my patients if I went away for a few days?"

His gaze met hers. "When are you thinking of going?"

"Friday morning. I'd be back on Sunday."

"The Bahamas? Cape Cod?"

"Boston," she said. "I'm going to go see Billy."

Twenty-six

"I think it's the next left," Deirdre said as they drove deeper into Cambridge on Friday afternoon. "Fourteen Hamilton Court."

"I don't see numbers on any of these houses," Ellen said, squinting at the mailboxes and front doors as they drove past. "How do they find each other around here?"

"Mary Pat said for you to look for the house with gray shakes and a gambrel roof."

They looked at each other and started to laugh.

"Do you have any idea what shakes and gambrels are?"

"You're the one with the education," Deirdre said. "I was hoping you did."

"I studied medicine, not architecture. All that talk about crown moldings and turrets makes my head spin."

"Slow down," Deirdre ordered. "It's not the next left. It's a right, then a left."

"I know I wrote down the directions. Look in my bag, would you?"

"We don't need directions. I've been here before. It's not like I won't recognize it."

"Mary Pat's going to be surprised to see you."

Deirdre's face was turned toward the window so Ellen couldn't make out her expression. "Safety in numbers." Her tone was light, almost as difficult to read as her expression. "I couldn't let you face her alone. It would be cruel."

So far that was the way Deirdre was playing it. No mention of Billy or the fact that he was dying. Nothing but jokes about Mary Pat, about her house, her neighborhood, her volunteer work, her taste in clothes and music and books and friends.

She knew it was Deirdre's way of coping, but the constant barrage of one-liners was wearing on her nerves more with every second that passed.

"Nice of Hall to take on Stanley while we're away," Deirdre said as they turned left onto Hamilton.

"He said he needs the practice." She told her about Hall's plans to adopt a dog from the rescue shelter in Idle Point.

"Maybe he could adopt Stanley."

"Stanley's your dog."

"Look!" Deirdre pointed toward a gray house at the end of the street. "I think that's her Saab parked in the driveway."

"Deirdre, I—"

"I'm not ducking the question, El. I was going to tell you when we got back to Shelter Rock. My agent found me a job playing the harp on a cruise ship out of Miami. I start June thirtieth."

"What were you planning to do with Stanley? Leave him on the street?"

"I was going to ask you to adopt him, but if Hall is looking, it's kind of the same thing, isn't it?" Deirdre studied her. "You're not mad, are you? I really was going to tell you when we got home."

There wasn't time to get into it, even though Ellen felt like the top of her head was going to separate from the rest of her body. Mary Pat was standing on her front porch with a toddler clinging to her leg.

"Declan?" she asked Deirdre.

"He's a sweetie," Deirdre said. "Another little redheaded O'Brien. I forgot you didn't make it down for the christening."

She sighed. "I figure Mary Pat will forgive me about the same time Social Security kicks in." Not even a very healthy savings bond for Declan's future had done much to break the ice.

The first thing she noticed as she climbed out of the Cruiser was that Mary Pat had gained weight. Her hips were a little wider, a little more womanly. Her breasts more prominent. Although she was sure the poundage was driving Mary Pat crazy, the truth was it suited her the same way it suited Deirdre.

Mary Pat was hovering right around forty and the look of the prosperous matron was all over her. She wore a beautifully tailored pair of black trousers with a deep green silk tunic that fell to mid-thigh. Her pale blond hair was cut short in one of those casual, choppy styles that Ellen would sell her curls to be able to wear. Small pearl earrings, a large watch with a leather strap, a blizzard of diamonds on the left ring finger. She was a well-groomed woman of a certain age and economic status who was deeply settled into a very comfortable life.

"I was getting worried," Mary Pat said as they approached. "I thought you would be here in time for lunch."

"Good to see you, too, Mary Pat." Deirdre bent down and swooped Declan into her arms. She rolled her eyes at Ellen over the little boy's head.

"You're looking well, Ellen." Mary Pat's dark blue eyes took inventory. "I hope you're not trying to diet. You're slim as a reed as it is."

"You look wonderful, too," she said as they gave each other a perfunctory hug and air kiss. "I love the new hairstyle."

Mary Pat inclined her head toward Declan, who was tugging on one of Deirdre's curls and laughing. "I needed something wash-and-wear. He's a bigger handful than his brother and sisters ever were."

Ellen opened her arms toward the little boy. "Hand him over," she said to Deirdre. "It's time we met."

Declan fussed a little, but Ellen's curls proved every bit as fascinating as Deirdre's had. He was big for sixteen months, with soft light auburn hair that glittered with gold in the afternoon sun. He had the O'Brien dark blue eyes and long curly lashes and that perfect peachy skin grown women paid a fortune to try to replicate.

Mary Pat was watching with open curiosity. "He looks a lot like you."

She felt a wide smile spread across her face. "You think?" A powerful surge of love seized her as she and Declan took each other's measure. They shared a history, she and Declan, a wonderful laundry list of details that linked them with those who had come before and the ones yet to be. Nothing she had learned in the classroom about DNA and heredity had prepared her for the violent, primal satisfaction that came with seeing your own eyes looking back at you from the round sweet face of a little child.

If this was even a fraction of the love Cy had felt when he looked into David's eyes, she owed him an apology. He had simply been responding the way nature had intended. You were meant to love your own.

"Same coloring," Mary Pat said. "But I think he's going to be cursed with the O'Brien thighs. He looked like a baby Sumo wrestler when he was born."

"I remember that picture," she said, laughing. "An eleven-pound baby is something to see."

"Try giving birth to one," Mary Pat said with a grimace. "You have no idea—" She stopped and gave her head a quick shake. "Of course you do. You see it every day, don't you?"

Ellen pressed kisses to Declan's buttery soft cheeks. "Believe me, I know there's a world of difference between assisting the delivery and doing the hard labor."

"Well, I certainly didn't mean to imply that—"

"I know that, Mary Pat. It isn't called hard labor for nothing, is it?"

"I hate to interrupt all of the bonding going on," Deirdre said, "but if I don't use the john in the next thirty seconds—"

"Straight through the hall, second door on your right."

Deirdre took off at a run.

"I half expected her to bring that dog with her," Mary Pat said.

"I convinced her that Cambridge was no place for Stanley."

She and Declan followed her into the house while Mary Pat gave her a brief rundown on the whereabouts of the other family members.

"James is at the office, of course. He'll join us at the hospital. Shawna has a job on the Cape. She probably won't be here this weekend. Sean is studying for finals with his friend Carl. Caitlin and Duffy are in school. They'll spend the rest of the afternoon at their friend Courtney's house. They're too young to go to the hospital with us."

"They're eight now, aren't they?"

"Almost nine," Mary Pat corrected her.

"You might want to check with your hospital. Ours would allow them to visit an adult patient."

"That's not the issue," Mary Pat said as she led the way to the kitchen. "They adore their grandfather. I think it would be too difficult for them to see him this way."

A powerful argument could be made against Mary Pat's position, but she wasn't fool enough to try it. They were her children. She would make the decisions without Ellen's two cents.

She ooh'd and aah'd over the recently remodeled kitchen. Mary Pat took her on a quick tour of the first floor. Within moments her head was awhirl with color schemes, window treatments, furniture styles, wallpaper patterns, and everything else that went into turning a bare-bones house into an inviting home.

"You should become a decorator," she said. "This place is absolutely wonderful, Mary Pat."

Her sister thanked her for the compliment. It was clear that the words, spoken sincerely, had pleased her. "From your descriptions, your house sounds fantastic."

"It's a great house," she agreed, "but it looks like an empty barn. I don't even have curtains on the bedroom windows yet. I ordered a bed for the guest room. Deirdre and I are a little too old to bunk together indefinitely."

Mary Pat had mastered the art of bland sarcasm. "You two always were very close."

"I've enjoyed spending time with her." She refused to rise to the bait.

Mary Pat considered that statement but refrained from comment. "If she ever comes out of the bathroom, we can set out for the hospital."

"Is Declan coming with us?"

"I'll drop him off at his baby-sitter's house on the way."

"I wouldn't mind staying here with him." *Actually I would love staying here with him.* It would mean avoiding a trip to the hospital to see Billy. What had seemed like the right thing to do when she was safe at home in Shelter Rock Cove suddenly seemed fraught with emotional peril.

"You didn't drive down from Maine to be a baby-sitter. That's what I pay Laura for. You're here to see our father, right?"

"𝕹ice try," Deirdre said *sotto voce* as they sat in the backseat of Mary Pat's Saab on the way to the hospital. They had stopped so their sister could drop Declan off with his sitter. "I was going to use the same line myself."

"Shh." She kicked Deirdre's ankle. "She probably has the car bugged." The truth was she would have loved to stay behind with her delightful nephew Declan, but that wasn't part of the plan.

Deirdre laughed. "You're beginning to sound like me."

"And I'm beginning to see why you sound the way you do. Mary Pat is a force to be reckoned with." She had never seen Mary Pat on her home turf before today. As adults, they had always met on more neutral territory. Restaurants. Clubs. Rented beach houses. Mary Pat was clearly a domestic genius who should have been chatelaine of a stately mansion or the *grande dame* of one of those sprawling multigenerational families whose story ended up sooner or later as fodder for a miniseries. "She could be CEO of a Fortune 500 company with those organizational skills."

"I'm surprised her kids aren't all in therapy," Deirdre said.

"Her kids are doing great," she reminded her sister. "Scholarships, awards, lots of friends."

"Enough to make you puke, isn't it?"

She gave Deirdre another soft kick in the ankle. "We're not fourteen any longer, Dee. We can admit she's doing something right."

Deirdre peered behind Ellen's ear. "No sign of a battery pack, so you haven't been Stepfordized yet."

They dissolved in highly inappropriate gales of laughter,

considering the reason for their trip to Cambridge. They were struggling to regain control of themselves when Mary Pat slid back behind the wheel and pinned them with a look through the rearview mirror.

"Why do I feel like I'm driving my kids around? You two are as bad as you were years ago."

"I'm sorry," Deirdre said, still bubbling with laughter. "Chalk it up to another Chuckles the Clown moment."

If Mary Pat understood the reference to the classic sitcom starring Mary Tyler Moore, she didn't let on. "I'm not a chauffeur. Why don't one of you sit up here with me?"

One look at the expression on Deirdre's face and Ellen knew she had been pressed into combat. Seconds later she was buckling the shoulder harness next to Mary Pat and trying to ignore the stifled sounds of laughter emanating from the backseat.

"When I was thirty-five," Mary Pat said, "I didn't have time for nonsense. I had four children to care for."

"When you were thirty-five, dinosaurs still roamed the earth," Deirdre shot back.

Ellen grinned. "Sorry," she said to Mary Pat, who gave her a look. "It was funny."

Was that the faintest twitch of a smile tugging at the corners of Mary Pat's perfectly lipsticked mouth? "I don't know why she bothers with music. She should be out there doing stand-up."

"A compliment?" Deirdre fanned herself. "Somebody time-stamp this moment because it'll never come again."

"Did you ever do anything about that mole on your shoulder?" Mary Pat asked Deirdre. "You know there's a strong history of skin cancer in the family."

"There is?" Ellen effortlessly slipped back into her doctor persona. "I didn't know that."

"You're as fair as we are," Mary Pat said, glancing over at her as if she had forgotten how she looked. "Do you freckle?"

"Unfortunately, yes."

"You doctors really are the worst when it comes to taking care of yourselves. You use sunblock, don't you?"

"When I remember."

"You're as bad as Deirdre."

"Thank you," Deirdre called out from the backseat. "I'm flattered."

"Tell me more about our family medical history." She knew her mother's history inside out, but she had never given a second thought to what her O'Brien genes brought to the table.

"We're a remarkably healthy, long-lived bunch," Mary Pat said as she flicked on her directional and glided into the right-hand lane. "My mother's—" She stopped. "Sorry. You want to know about the O'Briens. Well, Billy's brother lived to three months shy of his eighty-second birthday. His two sisters are still alive."

"I didn't know Billy had sisters."

"You're joking."

"He never mentioned anything about his family."

"I can't believe you never asked."

"Neither can I," she said. She had been so overwhelmed by the news that Cy wasn't her father, so shocked to learn that she had two sisters out there she had never met, that everything else had faded into the background where it had remained all these years.

Mary Pat was an encyclopedia of information. Billy's sisters, Maeve and Fiona, were both widows in their late seventies, who currently shared a condo in Fort Lauderdale.

Aunt Maeve. Aunt Fiona. She was finding it hard to take it all in.

"Do they have children?"

"They're O'Briens, aren't they? Maeve had six; five are still living. Fiona only had two, but they've given her eleven grandchildren between them." Maeve had twenty-two grandchildren and two great-grandchildren.

"We don't get to see each other very often," Mary Pat said. "We're scattered all over the world. I've been thinking about hosting a family reunion."

Deirdre's groan rattled the windows. "Oh, give it up, Mary Pat. We're not the Waltons and we never will be."

Mary Pat glanced in the rearview mirror. "I can't believe you never mentioned any of your aunts or cousins to Ellen."

"When was the last time they mentioned me to anyone?"

"I haven't a clue."

"I rest my case."

"That's your problem right there," Mary Pat said to Deirdre. "The world doesn't revolve around you. You should have told Ellen about her heritage."

"Maybe if you spoke to the Doctor now and then, you could've told her yourself."

The Doctor? Was that how they referred to her?

Mary Pat's face turned crimson, and Ellen felt like crawling under the floor mats.

"Are we having fun yet?" she said, and they all managed a weak facsimile of a laugh.

Mary Pat was the first one to regain her composure. No surprise there. Despite everything, she was filled with grudging admiration. "I've been working on our family tree," Mary Pat said as she pulled into the hospital parking lot. "I'd be glad to print out a copy of my information on the O'Brien branch."

"I'd appreciate it."

"I'll make sure you have it before you leave."

"Good night, John-Boy," Deirdre said from the backseat, and this time the laughs were a little closer to the real thing.

Ellen had learned early on in her training that hospitals had personalities same as the people who ran them. Some were austere and forbidding, the kind of place you wanted to avoid at all costs. Some felt like small hotels, where you weren't a patient, you were a guest. Others tried to be a high-tech extension of home with TVs and CD players and computers available for their patients' enjoyment.

There was an odd dichotomy at work when it came to hospital management. If the management staff was doing its job, the beds were filled with patients. But if the doctors were doing their job, the beds were empty because everyone was well and healthy. One of the trickiest tightrope walks was finding a way to balance the need to turn a profit with the very real needs of the patient population.

She liked the feel at St. Joseph's. It was close enough to Boston to attract high-quality staff, but far enough away to retain a real sense of community, not at all unlike what they enjoyed in Shelter Rock Cove.

Mary Pat's heels clicked loudly on the highly polished tiles in the lobby. She had a quick, long stride much like her own. Deirdre had to break into an almost-run to keep up with them.

They snagged an elevator and Mary Pat pressed 6.

"He's in ICU," she said, eyes focused on the lighted panel of numbers over the doors. "He had some trouble a few hours after the ERCP and—" She glanced over at Ellen. "You know how it is. Better to be safe than sorry, right?"

It was pure and utter bullshit and they both knew it. The diagnosis wasn't in yet, but the specialist had made it patently clear that Billy's chances were next to zero.

"He looks like hell," Mary Pat said as the doors slid open at the sixth floor. "They were able to open up his bile duct a little so he's not that ghastly deep yellow, but he's lost a lot of weight." She met Deirdre's eyes. "You should be prepared."

Deirdre looked as if she was going to pass out. Ellen placed an arm around her sister's shoulders as they exited the elevator. "Are you okay? Maybe you need to sit down and drink some water."

"Maybe I need to get out of here," Deirdre said.

That summed up Ellen's feelings right then as well. She found herself suddenly empathizing with every family member whose deer-in-the-headlights stare when she explained a diagnosis had gotten under her skin. It felt very different on this side of the stethoscope, something she would be wise to remember.

They passed through a pair of swinging doors marked ICU-CCU, walked past a small waiting room with a television suspended from the ceiling. Two women sat on opposite corners of the dark green sofa pretending to watch Emeril Lagasse do something unspeakable to a game hen. The women looked up as they approached. Their disappointment was palpable as they turned back to Emeril.

"They limit visitors to two at a time," Mary Pat said, "but they make allowances for family."

"That's okay," Deirdre said, her voice thin and shaky. "You two go ahead. I'll wait."

"If you disappear, so help me God I'll track you down."

"You've been watching too many old movies," Deirdre said and claimed a chair in the waiting room.

The ICU at St. Joseph's looked like every intensive care unit Ellen had ever seen. Bright lights. Lots of staff. The nurses' station at the center of a horseshoe of patient cubicles which were separated by blue curtains. That sense of hyper-alertness masked by a deceptively calm facade that would ignite into action at the first sign of trouble. A young dark-haired nurse looked up as they approached and smiled at Mary Pat.

"Good news," she said, pushing away from the computer terminal. "He's doing a lot better this afternoon."

"No more vomiting?" Mary Pat asked.

"Last episode was"—the nurse glanced back at the monitor—"last night around ten P.M. We might be able to start him on clear liquids tomorrow if he remains stabilized."

"He was vomiting?" Ellen asked. The urge to step behind the nurses' station and read the reports was very strong.

The nurse looked from Ellen to Mary Pat.

"This is my sister, Dr. Ellen Markowitz."

The nurse's eyes lit up. "Mr. O'Brien told us all about you. He'll be so excited when he finds out you're here."

Professional exaggeration, that was what it was. She had a hard time believing her presence or absence meant much of anything to Billy. She smiled at the nurse, then asked again about the vomiting.

"He had some trouble after the procedure."

"The ERCP?"

The nurse nodded.

"What type of trouble?" ERCPs were fairly simple procedures but not without risk, especially not for someone as ill as Billy was.

"He started vomiting blood about twelve hours after he came out of recovery. We had some trouble bringing it under control."

She had a score of questions, but the nurse looked so uncomfortable and poor Mary Pat was clutching the edge of the counter in a white-knuckle grasp.

"Has Dr. Loewe been in to see him today?"

"Not yet."

"Does he have the results from the procedure?"

"I believe he'll have them by four o'clock."

"Fine," said Ellen. "Please tell him that Mrs. Galvin and Dr. Markowitz would like to discuss their father's prognosis with him before he leaves for the day."

"Will do."

"I'm impressed," Mary Pat said as she led the way to Billy's cubicle. "I've never seen you in doctor mode."

"We've all grown up a lot since those first summers together."

Mary Pat stopped in front of the closed curtains of #8. "I should probably see if he's awake first. I told him you were coming, but I'm not sure how much he understood. He was still sleeping off the anesthesia." She reached for the curtain, then stopped. "He isn't the way you remember him, Ellen. I don't want you to be shocked."

She didn't have the heart to tell Mary Pat how little it mattered to her. All afternoon she had been waiting to feel something, anything, about Billy and his situation, but her emotions remained flatlined. Deirdre, who claimed to feel nothing at all, practically vibrated with love and fear and anger and every other emotion she could toss into the mix. Even though Billy was still alive, Mary Pat was clearly grieving. She managed to keep her sorrow contained by throwing herself into micromanaging every aspect of the situation that she possibly could.

And all the while Ellen felt nothing at all.

She waited on the other side of the curtain while Mary Pat moved next to the bed.

"Hi, Da . . . it's me, Mary Pat. . . ." Billy's responses were too muffled for her to make out. "You'll never guess who's driven down from Maine to see you. . . . Yes, Ellen . . . she's right outside. . . . Of course she wants to see you. . . . You look fine. . . . I'll go get her."

Was it possible to age ten years in fifty seconds? Mary Pat looked older and infinitely sadder than she had moments ago, as if the weight of all that lay ahead had suddenly landed squarely on her shoulders. How different things could have been if they had only found a way to look past Billy's sins and be a real family to one another. Maybe then she would know the right thing to say to ease the burden.

"He's tired but lucid," Mary Pat said. "He can't wait to see you. I'll wait out here."

Ellen stood up straight, summoned up a big smile, and wished she could fly away.

Twenty-seven

The two women were only being friendly, but their questions were grating on Deirdre's nerves.

"So what exactly is wrong with your father?" the older one asked.

"We don't know yet," Deirdre said, keeping her eyes fastened on Emeril's bald spot. "We're waiting for test results."

"You can wait forever if you don't nudge them along," the older woman said.

"They don't like being pushed," the younger one said, "but you do what you have to do when it's family."

She wondered what they would do if she ran screaming for the window and jumped.

She didn't do hospitals well at all. She never had. She liked to say it was that tonsillectomy when she was three years old—the one where they told her The Big Lie about all the ice cream she could eat—but it was more than that. Everything about them made her skin crawl. The smells. The sounds. The naked emotions flying around everywhere you looked. People came undone in hospitals. They went a little crazy. You never got good news in hospitals, not unless you were on the maternity ward, and even there things didn't always go the way you hoped they would.

Ellen thought Deirdre was worried about Billy, but that was so far from the truth that it was laughable. This didn't have anything at all to do with Billy. This had to do with the fact that if she didn't get out of there in the next thirty seconds, they would have to hose her down or put her in a straitjacket to keep her from doing something crazy.

Antonio had been claustrophobic and he said some of her symptoms sounded exactly like what he felt when he found himself trapped in a small room. Of course, that had made her wonder how often a grown man found himself trapped in small rooms unless he was in the habit of being interrogated by the police on a regular basis. Which, unfortunately, turned out to be closer to the truth than she had realized at the time.

See how good she was at spinning her mind away from her circumstances. Who said daydreaming didn't come in handy? She closed her eyes and tried to settle deep into that zone where she could tap into peace and harmony and block out the fact that she was trapped on the sixth floor of some crummy hospital in the middle of—

Oops. Now, that wasn't the right way to go about it, was it? She had to transcend her situation. What was it they used to say when she lived in Los Angeles and started hanging with the yoga-and-Zen crowd? Sublimate? Breathe deeply? Don't fire until you see the whites of their eyes?

She started to laugh, quietly at first, then a full-out bark of laughter popped out. She opened her eyes in time to see her two companions scuttling away like a pair of L. L. Bean land tortoises. When was the last time she had thought about land tortoises anyway? Grade school maybe. Maybe never. Land tortoises were a good thing to contemplate if you didn't want to contemplate the fact that you were trapped in a hospital waiting room while your sister the doctor had an audience with the great Billy O'Brien.

Notice how Mary Pat didn't press her to see him first? So much for all of that "he's been asking for you" bullshit she had used to bludgeon her into driving down with Ellen. Nothing had changed. She was every bit as invisible to Billy today as she had been since the day she was born. She'd bet her repaired-at-great-expense Hyundai that he had never once asked her whereabouts or expressed even a fleeting desire to see her. Deirdre who?

She should have asked Mary Pat for her cell phone. She needed to talk to somebody, connect with the real world beyond this stinking hellhole of a hospital. She could always call Scott the Mechanic or maybe Annie. Or how about her agent? She could pretend that she had forgotten the details of the cruise ship job. Once you got him on the phone, he was good for at least an hour of telling her everything that was going wrong in his life, from his hernia to his wife's snoring. Or better yet she could phone Hall Talbot and check up on how Stanley was faring, but she supposed it really wasn't good form to call an OB during office hours to ask about your dog, even if he was the only child you'd probably ever have.

Maybe she would walk down the hall and see what was happening in ICU.

Ellen didn't recognize him. If Mary Pat hadn't told her that this was their father, she would have walked back over to the nurses' station and asked where they'd transferred him. The big handsome man known as Billy O'Brien had disappeared, and in his place was this frail old man looking up at her with her eyes.

"Ellen!" His voice had the raspy quality consistent with the n-g tube that they had inserted down his throat.

"I see Dr. Loewe is taking good care of you." She bent down and kissed his left cheek.

He reached out and clasped her hands. His grip was surprisingly strong. He had always believed you could take the measure of a man by the strength of his handshake.

"Thank you for coming." The lilting rhythms of Ireland still lent music to his words. "I know you're a busy doctor."

"Babies follow their own timetable," she said, calling on every ounce of professionalism at her command to help her maintain her composure. "Especially around the full moon."

His richly vibrant laughter was a thing of the past. His eyes lit up, but his laughter was a rasping half-cough, half-sigh that she had heard before.

He was dying. She didn't need to hear test results to know that his time was near. The knowledge was there in his eyes, in the sound of his voice. She had seen it often enough to recognize the signs, and it filled her with regret for the things that would never be.

"I never stopped loving your mother." His voice was so low she had to lean closer to hear him. "She told me she was expecting you. . . . I was planning to leave Jeanne and Mary Pat so I could be with her."

Oh, God. Mary Pat was on the other side of the curtain. "Maybe we should talk about this some other time."

"It was the happiest time of my life. . . . We couldn't wait for you to be born. . . ."

"Mary Pat and Deirdre are here, too. Maybe I should—"

"Then Jeanne told me she was pregnant, too, and I had to choose."

"I know all about that," she said, unable to control the note of bitterness in her voice. "You chose your wife and family."

"She had nobody else." It hurt to listen to him. The raw sound of his voice matched the raw pain his words conveyed. "Only me. Nobody to turn to if I left. Her people were all gone." Ellen's mother had her parents and her friends, a network of support. She would never have to be alone.

And her mother had Cy Markowitz. Cy, a good friend who had loved her for a very long time and was eager for the chance to take care of her and her unborn baby.

"I wasn't a good husband to Jeanne," he said, "before your mother and after. So many mistakes. . . ."

His eyes glittered with unshed tears over choices made a long time ago. She saw him as he must have been then. Tall. Strong. Heartbreakingly handsome. The wild and poetic Irishman who could charm the birds from the trees.

Two choices and either way he lost.

They had all lost.

She wanted to love him, but she didn't. Too much time had passed, too little of it spent together without shadows of pain between them. His wife's humiliation. Her stepfather's jealousy. The fourteen years she had lived without the knowledge that she was his daughter. It had all been too much to overcome.

She pitied him. She wished him well. She would do anything she could to make him better, to see to it that he could live a long and healthy life, but when all was said and done, she didn't love him. But he was her father and she had one small gift for him.

"She always loved you," she said to him as he held on to her hand. "Right up until the end."

"You don't know that."

"Yes, I do." She squeezed his hand. "She saved all your letters."

He closed his eyes. Moments passed. Minutes. She watched his shallow respiration and noted the signs of life displayed on the machine in the corner. Pulse. Respiration. Blood pressure. Sinus rhythm. Her hand in his felt oddly comforting to her. She would be happy to stand there forever if it would do any good, but she knew it was too late for that.

His eyes fluttered open and there was that smile again. "You're really here," he said. "I thought I was dreaming."

"I'm really here. We were talking about the letters."

"Letters? I don't remember—" His smile made the years vanish as his dark blue eyes filled with tears. "I sent one every year . . . on her birthday . . . Yeats . . . I introduced her to Yeats. . . ."

"I know. She saved them all."

"*Go raibh maith agat.*" No human being should look at another with such pure aching gratitude. All she had done was give him back a memory. It seemed the least she could do for the man her mother had loved.

"You're welcome, Da." The unfamiliar word was on her tongue before she realized it. There was a first time for everything.

He smiled and closed his eyes again, and she settled down to watch him sleep.

Deirdre told her sisters she would meet them in the hospital cafeteria, but they dragged her down the hall to the consultation room as if she were five years old. She didn't want to hear anything this Dr. Loewe had to say. It wasn't going to be good news. Even she knew that, although she wasn't sure any of it was sinking into Mary Pat's head. Mary Pat was too busy racing around with her Day Runner clutched in her hands, trying to schedule Billy back to health.

What room would they take him to when he left ICU? How about a private nurse. TiVo. A CD player. A companion. A private chef.

Ellen had been very quiet since her visit with Billy. Deirdre had been expecting it to be a hello-how-are-you-doing kind of thing, the daughterly equivalent of visiting an ailing patient. Some good advice, a few upbeat words, a graceful goodbye. It hadn't quite gone that way. Instead Ellen had stayed with their father for almost an hour, leaving only when a pair of nurses told her she had to go so they could tend to Billy's needs. Now she seemed distant, as if she had somehow detached herself from her surroundings.

Deirdre glanced around. Who could blame her? The consulting room was painted the color of a baked potato. A nothing beige that was supposed to lull you into a false sense of security and hide the fact that nothing good ever happened here. Nobody walked out that door with a check from Publishers Clearing House or a gig on the *Tonight* show as the oldest living undiscovered talent in the universe. The room didn't even have a window, just a framed print of a Tuscan meadow.

They sat down at the long table. Mary Pat opened her Day Runner and uncapped her fountain pen. Ellen slipped her typed notes from her briefcase and fanned them out in front of her while Deirdre wished she had bought one of those PDAs, the kind that make you look all busy and efficient when you're really playing Free Cell.

Dr. Loewe blew into the room in a cloud of Phisohex and authority. He shook hands warmly with Mary Pat, who suddenly looked much older and much more terrified than she had just moments ago. He introduced himself to Ellen and made pleasant noises about her stepfather Cy and his family while Ellen made equally pleasant noises back to him. She supposed it was a doctor thing, an audible secret handshake.

"I'm Deirdre," she said finally, extending her hand.

"The harpist," he said. "I've heard a lot about you."

"My father's a musician, too," she said. "It's a crazy life."

Mary Pat neatly stepped in before she could start up an actual conversation. "I told Dr. Loewe you're leaving to work a cruise ship at the end of the month."

She laughed, which was probably inappropriate given the circumstances. "You make it sound like I'll be leaning against a smokestack in my miniskirt, trying to entice the wait staff."

Loewe, bless his chart-reading heart, got the joke. He allowed himself a quick eye twinkle before he got down to the business at hand. The good ones always knew how to pretend they were human. He started talking and before long Mary Pat was keening softly, so softly only a sister could hear her. Ellen took over, asking questions nobody really wanted the answers to. Loewe looked relieved to be talking to another doctor, someone who understood the jargon without requiring a translator. Someone who understood that emotion had no place in the business of dying.

The words volleyed across the table. A few of the serves went long. Some replies never made it to the net. She tried to listen without hearing, pulling only the necessary information out of the air and keeping the rest an arm's length away. Once again she summoned up every yoga class, every Zen lecture she had ever attended to help her quell the monkey mind inside that was always five years old and waving goodbye to Da as he set out on another adventure that didn't include them.

"We'll be moving him into a regular room tomorrow morning," Loewe was saying, "and I hope to discharge him Monday if he remains stabilized over the weekend."

"What about Hospice care?" Ellen asked.

He nodded. "It's time."

Mary Pat flinched and pretended to jot down a note in her Day Runner. Mary Pat was the good daughter, the one who had given him grandchildren, the one who always had a spare room ready for him. She would be lost without Billy and his problems.

Loewe looked over at Mary Pat. "I assume he'll be discharged to Mrs. Galvin's home."

Mary Pat nodded. "I'll talk to patient services before we leave tonight and get things moving."

Billy would need a hospital bed, a visiting nurse, access to sufficient painkiller to numb the discomfort but not so much that he lost touch with the world. Help to sleep. Help to move his bowels. Help to remember why waking up each morning was supposed to be a good thing.

They were all dancing around the one question that had to be asked.

"How much longer does he have?" Deirdre asked.

Mary Pat gasped. Ellen revealed nothing. Dr. Loewe took it in stride.

"With luck, six months."

"Without luck?" she asked.

"Three, maybe four."

"I disagree." Ellen's voice broke the silence that had fallen over the room.

"I understand how you're feeling, Dr. Markowitz," he said gently, "but the reality—"

"I don't think he has that long."

"You read the report. I showed you the scan results. He has a strong constitution. I think once we get him stabilized, he'll do surprisingly well for a fair bit of time."

"Medically I agree with your prognosis," Ellen said. "But I saw his eyes this afternoon. I think he's ready."

"Ellen, for God's sake!" Mary Pat's voice shook with anger. "What's wrong with you?"

"I'm not speaking as a doctor this time," Ellen said, still maintaining her even tone. "I'm speaking as Billy's daughter. He's saying his goodbyes. He's ready to leave."

"And since when does goodbye mean you're leaving?" Mary Pat tossed back at her. "Grandma Kathleen said goodbye fourteen times before she died. It became a family joke."

"I wouldn't know about Grandma Kathleen," Ellen said, "and I can't offer you any scientific proof to back up my words. I can only tell you what I'm feeling."

"Wow," said Deirdre minutes later as Dr. Loewe sprinted down the corridor toward the elevator. "I didn't think he could run that fast in those fancy Italian shoes."

"What the hell were you thinking?" Mary Pat demanded of Ellen. "How dare you jump in with all of your fancy medical training and embarrass me that way! You'll be going home to Maine, but I have to see Dr. Loewe every single day."

Ellen's cheeks reddened slightly, whether from anger or

embarrassment, Deirdre couldn't say. "As I said to Dr. Loewe, I wasn't speaking as a physician. I was speaking as a daughter."

"A little late for that," Mary Pat said.

"Get off your high horse, Mary Pat," Deirdre said. "Let's quit pretending we're anything but the dysfunctional family that we are. It will make this discussion a whole lot easier on all of us. Maybe Ellen is right. Nobody can predict exactly when a person is going to die . . . not even the great Dr. Loewe. Ellen's worked with dying patients before. Maybe she sees something we don't."

"I don't know how you could see anything," Mary Pat said. "You haven't even stopped in to say hello to him."

She had easily a half dozen excuses she could offer up to appease her sister's self-righteous anger, but lying seemed an utter waste of time and energy. She was getting too old to play this game. They all were.

"Did he ask to see me, Mary Pat?"

"Didn't I tell you—"

"The truth," she said. "Did he ask for me?"

Mary Pat fell silent.

Deirdre turned to Ellen and asked the same question.

"No," Ellen said. "I'm sorry, Dee."

"Why should he ask to see his own daughter?" Mary Pat found her tongue again. "What's stopping you from just walking in there and saying hello?"

"I don't know," she said, starting to cry. "Isn't that a kick in the head?"

Mary Pat whipped out her cell phone and told her husband James to forget about meeting them at the hospital. They would grab something at the local Olive Garden, then return to the hospital.

Ellen excused herself to phone her service for messages and to touch base with Hall. He was in the delivery room with Jill Franzese, whose easy labors and deliveries were the stuff of legend around the hospital. She left a long, rambling message that probably made no sense at all, but it was good to hear his voice, even if it was just his outgoing message.

She found her sisters in the gift shop. Mary Pat was thumbing through *Martha Stewart Living* while Deirdre flipped through *People*.

"If you need to make any calls, you're welcome to use my cell," Ellen said to her younger sister.

"I was thinking of calling Stanley."

"Don't bother," she said, draping an arm around Deirdre's shoulder. "You know Stanley. He probably has the phone off the hook."

The restaurant was crowded, but they lucked out and were settled into a booth near the window in record time.

"A glass of the house red and a bushel of breadsticks," Deirdre said to the painfully young waitress.

"Same here," Ellen said while Mary Pat opted for iced tea.

They busied themselves with the menus, making occasional comments about the relative calorie content of lasagna as opposed to fettuccine Alfredo until Deirdre put down her menu and said, "Who are we kidding? Let's order one of everything," and they shared their first real laugh since they pulled into Mary Pat's driveway hours ago.

The waitress arrived with their drinks, their breadsticks, and a salad bowl the size of a VW.

"It's a bottomless salad bowl, right?" Deirdre asked the waitress, then scowled when Ellen and Mary Pat laughed again. "I just wanted to make sure."

Mary Pat lifted her glass of iced tea. *"Slainte!"*

"Slainte!" she said.

"Slainte!" Ellen chimed in.

They touched glasses.

"Do you remember the first time Billy took us out to dinner together?" Mary Pat ripped open a blue packet of Equal and emptied the contents into her glass.

"That little Italian restaurant near the Five Corners!" Deirdre started serving up the salad.

"He ordered squid because he thought we all needed to develop more sophisticated palates," Ellen remembered. "Dee and I ended up racing each other to the ladies'."

"He was so disappointed," Mary Pat said as she added another packet of Equal. "He had this vision of driving down to

New York to take us to Le Cirque and introduce us to French cuisine."

That was Billy's style, all right. Sailing into a fancy restaurant with his three daughters on display. He would have loved every second of the attention. For a man who had the common touch, he was a terrible snob.

"It's a good thing he never got around to it," she said. "I don't think we were ready for escargot."

"It's been a long time since the three of us sat down together." Mary Pat sounded slightly wistful.

"I think it was the year Dee and I graduated high school," Ellen said. "You nursed Shawna at the table. I thought our waiter was going to need CPR."

"Oh, God," said Mary Pat, "I'd forgotten all about that. It took me awhile to master the art of discreet nursing."

"Put me off milk for months," Deirdre said, then yelped as Mary Pat smacked her with a breadstick.

They attacked their salads while Dean Martin sang about *amore* from the wall speakers overhead.

"I used to think that was the way love really is," Mary Pat said as she snagged an extra black olive from the humongous salad bowl. "Pizza-pie moons, floating down the street on a cloud. Every single silly pop song cliché."

"You mean it isn't?" Ellen feigned wide-eyed astonishment.

"At the beginning," Mary Pat said, "but it changes."

"For the worse," Deirdre said. "Like everything."

"Not for the worse," Mary Pat said. "It simply changes. You can't expect to walk on clouds for the next forty years, can you?"

"How would I know," Deirdre said. "I haven't been able to make it past the two-year mark."

"I haven't even made it that far," Ellen admitted. "Brian and I were engaged less than six months." At the best of times, in every important relationship, she had always kept one eye on the exit.

"Are you seeing anybody now?"

She hesitated. She found it difficult to think of Hall in that way. What she felt for him went so much deeper that it terrified her.

"She's seeing Hall Talbot," Deirdre said. "The doctor she works with."

Mary Pat's eyebrows lifted. "Is that true?"

If she hadn't eaten the last breadstick, she would've hit Deirdre, too. "I don't know if I'd phrase it quite that way, but I guess you'd say we were seeing each other." *All day, every day, for almost four years.*

"Do you think that's a good idea?" Mary Pat asked.

"No," she said, "but it seems I'm doing it anyway."

"You should see him," Deirdre said with a theatrical sigh. "The man is drop-dead gorgeous."

"I would never go to a gorgeous gynecologist," Mary Pat said. "Not with these thighs."

"I went to a gorgeous dentist once," Deirdre said. "When he said, 'Open wide for Mr. Thirsty,' I almost swooned."

They were collapsed in helpless laughter when their waitress brought their entrees.

"Are you ladies okay?" she asked as she deposited their meals in front of them.

"Never better," Ellen said, wiping her eyes with the corner of her napkin. "If you'd bring us more wine, we'd be downright perfect."

Just a second, Markowitz. There's a small chance you might be pregnant. Is that wine such a great idea?

"You know what?" she said as the waitress turned to leave. "Forget the wine for me. I'll have an iced tea."

"You're not driving," Mary Pat observed. "Feel free to have a second glass."

She shook her head. "I'd better stop. One more and I might belt out the score from *Chicago*."

"You're an O'Brien," Deirdre said. "Singing's in your blood."

"Singing might be in my blood, but talent isn't. I stink."

"We'll be the judge of that," said Mary Pat. "Sing something."

"I will not."

"Just a few lines, that's all, so we can judge."

Dino had segued into "Everybody Loves Somebody Sometime." She launched herself headfirst into the melody, and before she reached the chorus, her traitorous sisters were throwing wadded-up pieces of paper napkins at her and boo-ing.

"You're right," Deirdre said. "You really do stink."

"I told you so."

"You enunciate clearly," Mary Pat said. "That's always a plus."

"That's like saying the food was terrible but there was plenty of it," Ellen pointed out. Her sisters were honest. You had to give them that.

"I probably couldn't perform an episiotomy," Mary Pat said.

"That's our Mary Pat," Deirdre said. "Modesty becomes her."

Deirdre and Mary Pat bickered their way out to the parking lot, but for once it was a comic bickering that had Ellen weak with laughter by the time they reached Mary Pat's car. Nothing had gone quite the way she had expected it to. She had imagined a working supper, where they tried to iron out certain issues pertaining to Billy's care, but that hadn't happened. They had only danced across the surface of anything serious. Instead their fears for Billy and their uneasiness with each other somehow translated into waves of healing laughter.

The laughter, however, quickly faded into memory fifteen minutes later as the three of them approached ICU. The younger nurses averted their eyes. The head nurse looked up from her computer terminal with an expression of such deep compassion that a knot formed in Ellen's stomach. The curtain around Billy's area was tightly closed. She heard no familiar whooshes and peeps from the monitoring devices, and in that instant she knew that Billy was gone.

Twenty-eight

"You should be in the living room with your sisters."

Ellen turned away from the sink where she had been rinsing out her coffee cup and smiled at her brother-in-law. "I thought I'd finish washing up."

"That's why we have a dishwasher," he said, stifling a yawn as he entered the kitchen. "The kids are in there with them. Billy's death is hitting them all pretty hard."

It was a few minutes after midnight. At least a hundred years had passed since she and Deirdre rolled up the driveway and saw Mary Pat and Declan waiting for them on the front porch.

When James and Mary Pat married, they had both been starving students on scholarship to B.U. Now James was a tenured professor of anthropology at Harvard while Mary Pat took care of her family and maintained a 4.0 GPA as she pursued the degree she had abandoned years ago when Shawna was born. She had known about James and about Mary Pat's dedication to her family, but why hadn't she known the rest of it? Why hadn't she thought to ask?

"Come on," James said, stifling another yawn. "I'll walk you down the hall."

This was only the third or fourth time she had met her brother-in-law, but somehow she felt as if she had known him forever. "I need to make some phone calls," she said. "I'll be there soon. I promise."

"I'm going to hold you to it," he said as she excused herself and dashed upstairs to the guest room she was sharing with Deirdre.

The guest room was as lovely as every other room in the house. The bed was king-size with a padded headboard covered in the same lush fabric as the down comforter that floated above the pillowy mattress. The walls were papered in a watered silk in tones of dusty pink, dove gray, and cream. The crown moldings, baseboards, and windowsills were all enameled in a glossy vanilla that worked wonderfully with the antique armoire that looked like it had been refinished to resemble a white birch tree on a snowy day. Only Mary Pat could make something like that work, but there was no denying the fact that every aspect of the room delighted the eye.

And the other senses as well. The air was faintly scented with freesia. Trees tapped gently against the window screens. The comforter was soft and smooth beneath her fingertips.

You would never guess her father had just died.

She sat down on the edge of the bed and waited to feel something approaching the depth of feeling being expressed downstairs by the family Billy O'Brien left behind. Only a terrible sense of regret seemed worth noting. *If only ... maybe ... what if.* The litany of lost chances, mistakes made, opportunities wasted. He had been so happy to see her, so grateful for the memory of her mother that she had restored to him. Why did clarity always seem to appear when it was too late for anyone to benefit from it?

Somewhere in Mary Pat's beautiful house a clock chimed the quarter hour. They were all gathered together in the living room, taking comfort from the closeness, the shared memories, the stories. Even Deirdre was there with them. The family circle had opened wide enough for her to slip inside and reclaim her place. A place she spent her life fighting against but yearned for just the same.

Ellen didn't belong there. Now that Billy was gone, the connection between them would grow thinner, more fragile, until it vanished just as if it had never been at all. A fierce longing for home, for Shelter Rock Cove, for Hall settled deep in her chest. She needed to hear his voice, to hear him tell her there was some place in this world where she belonged.

He answered the phone on the first ring. "I was hoping to hear from you, Markowitz," he said, and that was all it took to open the floodgates.

She spilled her story to him, every last detail. Deirdre. Mary Pat. Declan and the towering joy she had felt when she saw herself reflected in his dark blue eyes. The consultation room with Dr. Loewe. Those last unexpected moments with Billy, as he lay sleeping with his hand in hers. The bitter taste of regret.

He let her talk. Every now and then he would ask a question or offer a viewpoint but mostly he listened with his heart.

"When is the funeral?" he asked when she had finally talked herself out.

"Monday." Her voice was scratchy, her eyes red from crying.

"Tell me where and what time and I'll be there."

"I appreciate the gesture, Hall, but I'd feel better if I knew you were there taking care of our patients."

"You know Arnstein and Williams would take over for us for a few days."

She told him about her visit with Patsy Wheeler that morning. "She's been pushing herself too hard. Doug said he found her sitting at her desk twice this week. She had a little staining which may have put the fear of God into her."

"She has in-home nursing care, hasn't she?"

"Absolutely. But Patsy is a strong personality, and she tends to intimidate the nurses. I'd feel better if you popped in on her every day, if possible."

"You don't want me there, do you, Markowitz?"

"It isn't that." At least not entirely. "I'll be home late Monday."

They listened to each other breathe for a few moments. It was almost as good as holding hands.

"How's Stanley doing?" she asked after a bit. "Is your house still in one piece?"

"We've been doing great," he said. "I locked up the beef

jerky, and that seemed to solve most of our problems." Susan Aldrin had offered to walk Stanley in the afternoon if Hall couldn't get home to take care of it.

"That was nice of her."

"You sound angry."

"I'm not angry at all."

"You don't like Susan?"

"I like her very much. I'm just surprised she has time to pull dog-walking duty."

"She's watched my kids plenty of times."

"Forget I said anything."

"Susan's crazy about dogs."

"Hmm," she said. "Could've sworn it was you she was crazy about."

"Susan? Get out of here."

"Just an observation." She didn't know if it was nothing more than a midlife crush on an old friend or something more intense, but Susan was definitely looking at Hall through new eyes these days.

She could almost see him smiling two hundred miles away. "You're jealous."

She was smiling, too. "Don't be an idiot."

"Susan and I have never—"

"I know that."

"Just wanted to make sure."

They fell into another one of those delicious silences that spoke volumes. Just listening to him breathe made her feel closer to home.

"One hour twenty-two minutes."

Jill Franzese's labor. "A boy?"

"Derek Jeter Franzese. Seven pounds, one ounce. The Yankees already have their eye on him."

Her eyes swam with tears. "Life renewing itself."

"Always," he said.

"I should go now."

"If you change your mind, I could be down there in a couple hours."

"I know," she said. "That means a lot to me." She took a deep breath. "You mean a lot to me."

She hung up before she could say another word.

*   *   *

Mary Pat coped by throwing herself into the details of fare-well. She called in the obituary to the major newspapers, phoned family and friends, settled on a casket, viewing hours, finalized arrangements for the funeral mass, and made sure the veteran's cemetery had all the necessary paperwork to receive Billy's remains.

Ellen made herself useful by making sure everyone was clean and well fed. Friends and neighbors had seen to it that they had a steady supply of casseroles, pots of chili, cakes and cookies and homemade bread. Shawna was due home in time for the funeral. Sean spent much of his time in his room, work-ing on a eulogy to his grandfather. Caitlin and Duffy alternated between teary outbursts and marathon sessions spent in front of the television. Caitlin had asked a few pointed questions of Ellen that had set her back for a while. Who are you? Why didn't you come see us before? How could Grandpa Billy be your father if Grandma Jeanne isn't your mother? She was grateful for Declan's wordless acceptance.

Deirdre was a mess. There was no other way to put it. She had quite literally cried herself sick, dissolving into tears every time someone mentioned Billy's name. Her heart went out to her younger sister. If only they hadn't dallied over dessert. Maybe then they might have gotten to the hospital in time for Deirdre to make some sort of peace with Billy. There was no point dwelling on it. Things were the way they were, and she could only pray that the services would help provide the clo-sure Deirdre was searching for. She spent a great deal of time with her lap harp. Mournful notes from long-forgotten songs provided a plaintive soundtrack to the days leading up to the funeral.

The house filled up swiftly with flowers. Mary Pat's friends sent enormous arrangements complete with mass cards and promises of adding prayers for Billy's immortal soul to their prayer group's list. Hall sent flowers, as did Janna on behalf of the office staff.

Hall was her touchstone. Their nightly phone calls re-minded her that she wasn't alone in the world, no matter how it might seem at the moment. She tried to explain how it felt to be alone in a house filled with O'Briens. People with whom she shared a bloodline but little else. The sorrows and joys and daily battles that made up their lives were a mystery to her and always would be.

She was clearly the stranger in their midst, the child whose existence had broken apart a family. Nobody was treating her with anything but consideration, yet the sense that she didn't belong not only lingered, it grew stronger. They didn't speak the same language. Every family had its own form of short-hand, unintelligible to the outside world. For all of their difficulties with each other, it was clear that when the chips were down, Deirdre and Mary Pat were members of the same clan.

Even their ways of grieving set them apart. Ellen's mother had been buried within twenty-four hours of her death, then Cy and her aunts sat shiva in the living room for seven days. It was a period of intense mourning and remembrance, designed to bridge the gap between death and the resumption of life. The Irish way was very different. She found the long hours spent at the funeral home greeting mourners and keeping up a cocktail party level of chat to be exhausting.

Billy's three daughters had been assigned certain roles. Mary Pat was the dutiful daughter. Deirdre was the prodigal daughter. Ellen, however, was the curiosity. She might be one of Billy's daughters, but she wasn't one of them. She hadn't been there for Christmas celebrations. She hadn't shared Thanksgiving with them or the Fourth of July. Most of the people who trooped through Flanagan's Funeral Home had only heard about her through the years, seen her face in the scratchy photographs Billy kept with him. They made a beeline to meet her, asking deeply personal questions that would get their faces slapped in any other venue but this one. How Billy O'Brien had managed to sire a Jewish obstetrician—and why this was the first time they had ever met her—was the stuff gossip was made of. Even there in Cambridge.

She knew it. She accepted it. But nothing could make her like it.

"I'm sorry you have to leave so soon," Mary Pat said as Ellen finished packing her bag. "I was hoping you'd be able to stay with us a few days."

"I wish I could," she lied, "but I have surgery tomorrow morning, so I need to get back."

"Declan's going to miss you."

Her smile softened into a more natural one. "Not half as much as I'm going to miss him. He's so—" She stopped and shrugged, afraid that the emotions she had been blocking so successfully would leap up and betray her. "You're his mother. You must know how terrific he is."

"They're all terrific," Mary Pat said. "Even if you have to keep reminding yourself of that once they hit puberty."

"Do you know if Deirdre's coming with me?"

"I haven't seen her since she went to put away her harp."

The house had been filled with people when they walked through the door, friends and relatives, business associates, neighbors who had come to love Mary Pat's father, the handsome and charming Irishman who told the best stories in town. Even Jeanne and her second husband Tom had shown up, driving all the way from Florida to be there to say goodbye to Billy. She had tendered Ellen a stiff hello, and then they had both retreated to separate corners for the duration.

Laughter rang out through the rooms as they shared memories of Billy, groaned over some of his old jokes, remembered the times he had blessed them with song. Deirdre, who had had little to say to anyone since Billy's death, disappeared for a few minutes. Suddenly the beautiful, heartwrenching sound of her lap harp drifted through the rooms, drawing everyone out to the foyer where Deirdre sat on the bottom step, harp across her knees, offering up her thanks to the man who had given her the gift of music.

One of the men began to sing "Danny Boy" as Deirdre accompanied him. She played old drinking songs, songs of struggle and need, songs of love and broken hearts. Finally, when Ellen thought her own heart was about to split in two from the sheer beauty of her sister's music, the first evocative notes of "Amazing Grace" sounded and Mary Pat's voice lifted in song. Mary Pat possessed a clear and innocent soprano. Deirdre's smoky alto added depth and emotion. Together they could break what remained of your heart.

"Billy would've been proud of his girls," one of the

O'Brien cousins said as the room burst into stomps and cheers of approval.

Nobody noticed when Ellen slipped quietly from the room to pack her bags.

Now Mary Pat watched while she zipped up her bag, then scanned the room for any forgotten items. "It must have been difficult, being thrust into the middle of so many O'Briens."

She met her older sister's eyes. "What was difficult was not knowing there were so many O'Briens out there."

"We're a big family."

First cousins, second cousins, second cousins twice-removed. "I wish I had been able to meet Fiona and Maeve." Billy's widowed sisters were both recovering from what they called "female" troubles.

"You should fly down there one day. They have a lot of stories to tell." Suddenly she did one of those forehead slaps and leaped to her feet. "How could I forget?"

Mary Pat disappeared from the room, then popped back in two minutes later with a thick brown envelope sealed with heavy tape. "They sent this up by courier," she said, handing it to Ellen. "Per Billy's wishes."

She took the envelope, surprised by its heft. "What's in it?"

Mary Pat shrugged. "For your eyes only, although I wouldn't mind if you opened it right now so I could see."

What difference did it make? She had no secrets from her sisters. They knew more about Billy and the rest of the family than she did. Why not open the envelope and get it over with.

The tape fought her, but she peeled it back and ripped open the envelope while Mary Pat watched with undisguised curiosity. She kind of liked that about her sister. You never had to wonder what Mary Pat was thinking: she would be more than happy to tell you.

"Oh great," Mary Pat said. "Another envelope."

"At least this one doesn't have eight layers of strapping tape on it." She slid her index finger under the flap and it gave way easily.

"Will you look at that!" Mary Pat met her eyes across the spill of letters and photographs that fanned across the bed between them. "What is it? A scrapbook without the scrapbook?"

"I don't know." She picked up a small square white envelope with her name on it and opened it.

"Is it from Billy?"

She didn't answer. Billy's flamboyant handwriting slanted across the page. He had always used a thick-nibbed fountain pen filled with vivid sapphire ink he said was the color of his mother's eyes. A ridiculously over-the-top statement that now, in memory, made her feel like crying.

"It's from Billy, isn't it?" Mary Pat persisted. "You can tell me."

She couldn't speak so she handed the one-page note to Mary Pat who read silently.

For my daughter Ellen, who was always in my heart even when I couldn't be in her life. Don't ever think that because I followed your mother's wishes and stayed away that I ever forgot you. Although you couldn't see me, I was there with you every step of the way.

Billy

"He watched you," Mary Pat said. "These are reports from a private investigator."

"That's my mother," she said, pointing to a small color photo of a beautiful woman pushing a stroller through Central Park.

Mary Pat reached for the photo and studied it. "She was beautiful."

Ellen nodded. Her throat felt tight, painful. "She turned heads everywhere." Even as a little girl she had been aware of her mother's star power.

"I never thought about her as a real person before," Mary Pat said quietly. "She was always 'That Woman' around our house." Her eyes filled with tears. "You must miss her terribly."

"Even more now that I'm older," she said. "There are so many things I wish I could ask her."

They sat together, sifting through a lifetime of memories captured in snapshots and written reports that read more like a letter from home than a detective's summary. Her first day at school. Girl Scouts. Riding her bike through the Park. Horseback riding lessons. Skating with her friends at the rink at Rockefeller Center. Letters from Cy, begging Billy to allow him to formally adopt Ellen, the "child of my heart."

"I never really understood," Mary Pat said quietly. She met Ellen's eyes. "Maybe I didn't want to."

"Maybe you couldn't," she said. "Maybe none of us could."

"Maybe we didn't try hard enough," Mary Pat said.

Ellen looked at her and her breath caught as she saw their father in Mary Pat's eyes, she saw Deirdre and Declan, and for the very first time she saw herself as well. Past and future. All the mistakes, all the pain, all the promise.

"Do you think it's too late to try again?" she asked.

Mary Pat reached across the bed and took her hand. "Not too late at all," her big sister said.

Deirdre was waiting by the Cruiser. Her duffel bag rested at her feet. Her lap harp, protected by a leather carrying case, rested against her side. She had changed out of her funeral clothes and into a pair of softly faded jeans with a patch on the right thigh and a sleeveless sweater in a pale shade of lavender. Her wild mane of curls looked even more untamed than usual as the afternoon wind played havoc with them.

Ellen took in all the details as she approached her sister.

"Shades?" she asked as she unlocked the back of the car. "Since when?"

"I have a headache," Deirdre said, then offered up nothing more.

They tossed their bags into the Cruiser, then hit the road.

Deirdre was asleep before they reached the Mass Turnpike.

She wasn't much in the mood for silence. Silence left room inside her head for all the thoughts she didn't want to deal with. She switched on the radio, adjusted the volume low, and settled on a call-in show that seemed to revolve around old movies and classic TV shows. Absolutely perfect.

They zipped through Massachusetts, sailing across the southern tip of New Hampshire, and had just waved goodbye to Portsmouth when the cramps started up. She tried to ignore them, but she knew that wasn't a bright idea, so she exited the Maine Turnpike in Kittery and pulled into a McDonald's parking lot. She turned off the engine and waited a second for Deirdre to rouse herself from sleep. Finally she placed a hand on her sister's shoulder and shook her gently.

"Dee, wake up for a second. We're at McDonald's. I need to use the bathroom."

Deirdre muttered something but didn't open her eyes.

"Deirdre!"

Deirdre peered sleepily at her. "McDonald's. Pee. I heard you."

"I'll be right back."

How could you expect a woman to sleep when there were French fries less than fifty yards away?

Deirdre yawned, dug around in her duffel bag for her wallet, then stumbled sleepily through the parking lot to the entrance. French fries were ambrosia, manna from the gods, all-purpose, can't-fail comfort food extraordinaire.

"Supersize diet and king-size fries," she told the ten-year-old counter clerk.

She hid a yawn behind her hand and leaned against the counter for support. She hadn't slept more than an hour since the night Billy died. Every time she closed her eyes she saw him lying in that hospital bed, and she jerked up from sleep as if she were escaping the jaws of death herself.

She paid the clerk for her bounty, then bumped into Ellen near the exit door. "Want some fries?"

"Thanks, but I don't think that's such a good idea."

"Oh, please don't start with the cholesterol talk. I heard enough of that from Mary Pat. They're using canola oil these days."

"I meant, I'm not feeling too great. My period just started."

"And you're still vertical? Mine always knocks me flat the first day. Listen, if you want me to drive, I'll—" She stopped. "Shit. I'm sorry. This means you're not pregnant, doesn't it?"

Ellen gave her one of those looks she had been perfecting since the summer they were fourteen. "Go back to sleep," she said.

Twenty-nine

"They mean well," Hall said as Ellen cuddled closer to him on the old leather sofa. "They want you to know they care."

Ellen buried her face against his chest and breathed in deeply. "I know, I know. I wish I could find a way to handle it better. I feel like I just don't seem grateful enough for their concern."

"You're handling it fine." He pressed a kiss to the top of her head. Her curls felt like swirls of silk against his lips. "Don't beat yourself up about it."

She had the idea that she wasn't presenting the proper picture of the grieving daughter, and it bothered her. Deirdre went around pale and wan, settling into her grief as if it were a starring role in a movie while Ellen fought with her own natural inclination toward keeping her deepest emotions private.

"We really shouldn't be doing this," she said. "What if—"

"Fuck 'em." She laughed against his chest and he grinned. "It's lunchtime. This is our office. The door's locked. They can all go to hell."

"This is a side of you I've never seen before."

"I have a lot of sides you've never seen."

"Apparently." She sighed deeply. "It's so good to be home again." She had been home for a week and she was still saying it.

"Home," he said. "I like that word."

"I do, too," she said. "Now." She told him again how much she had missed him while she was in Cambridge.

"Wait a second," he said. "I want to get that on tape."

She sat up, cradled his face in her hands, and kissed him. "You don't need to get it on tape. I'll tell you any time you want. I missed you, Hall. More than I ever thought possible."

They fell silent for a while. They did quiet better than any couple on the planet. Their quiet hid a symphony.

She stretched a little, then placed a hand low on her stomach.

"Cramps?" he asked.

"Six days of them," she said. "I have newfound respect for the power of stress on the human body."

"There's an opinion ready for *The New England Journal of Medicine*." He placed his hand on top of hers. "Think there's anything to touch therapy?"

"Your hand is warm," she murmured. "It feels good."

He slid his hand under the waistband of her trousers, then splayed his fingers across her bare skin. "That should feel better."

"It does."

His fingers crept lower, sliding under the waistband of her bikini panties. He could feel her heat rising.

"Are you disappointed you're not pregnant?" he asked.

"I was, but it's probably for the best." She leaned back and looked at him. "How about you?"

"Disappointed. The thought of a little redhead had its appeal."

"You could always adopt an Irish setter."

He shook his head. "You're a lot like your sister, Markowitz. Always the smart remark when the conversation gets a little too close for comfort."

"I don't do that."

"Yeah, you do."

"We can take things slowly now," she said. "Get to know each other."

"We know each other better than most couples who've been married twenty years."

"Shh," she said. "This is perfect. You don't have anything against perfect, do you?"

She'd had a rough week. He didn't want to push her, but the answer was yes. He did have something against perfect. Perfect didn't last. He wanted messy. He wanted loud. He wanted passionately imperfect if it meant having her by his side. Seventeen hours a day weren't enough. He wanted all twenty-four. He wanted seven days a week, four weeks a month, twelve months a year.

He wanted forever.

Janna gave her one of those appraising looks when she and Hall stepped out of the office after lunch, but Ellen found she didn't really give a damn. Maybe he was right and it was time to start seeing each other publicly and let the chips fall where they may. Compared to the rest of her life, the opinions of a few rigid human beings really didn't matter. Or they shouldn't.

Tori and her mother had a three o'clock. They had decided to start her on birth control pills, a decision that churned up mixed feelings for Ellen. She had to make sure the girl understood that while the Pill, properly used, would prevent pregnancy, it still didn't offer the necessary barrier protection against sexually transmitted diseases. Try explaining that to a girl just a couple of years away from playing Barbies.

And there was the problem of Patsy Wheeler. Patsy was stretching the limits a little bit more every day. That was just human nature at work, but it surprised her that Patsy, who so desperately wanted to carry her child to term, would take unnecessary chances. Explaining the dangers of sex to a sixteen-year-old girl was easy compared to explaining to a forty-something-year-old woman why sitting quietly at a desk for thirty minutes might be enough to end her pregnancy.

Add to those problems the fact that she felt like hell. The cramps were showing no sign of stopping. In fact, cramps might not be the right term for what she was feeling. The pain was sharper, less rhythmic, and it seemed to be settling on the right side of her lower abdomen. She wasn't spiking a fever, so appendicitis didn't seem too likely, but if it continued into the weekend, she would definitely have to see someone about it.

Deirdre was planning to leave in the morning for the long drive down to Florida, where she would board the cruise ship and embark on her latest adventure. They had decided that Stanley would stay in Shelter Rock Cove with Ellen. They called it "temporary custody," but they both knew there was little that was temporary about it. Stanley was there to stay.

Talk about leaving footprints in the cheesecake.

First rule of chasing a man: Don't ask a pair of nosy women for directions to his house. She thought Annie and Claudia were going to pass out on the floor when she asked them if they had any idea where Scott the Mechanic lived. Annie was clueless, but that Claudia was a regular Columbo. She grabbed the latest edition of the local phone directory, flipped to P for Peretti, and there he was.

"We won't ask," Claudia said as she copied the address and phone number onto a sheet of Annie's Flowers notepaper for her.

"That's right," said Annie. "We'll just make up something juicy."

They would, too, but she didn't care. Tomorrow morning she would point her Hyundai south, and they would be nothing but a memory. And in another two weeks, she would be boarding a cruise ship where she would spend her days and nights playing the harp for a bunch of people who cared more about the midnight buffet than music. Still, it paid well and it came with room and board, which, considering the fact that she was technically homeless, was a pretty good deal.

Her manager had asked her if she got seasick, and she had laughed out loud. O'Briens didn't get seasick. Billy used to say she was part mermaid, the way she'd stay in the water all day long during the summer.

Nope. Strike that. She wasn't going to think about Billy. She had done enough thinking and crying over the last week and a half to last her a lifetime. Fiona had spelled it all out for her on the telephone when she called to let the aunts know their flowers had arrived. "Mary Pat was his firstborn," Fiona said, "and a daddy's girl at that. There isn't a man alive who can resist. And Ellen is the spit of her mam. Every time he looked at her, he saw the woman who was the love of his life."

"And then there's me," she had said, almost spitting the words into the phone.

"I won't be lying to you, child. You were never his favorite, but the fault wasn't with you. Your mam should've thought it through before she laid her trap for the boy-o. He never claimed to be anything but the rogue he was, and bringing a new one into the world wasn't about to change a thing."

They were all so filled with excuses for him that it made her sick. He didn't . . . he couldn't . . . no one expected him to . . . maybe you should have . . .

Well, she hadn't. That was the truth of it. They had ended the way they began, separated by expectations neither one of them had the power to control.

Not that she was going to say any of this to Scott the Mechanic. She had been deeply touched by the beautiful bouquet of wildflowers he had sent to her at Ellen's house, and even more deeply touched by the short handwritten note of sympathy. For two people who didn't know anything about each other, they had shared an awful lot in a very short time. She wanted to thank him for the flowers, for the lift up to Bar Harbor, for giving her a shoulder to cry on, and not making her feel guilty or embarrassed for using it. They were alike somehow. She knew he could feel it, too. Something had drawn them together right from the first instant, and she couldn't leave without acknowledging it.

His truck was in the driveway. She placed her hand on the hood. It was still warm. *Gotcha,* she thought. She knocked on the door. No answer. She rang the bell. Still no answer. She peered through the curtainless window. There was no sign of life anywhere.

"I know you're in there," she called out. "I can see you hiding behind the sofa."

Even if that didn't flush him out, the potential for embarrassment was a nice touch. She peered through the window one last time, then turned to leave.

"Going somewhere?" Scott the Mechanic blocked the path. He wore a pair of jeans, no shirt, and had a phallic-looking telescope balanced on his brawny shoulder.

"I was afraid you were lying unconscious in there and needed me to call 911."

"You're a real Samaritan."

She tilted her head. "I like to think so."

"Did you get the flowers?"

"That's why I'm here. I'm leaving tomorrow for Florida and I wanted to thank you."

"Glad you liked them." He shifted the telescope to his opposite shoulder. "How're you doing?"

She made a so-so gesture with her right hand. "Good days and bad days," she said. "I think the change of scene is exactly what I need."

"Was your father sick very long?"

"One day they told me he wasn't feeling the greatest and the next day"—she snapped her fingers—"he was gone."

"Were you two close?"

Say it, damn it. Don't pretend. Don't sugarcoat it. Tell the truth and maybe the hurting will stop. He had three daughters and I was number four on his list. How's that for not being close?

"No," she said. "We weren't close at all."

ℋℯ had never been great when faced with raw emotions. When Megan used to fall into one of those blue funks she was prone to, he would rack his brain for a way to make her laugh, anything to keep it from spiraling down into tears.

He wasn't any better with his own emotions. He had been ducking the harpist since that night in Bar Harbor when he cried in her arms. He had feigned sleep, but they both knew that was a lie even though neither one acknowledged it. It was easier to deal with her meltdown over the loss of her job than with the fact that he was only human.

Now here they were again in another one of those emotional pressure-cooker situations they seemed to specialize in. One minute she was standing there speaking to him in a perfectly normal voice, and the next she was crying so hard she could barely breathe. Maybe it was him. It seemed they couldn't be in the same room without an eruption.

"Come on," he said as he unlocked the front door. "I'll get you a drink of water." He couldn't leave her standing there on the path and she sure as hell couldn't drive in that condition.

"I don't want any water," she said, following him inside. "Why do people always think you need water when you're upset?"

"Same reason they tell you to put your head between your knees."

She laughed and cried at the same time. On her it looked good. It looked better than good. It made him want to pull her into his arms and hold her until the world stopped spinning out of control.

"I don't know why I'm crying so much," she said as she poked around the room, flipping through the stack of newspapers on the end table, fanning the stack of magazines on the couch. She looked up at him with stormy blue eyes. "He knew I was there at the hospital, but he didn't even ask to see me. He left Ellen a bundle of photos he'd taken of her—I don't know why I'm wasting my tears on someone who didn't give a damn."

She was looking for a way to control what was ultimately beyond control. Only time and distance would help. "He was still your father," he pointed out, "and it's only been a week. Crying jags sound pretty normal to me at this stage."

"Normal? I wouldn't know normal if it bit me on the ass."

"*Normal* being a relative term."

"There you go again. What are you doing repairing cars? You should be doing"—she waved her hand in the air—"something else."

She was right. He should be doing something else and come September he would be.

"You snooped through the wrong stacks," he said. "Try the stack in the corner while I get you the water."

What was wrong with her? Every time she saw him, she ended up collapsing in a sodden heap of tears. She wasn't like this at all. Sure, she cried at sad movies or over a particularly powerful piece of music, but when it came to real life, she was drier than the Mojave. Still sniffling, she wandered over to the stack of papers in the corner and started shuffling through them. *Baxter College* was imprinted on the front of a deep blue folder. Was that one of those vocational schools that gave you life credit for knowing how to tie your shoes? Not that she was being critical. She didn't have a credit to her name and probably never would. Last she heard they didn't give life credit for being a fuckup.

She opened the folder. A list of courses. Per credit charges. Scott the Mechanic's name was typed right there at the top with the word *Student* after it and the words, "Bachelor of Science, major in Astronomy" beneath it. Apparently he was going back to school in September and planned to work toward the goal he had given up years ago.

Those damn tears started up again. She wished she hadn't teased him about being a mechanic. God, what was she after all but a down-on-her-luck ex-blues singer turned harper who was about to sail away on a low-rent version of the *Love Boat*.

Good on you, Scott Peretti. She flipped through a few more pages but didn't stumble upon any more surprises. She was about to put the folder down when an envelope slipped out and fluttered to the floor, and she bent down to pick it up.

Nice heavy-laid finish. Perfectly typed address complete with bar code. A commemorative stamp, one of those Old Glory ones, and a handsome logo in the upper left-hand corner that almost brought her to her knees.

The 9/11 Families Relief Organization.

"Oh God," she breathed, staring down at the envelope. "Oh, no . . ."

She didn't hear him come in. She looked up and he was standing in front of her, holding a glass of water in his left hand.

"I'm sorry," she said. "I didn't know . . . I didn't mean to . . ." What was there to say that could make the slightest difference?

"I told you that you could look. I wasn't sure Baxter would be able to accommodate my schedule, but it looks like we can work something out. Jack—" He stopped and in that instant she saw the realization spread across his face. The glass shattered in his hand in a spray of water and glittering shards.

"Your wife," she whispered, "your little boy."

The muscles in his throat, his jaw, clenched and unclenched as he struggled to control his emotions the way he hadn't been able to that night in Bar Harbor. He said nothing but his eyes gave him away. She didn't need the details. He had lived near Boston. The two planes that slammed into the Twin Towers had both originated from Logan.

"I'm so—"

"Shut up." His voice was harsh, raw with the struggle against his sorrow.

"Don't fight it," she said. "It's okay to—"

"Shut up." The ragged edge of sorrow was blunted by something else, a tidal pull of longing that wrapped itself around her and wouldn't let go.

Nobody had ever looked at her that way before. Rage, sorrow, a loneliness that ran deep and wide and long. She felt as if she was seeing into her own soul, past the lies and the defenses meant to keep the world out, seeing straight into the vulnerable beating heart of truth she had spent a lifetime running from.

He crossed the room to where she stood waiting for him.

Their fingers touched and for a second it seemed as if the world and everything in it fell away. They had been circling this moment from the day they met.

"You're bleeding," she said, examining the palm of his left hand.

"You're crying," he said, touching her cheek with the callused tip of his forefinger.

The cut on his hand was small, nothing more than a scratch really, but she needed time. After waiting all her life for this moment, she needed more time. She took him into the kitchen and washed and dried his hand, fussed about Band-Aids and hydrogen peroxide as if adhesive and gauze could heal their broken parts as neatly as they could heal a scratch.

"I didn't want this," she said.

He cradled her face in his hands and said, "Nobody does."

Then, because there was nothing else they could do, no other way to postpone the inevitable, he swept her up into his arms and carried her into the bedroom where he gently stripped away her clothes and began to make love to her body and soul.

"It's been a long time for me," she warned him as she helped roll on the condom.

He cupped her with his hand. "We'll take it slow." He told her it had been a long time for him, too, and he wanted them to enjoy every second.

Hot. Wet. Long and slow until they were drenched in sweat and the heady, erotic smell of sex. She slid down his body, aware of the way her nipples felt against his chest, his belly, his erection, drawing pleasure from the sounds he made deep in his throat when she cupped him with her hand, then drew him deep inside her mouth. She used to think of this as a parlor trick, something you did because men loved it and expected it and you never disappointed a man, not if you wanted to see him again.

She did it this time because she wanted to, because there was as much pleasure in it for her as there was for him.

And oh, God, the things he did to her with his hands and his lips and his tongue. Wild forbidden things she had only dreamed about. Tasting, sucking, sharp little bites that sent her spiraling out of her mind, away from the world, away from sorrow and disappointment just long enough for her to remember how sweet life could be if you let it.

Sweet and precious and terribly short.

"I'll be back later," Susan said to her husband as she grabbed her purse and car keys from the hall table. If she kept fussing with her hair and makeup, she would never leave.

Jack looked up from the Red Sox game he was watching. "Where are you going all dressed up?"

She considered lying, but she was still too much of a Catholic schoolgirl to do that. "I'm stopping by the office for a while, and then I'm going by Hall's."

"What for?"

"I need to sign some papers."

"I mean, why are you going to Hall's place?"

"He made a big contribution to the town preservation fund. I wanted to pick up the check."

"It can't wait until tomorrow?"

"Jack, if you don't want me to go, just say so." She held her breath.

"Do what you want," he said. "There's no talking to you lately."

She didn't even bother to hang around for a fight. Lately fights were like buses: If she missed one, there would be another along any minute. She flew out the door, leaped into her car, and zipped over to the office, where she signed some contracts, returned a phone call, then raced back out to her car. She supposed she was taking a chance, just popping in on Hall this way, but it was now or never.

𝐼𝑡 was a little after seven P.M. when Ellen pulled into Patsy Wheeler's driveway. Doug was away on another business trip. She was surprised to note the private nurse's car was missing. She added that to her list of items that needed to be dealt with during the visit.

She had made arrangements for a technician to bring over a portable sonogram machine tomorrow so they could perform a status report on the baby's progress. Her reasoning was twofold: They needed to know how well the baby was developing and she hoped that seeing her child right there on the monitor might spur Patsy to take fewer chances, no matter how minor they might seem to be.

She climbed gingerly from her Cruiser. The pain in her abdomen had intensified since the afternoon. Sharp, searing, it was beginning to seem more and more like appendicitis. Acute appendicitis was nothing to fool with, and she was seriously considering a quick stop at the hospital after her visit with Patsy. Better safe than sorry. It would be pretty embarrassing for a physician to be hauled into the ER on a stretcher because she was too arrogant to pay attention to her own symptoms.

Patsy and Doug had given her a key to the house, but she didn't like to use it without announcing herself first. She rang the doorbell, then waited for Patsy to click on the intercom and inquire who was there. A minute passed, but no Patsy.

She rang again and waited. Still no Patsy. Okay. That did it. She unlocked the door and stepped into the shadowy hallway.

"Patsy!" Her voice seemed to echo in the silent house. "Patsy, it's Dr. Ellen!"

No answer. Sweat broke out on the back of her neck as a sharp blade of pain sliced through her midsection. She moved through the darkened house, switching on lights as she made her way toward the master bedroom. Patsy wasn't a deep sleeper. She certainly would have heard her approach.

"Patsy! Don't be alarmed. It's just me . . . Dr. Ellen."

Still nothing. Her heartbeat leaped forward. She placed her hand against her abdomen and almost jumped at the shock of heat against her palm. Something was very wrong. A wave of nausea assailed her and she forced herself to breathe deeply in order to quell it. She pushed open the bedroom door and gasped at the sight before her.

Patsy was lying on the floor near her desk. She was conscious, but there was an ominous pool of blood beneath her.

"It's okay, Patsy," she said, putting her arm around the woman. "I promise it's going to be okay."

"My b-baby . . ."

"We'll get a sonogram done at the hospital. I've told you before how resilient babies are." She glanced around. "Where's the nurse?"

"She had to leave early. I—" She clutched her belly. "The battery on the cordless was low. I needed the phone to—Dr. Markowitz?" Her voice rose in fear. "Dr. Markowitz, what's wrong?"

Pain shot through Ellen's middle with ferocious intensity. White hot pain that seared away everything else.

"Dr. Markowitz—"

Those were the last words she heard.

Thirty

Hall was surfing the Web for information on the restaurant where Kate and Lizzy would be working this summer when he heard a knock at the front door. He glanced at the clock on the bottom right of his computer screen. Almost nine o'clock. A grin spread across his face and he yanked off his reading glasses and dragged a hand through his hair. Ellen, he thought. It had to be.

It wasn't.

Susan brushed past him into the foyer. It would never occur to his old friend to ask if it was a good time, something he had had to explain more than once during the course of his marriages.

"So what're you doing out this late?" he asked as he followed her into his kitchen.

"Late?" She wrinkled her nose and he noticed she was wearing more makeup than usual and had taken great pains with her hair. "It's not even nine."

"You look good. What were you up to?"

"Nothing special. I had to sign a few papers at the office. I was on my way home when I remembered I left one of my date books here when I was pulling afternoon duty with Stanley last week."

"I haven't seen a date book around here."

"Small. Red leather. You must've seen it."

"I'd notice a red leather date book." Mainly because he wouldn't be caught dead with one. "Sorry."

Some of her brassy self-confidence faded. "Am I interrupting anything?"

"I was doing some background on the place where the girls will be working this summer. I wanted to get a feel for who runs it, that kind of thing."

"You're such a worrier."

"Yeah," he said, "and you're not."

She laughed. "That's why we're friends, isn't it? We have a lot in common."

"How's Jack? I heard he sprained his wrist yesterday and ended up in the ER."

She made a dismissive motion with her hand. "It's always something lately. Since he turned forty-five, it's been one thing after another."

"As someone who kissed forty-five goodbye, I can relate." *You were right, Claudia. Something's definitely wrong with the Aldrins.*

"Not you!" Again that unfamiliar laugh. "You haven't changed a bit in the last twenty years."

"Okay," he said. "What the hell's going on?"

"I paid you a compliment."

"I know," he said. "What gives?"

"Do I have to spell it out?"

"Yeah," he said. "I think you do."

That was his first mistake.

Ðeirðre sat up against the pillows and stretched. All of those wasted classes, trying to understand how to be in the moment. The answer had been right here in Scott the Mechanic's bed all the time. She felt completely connected in body and soul, alive in every atom of her being.

"You're not much of a talker," she said, running her fingers through her tangled curls. "Believe it or not, I'm a pretty good listener."

"I know," he said. "Maybe some day."

Or maybe not. They both knew life would make that decision for them.

"Come back here," he said from the other side of the bed. "You don't leave until tomorrow morning, right?"

Oh God, she was tempted. A night in his arms would be enough to carry her through the next decade.

"I have to go," she said. "Ellen had to work late, but I'd like to spend a little time with her before I leave."

"I could try to change your mind."

"And you'd probably be able to do it."

"But you want to spend time with your sister."

"I really do."

He watched her as she climbed from the bed. "What would it take to get you to stay?"

"For the night?"

"For the summer," he said.

She sat down next to him and brushed a lock of hair off his forehead. "Not many things in life are perfect, but tonight was. We should keep it that way."

An hour later, freshly showered and with her damp curls loosely gathered on top of her head, she started back to Ellen's house. She felt lighter in spirit than she had in months, as if just maybe things were finally going to make a turn for the better.

She was going to miss Scott the Mechanic, but then she was going to miss the entire town. She had grown very fond of the place over the last few weeks and was beginning to feel as if she belonged there. There was something to what Ellen had said about the lack of privacy, though. She wondered how many Shelter Rock Cove townspeople had noticed her Hyundai parked in Scott's driveway. Not that it mattered. They were both free to do whatever they liked. Still, it was a thought. In three blocks she had already noticed Sweeney's Harley in front of Artie's house, Roberta's Lincoln angled in front of the Stop 'n' Shop, and Susan Aldrin's SUV tucked next to Hall Talbot's Rover at the foot of his driveway.

She laughed as she drove past the cluster of new homes at

the edge of Shore Drive. Score another point for Dr. Ellen. No wonder she had been paranoid after that night she spent with Hall. Her red PT Cruiser really did make a statement you couldn't miss. The car was parked in the driveway of the last house on the corner, one of those gorgeous saltbox rip-offs that went for more money than she would probably earn in her lifetime.

A little late for house calls, she thought as she stopped at the traffic sign. Ellen had said she would be home by nine, which was one of the many reasons why she didn't stay longer at Scott's. She reminded herself that obstetricians didn't work on their own schedules; they worked on the babies' schedules.

But what was with the house call anyway? Nobody made house calls anymore.

She looked back at the house through the rearview mirror. It had been ablaze with light. Nothing abnormal there. But something wasn't quite right and she couldn't put her finger on it. The road was empty. All she had to do was throw the car into reverse, back down the block, and take a look. What could it hurt? Ellen wouldn't even know she was there.

She backed her way up the street and came to a stop in front of the house with Ellen's Cruiser in the driveway. The front door was wide open. Not open a crack, mind you, but wide open with the foyer lights blazing. She threw the car into park and dashed up the walk. Okay, so maybe this town really was Maine's answer to Mayberry RFD, but things happened. Even Paradise had its share of snakes. The worst that could happen was that she pissed Ellen off. It wasn't like that hadn't happened before. She was leaving town tomorrow. She would take her chances.

"Ellen!" She called from the doorway. "Are you in here?"

No answer.

She stepped into the foyer. It was almost too quiet in there. Prickles of alarm erupted up and down her arms.

"Ellen! It's Deirdre. Are you here?"

She jumped at a sound coming from somewhere down the hallway. Footsteps? A television? She couldn't be sure. Cautiously she moved through the foyer, past the living room, until she reached—

A hugely pregnant woman lay sprawled on the floor, blood

pooling beneath her ivory nightgown. Her face was dead white and she clutched her belly.

"Call 911," she begged Deirdre. "Hurry! Dr. Markowitz—"

And then she saw Ellen. Oh, God. Oh, God. Not Ellen. Please not Ellen. Her sister's slender form lay at the foot of the dresser in the corner. She was motionless. Her eyes were closed. No no no no no—

"911!" the woman begged. "Do something please!"

"Where's the phone?" she asked, struggling to keep it all together. "I don't see a—"

"Kitchen . . . try the kitchen. Hurry!"

𝓗OW did you tell your oldest friend to keep her shirt on without losing her friendship forever?

Susan's fingers trembled at the buttons of her silk blouse as she waited for him to respond to her invitation. Truth was, he was shocked. He wasn't an unsophisticated man and God knew he had known his share of women, but the sight of the woman he loved as a sister getting ready to bare her breasts shocked the hell out of him.

And it wasn't even as if he hadn't seen her breasts before. He was her gynecologist. He had delivered her children.

"Susie, stop." He tried to soften the words with a smile, but he couldn't quite get it right. "Don't do something you'll regret."

"That's where you've got it wrong," she said as the first button popped open. "You only regret what you don't do."

"You don't really want to do this."

The second button popped open. "Yes, I do."

He could see the lacy edge of her bra. "You're like my sister."

"I'm not your sister."

"We grew up together."

"Claudia always wanted to see us get together. Better late than never."

"You're married."

"I've never not been married," she said. "I was born married."

He wasn't a psychologist, but he recognized a clue when he saw one.

Jesus, there went the third button. Would she think he was a weasel if he sprinted for the door? This was more than he had bargained on. The woman was his oldest friend, his confidante, the person he had turned to for advice and consolation before Ellen came into—

Wait a minute. Wasn't this the same way she had reacted a few years ago when Annie and Sam first got together? She tried to push change away with both hands and, to his embarrassment, so had he. That hadn't been the finest hour for either one of them. He had actually looked into Sam's background, hoping to find something that would send Annie running straight into his arms. Annie had been a lot kinder and more understanding than they had deserved, something he saw now with painful clarity.

"Susan, we'd better—" He stopped as he realized she wasn't listening to him. She was looking over his right shoulder toward the doorway with a look of utter horror on her face.

He turned around and found himself looking straight into the angry eyes of Ellen's sister Deirdre.

"They're taking Ellen to the ER," she said without preamble as she glared at Susan. "Next time, try closing the door."

She turned and left without another word.

"Dr. Markowitz!" The voice came to her from very far away. "Dr. Markowitz, can you hear me?"

She opened her eyes. A young man was looking down at her. He seemed familiar, but she couldn't remember his name. "Where—?"

"You're in an ambulance, Dr. Markowitz. We're taking you to the hospital."

"Patsy . . . how is . . ."

"Mrs. Wheeler is stable. She's en route to the hospital in our other vehicle."

"Hall," she whispered. "Hall?"

"Hospital," the young man repeated, a puzzled look in his eyes. "We're taking you to the hospital."

She tried to sit up, but the pain wouldn't let her, so she sank back into oblivion where it couldn't find her.

"Go," Susan said. She fumbled with the buttons on her shirt. "Get to the hospital."

Why did he have to look at her that way, with that combination of love and friendship and compassion that made her so damned ashamed of herself that she wanted to crawl out the door and disappear.

"Susie, I—"

"Just go, will you? She needs you."

He kissed the top of her head and was gone.

Now what? How was she going to walk back into her life? How could she climb back into bed with Jack tonight like nothing happened? She had never been very good at lying to herself, and she knew that if Hall had said yes, if he had shown the slightest interest, nothing on earth would have stopped her. And it wasn't because she loved him that way, because she really didn't. He was gorgeous, he was her friend, and he was safe. Her secrets had always been safe with him, and this one would have been no exception.

A safe fling. A walk on the wild side without crossing the street. Infidelity without repercussions, where nobody got hurt and everybody but the clueless husband was happy.

Get real.

Not a very pretty picture. Not a terrific thing to find out about yourself.

And, even worse, not something you wanted his future sister-in-law to know.

Hall burst into the ER and demanded to know where Ellen was.

"Number three," one of the residents told him. "Arnstein's with her right now."

He heard Ellen before he saw her—a sharp high-pitched cry of pain he felt in his own gut.

Arnstein looked up as he stepped into the cubicle. "What happened?" he asked his colleague. Car accident? Broken leg?

"She had a small cyst on her right ovary the last time she was in. We weren't too concerned, figured we'd watch it through three cycles before we made any decisions."

"Torsion?"

"I think so. The pain is at the high end of the scale and all the other symptoms are there." Arnstein met his eyes. "She's been calling for you."

He nodded, afraid Arnstein would see his heart beating on his sleeve.

"I keep asking her if she has any family she wants me to call, and she keeps saying you're her family."

Goddamn it. His eyes welled with tears, and Arnstein was there counting every single one.

"I'll take care of it." Deirdre was probably on her way to the hospital. She could call the other sister in Cambridge while he called Cy.

Arnstein nodded. "I need someone to sign the surgical release for her. She's not in any condition to sign herself in."

The ER crew had shot her up with some powerful drugs to dull the worst of the pain, and she wasn't tracking well.

"Her sister's on her way here. Can she do it?"

"Any port in a storm." Arnstein cleared his throat. He was a young man who didn't wear his discomfort well at all. "Any chance Dr. Markowitz is pregnant?"

"No," he said, then caught himself. "Strike that. Yes, there is a chance."

"We'll run a test." Arnstein ducked out to order a pregnancy test added to the list.

Hall knew too much. That was the problem. He knew all of the things Arnstein wasn't saying. The risks to Ellen. The risks to a pregnancy, if there was one. A torsioned cyst caught early was relatively minor. A torsioned cyst at the stage this one appeared to be at was something else again. The sheer weight of the cyst caused the ovary to twist on its stem, effectively blocking the blood supply to both the ovary and the fallopian tube and causing both to die. The next stage was gangrene, a painful and potentially dangerous situation.

For the first time he was grateful she was most likely not pregnant.

He held her hand while she drifted in and out of a drugged sleep.

"Hall . . ."

"I'm here." He bent down and kissed her gently. "I'll always be here."

They grabbed Deirdre immediately and set her to work signing consent forms for Ellen's surgery. Her hands shook as she tried to comprehend the endless paragraphs snaking across the pages.

"Your sister and Mrs. Wheeler owe you big time, Ms. O'Brien." The clerk, a sweet-faced woman named Tina, shuddered. "I hate to think what would have happened to the two of them if you hadn't gone back."

The whole thing made her think of a line of dominoes. Touch one and the whole thing tumbled down. Patsy Wheeler's husband was away on business. The day-shift nurse left early. The evening-shift nurse was delayed. Patsy's cell phone battery died. And so it went. A series of minor annoyances that added one upon another led straight into the heart of what could have been a tragedy.

She finished signing papers, then went off in search of cubicle three, where Ellen was being monitored. Hall parted the curtains and stepped outside as she approached.

"Don't worry," she said. "I figured it out."

The look of relief on his face made her smile.

"How is she?"

He spelled it out in a combination of medicalese and plain English.

"They're waiting for some test results, and then they'll start prepping her for surgery."

"Is it serious?"

"Serious enough," he said, "but not life-threatening."

She would lose a tube and an ovary, but her ability to become pregnant and carry a child to term shouldn't be compromised.

"How about the other woman?"

"Patsy is fine, but it's touch-and-go for the baby. They admitted her."

Deirdre inclined her head toward the cubicle. "Can I see her?"

He held open the curtain for her, and a wave of relief came over her at the sight of her sister in the hospital bed, hooked up to all manner of monitors and IV tubes. Anything was better than the sight of her unconscious on the floor.

"I'm here, Elly," she whispered into her ear. "Don't tell anyone, but I'll try to smuggle Stanley in tomorrow."

She hoped she hadn't imagined the smile.

Ellen opened her eyes and saw flowers. Roses. Daisies. Carnations. Big splashy flowers. Little delicate flowers. Flowers she had never seen before. Flowers with big long Latin names she couldn't pronounce.

"I must be dead," she murmured and closed her eyes again.

The next time she opened them there were even more flowers. Flowers on tabletops, windowsills, in big colorful tubs lined up against the walls. And sitting in the middle of this indoor garden was Claudia Galloway, thumbing through a copy of *Cosmopolitan.*

"Welcome back," Claudia said, beaming a bright smile in her direction. She put down the magazine and reached for her hand. "You've been gone awhile."

She was a little fuzzy-headed, but the images were beginning to arrange themselves into a recognizable pattern. She remembered pain. Patsy Wheeler on the floor of her bedroom. An ambulance ride. Hall, his face gray with worry, holding her hand as they wheeled her into surgery.

"What day is it?"

"Saturday morning. You've been catching up on your sleep."

She glanced around the room and saw the computer monitor tucked in the corner. "I want to read my chart."

"What you need is more sleep."

She tried to protest, but it took too much energy. She fell back again into healing sleep.

She dreamed there was an endless stream of visitors trekking in and out of her room. A crazy quilt of people she couldn't imagine together in the same room no matter how hard she tried. Cy and Nancy. Their son David. Claudia. Roberta. Annie and Sam Butler. Susan. Janna and the office staff. The OB-GYN residents. Doug Wheeler. Deirdre and Mary Pat and baby Declan. Sweeney in her motorcycle-mama gear. Scott the Mechanic.

A dream with a cast of thousands, but not the one she most wanted to see.

She opened her eyes again and what she saw was better than any dream imaginable. Hall was sitting next to her bed, her hand in his, his beautiful face aglow with happiness.

"You're really here," she said, sounding sleepy but clear-headed. "I dreamed that everyone in town showed up but you."

"Thanks a lot," he said, leaning forward to kiss her gently. "Everyone in town really was here, but I had a baby to deliver."

"Holder?"

"Baby girl," he said. "Seven pounds even. Nineteen inches long."

"Black hair?"

"Raven's wing."

"Healthy?"

"Very."

She smiled and closed her eyes for a second. "I'm glad." She rested her free hand on her belly, over the cushion of heavy gauze that shielded the incision. "So what happened? Is Patsy . . . ?"

"She and the baby are holding their own." He told her the rest in detail—from Deirdre's discovery to her recovery.

"Your red Cruiser saved the day," he said. "Deirdre saw it in the driveway and began to wonder if something was wrong."

"They took the ovary and tube, of course."

He nodded. "No choice."

"I know," she said, feeling weepy. "I know we always say it shouldn't impact fertility, but—"

"Not a problem."

"I know that's the party line, but—"

"Listen to me, Markowitz: not a problem."

She looked at him, focused all of her concentration on his

beautiful blue eyes, the look of joy radiating from them, and she knew.

"We're pregnant?"

His smile could light up the entire state of Maine and have enough power left over for Vermont and New Hampshire. "How does late February sound to you?"

"But what about the surgery? Is the baby in any danger?"

"Arnstein is a hell of a surgeon. He wants to keep you on bed rest for four weeks and then we can rest easy."

"Something's wrong? Is that why?"

"Nothing's wrong. It's known as preventive medicine. You should know all about that, Markowitz." He sat down gingerly on the edge of the bed. "You asked for me."

She couldn't wipe the silly smile off her face. "Did I?"

"They asked you for the name of a family member and you gave mine."

"I was delirious."

"You called out for me in the ambulance."

"They had me on painkillers."

If her smile grew any wider, she'd need an extra room for it.

"You told me you loved me."

"No, I didn't," she said softly, "but I'm telling you now."

He brushed a curl away from her cheek and drew in a deep breath. "I love you, Markowitz. I've spent my life looking for you. I wish you hadn't taken so long to get here." He reached deep into the pocket of his lab coat and pulled out a small box. "There's probably a more romantic way to do this, but life is too short to wait another second."

Her breath caught as he dropped to his knee next to the bed and removed the ring from the box.

"We have the house, the dog, and the baby on the way. All that's left is to stand up in front of our friends and make it legal."

"This time it's going to be forever," she warned him. "I love you too much for anything less."

"Will you marry me, Ellen O'Brien Markowitz? Will you take a chance on forever with me?"

She placed his hand on her belly and met his eyes. "I already have," she said.

Thirty-one

"Willa! Mariah!" Ellen leaned over the deck railing and motioned to the two little girls. "It's time!"

"Five more minutes," Mariah begged as she danced around Stanley, who was on his best behavior.

"Please!" Willa added. "Stanley's doing his best tricks for us."

"Everyone's waiting for us," Ellen called out. "The wedding's about to start!"

Deirdre joined her on the deck. She looked lovely in a floaty dress the color of sea foam shot through with stars. "Having second thoughts?" she teased.

"Only that it took me so long to find him."

Deirdre gave her a hug. "I'm so happy for you."

"For all of us," Ellen said. It had been touch-and-go for a while with her pregnancy, but she had passed the first trimester and all looked well for a healthy baby in late February. Those first months had been difficult, but she hadn't faced them alone. Who would have guessed that family could manifest itself in so many different ways, each one of them as real and as important as the bonds forged in blood and bone?

Deirdre had canceled her job on the cruise ship and taken over caring for the house and Stanley while Ellen remained on total bed rest. Hall took over her half of the practice, working long days and nights, and spending every spare second of his time by her side. Mary Pat was a frequent visitor, with and without her husband and kids. Her solid, unruffled personality had been exactly what they needed to keep themselves grounded.

Cy and Nancy had stayed with her during her entire hospitalization. Cy was in his glory overseeing her care. Who would have guessed he would embrace impending grandfatherhood with such enthusiasm?

Since Billy's death, she had learned so much about the forces that had shaped her life. Things she hadn't understood before became clear. Sometimes the details were heartbreaking. The regrets would probably never leave her, but the bitterness had been replaced by love and understanding. Not a bad tradeoff at all.

Deirdre continued to struggle against the past. There had been no happy resolution for her, no letter from Billy or scrapbook of her accomplishments hidden away. Ellen would give anything to be able to ease her sister's heartache, but only Billy could have done that. Now time would have to take care of the rest.

She and Scott the Mechanic were seeing each other. Deirdre said it was just a summer thing, but there was no denying the deep connection that seemed to exist between them. Once again, with Deirdre only time would tell.

"What on earth is taking you two so long? Maeve and Fiona are pushing ninety. Let's get moving!" Mary Pat clattered across the deck in her brand-new Jimmy Choos. "So help me, if you don't get out there right now, Ellen, I'll marry him myself."

"Not if I get there before you do," Deirdre said.

Ellen looked down at her blossoming belly and laughed. "I think I have first claim on him."

Mary Pat leaned over the railing. "Girls! Leave that dog alone and get in here NOW!"

Willa and Mariah kissed Stanley on the nose, then ran into the house.

"Wow," said Ellen, shaking her head. "Looks like I have a lot to learn."

"You will," Mary Pat said. "You just need a little practice."

"I'm feeling very left out," Deirdre said. "I don't even have Stanley anymore."

Ellen draped an arm around her sister's shoulders. Mary Pat took her hand.

"You did a great job," Ellen said to her sisters. "The house looks wonderful."

"A little paint, a few flowers." Mary Pat grinned at Deirdre. "That's all it takes."

Their laughter rang out on the late summer air. The parlor had been transformed into a garden of flowers where Reverend Edwards and Rabbi Glassberg would perform the ceremony.

"Is everyone there?" Ellen asked.

"As far as I can see, the entire town showed up," Mary Pat said. "I hope we have enough champagne and—"

"We'll do fine," Ellen said. "You've done a spectacular job on this wedding."

"Did Susan show up?" Deirdre asked.

"The real estate agent?" Mary Pat asked. Deirdre nodded. "Yes. She brought her kids."

"Jack came with Scott," Deirdre said. "I guess they really did separate."

Both Hall and Deirdre told her the story of Susan's attempt at seduction, and it still made her terribly sad to think of Susan throwing away a twenty-year marriage while she went searching for the love she already had.

Mary Pat checked her watch. "Cy's waiting upstairs to walk you down the aisle." Or the front staircase, as it were. "He's a good man. He loves you very much."

She knew that now. All of the bits and pieces she had been too young to understand, too angry to hear, too lonely to pursue, finally made sense. Cy had thought he could bring enough love into his marriage for all of them, but life didn't always work that way. Sharon had never been able to let Billy O'Brien's memory go long enough to see the love that was waiting for her right in her own backyard. How difficult it must have been for him to be reminded of the man who owned his wife's heart every time he looked into the eyes of Billy's daughter.

"So here we are again," Deirdre said as they linked arms to walk back to the house. "Who knew we'd have one more summer together?"

"I wouldn't have missed it for anything," Ellen said, her eyes misting over with tears.

"Don't you dare cry," Mary Pat warned her. "I'm not sure that mascara is waterproof. I told Shawna to—"

Deirdre groaned. "Mary Pat, so help me God, if you start bitching again I swear I'm going to . . ."

"—you're supposed to play them in. . . . Shouldn't you be at the harp—"

". . . it isn't like they can start without us, is it. . . ."

The sound of her sisters bickering was better than Beethoven to Ellen, better than Mozart, better even than Deirdre's glorious harp. It was the sound of family.

Good on you, Billy O'Brien, she thought as she hugged her sisters close. Those long ago summers had made this moment possible.

"Ellen!" Willa popped up at her side, a spun-sugar fairy in butter yellow. Mariah, Kate, and Lizzy weren't far behind. "Grandpa Cy says if you don't hurry up, you'll have the baby on your honeymoon!"

"Daddy looks like he's going to faint," Lizzy said. "You'd better hurry."

"Listen to your girls," Mary Pat said with a wink for Deirdre. "They know what they're talking about."

And so did Ellen. They were talking about love. It was all that really mattered.

Hall *and* Ellen Talbot

announce with pride
the birth of their daughter

Emilie Sophia

on the twenty-fifth of February
six pounds four ounces
twenty-one inches long

absolutely perfect